ALL
THE
HEARTS
YOU
EAT

HAILEY PIPER

ALL THE HEARTS YOU EAT

TITAN BOOKS

All the Hearts You Eat
Print edition ISBN: 9781803367644
E-book edition ISBN: 9781803367651

Published by Titan Books
A division of Titan Publishing Group Ltd
144 Southwark Street, London SE1 0UP
www.titanbooks.com

First edition: October 2024
10 9 8 7 6 5 4 3 2 1

A CIP catalogue record for this title is available from the British Library.

Printed and bound by CPI (UK) Ltd, Croydon, CR0 4YY

"We are the saddest of all the animals."

—Lindsay Lerman

"Most people have a ghost story of some kind,
even if they don't believe in ghosts."

—Alison Rumfitt, Tell Me I'm Worthless

Once there was a ghost who fell in love with a lady by the sea. It happened here on the sand and rock, against the brine and rhythm and salt.

The ghost first fell in love with her forlorn beauty. And then her smile. And as the ghost haunted her, it fell in love with her spirit. It loved her so hard that it clawed a hole from the world of the dead into the world of the living and tried to take her home to that dead place.

But the ghost was part of the sea, and the sea wants blood. Everyone who lives on the coast and alongside its waves should know that.

The cold of the sea sank its fingers into the lady's once-warm flesh, into her slowing heart. For a moment, the ghost and the sea were one, and she became one with them, and in another kind of story, this might have been an ecstasy.

We only know the one kind of story: the life in her seeped away, and she died, like all tragic lovers torn between worlds.

The romantics would say they are now ghosts together in the world of the living. But those who walk the coast and brush against its enigmatic nature know the story better. We say that when the ghost broke through the worlds, something shattered in the way people die here, and no one can mend the wound. The romantics might also say that lovers who've been torn apart between worlds can at least reunite in the world of the dead.

But those aren't the kinds of stories we tell in the uncertain places by the sea.

PART ONE: THE GHOST

1. THE BODY

The sea wanted blood. Ivory Sloan had known that all her life, traveling from one coastal town or another along the eastern United States. She had spent most of her twenty-nine years with a passable understanding for the Atlantic Ocean and its hazards— jellyfish, undertow, strangers.

She should have expected to find death at the shores of Cape Morning.

A gray overcast painted the sky as she approached the water; New England coastal summer made for uncertain vacations against its sudden storm fronts, and there was no better deterrent for tourists than a chilly early twilight mixed with chances of unpleasant weather. Unlikely for other locals to wander the shore yet, either.

For a few minutes each morning, this stretch of beach belonged to Ivory. One of the rare perks of renting her stuffy attic room— ready access to the water. Before true daylight lured overheated tourists to the beach and cooped her up in the café until evening, she wanted her morning swim.

Down wooden steps and a grassy slope, white sand led the way to chopping waves. Ivory passed an enormous driftwood tree that had been lying on the shore the past few months. It had supposedly floated down from Canada, but no one could be sure.

Scars marked its trunk where barnacles once clung to the bark.

Ivory crossed her arms and slid her pastel pink hoodie up her midriff, past her chest, and over her head. She folded it with care and laid it in the sand beside the driftwood tree, and then she set her boots and socks on top. Her jeans joined the pile last, revealing in full her black one-piece swimsuit and her inner thigh tattoo.

I am a creature of life, it read in curving letters and black ink.

Her swimsuit's dark hue made each part of her torso look smaller, shrinking her chest, belly chub, and the swell between her legs. She didn't want anyone to see that part of her, especially after she emerged from the water, swimsuit clinging to her skin. Neither locals nor tourists would understand. Or worse, they might understand, and she had no control over what they might decide to do with that understanding.

One quick swim, that was all she wanted. In and out from here to Ghost Cat Island, the tiny sea-slick patch of rock standing not far from shore, and no stranger would stroll close enough when she fetched her clothes off the beach to eyeball the outline of her tits or her dick.

The sand was cold against her feet as she padded toward the Atlantic. Wet impressions dotted the shore's edge behind her before the next wave splashed her knees and flattened the sand. A chill hit her skin, but it would fade once her muscles went to work.

She had reached waist-deep water, the waves frothing at her arms and chest, when she noticed the man standing on the beach.

Her knees buckled, tugging her down so that the surf pushed at her chin. She hardly ever saw anyone out this early, at least not in June. Maybe in July or August when the daytime sun boiled the air, but not in the beginning stretch of summer.

Had the man seen her swimsuit, its details? He might spot her now if she slid away. She didn't know him, his intentions, anything. Why the hell was he here?

Maybe because the sea wanted blood.

She couldn't hold here in the shallows to wait for him to leave, no telling how long that might be. Better she risk going back for her clothes and heading home now.

She kept one dark blue eye on the beach as she retreated from the water. The man stood stiff in his khakis and coat, a white ballcap hugging his gray locks. He didn't seem to notice her, all his attention zeroed in on the tide three feet past his boots. A pale tangle of driftwood lay ahead of him. Was he local? One of the summer people? A drifter? Ivory had never seen him before, but that hardly mattered with eight thousand people living here, not to mention the legion of tourists. The man held a phone to his ear, scowling as he spoke.

Ivory only realized who he'd been talking to when the sirens sounded from afar. Within moments, flashes of red and blue flickered over the grassy slope between the summerhouses and the beach. She froze halfway between the water and the driftwood tree and looked—really looked—at where the man was staring. And exactly what he'd called in.

The white shape lying in the tide was a dead body.

Ivory stumbled toward the driftwood tree, eyes locked on the frothing water, splashing at pale skin.

Over the past few days, families and college kids had swarmed Cape Morning's tree-choked roads, cramped town, and windy beach to swim and tan and drink themselves brainless. A different scene from Florida, but a clean beach on a warm day drew tourists nonetheless. Did this body belong to one of them?

Ivory kept backing up until her hip banged against the driftwood tree. Her clothing pile collapsed in her shaking hands. She pushed her head into the hoodie and yanked her damp hair through in clingy dark red locks. Never mind the wet swimsuit getting her clothes and boots soaked as she hurried into them.

There would be time to dry and change into something else when she reached home before her barista shift.

But she couldn't leave yet. A sudden heaviness tugged her toward the prone trunk of the driftwood tree.

She sat and watched as the man with the phone turned toward the distant uniformed strangers, descending the wooden steps to the beach. No rush—dead was dead. Nothing they could do but investigate and then carry the dead away.

Ivory sucked at the wind, trying to catch her breath. Lightheadedness sent her doubling over, and it became easier to breathe with her eyes focused on the sand.

Where she spotted a piece of pink-tinted paper at her feet, partway pinned beneath the driftwood trunk.

She pinched its corner and worked it free. The wind tried to snatch it, but she held on firm. It looked torn from a journal or diary. A transparent flower pattern wreathed its edges, and curls of black ink scrawled over its front.

> *Don't call me a suicide. I want to live.*
> *I've simply chosen one death over another*
> *After I've been robbed of life.*
> *—Cabrina Aphrodite Brite*

Ivory glanced at the dead body, and then back to the words. The authorities had neared the man who'd called them to the beach. If they spotted Ivory, they might want to question her, and she didn't care to talk.

What about her secret find? A suicide note might determine the future of Cabrina's body, how her family saw her life. But it wasn't really a suicide note, the first line said as much. It was more a death poem, and a poem couldn't count as evidence, could it?

Ivory understood, but others might not. The family would ache to think their dear girl, Cabrina Brite, had taken her own life. Broken hearts. Only pain.

But Ivory could help. She folded the poem in half and tucked it inside her hoodie pocket.

Her legs shuddered as she stood from the driftwood seat. Not ready to go, but she couldn't stay here. She didn't want to watch the authorities, closer now, take photographs of Cabrina Brite, or inspect her every inch, or draw her from the water like scavenging gulls picking at beach debris.

As she walked back the way she'd come, Ivory turned to watch the sea. She scarcely made out Ghost Cat Island beneath the overcast. It was so tiny that she never tried to stand on it when she swam out, only touching it and then returning to shore.

But that was the nearest land to where Cabrina might have died in the night. Had she, too, meant to swim out to the small scrap of rock?

Ivory had heard stories of locals glimpsing feline shapes upon the island. There were tales old and new of their lithe paws walking on ocean waves as if the bobbing water were gray-blue hills, fur glimmering with sunshine. No one ever found them—there was nothing on that lifeless rock to find—but that didn't stop anyone from looking. Or from telling the stories.

Cabrina might have been the same, looking for ghost cats, no more solid than flying saucers or that monster at Lake Champlain. Mirages at best, lies at worst, but sometimes people liked the lies.

Ivory knew she shouldn't entertain fantasies of ghosts. They might show up and then stick around.

Gray clouds parted, and the sun cast a sharp glare off the water. Shapes flashed across the glittering waves. Ivory shaded her eyes under one hand and squinted for a better look at Ghost Cat Island.

A figure slid over the island's rocky nub, its shape bowing under the sun like a distorted shadow play on a bedroom wall. One sleek leg stretched in a molten glow, almost human. The figure's next step dragged it down, close to the rock, and sprouted new limbs, melting its shape into that of a pacing four-legged beast.

It briefly sloshed and crawled above the watery sunshine. Then the figure's next step sent it climbing a slope of light until it stood tall on two legs, with two arms at its sides, its glowing silhouette thin and pale. Like someone Ivory might have seen lying in the surf. Someone who'd left a death poem wedged beneath a driftwood tree.

Cabrina? she wondered.

The sunlight glinted off a fresh wave and stabbed Ivory's eyes shut. She threw both hands over them, croaking with pain, and then she blinked into the shadows of her palms until the dancing white dots settled behind her eyelids.

When she looked again, grayness had retaken the shore, and only rolling waves broke across Ghost Cat Island. No light, no animal, no human. Nothing at all.

Someone laughed in the wind, and Ivory turned from the water. Beachgoers were strolling far down the sands. They were only vague puddles of likely tourists in hoodies snatched from different state colleges, but soon they would pincer her against the authorities. Someone might say they'd spotted her, a woman in a pink hoodie, acting suspicious even though she'd done nothing wrong.

Others would soon join them. They would be waking up across the summerhouses to wailing sirens and flashing lights, and they would come to see the sights of Cape Morning. Even a dead girl could become entertainment for bored tourists.

Ivory headed for the nearest wooden steps and climbed past the grass back to town proper. A soft breeze chased her, and she couldn't shake the sense of footsteps behind her, first sandy and soft, and then padding on pavement at her heels. She expected to glance out the corner of one eye and spot a pale shadow, but nothing followed that she could see. Only scattered pedestrians dotted the sidewalk.

The feeling of being alone, and yet not alone, refused to leave. A presence weighed on Ivory's back, like someone jamming a cold fingertip to one side of her spine. She couldn't blame herself for feeling unnerved after seeing the man, and then Cabrina's body, and that sunlit mirage over Ghost Cat Island, but she needed the feeling to die now, let her get on with the day.

It faded with each step, and the walk home was only a block from the beach. Ivory met no one she knew on the way, and she was grateful for it.

She didn't need anyone to tell her she looked like she'd seen a ghost.

From the Diary of Cabrina Brite,
April 8, 2018

I tried to stop writing my thoughts, but then it was like I swallowed a scream, and it kept getting bigger inside me, and either it would kill me or it would turn me out like Dad, and that would be how she ruined me.

She and Dad won't see this time. I hate that I lost the online entries after my birthday video, but we lose everything eventually, the kind of thing you learn when you turn nineteen, and anyway, I couldn't let her keep seeing my thoughts.

This one will be secret. Paper and pen and a hidden place. I can scream inside here. All the thoughts and truths she can't handle or doesn't want me to know.

If I could run on water, she would never see me again.
Goodbye, Cape Morning!
Goodbye, Massachusetts!
Hello, Atlantic Ocean, then Europe, Africa! And keep running.

The closest I can get is crashing into the water, soaking my body like it soaks the sand. Sometimes I daydream about swimming into it and never coming out. But I always do. The ocean never keeps me. I keep it instead, dripping in saltwater drops, lingering in my throat. I'm still shivering with it. If the ink runs, that's why.

She tries to keep me here, but she can't stop me at night when there's the beach and spring break. Don't I deserve a moment's peace too?

Rex wanted us out at the water, and this far into April, the spring-breakers are headed home. He said his Ma told him Cape

Morning has a magnetism which attracts too many people, but I guess the magic comes and goes with the sun. Maybe the magic is broken. Lots of things are.

Xi came with us. She wanted to enjoy the last of spring break before school hit. Summer will be full of summer people, and then she starts college in August.

I snuck out. Xi knew, Rex knew, maybe everyone knew. I told them I didn't bother asking permission, so no one had to worry about my dad rolling up with cop sirens chirping, looking for me under a certain town councilmember's command.

Xi pulled me aside once and asked *How bad is it?* but I faked a laugh. I wouldn't have wanted to talk about what happens in the house anyway. Rex took us out to forget everything else.

It got weirdly cold, and we were bundled up in winter coats like it was January instead of April, all of us around the fire Rex likes to build on the south tip of the beach. It doesn't really help, but sometimes we pretend it does.

Well, the fire might help the others. I'm the one who has to pretend. I would have been warmer that night if I had put on jeans, but I never get to wear a dress anymore. Xi asked what happened to my makeup, dresses, blouses, and I said, *She threw most of it out*, and Xi knew who I meant. The jewelry went in the garbage too, even my seashell necklace. All I've got left is the Bride of Frankenstein costume dress I hid under the mattress and the nude lipstick I hid in the vent. She never looks there.

I wore them both tonight, and I felt something close to right again.

There were other kids from school, just chattering and milling around, a phone blasting Blood Red Shoes so loud it fuzzed the audio. I think someone brought drinks. If Rex and Xi ask what happened, I can say I drank too much. Shouldn't underage drink, yadda, yadda, guess our parents are right about one thing, good talk.

They might not believe me, but like the fire, we'll pretend it helps.

It was my fault. I had that heavy feeling in my knees like I might go through one more late growth spurt. With Germaine in prison and still waiting for trial, I'm out of options to get the pills I need. There's no hope of him getting out. He was dealing coke to others. Never me, but I get cut off from my meds the same.

She had something to do with it. Either she found him out and told the rest of town council and Dad and his cop buddies, or she threatened to bash Germaine's brains in and toss him out to sea unless he turned himself in. Cape Morning takes care of secrets, even hers.

The ocean sends a whisper,
That the outsider feeling isn't just me,
That our bodies and souls are borrowed,
And one day we give everything back.
I longed to look at the ocean,
And I was afraid to look, too,
Like when you have a crush in middle school,
And to have class with them both lights and destroys you.
The ocean longs to crush my heart,
And part of me wants to let her.

The poetry needs work, but that's how it felt. I could barely look at the water, like it was the sun at night. Still, I told everyone to come closer and get their boots in the tide. I had a spring break game for them. They had to have been drinking. No one would have done what I said without at least being tipsy.

The rule of the game was: see who could keep their faces under for the longest without coming up for air. Nobody really wanted to get their faces wet when it was so cold out, but I got Xi to play, and then Rex and a couple other guys joined in, and Brian said he wasn't going to be shown up by two girls. It was brutish, but it made me feel more like I belong, even though I don't.

That's not their fault. I am an outsider, stuck inside. At the house, she wants me to pretend her and me and Dad have a perfect little home, like we're in a stage play called *Election Campaign*, and we put it on 24/7, like I pretend the fire keeps me warm, like I'll pretend the game was a drunken mistake and not an honest one.

We all got on our hands and knees a little into the water, and then we put our faces in. I forget if I took a good breath. Rex did, I heard him. I thought he would win, but I also thought it was just a silly game.

A little drowning goes a long way.

The cold makes it easy to keep holding your breath. Not right away. First it stabs your skin everywhere and makes you want to scream, but after that? It's peaceful. Slows you down.

Cabrina, how long were you down?

We were too busy drowning to time ourselves, but I kept my face in the water long enough to see things.

Down in the dark, someone reached out for me. It might have been a person. I thought it looked a little like a cat. But then I had another thought: I was seeing into the afterlife. Is there such a thing as a death psychic? I could be one.

One of the bio teachers from back in high school, before I got pulled out, said we all come from the sea, and maybe we go back there when we die, no matter where we die. Like an ocean of ghosts.

The something inside the water reached for my lips and let a piece of ocean drip into me. It was thick, like sticking my mouth around raw meat, and there was a darkness, and I wondered if I would be part of the Atlantic soon.

And I swallowed it. A little bit of ocean to play with my inside screams.

Rex tackled me. I fell sideways into the tide and took a breath. He was shaking his fists and shouting at me. He thought I was dying. Xi shouted too and kept aiming a finger at me, like every word was supposed to be a bullet gunning me down. I pointed back at her, tried to play it off like a joke, but no one believed me. Most of the guys who played the game with us had punked back to the fire, even Brian. Poor nervous boys.

Xi and Rex stayed angry, but they stayed with me too. It wasn't right to scare them. I told them I was sorry and that I loved them. I wanted to cry, but sometimes a fist holds every feeling back, and it'll crush my bones if I dare give the world one teardrop.

So I showed everyone a new game. I wiped the ocean off my face, turned to it, and screamed as loud as I could out over the water.

Xi screamed with me, and then Rex screamed too. Some of the others whooped or made little fakey shouts to join in, but they didn't get it. Ours were real screams, the kind that break your throat and steamroll your lungs. Mine were high-pitched cracked little shrieks.

I had to get them out of me right then. If I didn't, each one would've got stuck inside me. There's something wrong in the world when you can't scream right.

The ocean understood,
And it offered to swallow the screams for me.
I thought, how Atlantic of you.
But what could the Pacific do?
I could let my screams loose,
On a different ocean.
Would I be a California girl?
Or would I just be this same girl,
Decaying on a west coast shore?

That might be something later if I can make it make sense. Water is just molecules and atoms and all the stuff in it. There's no kindness to water, and it didn't have any reason to take my screams. So maybe it wasn't the water itself doing me that kindness.

Maybe it was the ghosts.

2. THE FOOL

Ivory finished her question and then took a drink, like that meant she wouldn't have to repeat herself no matter what she heard. It wasn't the sort of question she would ordinarily ask while nursing a sweaty beer bottle at the end of a man's bed, but she'd started the day on strange tides and saw no reason to end it any different.

Wolf wore a confused expression, one eyebrow raised. He looked like he didn't think he'd heard the question right.

"I asked if you believe in ghosts," Ivory said.

"Maybe." Wolf lifted the glass neck of another beer to his lips. "Why?"

"Do you think there would be a ghost for no reason?" Ivory turned to the floor as if it could answer her instead. "Like, one would come around for the fun of it?"

"What are you on now?" Wolf had asked Ivory more questions tonight than he usually asked her in a week. She should fall into a weird mood more often.

"I'm not on anything," Ivory said. "If a ghost came around, she—there would have to be a reason, right? Unfinished business? A ghost wouldn't show up for nothing."

Wolf leaned into the flat wooden headboard and drank deeply of his beer. He was a big man, built of firm bone and stony muscle, and took up much of the bed, its sheets and blankets forming hills around him.

Ivory never asked if Wolf was his first name, or his surname, or a nickname. She'd long ago decided his business was none of hers. Almost easier to think him like his namesake, a wolf accidentally born as man. She once believed wolves could live anywhere, even the coastal towns where she grew up and then hopped between as an adult. Even the cities. Werewolves, too. Both existed in her childhood stories, and when she was little, that had meant both were real somewhere. They sometimes wandered, maybe vacationed, and even decided to linger.

She realized Wolf was looking at her again. A stoic expression had formed between his cropped hair and gray-black beard.

"I think the world is complicated," Wolf said, and he set his beer bottle onto the glass-topped nightstand with a firm clack. "Everything we know of the world is a mess. Maybe everything we don't know is a mess, too."

His answer pasted a smile into the corner of Ivory's lips. She might have been too hard on him. He hadn't invited her over for ghost talk, but willingness to play at spectral epiphanies went a long way.

"Why ask about ghosts?" Wolf raised a dark eyebrow. "Seen one?"

"No big reason." Ivory swirled her bottle's last puddle of beer. "But yes, maybe I saw one."

Wolf coughed out a laugh. "You're not on anything now, but what about earlier?"

"It isn't like that," Ivory said, exhaustion creeping into her voice. "It's been going round and round in my head all day, and I can't talk to Joan about it without getting a lecture."

"Joan might have it right," Wolf said, his tone dismissive.

Ivory wanted to mention that Joan wasn't exactly Wolf's biggest fan. And she wanted to mention the body of Cabrina Brite, the death poem she'd pinched from the beach, and what she'd seen—might have seen—in the sun's glare across Ghost Cat Island.

But she might have misworded her questions. She'd been holding her morning encounter behind pursed lips the whole workday, and by nightfall it might have overcooked on her tongue.

Wolf sat forward, and the headboard groaned like an abandoned lover. His feet slid past Ivory's legs, and his thighs tucked around hers as the bulk of him pressed across her back. One arm encircled her chest, and his beard and lips brushed her neck.

"Why don't we quit the dead talk for tonight, yeah?" Wolf asked.

But his question was a statement. Ivory's ghosts had pricked his blood in the wrong way. Only she could set it right.

"Let me freshen up," Ivory said, sliding his arm away and easing off the bed.

She kicked past abandoned cardboard fragments and loose laundry, detritus of a single man's bedroom, and slipped into the bathroom. If she waited for his assent, she wouldn't make it this far. She needed a moment to herself behind a locked door.

A crucifix hung from the wall opposite the mirror—Wolf kept one in every room but the bedroom—and Ivory shifted her head to blot it out. She studied her reflection across the toothpaste-speckled glass. The day had clouded her makeup, hung blue-gray bags beneath her eyes, and glued a stony frown over her lips.

She shouldn't have been pushed to worry tonight. Asking these questions, dissecting her face—it was wrong and unfair at the end of a rough day. She should have called off visiting Wolf's place tonight. Serving food and drink left a special kind of exhaustion in anyone's skin and bones, the body absorbing furious cravings and bottomless demands.

Ivory studied that special exhaustion in the mirror. Nudged it. Tried to smush it around with her fingertips and find the woman she'd been before today's shift.

The woman who might've seen a ghost.

But her fingers carried neither the time nor parasitic quality of hours on her feet asking, *Can I get you anything else?* with the answer almost always, *Yeah.*

Hers was a conditional humanity. Not the sort where she demanded better of herself, but where the world demanded she prove her worth. She could be human if every stranger found she measured up to the right expectations.

Am I nice enough that they'll let me live?

Am I pretty enough that they won't burn me?

She thought she'd figured out the answers. Wolf seemed to want her, sometimes more than she felt wanted. Weren't these human measurements? She couldn't say for sure when someone as young as Cabrina could—what? Die by accident? By choice? Ivory hadn't even named this uncertainty, almost refused it.

Thinking about death wasn't right tonight. Wasn't she a creature of life?

She backstepped from the mirror, and her reflection did the same. Her hands pawed down her front, testing every curve and corner. Were the meat shapes at her chest the right roundness for Wolf? The right position? Ivory pressed both hands against her thighs, kneading her fingers against either leg, and then she slipped between them where everything hung small and soft. What about *these* meat shapes? She never tucked into a gaff at Wolf's house, by *his* preference, but uncertainty haunted her insides anyway.

Why the hell was she like this?

And worse, what if someday she wasn't like this? Her rocky non-relationship with Wolf might die when she was no longer a combination of cock below, tits above, softly this and firmly that, a puzzle piece of unique sides that fit his attraction *just right*. No more pretending she was more than a maid and a fetish, that he wasn't validation in this blood-sucking town.

She couldn't believe in love, and she couldn't ask him to love her.

"Ivory?" he called.

"On my way," she said. Fuck the mirror.

The bathroom door opened on dim lighting, the center of Wolf's bedroom blanketed in fuzzy darkness. He waited on the bed, heavy and warm in the gloom. Music breathed gently from the window-side wall, the easy kind of wordless tune you might expect beachside, but he'd brought it here.

Ivory couldn't help but smile. All her fretting about her looks, only to do this in the dark.

She let the instrumental music lead her onto his bed again, one foot gliding past the cold glass curve of a beer bottle. His firm hands found her waist, her thigh and its tattoo, and drew her weightless off the floor, into his arms, onto his lap. He had a rough touch tonight, the true wolf coming out. Eager to unzip and roll down her jeans, slide off her tank, almost tearing her bra. She kissed his neck, ran fingers through his short hair, and then squeaked as teeth scraped her shoulder.

"It's only me," Wolf said, and his smirk crossed the darkness. "Didn't mean to bite you." But he wasn't apologizing for it, either.

"I might like to be bitten," Ivory said. She wanted to sound cocky, but it came out in a shaking breath. More than anything, she wanted him to like how she felt about everything he did.

He kissed her hard again, first across the lips, and then down her jaw and neck. His fingertips dragged at her waist, crumpling her panties. He might rip them if she let him. Her breath rocked her body in a gentle in and out. One of his hands sank against her breast; the other crossed between her legs, gentler now, stroking her soft cock.

She almost wished the lights shined bright enough to see his face better, get a solid sense of how he looked at her, if she'd see anything in his eyes beyond attraction to her surface self. What had his past intimate partners looked like? He kissed her pretty belly, ample hips, and sometimes her shy member and the tops of her feet with their blue lagoon toenails.

This wasn't love. It was worship. She wasn't human right now but a divine figure carved from flesh. Some kind of complex goddess he couldn't have named, only given himself over to, and then given back to himself as a gift.

Some nights, she enjoyed it. Tonight, she wanted to be more than an effigy of a woman, subject to careless fingers and ravenous appetites.

If you don't want it, you can end it, she reminded herself. But she didn't want to stop either, even when he was rough and thoughtless.

A man pure of heart did not need a wild animal bite or a lycanthropic curse to become a wolf under the full moon. He only needed life to whisper in his ear, *You're the best, the absolute best, the most specialest boy, and then you'll be the most powerfulest man, and everything you choose to take belongs to you.*

Even Ivory's humanity.

Wolf's hands loosened, and his face climbed from her body. "Distracted tonight, huh?"

He had noticed she wasn't touching back. This might be a rare moment when he understood Ivory had oceans beneath the parts he liked to play with, full of questions and strangeness, fears both real and superstitious.

But she couldn't tell him that. "Oh," she said, brushing a red lock behind one ear. "Guess I was someplace else."

Wolf smirked again, and his teeth gleamed in the window light. Ivory melted into that look without meaning to, and she could believe her head was full of paranoid soup instead of brains. That his heart might be bigger than she gave credit for, and he might even have it set on her.

She would never know for sure.

"Come on, cute thing, get out of your head and be with me," Wolf said, and he kissed her again.

Ivory pressed him toward the headboard again. A fresh eagerness rained down her muscles. Her sensitive lips and tongue lit when she leaned between his legs. She could get out of her head and into the moment, as if pushing his hard cock inside her mouth left no room in there for thoughts.

Simplicity overtook the evening as she drank of him. She almost believed they could work like this, and maybe she could tell him how she wanted things to be. He might even care. She could be safe laying out her true desires, and then her thoughts, and then the grounds of a real relationship.

But if she was wrong, her desires would mean the end of it all. She would know for certain she was an idol, and a toy, and when he finished playing with her, he'd go looking for another woman who might fit his criteria.

Down she'd go, to sand and surf, another forgotten goddess, like those buried in dead empires across the world.

These were the messy thoughts of post-intimacy euphoria. The moment was done, and she sobered her mind as she rinsed with mouthwash.

Wolf's firm hands found her again as she left the bathroom, and she giggled in surprise when he grabbed her up in his arms. She had thought they were done, time to turn her out the door, but he was kissing her again. Hard, again. The bathroom light cast a wolfish hunger in his eyes before she hit the switch and flew from the doorway. A bottle of slick fluid passed from hand to hand to skin, and the rest happened in a humid maelstrom.

Back to bed, he pressed her face down, his weight on top of her, inside her, his every muscle crushing and fusing her to the mattress. She could scarcely breath beneath his sweat and skin, her nose and lips plunged against fabric, and she reveled in the thrill quaking through every nerve, her skin alight with burning sunshine. Her world climbed, crested, filled with his breathy moan and then her high-pitched rattling squeal. She hadn't meant to burst against his bedsheets, but sweetness was hard to find, and this night was much-needed honey, in both body and soul.

For a brief ecstatic moment, yes—she could believe in love.

3. THE HEART

A tidal rhythm beat in Ivory's ears. She sloshed atop fitful waves, and sometimes beneath them, at once wanted and unwanted. Had she been drowning for a long time? She should finish already, get this death business wrapped up.

Countless stars lit the sky and sea as the waves splashed her onto a black-sanded beach. White bones rattled against the incoming tide in a broken skeletal jig. They were tiny chipped fragments at the ocean's lip, but they grew larger inland, and footsteps approached, kicking and crunching them.

"Who's there?" Ivory asked.

She hoped to see a pale thin girl walk the beach. Cabrina Brite of all people would understand the feeling of washing ashore.

Except Cabrina had washed onto the sands of Cape Morning. Ivory had washed onto its sister of night, a Cape Shadow with its own sky and ocean, hidden from the red sunrise.

She rolled over and sat up, eyeballing a great white skull the width of her chest that lay not far away. It was catlike, only far too large, the remains of some prehistoric sabercat with two curved teeth boring into the sand.

Something laughed from inside the skull's sockets, shrill and mean.

"Cabrina?" Ivory said, her voice nearly a croak.

She doubted Cabrina laughed like that. But then, how could Ivory know? They had never met while Cabrina was alive.

The skull twitched, and Ivory made to turn, stand, get away, but her head felt full of seawater, leaving her a waterlogged doll. The skull watched her squirm in place. She could only stare back unblinking as a hairy yellow-black teardrop slithered down the skull's alabaster cheekbone and onto the sand.

It was a cat. Short tawny fur covered most of her lithe body except where a black stripe split her down the face, spine, and tail, like a chasm gaping open through the cat's body.

The chasm cat arched her spine in a taut stretch and then padded toward the water on cautious steps. Red drops trailed her hindlegs, and Ivory had the ludicrous thought that the cat had gotten her period. She was pretty sure cats went into heat instead.

The same red fluid dripped from Chasm Cat's mouth. An object trembled between her teeth. She might have caught a small bird, or a fish, but the wet form wriggled without any clear shape.

Even when the cat hopped onto Ivory's chest and slinked up her body, Ivory couldn't make out the nature of the cat's crimson prize. No fur, feathers, or skin. Only a raw gleaming muscle, its edges swimming in thin tendrils like tiny hairs underwater.

The dark lump swelled with heat where it touched Ivory. Its drops dotted her chest and flared past her collarbone and up her neck, where the lump's odor invaded her nose. Either Chasm Cat herself had no scent, or this sour animal stink overpowered all others.

She slid the wet lump against Ivory's lips. Mixed sensations made her think of newborns, and red-tinged milk, and dark blood dripping down a needful throat. They were alien thoughts, as intrusive as the lump itself.

The cat pressed harder against Ivory's face, greasing her lips and chin with warm fluid. Knifelike slits in the cat's eyes cut an insistent wedge into Ivory's mouth. Her entire body would cover Ivory's face if she kept sliding upward, and Ivory remembered old folklore about cats smothering infants in their cribs.

She could almost believe it as the lump sprouted tiny limbs and crawled inside her mouth. Each touch was a spider leg across her gums, between her teeth, exploring the insides of her cheeks. Once squeezed all the way inside, the lump sank onto her tongue, and its hair-like tendrils flicked at the edges of her throat.

If she resisted, those tips would keep prodding inside her mouth. It was simpler to bite down. Soft flesh coated the lump's outside, but inside, her teeth crunched messily on thin fishlike bones. The sound clicked in her ears and made her jerk and twitch and want to vomit.

Chasm Cat pressed her face to Ivory's lips to keep the meal from coming up, and then she nuzzled Ivory's neck as if showing her how to swallow.

Harsh wind rolled off the still-coming tide and whistled through the sockets of the beach skull. *Swallow*, its notes sang. *And don't forget.*

Ivory hurried through crunching and then forced the stinking lump down her throat. Its fleshy hairs squirmed all the way to her stomach.

Chasm Cat sank from Ivory's face. Small paws padded down Ivory's limbs, past her tattoo, smudgy and unreadable here at Cape Shadow, and then Chasm Cat slinked past the grand skull, where the darkness cleaved her into two tawny half-cats with a black line between them. The tide sent bones clacking across the sand.

Beyond the shore, a black silhouette cut a starless patch from the night-blue sky where a mountain climbed from the ocean.

Ivory had to be imagining this distant shape. There was no island off the coast of Cape Morning besides the tiny remaining nub of Ghost Cat Island. Nothing like the looming presence in the distance.

But then, she had to be dreaming, right? The rock Ivory knew might only be the pathetic reality to a cat's infinite dream. Ghost Cat Island might be grander than Ivory had ever known.

The blue-black sky rippled, and the stars shot apart, a clump of luminous sand dispersing through a cosmic ocean.

Ivory began to crumble too. Her vision washed from the world under a black tide, and she became sand in an hourglass, bleeding at hour's end to the far side of time. Away from Cape Shadow.

Back to Cape Morning.

4. THE INVITATION

Something moved in the dark.

A noise hit Ivory as she surfaced from the dream. She wanted to cry out for the cat, and then for someone to come to her attic bedroom, before she remembered she wasn't home. This was Wolf's house. She rarely stayed over at Wolf's, but a new exhaustion had slipped into bed, and they had both crashed together in worn-out sleep.

Sweat dotted her skin as she curled against the bed. A scent she'd once savored had gone bad somewhere nearby, and now a miasma coated the cool sheets and warm air. Wolf's heavy breath teased toward snoring beside her.

Which meant the noise couldn't be either her or Wolf.

He would be pissed if she woke him up over nothing, and did she really want to spoil a good night? Better to see if there was anything worth bothering him about. She climbed out of bed on careful tiptoe, slid on her underwear, tank top, and jeans.

The zipper chewed its teeth shut as the noise came again. Hard surfaces, scraping together, like the soles of rough feet brushing against floorboards.

It could be a window rocking loose in its frame. Wolf's house was old, wasn't it? These wooden floors and narrow halls had watched generations come and go.

Ivory listened at Wolf's bedroom doorway. A cry stirred in her chest like a war horn calling across an ancient battlefield.

Except to cry out might draw an intrusive presence.

She crept into the hallway, paused outside Wolf's office to listen again, but there was nothing on the other side of the locked door. If she called it quits now, she could strip naked again, slide into bed, and soak in Wolf's warmth until morning. She should take what she could get. That was how life worked.

The next scrape dragged a soft shriek up Ivory's throat. She swallowed it hard. She had to be hearing branches against glass, her own heartbeat, not footsteps elsewhere in the house.

At the hallway's end, she glanced into the kitchen and turned on the light. No sign that anyone or anything had entered since her arrival tonight, but the kitchen's luminance only reached so far into the nearby living room. One more wall switch, anchored between the living room's crucifix and the sofa, and Ivory could put this trouble and herself to bed.

Scraping came again, closer and louder, a sharp nail against glass. Outside.

Ivory padded over the living room carpet and parted the weighty curtain from the picture window, where Wolf's house looked out on his neighborhood.

A white figure rushed away from the glass.

Another shriek tore up Ivory's throat. Her hands flew to cover her mouth and pawed uselessly at her neck, but they couldn't choke away her cry.

The figure swept toward the end of Wolf's driveway like a leaf snatched by the wind. It twisted there, lost in a stormy spiral, and then turned around as if hearing Ivory's shriek.

Looking back at the house.

Waiting.

A stillness settled between them, caught in the picture window glass. Was this a thin human far away, or a hunched animal close by? Ivory couldn't tell for certain in the dark. She leaned forward to get a better look and then sank against the window. Exhaustion tugged her eyelids down.

When she opened them again, there was nothing but the white reflection of her face against the black night.

Like bone upon sand. Her dream of catlike phantoms returned, carrying a force-fed heart. Swallow a small heart, offer blood, and off to a world of shadows, if she would only follow that uncertain figure into the night.

"*Whaaat—*"

The noise shot another shriek through Ivory, and she'd already spun from the window and raised her hands before she realized it was only Wolf, speaking through a yawn. Her second scream blocked out the rest of whatever he said. He was a silhouette against the kitchen light, rubbing the heel of his hand at his forehead.

"Ivory," he said, fighting another yawn. "It's just me."

He should try telling her heart that, maybe then it would quit slamming one-two fists against her ribcage.

She forced in a deep breath. "I heard something," she coughed out.

Wolf tilted his head to show he was listening. "Wind. Nothing else."

She looked out the window again and listened to him pace the room, grumbling to himself. He turned on the lights, and she came eye to eye again with her own transparent reflection and the sliding shapes of the living room against the darkness.

Maybe she'd heard the wind. Or a cat, not in her dreams but something solid and mischievous running around in the night. People weren't supposed to believe in ghosts, and a visit by some large feral cat made a hell of a lot more sense than a visit from the dead. And Ivory had never given a ghost reason to haunt her anyway.

Besides grabbing the death poem.

She chewed her lip, and her vague reflection did the same. Wind, cat, ghost, her own imagination? The only dead people she'd seen before were in funeral homes. She'd never witnessed one out in the world until this morning, let alone stolen the deceased's writing. What had she seen on Ghost Cat Island? It could've been a cat. Or a ghost. And if it were a ghost, couldn't it be Cabrina? Curious and perhaps not too happy at having her poem taken from the beach.

Why did that matter if her death wasn't a suicide, as the poem claimed? What really happened to Cabrina Brite?

The death poem gave no answers.

"What are you looking for out there, another ghoul?" Wolf asked.

"Ghouls aren't ghosts," Ivory muttered, but she couldn't remember the distinction.

"Pretty sure they're the same." Wolf slid close, warming Ivory's back. "And this is why we don't tell ghost stories before bed."

He was making fun of her. Thought she'd had a nightmare, and maybe that was so, but he should take her seriously. He instead tried to pick her up and carry her back to bed, as if nothing had happened since.

Ivory pressed him back and curled into herself. "I was scared," she said. "It doesn't matter what it really was."

"Come on." Wolf offered a smirk instead of comfort. "Can't you take a joke?" He laughed as if he could infect her with the noise.

The best she could muster was an olive branch of a smile, and even that made her tongue taste rotten behind her teeth. She looked down at her clothes, and then to the front door. To walk away in the middle of the night would be dangerous, ghosts or not. Ivory would need Wolf to drive her.

His hands encircled her wrists in rough but familiar fingers. "Come on," he said again. "Back to bed where you belong. With me."

Pleading haunted his eyes. *Be the good one, pretty Ivory*, they said. *Or pretend. Can't you at least pretend? Be convenient for me. Please.*

The window beckoned, the night waiting with its ghosts and ghouls.

Ivory relented, kissing Wolf's hands. Tonight had been good. Wasn't that worth being convenient for his sake? She could shrug off his disregard, especially when she would rather hold his body than a grudge.

He drew her in, and she let him, and the bed took them again. Even if she couldn't get back to sleep, his wanting her might be enough.

From the Diary of Cabrina Brite,
April 17, 2018

You can treat anything like flower petals
Plucking away the pieces
She loves me
She loves me not
She loves me
She loves me not
She f

I shouldn't have done that with Xi. I knew better, I'm smarter than this, but she's smarter than me, and we both knew what we wanted, and my heart was so full when I looked at her that night, and we kissed, and everything went from there.

It was a good kiss. A good everything.

[a section is missing, cut away by fabric shears]

wrote it then I wouldn't stop thinking about it, but I already can't stop.

I kissed Xi. In different places. Ordinary kisses, sweet kisses. A special kiss.

She was soft, and I've been second-guessing myself since. Did I do this because I have feelings for her? Or because we're friends and I don't know how to show affection right? Or because I want what she has? She can't slice open a vein and share meds with me, doesn't matter which parts of her I taste or take inside me.

I'm so fucked. Xi's been looking at me weird since. I don't think she told anyone. But she knows one thing, and Rex knows another, and they talk, but none of us would kiss and tell.

Which means nothing about this can get to the house. To her.

It stays between Xi and me, and I guess Rex in whatever he figures out or hears. I can't even keep my lies straight anymore. But Xi and Rex and me are forever, if forever can be a for now kind of thing. I hope it can.

~~Xiomara~~

~~Alyssa~~

I'm going to die in this house.

5. THE VISITOR

Five days after an elderly Cape Morning resident found the body at the beach, and one day after the wake, Alyssa Xiomara Munoz attended the funeral service for one of her best friends in the world.

She hated every moment of it. All the wrong things came out of people's mouths in the church, at the cemetery. Especially from Viola Brite, acting the perfect grieving mother as if the funeral were a scheduled event in her reelection campaign to town council, while her husband Gary stood by in approving silence.

Xi spent the evening cleansing her brain with a long scroll through photos of herself, Rex, and Cabrina. Cabrina never took selfies, had no social media presence anymore, and she wasn't fond of letting others take her picture, but Xi had managed to guilt her into group shots. Sometimes she had taken candid photos of Cabrina while pretending to text or browse videos. And she sometimes felt guilty for taking them.

But not tonight. Right now, she needed every true photo of Cabrina she could get. Her head turned away while sitting at a high school cafeteria table. A distant figure on the beach at night. A forced smile seated between Xi's big grin and Rex's smirk on Cabrina's birthday back in April.

If Xi sat on her bed in her pajamas and kerchief, scrolling through photos until she passed out, maybe she could push this terrible day out of her head.

Rex hadn't shown up at the funeral. Less likely chickening out, more likely because one or both of his mothers refused to let him go unless he promised to hold his tongue, a promise Rex could never keep. Cabrina used to blame it on Rex being a Virgo, but really, he was the youngest of the trio. Xi had turned nineteen in February, and Cabrina in April, while Rex remained eighteen until September, and that appeared to make a big difference in restraint.

Xi really could have used him at her side today. Yes, he was grieving too, and he had his own way of digesting that grief. He had come by later for their beach ritual, a symbolic burial at sea involving offering Cabrina's belongings to the tide while he chanted some made-up ceremonial spell, and briefly Xi had pretended the three of them were together again. That didn't make Rex's absence earlier in the day easier. The beach ritual was a personal goodbye in the place Cabrina's body had been found, but it wasn't the same as donning black at that sunbaked cemetery while the weight of a lowering casket sank against Xi's bones.

The next photo, from some time ago, showed a day when Xi's mother Josephine had taken the girls dress shopping, and Cabrina had bared her pasty white chest beside Xi's olive one when they both lifted their tops and stuck out their tongues in the changing room mirror. Xi had transitioned from blockers to estradiol shots eleven months earlier and had been proud of the changes. In another photo, more recent, Cabrina sat writing in her pink-paged diary with the green cover beside a swelling beach fire.

Yet another showed Cabrina dozing here, in Xi's room, on the night of the kiss. Recent enough that Xi could still feel it. An easy memory to sink toward, maybe to dream about.

She didn't realize she'd fallen asleep until the rattling glass in one of her bedroom's windowpanes shook her awake. Her eyes flew open to find her glasses had slid off her face. Her phone had slipped through her fingers. She had the drowsy notion of an animal banging in its cage for food or freedom; the wind could play such tricks. Or maybe the wind was the animal itself, hunting her on this awful day.

Her eyes rammed shut and then open again. She needed to jot down that thought. It might lead to a decent poem.

She struggled her glasses onto her nose and ears, and then reached for the pen on her nightstand when she heard the second rattling.

The sounds didn't make sense. Usually when Xi heard noises at night, she dismissed them for the family on the other side of the duplex walls. One side of her bedroom held both her windows, covered by violet curtains and separated by a stretch of wall coated in off-gold wallpaper. If a stiff wind came howling against this side of the house, both windows should have quaked together, but the one down at the corner had rattled first, alone, and now the other rattled across from her bed.

Like something wanted in.

"He's found us," Xi muttered, and then she shook her head.

She and her mother had left New York when Xi was young, and they had been living in the duplex at Cape Morning, Massachusetts since Xi started middle school. Little chance for the past to creep her way. Zero chance it would recognize her at nineteen when her childhood had worn a different name, different presentation, different everything.

Her father was dead, nothing but a boogeyman. There was no protective bubble surrounding Cape Morning, let alone any reason to believe she'd burst said non-existent bubble by leaving for Dartmouth in two months to begin her freshman year at college.

But the thought hit anyway. Another consequence of sitting up too late, as if nocturnal grief might wake the dead.

Xi glanced over her room, watchful for spectral signs. Her walls wore framed photographs, scraps of highlighted magazine pages, and a mounted bookshelf loaded with chosen texts like *White Is for Witching* and *The Haunting of Hill House* which sat beside gifted books like *100 Great American Poems*, because her mother was trying her best. Xi had been teaching Cabrina about poems and scrapbooking, trying to hobby her way through Cabrina's depression before—

Before. And they had both expected tragedy for far longer. Maybe always.

Only books and papers and memories dotted the bedroom. No mysterious presence. Raindrops tapped the windows. Either the wind was the hungry predator, or it was prey leading a predatory storm against the Munoz side of the duplex.

"Stop," Xi warned herself.

If she kept thinking like this, she would never sleep. Let the past lie, let the dead stay dead, let her head fill with soothing voices and calm rainfall.

She was about to pull off her glasses when a new sound slid from outside, the kind she couldn't dismiss for rain or wind.

A light hiss climbed a tensed throat.

Xi knew that sound best coming from Cabrina Brite, when she would quietly muscle her vocal cords toward a higher pitch before speaking. A hurried exhalation; you had to know Cabrina to notice. Even her vindictive mother couldn't take that away.

But that sound had no place tonight.

Between the wet-streaked glass and her vague reflection cast by lamplight, Xi couldn't see outside her window. She unlatched the top and forced it squealing open to the fresh sound of rain and a low thunderous rumble. Beyond the screen mesh, a shingled awning sloped toward the darkened lawn, where tendrils of night curled around nearby houses and a pale figure below.

Cabrina.

She stood on the lawn, impossible and hazy. A walking dream, let into the waking world by Xi's heartache. This had to be the kind of night for miracles, when a beloved friend could come back.

Xi's heart quivered, and warm relief flooded through her. Explanations wrestled through her thoughts—*the body's discovery was a case of mistaken identity, the funeral was an expensive error, the last few days have been a nightmare and now I'm awake*—but reminiscence drowned them out. Memories and immediacy stewed an amalgamation of this moment and that April night when they had kissed, and held each other, and more.

Like part of that night, Cabrina was naked. Xi retreated to her drawers and pulled out clothes—a gray hoodie and white sweatpants. Wide for Cabrina, but they would help.

Xi lifted the window's screeching mesh screen and then carried the clothing bundle over the sill and onto the damp shingles. Rain splashed her pajamas and kerchief, dampening skin and hair. She should head back inside, forget this, except she couldn't leave Cabrina standing cold and alone below.

"Cab?" Xi called into the storm.

The pale figure came half-climbing, half-drifting up the side of the house, toward the awning's slope. Yes, this had to be a dream, one in which Cabrina could fly.

She stepped with birdlike grace onto the awning's edge. Bedroom light shined across her damp skin. She had always been pasty, but she was paler now, like the night had grown a sharp tooth of a young woman outside Xi's window.

"Here," Xi said, holding out the hoodie and sweatpants. "You're cold."

Cabrina turned over the clothes between her hands and then hurried into them. Xi studied her for signs of decay, of having drowned and washed ashore, but Cabrina looked like a living girl. Not someone to bury but someone Xi wanted to hold against her.

Another reminder of that night two months ago—Xi and Cabrina, wrapped in a tempest of each other's scents and touches. Cabrina's hand in Xi's hair. Xi's tongue in Cabrina's mouth. Cabrina's breath down Xi's front. The two of them rushing into their clothes afterward with shallow breath and soreness.

Xi took a step closer, and her foot skidded over the slick awning. Cold fear fingered through her nerves, freezing her in place. The sense of slipping and falling tingled too clearly across her dampening skin. Too real.

This was no dream.

The wind blew Cabrina closer, her presence nipping at Xi like an ice cube kissing her spine. If tonight was not a dream, then it should be impossible. Cabrina Brite couldn't glide on the wind, could never frighten Xi. More than that, Cabrina was dead.

And yet she was perched outside Xi's bedroom. Real? A dream? Or something else?

The thudding quickened in Xi's chest, her body noticing something her thoughts hadn't caught up with yet. Stormy tension gripped the air around Cabrina. Her chill didn't seem to bother her, and a stiff look in her eyes warned she'd found a better source for warmth than clothes, the glint of a big cat somehow knowing it was about to catch an antelope.

Xi scuttled backward over the sill and slammed her window shut. Raindrops slid from her feet onto the gray bedroom carpet. A black curtain coated the outdoors, the night hungry for the house, and a chill crawled over Xi's skin.

She must have imagined the ghost. Guilt could twist somebody up inside—except Xi had nothing to feel bad about.

Not guilt then, but anxiety that someone might find out what she and Rex did today after the funeral, at the beach where Cabrina's body had floated ashore. It would have offended Cabrina's mother and probably most other funeral attendees to see amateur witchcraft for a dead girl, but few of those attendees had loved Cabrina. They wouldn't have understood, and none of them could know. Rex would never tell. Neither would Xi.

But an anxious illusion couldn't have accepted Xi's offer of clothing.

A palm struck the outer glass with a hard thump, making Xi leap back from the window. The skin was not pink-pale like Cabrina's when she was alive, but eggshell-white.

Two eyes surfaced from thick nighttime, Cabrina's once-gray irises now ringed in honey. Her eyelids narrowed to menacing, and then her jaw snapped open with a throaty catlike hiss. The narrow shape of her face glowed white, androgynous in her violent thinness. A fresh gust sloshed rainwater against the glass and shoved another palm beside the first, as if both the storm and the dead friend had been dredged up by the sea.

Both the storm and the dead wanted in.

Xi snapped her hand to lock the window's latch the moment Cabrina's palms pressed up.

The window jiggled in place, but it did not open. Cabrina's gaze flicked toward the latch, and then she hissed again. Her eyes and palms sank into the night, leaving finger-shaped smearing on the glass.

Xi rushed to the other window and twisted the latch seconds before an open hand struck the screen mesh. No face emerged, only that hiss against the rattling wind.

Genuine guilt sank through Xi's insides. She had never shut Cabrina out before. No one Xi knew needed a safe haven like Cabrina. If the past several days of death, wake, and funeral had been nightmares—nothing more—and a living Cabrina now clambered outside Xi's room, she would have opened the windows in a heartbeat.

Except Cabrina was dead.

The night closed fingers around a vague pallor and drew Cabrina's palm off the screen mesh. Shadows snaked through Xi's bedroom, beneath her dresser, bed, in the open closet. Cabrina's presence haunted the walls, either invading the other family's side of the duplex or giving up corporeal form to join the wind itself.

Xi staggered backward to her nightstand and snapped up her phone. Rex might be awake. That shoreside ritual had been his idea. He was the witchcraft aficionado; maybe he could fix this. And even if Cabrina's presence tonight had nothing to do with the post-funeral ritual, who else could Xi turn to?

Another rumble of half-hearted thunder chased a squeaking wet noise outside—feet leaving the awning. Cabrina was on the move.

Every door and window on Xi's side of the duplex gaped open in thought like fresh holes in her head. She dashed into the upstairs hallway, lying dark in either direction. The windows in her mother's room would be locked, the bathroom window didn't open, but what about the other side of the duplex?

Xi scrambled toward the slim staircase and paused halfway down to peer over the banister, where the foyer led to the kitchen and living room.

At the far side of the kitchen, a white figment rushed toward the window over the sink. Wet palms squealed against unyielding glass, and then Cabrina hurried on. She struck the next window hard, desperate, and then swept by on another stormy gust.

Xi flew down the stairs and crashed into the foyer as a bony form slammed the front door from outside. It jostled in the frame, the thick wood turning furious.

Twin deadbolts and the knob lock should have held, but Xi pressed her hands against the door anyway, almost superstitious that without living flesh to help, the house would lie open for every vampire and ghoul and ghostly friend who crept in the night. The door bucked horse-like beneath frail hands.

"What do you want?" Xi cried. She sounded alien, her voice cracked and panicky.

The door quit fighting, and a needful fist pounded hard in time to Xi's heart. *Thud-thud. Thud-thud.* Like Cabrina was afraid.

Deeper guilt stretched open inside Xi, hungry enough to swallow her, but she was too scared to unlock the door. Never mind Cabrina had never hurt anyone but herself. Xi should be ashamed. How was she any better than everyone else in Cape Morning?

That guilty inner maw seemed more friend to this pale Cabrina than to Xi, wanting her in, in, in as if Cabrina's ghost could replace Xi's heart and come alive again in Xi's chest.

The night wind rolled off the house, an echo of the receding tide, and the front door went still. Xi's hands held stiff against the wood in case the calm was a trick, though Cabrina could try the living room next. If she pounded those fists against the picture window, she might break it.

Light flashed down the stairs and into the foyer. "Alyssa, what are you doing?"

No ghost this time. Cab would never call Xi by her first name.

She rolled her shoulders back, pried her hands from the door, and sank toward the staircase as Josephine reached the bottom step. The wind settled, the night forgetting Xi's age in favor of obeying one of her childhood's hallowed rules—when her mother came near, the monsters had to flee.

Xi needed to believe that rule now more than any other night in her life. She shrank against Josephine and tangled her arms around her mother's trunk.

"Alyssa, please," Josephine said, but she wrapped her thin arms around Xi's shoulders. "What's with you? I thought someone was trying to break in."

"A nightmare," Xi said, still a tremor in her voice. "Sorry, Mama."

Her mother seemed unsteady beneath her arms. Unlikely that Josephine had frightened anything off, mother rules be damned. She was a runner more than a fighter, one reason she and Xi had fled from Xi's father years ago, when he was still alive. Even then, Josephine remained nervous, like she thought he was faking. Or maybe she believed in ghosts.

She might have been in the right. Cabrina had wanted in, and she'd vanished less by motherly rules, more like she'd been torn from the door along with the storm.

A little bit of a nightmare, and something in the wind.

Josephine ushered Xi upstairs step by step, muttering about old times under her breath, as if hiding the past from Xi would likewise hide Xi from the past. As if there weren't much worse things than memories seeking warm bodies in the night.

Ghosts shouldn't be able to accept clothes and wear them. A true specter shouldn't have any need for windows and doors.

What the hell had come to the house tonight then, and why?

Xi meant to text Rex, warn him, but Josephine led the way back to bed, where the night and drowsiness hit hard.

Morning poured summer sun into Xi's bedroom. She woke up late to striking daylight, the kind that made ghosts seem silly. She could almost pretend her Cabrina sighting was only a nightmare brought on by guilt, regret, and nostalgia. Maybe she would have forgotten the encounter entirely.

If not for the handprints smearing the glass outside one bedroom window.

From the Diary of Cabrina Brite,
April 18, 2018

When we're closest to what we want,
That's when gravity changes its mind.
The world performs a handstand,
Shaking us off at last.
And in the beautiful embracing emptiness,
We pretend we can fly.

6. HAUNTED

In the early dawn, Ivory meant to get her swim in before work. Days had passed since that fateful discovery and the sighting over the sun-stricken water on Ghost Cat Island. The odds of finding another body, seeing another ghost, whatever it was, should be low.

Ivory was about to leave her attic bedroom, bathing suit under her clothes, when she heard a familiar scraping downstairs.

The house had kept her since she first moved to Cape Morning, before she'd even found a job. It had been a Craigslist opportunity from two landladies who'd converted their small split-level attic into a bedroom; sisters Stella and Chelsea Burke had grown up in this house and taken it on when their parents moved to Florida. Both were in New York on vacation, same as this time last year, as if the summer people still to come in July and August would be easier to stand than the June tourists invading Cape Morning now.

Ivory froze in place and listened hard for footsteps, creaking floorboards, a voice. "Stella?" she called. "Chelsea?"

No answer. Had the sisters come home early? Ivory doubted it; the house should be landlady-free for another couple of days.

She cracked open her bedroom door, overlooking a descending set of wooden stairs. "Chelsea? Stella, is that you?"

Nothing. Ivory padded down the short steps from her attic room to the second-floor hallway. The house was narrow, its living spaces packed tight against each other. No one up here between Stella's room, which had once belonged to both sisters, and Chelsea's, which had once belonged to their parents. The bathroom door hung open— nothing inside. Ivory peered over the banister to the first floor. The picture window faced west, leaving the downstairs gloomy even in the early morning, but best Ivory could make out, there was no visible sign of anyone in the living room, kitchen, or foyer.

Only the sound of scraping. Less like rough feet on floorboards now, more like someone brushing against the front door. The wind rattled it against its frame, and Ivory felt the curl of an inviting finger in the intrusive gust.

She swallowed hard, muttering "Fuck it" under her breath, and then raised her voice into the darkness. "Cabrina?"

No answer, but there was no mistaking that scraping sound. She'd heard it last week at Wolf's house. Cabrina or not, this could be the same haunting.

If Ivory could call it a haunting at all. Wolf's mocking denial hadn't helped a few nights ago, but lying down with him afterward had at least settled her nerves, and she'd started to wonder if he could be right, that she'd mistaken a neighborhood pet, or her own pale reflection, for the ghost of a dead girl running through town, trying to get into people's houses. Wolf's, then. Ivory's, now.

"Are you Cabrina?" she asked. "Is this about the poem?"

She started toward the stairs and felt her bathing suit chafe beneath her clothes. She'd been heading to the beach. Couldn't she grab the death poem and wedge it back beneath the driftwood tree? No harm done? She retreated upstairs and looked out her attic window, past the next block and the summerhouse rooftops. Ghost Cat Island eluded her view from here, but she could just make out a patch of the sand and water.

Red sunshine glared over the horizon. Maybe its light was dancing on the waves again, forming illusory cats on that scrap of offshore rock. Ivory tried to laugh. Scared of shadows—no, worse, scared of the damn sun itself.

But the laugh caught in her throat, refusing to believe any of this was funny. Instead, her hands began to tremble.

"I'm being such a baby," she whispered, annoyed.

But she couldn't make herself believe that either. Something was waiting for her, and if she went to the beach alone, she couldn't be certain what would happen.

She hurried out of her clothes, tossed aside her bathing suit, and then dressed for work. There would be no swim this morning. Maybe never again.

Downstairs, the living room seemed brighter. Ivory might've been scaring herself silly with paranoia, but she didn't trust that possibility either. It seemed the kind of thought meant to deceive her only long enough for some other symptom of haunting to rip the belief to pieces.

Movement slid in the corner of her eye. Something at the picture window. Maybe looking through. At her.

"A bird," she said, stirring up courage. "A cat. A big bug."

Her head twisted fast, shooting a twinge down her neck. Through the glass, the only movement was the hedge rising just above the height of the sill. Something there, then gone. It reminded Ivory of childhood games, little kids yelling *Chase me!* at tired adults.

She didn't think there was a child out there. And it wasn't the wind.

She could tell by the smudge. A curving shape to suit a brow over two eyes, pressed against the glass. It might've been a face small enough to fit wholly against Ivory's palm. Or it might've been only a partial smudge, where a girl could've been looking through the window for the woman who'd stolen her final words.

Someone, or something, waiting for Ivory to come back to the beach.

Cape Morning formed a crooked hook of Massachusetts curling into the Atlantic Ocean. Ivory liked to imagine that from the sky, on a cloudless night, the cape's lights might twinkle into the dark ocean like fairy lights against a wall of black paint, but she never saw anything like that from the ground.

One side of the cape faced the mainland in an unpleasant shoreline of small stones and shards of sea glass. The other side faced the ocean, where it lay beaten into stretches of white sand, overlooked by summerhouses. A fishing dock lingered at the cape's tip, where the hauls became scanter every year.

The land widened heading away from that tip and toward town, where Ivory could almost forget the peninsula's shape. No sea, no shoreline, no ghost. She might not have thought of the beach while on shift if not for the summer people it drew.

Some of them arrived to drink and relax. Others seemed to visit solely to unleash themselves on the locals.

Ivory's first shouter appeared half an hour into her early Thursday shift at Sunshine & Chill. Like most Cape Morning businesses, the café saw a flood of summer people in June. Their numbers would taper off by late July, but right now Ivory was stuck behind this cramped counter, facing customers built of salt and annoyance.

"I wanted a caramel double espresso," the woman snapped. Teeth glared between her lips, colored with a striking shade of scarlet lipstick. She wore a likewise scarlet wide-brimmed hat, and thick sunglasses guised her face, pale except where the sun had already licked her tiny nose a faint pink. "This has peach in it. Why would you do that?"

Ivory wasn't surprised she had messed up an order. Sleep had come hard the past several nights since her scare at Wolf's house, her bad dreams full of a dark shore, an oceanic mountain, and golden eyes. Work had come even harder. She could barely keep her thoughts straight. Scarlet here might not have been the first mistake, only the first to speak up.

"I'm so sorry," Ivory said, taking Scarlet's tray, where a thick mug steamed with the wrong coffee. "I'll get your correct drink right away."

"But you shouldn't have done it in the first place," Scarlet said through her teeth. "I've been waiting behind all these other people, and after all that, my drink's wrong. Just because you don't want to come work your shitty job doesn't mean you should give me a shitty morning."

Ivory pretended the café's machines were making too much noise for her to hear. She could have turned around and snapped back that she made mistakes like anyone else, or that she might make fewer mistakes if she hadn't been having nightmares, or that she was a person and that should be enough.

But snapping would break Ivory's protective shell. She had to be nice, had to be pretty, even in this ugly off-yellow cap and apron worn by every Sunshine & Chill employee. To be unpleasant, even for a moment, was to turn pariah in another's eyes, and ugliness was unladylike, and to be unladylike was to be burned.

Years after high school, she remembered the trick campfire keenly, no matter how much she wanted to forget. Shannon, Carrie, Lana, Trevor, Casey. What they pretended to be, and the moment they showed their true faces. Funny—Ivory had forgotten their names for the better part of a decade. Why had they come back now? Maybe to trick her again.

"Stop," she whispered.

"What?" Scarlet snapped. "What'd you say?"

"I said, here you go." Each word quivered as Ivory turned around and passed a new mug and tray across the counter to Scarlet. "Sorry again."

Scarlet turned away, muttering something Ivory was grateful to miss. She forced her attention to the next pair of customers and pushed high-school era memories down into the depths of her brain where they belonged. Underwater. Drowned.

The morning rush began to die down when she heard a familiar voice.

"I'd have banged my car into hers before she left if I still had the old plates."

Joan Fang appeared like a dream at the counter's head. Similar sunglasses to Scarlet's dangled on a strap from her neck, and she scratched at the fade along one side of her head beneath a patch of trimmed black hair. She was stocky with a square tan face, a sturdy mountain of a woman.

"I wouldn't get in trouble for it either," Joan went on. "Nobody can blame you for shit driving if you're from Boston. That's street law." A Cape Morning resident for ten of her forty years, but she couldn't shake her prior city's accent.

"You heard all that?" Ivory asked. "How long have you been here?"

"Since before your shift." Joan cocked her head at one of the tables. "Semester's done, so I'm pleasure reading while I can before summer tutoring kicks in. Would've said hi whenever you came in if I'd seen, but you might've been too stressed to notice anyway."

Ivory gave a rough sigh. "I didn't see you." She wanted to collapse across the counter, let Joan pat her head, but the best she could get away with on the clock was a stealthy half hug before refilling Joan's coffee. Still, it looked like the customer herd had thinned, most of the summer people now making for the beach. There was a chance to talk.

"Been busy?" Joan asked.

"Sort of," Ivory said. "The house is empty with the landladies away, so I've been at Wolf's more."

Joan's tone turned disappointed. "Ives."

Ivory began shuffling cups and trays. "He's not that bad."

"What a terrific bar for relationships, *not that bad*."

"It's hardly a relationship."

"I'll say." Joan turned her silver wedding ring between two black-painted fingernails. "What happened to that dancing girl?"

"You mean Lucinda?" Ivory balked as a *ping* let her know the water had reached a near-boil. "That was two years ago, and she was only here for that summer. You told me not to fall for summer people anymore."

"Sounds like me." Joan lowered her voice. "But take a break from him, or he'll think you owe him, or that he owns you. He don't respect you, Ives."

Her coffee was ready, and Ivory took the moment of toying with the cup, spoon, and tray to let the subject die. Joan's dark fingernails were scratching too deep.

"How about you?" Ivory asked, passing the order across the counter. "Peaceful summer?"

"Been rough at the house," Joan said. "They had that funeral yesterday, for the Brite girl. I didn't let Rex go. Too much of a smartass. Went in his place, to pay respects."

The death poem flashed through Ivory's head. "I heard about her. The one they found on the beach?"

"Yeah. Drowned, washed ashore. Rex is taking it hard. They were close." Joan tossed up her hands. "Right after graduation, practically. Finally through high school and then bang, lose one of your best friends. Now he's got to step into the adult world with a fresh catastrophe."

Ivory met Rex in passing now and then when she visited Joan and her wife Marla; a teenage boy had better things to pay attention to than his mother's friend. No chance until now for Ivory to realize she knew anyone with ties to Cabrina Brite.

"Now that boy's getting deep into Marla's mystical crap." Joan clinked her wedding ring against the counter in a *tink-tink* rhythm. "He should be visiting his father next month. If he gets too stuck in the weird, I don't know if he'll get out of town. He should drive down to Boston, get some miles under him."

"His dad won't come here?" Ivory asked.

"I took the motivation in the divorce," Joan said, smirking. "George Murphy is a glacier. A wonder he even commutes himself to work. I don't like Rex driving down, but I got to push my case. When he's got one mother saying to go, and another mother saying to get the Ouija board, what's he supposed to do? Shouldn't matter so much to me when it's all fakey garbage, I suppose. I'd rather he get high and play with Marla's nonsense than anything real and dangerous."

Ivory thought of a white shape caught in the sunshine. "What's something not fake?" she asked. "Something dangerous?"

"Cape Morning," Joan said. She shuffled aside as another customer approached the counter and gave Ivory his coffee order. When he left, she took his place. "Marla says this place draws people in. And there was this old fisherman, Roy Long. Nice guy, used to give Rex neat stuff. Passed away a couple years back. Anyway, Long would tell me the undertow here has an appetite. Weird shit, huh?"

"The sea wants blood." Ivory's voice was almost a whisper. "Do you think Cabrina knew that?"

Joan gave Ivory a hard look, eyes falling dark. That question might have pushed too far.

"I heard she might've been swimming between the beach and Ghost Cat Island," Ivory hurried out. She swept a rag over the countertop. "That's the only weird place at Cape Morning I can think of."

The concern faded from Joan's eyes. "Sure, sure. I mean, it's all secondhand these days, but there used to be a decent-sized stretch of scrubland off Cape Morning's coast. Might've had another name then. Some ship sank out there in the 1920s, passengers got on lifeboats, and as they were rowing ashore, people said they spotted cats on that little island. Supposedly there never were any cats on that ship that went down, though. Locals started believing the cat sightings were ghosts, running out their nine lives on the Atlantic. Hence, Ghost Cat Island."

Ivory spied another customer coming in and willed him to venture toward another stretch of counter, let him be someone else's problem. The customer did as Ivory hoped.

"Time goes on, the stories get bigger and stranger," Joan said. "Sightings of different things under the sun's glare. Other kinds of animals. Cougars, lions, tigers, hyenas—"

"They saw dogs on Ghost Cat Island?" Ivory asked.

"Hyenas are cats. Part of that ancestry." Joan grinned. "They just look funny. Except they couldn't look like anything since people weren't really seeing animals. You go out there, you'll find nothing. Like UFOs, the Loch Ness Monster, this and that. Somebody catches movement out the corner of their eye, mistakes it for one thing, tells people. Someone else's mirage looks like what they expect. Soon enough you got everyone seeing aliens and dinosaurs. Or a ghost cat. An illusion. But that's the dangerous part, you know? Expectation and mystique."

Ivory guessed that was true, if Cabrina had drowned trying to reach that island and find the impossible for some reason. A mirage would explain the shapeshifting figure Ivory had seen in the sunshine that next morning.

But expectation couldn't explain her Cape Shadow dreams.

"People see less these days." Joan sipped her coffee and winced—still too hot. "The ocean's been eating the rock. No more shrubs, barely any ghost sightings. It's still out there, and you could probably get on top and pretend you're standing on water from a distance like some New England Jesus. But Ghost Cat Island is pretty much sunk."

"So there's nothing to see," Ivory said. "Nothing to swim for."

"Yeah, mystery to me why the Brite girl might've swum out," Joan said. "Got rumors, though. People talking accident, maybe she took her life."

Sunshine & Chill's atmosphere grew heavy on Ivory's skin. "How was the service?"

"Bright. Humid." Joan pointed at the café windows, as if you could see the cemetery from here. "It was up in that treeless corner of Fairview West, a lot of new plots there. No shade in a summertime funeral, because of course. Can't tell sweat from tears, except with Viola, that poor mother. That's why I kept Rex home. Got that mouth on him from me, none of the wisdom to keep it shut."

Ivory nodded along. That poor mother, yes. That poor family. And what about that poor ghost who might have come creeping outside Wolf's house last Friday night and Ivory's house today? If it had been Cabrina, that is. Other thoughts bullied for space in Ivory's head, of Cabrina Brite taking a nighttime swim, and Ghost Cat Island, and a service in a cemetery's treeless corner.

An idea struck Ivory of where she needed to go after her shift ended this afternoon.

"Joan?" Ivory said. "I have a weird favor to ask."

7. THE ANGEL

The house was a sea-worn two-floor colonial with narrow rooms and halls. Joan had said a dozen times that the outside needed a fresh paintjob, having been scored by ocean winds and storms, and Ivory knew from entering the home-side entrance in the past that the inside lay lushly cluttered with ornate lamps, overlapping throw rugs, and boxes of antiques and junk for Marla's occult shop, Secret Spell.

Ivory and Joan came through the shop-side entrance today. Wooden windchimes hung above the door, and it knocked the low-hanging sail as it opened, sending the tubes clunking together beneath the planked ceiling.

Rows of shelves stood tightly packed together throughout the shop. Secret Spell held an eclectic collection where you could find typical new age mass-marketed crystals and tarot cards mixed in with genuinely unique pieces and rare finds. From how Joan told it, while some tourists liked the usual witchy assortment, more often they favored ocean-themed trinkets, talismans, occasional scrimshaw, and other baubles made of sea glass, driftwood, small seashells, and shark teeth. A glass case near the register toward the back displayed the shop's more expensive jewelry. Other decorations hung from four rows of nails beneath the register, and various windchimes, tapestries, and threads with purposes Ivory couldn't identify dangled from the ceiling.

Out of this collection, she needed to find something to help with a spirit, and before her short lunchbreak ended.

"Good afternoon!" a cheery voice belted out.

Marla Sinclair appeared from around one of the taller shelves. Silver and darkness danced through her waist-length hair, caught in a red kerchief. She was a broad woman nearing fifty and wore a heavy leather apron over her blouse, likely to work on one restoration project or another.

Her eyebrows bounced when she spotted Joan, and then Ivory. "Oh, I thought I heard tourists again. Here for lunch?"

"I need to pick something up, and then it's back to work," Ivory said.

Marla coasted toward Joan. "Which makes you the chauffeur."

"Shuttle driver, bringing you customers," Joan said. She kissed Marla's cheek, looked at Ivory, and then cocked her head toward the rest of the shop. "Be a star and buy something nice."

Ivory hoped to. She also hoped she would know what she needed when she laid eyes on it.

Marla nudged Joan aside and pressed close to Ivory. "Clue me in. I'd love to help."

Ivory chewed on her tongue. Saying she wanted a token to help give peace to Cabrina might be an issue for Joan and Marla when their son had been her friend. But lying might not get Ivory the item she needed.

"I had a friend," Ivory said. "She passed away a year ago, and I wanted something to commemorate her? No, that isn't it—to say goodbye? A sendoff? If that makes sense."

"You're such a sweetheart," Marla said. "I can walk you through it. Tell me more about your friend."

Ivory set her teeth. She knew practically nothing about Cabrina besides spotting her body on the beach and feeling that presence on the way home, outside Wolf's house, and this morning, a haunted heaviness that might have had nothing to do with the girl who'd left a death poem under driftwood.

"She liked poetry," Ivory blurted out.

"Okay." Marla flashed a smile. "That's a start."

They left Joan fiddling with a trinket by the register and approached a thin line of smoky windows. Sand and grime coated the outer edges, but sunlight shined cleanly on a series of statues and carvings. A column of shelves jutted from the wall underneath, filled with statuettes and idols.

Marla hummed as she floated her hand over the shelf, readying a suggestion. "How about—"

The above-door windchimes clunked their music again, this time for a longer spell as six people stepped inside at once wearing the summer vacation look of tourists in identical sunglasses, tote bags, and Cape Morning T-shirts. They must have already visited one of the more obvious beach-side gift shops. Now they thought they wanted something more exotic.

"Here come the connoisseurs," Joan muttered.

Marla slid pincered fingers across her lips before excusing herself, leaving Ivory to her own devices. She couldn't exactly wait through Marla's niceties with the out-of-towners. Her break wouldn't last forever, and neither would Joan's offer to drive her back to Sunshine & Chill. Joan had her own day to get to.

Ivory leaned over the figure-stuffed shelves. A curvaceous mermaid lay beside a wooden heart, and beneath them sat a small lion-like sea monster. Any one of these could make the kind of magic Ivory needed. Or they could be as useless as good luck you bought in a store, all mass-produced rabbit's feet and four-leaf clovers made of plastic.

But she kind of loved that people purchased treasures like that. To adorn themselves with hopeful trinkets was like pretending there were gods of fortune they could coax into loving them.

Ivory's eyes lit up as she zeroed in on a particular statuette—a wooden angel, about the size of her hand. Its warped creases and washed-out coloring suggested it had been carved from driftwood.

Was this more of Marla's nonsense? A touristy bauble? Or something real and dangerous? Something in between, Ivory hoped. Something to watch over and guide the dead. She had to go with her gut.

And hopefully her gut went with her purse. There was no price tag.

She waited for the tourists to spread through the shop and leave the counter open, where Marla and Joan chatted over the register.

"Why?" Joan asked, questioning a sentence Ivory couldn't hear. "It's my summer."

"Because you're too gorgeous to lounge around all day," Marla said.

Joan patted her cheek. "I'm too gorgeous to do anything else."

Marla gave a loud, barking laugh, glanced for whether the tourists could see her, and then kissed Joan's lips. This was not a moment for Ivory, but she found herself smiling anyway.

Joan noticed her and slid back on her heels. "How goes it?"

Marla plucked Ivory's prize from her hand. "A driftwood angel. They might watch over a journey."

"Is it good?" Ivory asked.

"The ritual of mourning is what matters," Marla said. "And I think an angel is a safe choice for that."

Safe—Ivory liked the sound of that. She could use cautious stability if she was going to try appeasing ghosts. And something safe might protect her in case this haunted feeling signified a presence that wasn't a dead teenage girl.

"It's thirty?" Marla said like a question and started to ring Ivory up. "I feel like putting a price sticker on it saps the magic."

"Oh, totally," Ivory said shakily, and she felt Joan rolling her eyes.

Ivory's reluctant hand dipped into her purse. Thirty was more than she'd meant to spend.

But then, could she put a price on the end of a haunting? That had to be worth eating ramen a few nights until her next paycheck.

Was the driftwood angel enough then? Ivory glanced over the countertop, the shelves of bottles behind it, the woven basket of hard candies, seeking anything she could use.

Her gaze fell left of the counter, where various bracelets, necklaces, and flower crowns hung on iron nails. Some were made of sea glass, others from old shells. One of the crowns appeared to be done up in dried seaweed, though a closer look revealed the kelp-colored leaves to be plastic. The nails bore a mix of the authentic and the touristy.

Along the bottom row dangled a small wreath of stems and three poppies. The flowers looked to have been dried out, and the wreath gave a crispy sureness when Ivory plucked it off its nail.

"And this," Ivory said. "It's beautiful, don't you think?"

She paid in cash, dollars she usually kept in her purse for a cab or tipping a Lyft driver on those just-in-case nights when Wolf turned her out with no offer to drive her home. It had only happened twice before. She would try to stuff a little more cash inside before it happened again, but that would come another night.

Right now, she meant to honor a ghost.

From the Diary of Cabrina Brite,
April 21, 2018

<u>Daytime People</u>
Cabrina the Caged
Dad
Her
Mailman
Campaign Claude

<u>Nighttime People</u>
Cabrina the Uncaged
Dad
Her
Sometimes Xi
???

<u>Nighttime Theories</u>
I am dreaming
I am nightmaring
I am sleepwalking
~~I am losing it~~
~~I am being punished~~ FOR WHAT?
I am being paranoid
I am being watched
I am being followed
I am being possessed
I am being haunted

8. THE CEMETERY

After Ivory finished high school, she had decided to be a creature of life. She first jotted the words on her Class of 2006 senior yearbook's inside cover, beside a violet lipstick kiss. The next day, she threw the book into the Rhode Island Sound, letting the water swallow her old face, old name, and everyone she wanted to forget. Shannon, Carrie, Lana, Trevor, Casey, even her parents. A kiss of death to the past, to that high-school era trick campfire; a proclamation of life for the future. She had stuck with those principles since.

To set foot among headstones and graves was not her way.

She left Sunshine & Chill at four, slathered sunblock down her arms, face, and neck, and then started up Main Street. Her walk took her past the fast food chains, Starbucks, the library, Peyton's Ice Cream, government buildings, and more. A small cluster of plastic roadside ads swayed in the wind, each wearing a politician's name, slogan, or photograph filled with false cheer and false promises. High above them, a white billboard wished out-of-towners a fantastic summer at Cape Morning's beaches.

The western stretch of town liked to pretend there was no such thing as the sea. Spruce trees braced the roads to neighboring avenues from Main, and maples led down residential offshoots. The town splintered from its necessary parts the farther west Ivory walked, its primary thoroughfare branching into suburban lanes and hidden gathering places, like Fairview West Court and its cemetery.

Ivory's boots flattened the sand-flecked grass at every step. How did bits of beach get this far inland? She couldn't imagine most tourists wishing to see rows of gray, black, and white headstones, especially not summer people. They came to Cape Morning for the beach when Cape Ann sounded like too much trouble, Cape Cod was too busy or too far, and Salem wasn't their style. They did not come to stroll between the graves of Cape Morning's dead.

No matter how recently interred.

The air turned heavy with a New England grayness, almost mournful, ready to cry rain against Ivory's skin. New plots opened in the cemetery's treeless far corner, where Joan had described Cabrina's service.

The poppy wreath dangled from Ivory's uncertain fingers. She could have worn it as a bracelet were it for her, but she had brought it for Cabrina. Amends for seeing her body on the shore and taking her death poem.

Appeasement for a ghost, if that was what Ivory had really seen.

Someone else might have had the same idea. Past a tremendous angelic monument with the surname *Thompson* carved at its base, two voices whispered back and forth.

Ivory slowed in the grass and listened to it crunch blade by blade, felt the alien grains of sand dig and stick within the textured soles of her checkerboard shoes. They were trustworthy sensations, realer than any spectral chill. She didn't want to believe in ghosts and mysticism, but a lot of people refused to believe far more evident things. How could she be sure she wasn't one of them?

She rounded the gray-stoned monument and came upon a stretch of unsettled earth and a plastic grave marker. The marker did not linger alone.

Two teenagers hunched over it, their backs to Ivory, their sneaker heels digging into the upturned soil at the grave's edge. One held a canvas bag, the other a purse. The one with the purse turned, her green-and-white glasses shooting a look over the purse strap. Dark curls ringed her round olive cheeks and pursed lips, and ruby-colored plastic studs dotted one ear. Her hand shoved the other teen's arm.

"No rushing me, Xi," a voice of sandpaper said. It was familiar, with traces of Joan's Boston accent. "Almost done."

"No, we're completely done," Xi said. She sprang from the grave and shoved a plastic baggy into her purse. The hem of her wine-red blouse swayed over blue jeans, and sunlight glinted in the lenses of her glasses.

Her friend grabbed his canvas bag and glanced over, baring his round tan face. He was fresh out of high school, his hair shorn short, his stocky form wearing black jeans and a leather jacket like he was some 1950s greaser transported to June 2018.

Yes, Ivory knew him—Rex Murphy, son of Joan and Marla.

"You'll forget your mom's brushes," Xi said, smacking Rex's arm.

He bent again to scoop the abandoned brushes down his canvas bag's throat. The jostling contents revealed a dark wooden corner with the word HELLO curling toward the center of a flat board. Both teens caught Ivory's stare.

"What's the matter?" Rex asked, smirking now. "Never done a séance?"

Ivory settled into herself and shook the eerie atmosphere out of her head. "It's okay if I startled you," she said, raising a friendly hand. "I'd have thought I was a ghost too."

"Ghosts don't care about graveyards," Xi said. She had pensive eyes, too old for her teenaged face. "This is where we put the bodies, not the souls."

Both teens retreated in slow steps. Rex was all nerves and fists, a bristling little hedgehog who thought himself a giant porcupine. Xi's glasses half-caught the gray light, bending one eye against the other like a pair of laughing/crying masks.

"What would haunt a cemetery, then?" Ivory asked.

"Ghouls," Rex said, almost reflexively. "Looking for bodies to eat."

Xi tugged Rex's arm. His posture suggested he knew he should run, but Ivory had dangled his interests, and he was taking the bait. Too much like Marla to resist.

Ivory gestured at the earth. "And zombies? Don't they climb out of graves in the movies?"

"Mainstream movies are for imperialist indoctrination." Rex's surly expression resembled a teacher disappointed with his class. "But yeah, they'd probably want to leave their graveyard, and quick. When you put that much work into getting loose from somewhere, you don't want to risk getting caught again."

"Was Cabrina interested in this stuff?" Ivory asked.

"Sometimes." Rex stumbled back a step, led by Xi. If he was surprised Ivory knew that he'd known Cabrina, he didn't show it. "Depended on her mood."

"She had a lot of moods," Xi hurried out. "Come on. We're done."

Ivory followed them a step. "Have you seen her too?"

Xi froze between the headstones. She glanced over her shoulder into the cemetery's distance, wearing the look of someone who believed more than she liked. Rex might believe too, but he kept a stern face.

"Did she keep a diary?" Ivory reached into her purse. Her fingertips teased at the folded scrap of pink paper there, a death poem read by her and her alone. "Do you know where it is?"

"Do we know how to betray her?" Rex snapped. "No, we don't."

Ivory couldn't blame him for being defensive. Their friend was gone—what else could they do?

"You've seen her, haven't you?" Ivory stepped closer.

"My room," Xi said. Her eyes widened to sky-swallowing pits. "My window."

Ivory's nerves quaked. She still wasn't sure what she'd seen outside Wolf's window, or this morning, but her suspicions were growing. There was too much sense of a Cabrina-shaped haunting to be coincidence.

"There has to be a reason she came to you," Ivory said. "I want to know—I want to understand. What really happened to Cabrina Brite?"

"Doesn't matter," Rex said. He grabbed Xi's arm and ushered her farther back into the cemetery. "Nobody can help Cab now. She's gone."

They slid deep into the rows, toward a line of trees. Neither glanced at Ivory, as if they had really seen a ghost this time.

Or perhaps they were the ghosts.

Ivory strode alongside the tilled earth and laid down her poppy wreath. Blades of grass curled around the stems. Ivory prettied the wreath in place and then took in an eyeful of Xi's and Rex's handiwork.

The placard lay maybe a foot and a half across, its white face printed with firm dark letters, but Ivory could scarcely read them beneath the layers of dripping paint. It was the wall-grade kind, smeared in a clumsy rainbow. Within the mess, elegant yellow letters formed a name.

Cabrina Aphrodite Brite.

"Beautiful," Ivory whispered, without meaning to.

Other names lingered beneath the vandalism. Vague suggestions near the grave marker's base offered Cabrina's birthday—April 2, 1999—and her significant date from a week ago, June 14, 2018. Beneath that showed Cabrina's parentage, *Gary Brite and Viola Brite*.

Another name hung above everything else in larger letters, but

Ivory couldn't make it out through the paint. She picked out letters not belonging to *Cabrina Aphrodite Brite*. What bizarre alias had the family printed on the grave marker?

Crunching footsteps stiffened Ivory's limbs. She wheeled around to standing, half-expecting to see the shifting white shape from outside Wolf's house that night a week ago.

Only a silhouette haunted the foot of the grave at first, some small bare-limbed tree, black against the sunshine. The features then sharpened to a thin woman in her late forties, wearing a navy-blue blouse and mom jeans. Puffs of strawberry blond hair sprang in magnificent curls. A battered expression hung loose on her lips.

Ivory knew firsthand that this woman's expression had seen better days. She'd witnessed it herself, beaming with false cheer from the campaign standees dotting Main Street and other roads. She knew this woman by name, face, and the body of her dead daughter.

Viola Brite.

And Ivory had to look as guilty as the teens, an overgrown vandal who'd dumped high school into the sea years ago and yet apparently needed to flex rebellious muscles over a dead girl's grave.

An excuse stammered on her lips. "I'm sorry," she said. "I came to pay respects, and you startled me—not that it's your fault! There's something about cemeteries, don't you think?"

Ivory bit her bottom lip. Of course Viola didn't think that. Graveyards only offered ghouls and ghosts when they were strange places. When you buried a loved one, that graveyard had to feel like a home.

"You can breathe easy," Viola said, her tone polite. "I know this wasn't you. Neither of those two are strangers. They think they're being friends, but they're too young to know the cost. Defacement, violation—it doesn't honor the dead. It hurts everyone left behind. I hope they never know what it's like to outlive their children."

She knelt at the grave marker and ran a finger over the plastic. It came away wet with paint. She reached into her purse and dug out a pair of tissues.

"I'm sorry," Ivory said again. She was abusing that poor word today like a fourth grader who'd just learned they could swear.

"Do you have anything to wipe with?" Viola asked. "Napkins, anything like that?"

Ivory's hand crawled into her purse, past the death poem. Her fingertips brushed the angel carving, but right now seemed like a bad time to give it to Cabrina. She drew up a papery wad of white instead.

Viola took the wad and kept wiping up yellow paint. "Bless you—?" The sentence dangled expectantly.

"Ivory Sloan."

"Thank God for you, Ivory." Viola reached out, took Ivory's hand, and gave it a politician's firm shake, smearing dots of yellow paint on Ivory's fingers. "Apologies, I'm a mess. I'm your town councilmember. You've probably seen my reelection posters. *Viola Brite will make it right*? My campaign manager likes a rhyme."

"I—yes." Ivory hardly squeezed Viola's hand as she glanced up and down the rows.

There was no sign of Xi or Rex; they knew better than to trap themselves over a near stranger. Maybe Rex would tell Joan and Marla he'd seen Ivory. Maybe not.

"He never wanted to hurt anyone," Viola said. "I think that's why everything confused him. You expect boys to cause pain, and to like it. Boys will be boys—except sometimes they won't. Because the boy is gone."

Ivory opened her mouth to ask how much Viola knew about Rex, why she'd think this. The sound rippled in her throat and died there. Her front teeth dug into her lower lip.

"He was sweet." Viola swiped again at the paint, stroke by unmaking stroke. She grew silent and closed her eyes, falling into the motion of it, as if rocking a baby in her arms.

Paint smeared together, reds and yellows forming orange, yellows and blues forming green, purples mushing into the lot of it as rainbow streaks ran as brown as clotted blood. Little by little, another name climbed from the grave.

Jesus, she was trans too, Ivory thought. Viola was talking about her daughter.

Ivory glanced away. She didn't want to know this deadname. Cabrina had signed her true name on the death poem, the ink on pink paper more meaningful than whatever her mother had forced onto her grave marker.

An unwanted thought sank through Ivory: *I could've been her.*

And then another: *Had she lived, she could've been me. A creature of life.*

But Cabrina seemed more a creature of death now. Still, didn't the dead have a right to themselves? Or did someone quit being human after passing away?

"Anyway, put those troublemakers out of mind, won't you," Viola asked, in a way that wasn't a question. She crumpled the tissues into a paint-streaked wad, tucked them into a sandwich baggie, and then tucked that into her purse. "We each grieve in our own way."

Ivory chewed her lip into a wobbly smile. What a perfect defense. Viola was in denial, and no one could fault her for it without looking like a monster. Who'd dare contradict a grieving mother? Vandals and beasts. Not nice and pretty ladies like Ivory.

Viola petted the poppy wreath, as if she'd brought it herself. "This is sweet," she said. "Lovely. A symbol of remembrance after wartime, and my child's war is over. It belongs here."

Ivory's fingertips teased the death poem in her purse. It belonged here, too. She could draw it out, show Viola, and even through a shield of denial, the doubt would hurt her.

Don't call me a suicide.

Except Ivory didn't know the truth herself. The death poem was a mystery, as was what had truly happened to Cabrina Brite beyond the beach, in sight of Ghost Cat Island.

Viola looked thinner kneeling than she had standing. If the death of her daughter couldn't eat at her spirit, it would devour her flesh instead, leaving only a skeleton to tend this grave. Her smile would go unchanged, and the grave would freeze in this presentation, a stretch of tilled earth leading to Cabrina's deadname on the plastic grave marker, a placeholder desecration before her family had it carved forever in marble. Viola might sit in denial, but she might also have been a mother who felt everything. Vanity, grief, pride, hatred, defeat— all at once. Was that enough to feel sorry for her?

Ivory studied Viola—no flowers, no visible card, nothing she meant to read. She might have come to speak with Cabrina, lay untruths upon her grave, but a less charitable side of Ivory wondered if Viola had come solely to guard Cabrina's grave from her friends.

"Forgive me, but I should get going," Ivory said. "I have work." She didn't, she'd finished at the café today, but there was no reason for Viola to know that.

"You'll visit, won't you? At the house?" Another Viola question that sounded like a command. "You'll stop by? I don't think anyone else has come to his grave since the funeral, like they think it needs time to cool. But you're here, and I appreciate it."

I didn't do it for you, Ivory wanted to say. And she had harsher words, bubbling in her throat under a smothering caul of niceties. The angel carving formed a bulge in the side of her purse. She would have to save it for another time.

"We're at 36 Harper," Viola said. "A little ways from Main Street."

"I can find it." Ivory wished she couldn't.

"You might be surprised to hear, but you come to miss arguing with a child around the house." Viola patted her palms over the still-grassless soil of her daughter's grave as if tucking a blanket over a child's bed. "Silence will do that."

Ivory studied Viola again, wishing she could read past those blue eyes and pert lips. Viola was a pitiable wall, the avatar of familial loss. How could any decent woman deny a grieving mother a little company?

"I could visit sometime, sure," Ivory said. Not strong enough. She forced a wider smile and a grander lie. "I'd love to."

9. SECRETS

For all his hurry in leading Xi away, Rex was the one to stall at the tree line where Fairview West Cemetery met a low cement wall. Too far to hear Ivory talk with Viola, but he watched them. Ivory reached into her purse for a cloth or tissue and handed it to Viola, who went straight to work defacing the grave marker's painted corrections.

"Rex?" Xi tugged at his arm. "Do you know her?"

"My Ma's friend," Rex said. "Supposedly Ivory's one of us, but she doesn't look it from here."

"She might not know any better," Xi said. "Maybe she just thinks she's helping a local politician."

Sure, Rex supposed Ivory could be trans *and* not very bright. Cab had been the same. But there was ignorance, and there was being so dense that you couldn't feel a tightly wound viciousness radiating from Viola Brite.

If she caught Rex or Xi correcting Cabrina's grave again, she'd send her cop husband to prowl the headstones. He might not have evidence to pin a graveyard paintjob on Rex or Xi, their word against his wife's, but he could catch them in the act and make their summer a living hell in the meantime. Anything to keep Viola off his back.

And when Xi left town for Dartmouth at the start of the college semester, Rex's hell would go on and on unchanging. Same as Cabrina's death.

"Rex, please," Xi said, pulling again. Unless he ran, she wouldn't either.

"Right, fine," Rex said. "Got what we need."

His sneakers crunched through the mulch beneath the nearest tree. He and Xi would hop outside the cemetery's grounds, circle around to his car by the bait-and-tackle shop, and be on their way.

"Did you think Ivory was a ghost?" Xi asked. "At first?"

"Oh yeah, town's full of them." Rex wasn't sure if he meant it or not. He liked to keep the possibility in mind while leaving any definite wraiths to comic books like *Hellblazer* or the occult section of his stepmother Marla's shop.

Xi should have laughed but didn't. "Why did she ask about Cab's diary? Do you think Viola passed the old one around?"

Rex didn't answer.

Cabrina had kept an online blog full of videos and text—what she'd called her diary—up until her mother discovered it. The next day, Cabrina deleted the whole thing. Better to scorch that digital earth without knowing how much Viola had read than risk her seeing another second of video or sentence of text. That was in early April, right after Cabrina's birthday.

Rex understood. He had destroyed his social media accounts sometime after starting testosterone, after a couple shits from school clogged his comments calling his incoming goatee a *face pussy*. That made Xi the lone digital holdout, but the silly gay people in her phone couldn't hold a candle to the ones she knew by sight and by heart.

After erasing herself online, Cabrina had started writing in a paper diary of pink pages and a green cover. Her secret. Not even Xi or Rex knew where to find it.

No way Ivory could know about it. She probably hadn't even known Cabrina existed before her death, and vice versa.

But then, Cabrina had kept secrets even from her friends. If Ivory was one such Cabrina secret, she might pop up in the diary. Maybe she'd passed hormone meds to Cabrina after her dealer Germaine's arrest.

Not a mystery Rex or Xi could solve without Cabrina. If anything had happened to her beyond drowning, they would find out tonight for themselves.

At the séance.

She thinks if I like girls then I can't be one, so if she knew what happened with Xi—I don't know, it can't get worse, can it? None of it would make sense to her anyway. She can't understand how two trans girls touch.

I'm always scared I'll come back to the house one day and she'll be here in my room, pawing through this book, and she'll ask me about Xi, about a lot of things.

No, worse, she'll put it right back where it belongs, exactly the way it was, so I'll keep writing here without knowing she's watching me. She won't make the same mistake like with the videos. She'll think up ways to have found things out, and I'll think she's psychic, or

[a section is missing, cut away by fabric shears]

I think Xi gets worried what everyone thinks too. She used to crush on Brian and a couple other guys at the school. I've been forgetting their names since homeschool started.

Sometimes Xi plays it up real obvious. I don't blame her. Liking boys is supposed to be the girly thing to do. The only boy I've liked was Rex. At least when I went to their school.

There used to be a guy I liked who wasn't at school. Or was he a man? I don't know how he liked to be called. I never told Xi and Rex. Would they be jealous? Would they even understand? Maybe I'm selfish, but I want them and him and the ocean and everything.

How am I nineteen years old with too many lovers and too few?

Xi would turn that into a poem. She's been trying to get me to write them again, I haven't since sophomore year, but I've been playing with snippets in these pages. I don't think she understands we're walking different roads. College is a real future for her, putting Cape Morning behind her. I don't even have my GED yet. Poetry won't save me from this house.

Neither will the cinnamon scent man.

This was summer before last, so I was still seventeen. It's hard to remember. Germaine was still selling hormones then, and I got pretty good at hiding my breasts under baggy clothes around the house, but I wasn't ready for a bikini top. I don't know what drew the man to me.

He was older, a little gray in his beard. Big and dapper, could give a bear hug, and he had a distinct scent, like cinnamon. We met when it was cooling off from summer and the tourists were leaving, most of them. He mistook me for a boy like they all do, and then he got confused at my chest. I told him I'm Cabrina Aphrodite, and he told me a name I think he made up on the spot. Maybe it will turn into his real name, the way I got mine. Sometimes placeholders get stuck to you, and it could happen to him. I didn't mean to name myself Cabrina forever. The name was part of a poem, or a trial poem, the bad kind you write in middle school, but the more I thought about it, that was me.

Once the cinnamon scent man and I started talking, he understood. God, it felt good that he understood. Xi takes it for granted. That's not fair, but I think it's true in a tiny way. She's always looked incredible, and I've always looked like me.

The man with the cinnamon scent talked about how nice Cape Morning is in summer, and I guess that's how every stranger thinks. They never see the ugly side of this place. He talked about the water being magic, but then he also said it wasn't ecologically sound to collect seashells, so I think he feels that way about all beaches. I've stopped picking them up since then. Not because I understand, but kind of in respect toward him. He deserves it.

We ended up talking about my stuff later. We talked about a lot of things, I can't write them all here. I forget some, thanks to the anti-depressants. Maybe I'll remember later?

But I won't forget how he made me laugh. I was complaining about how I was too late for blockers by the time I knew what those were, how she wouldn't let me take hormones, so I had to scrounge and get what I could from a dealer. I didn't name Germaine.

The cinnamon scent man didn't want to talk about my home life. He looked me over and said I was a Laura Dern-shaped girl. I didn't know who that was, but I wanted to look smart, so I pretended. My smile got too big and fake, and he called me out, so we started laughing.

It was sweet. A real laugh. I forgot I was allowed to have those. Never in the house.

He'd show up there sometimes, and somehow I'd sneak out, or lie my way down the driveway. She didn't know, or she let it happen. I don't know.

The magic water thing came back up when we were watching a movie at his rental house. I forget the name, but there was a woman who was a mermaid—or a mermaid who was a woman? I don't know how those work. But on land, she had legs. In the water, she had fins. Not like in the Disney movie.

I kind of stopped paying attention here and there, got stuck in my head. Xi would call it an overactive imagination, and she's probably right. But I couldn't get out of my head the magic water thing, or the magic fins and legs. Thinking it could be me.

If I dived into the water, something wondrous would come out.

The cinnamon scent man took me on a lot of dates like that. I think he knew I was off in my head, but he was okay with it.

Things didn't end right. He left town at the end of that summer, came back that October. Everything would have been fine, but I think Xi or Rex noticed him. They had to have seen before. Maybe they were okay with it for summer '16, because he was in town anyway, but he had no reason to be here in October.

Except me.

He told me he couldn't see me again. That it wasn't right, and he had to be the adult and say so, be a good influence. That made it sound like he was any other man, like he knew my dad, knew *her*, and maybe she had paid him to hang out with me, and I couldn't accept that, so I screamed at him.

I was such a child, that was the real problem. I was infatuated, and he noticed and decided we couldn't be friends anymore. Maybe it was the responsible thing to do, but now there's a part of me that hopes he'll come back. It's been over a year and a half. I'm nineteen now.

He gave me this diary. I didn't think I'd ever use it, one of those things you keep but it's too nice to write in. But he told me I had to use it, if I needed it. I could call it a poetry book or an art project if I liked, but I couldn't treat it like it was too nice to write in or else I wasn't really accepting the gift. He asked if I thought it was pretty, and I said it was beautiful, and he said if I felt something was beautiful, then it shouldn't matter what it's called.

I don't know if he was talking about the diary or if he was talking about us. What we couldn't be. I cried a lot then. He was right to cut me off, and I know that now, but I didn't know it then, and I still feel so sorry for that girl I was, crying on the beach.

She would feel sorry for me, too, if she knew how bad things would get. No more hormones. No more high school. Everyone busy and scattering.

That's why I still think about the cinnamon scent man sometimes. He could come back. We could go to the magic water together.

But now I've done much more with Xi. A kiss, and things I can't write here, but they make me blush and tingle like a kid with a crush.

It feels like I'm waiting for her to finish school, like that will change anything. But then, it might? She can come by in the early morning, in the night, or I can run off again without worrying I'll mess up her studies, college prep, beauty sleep. It's going to be a long spring waiting for her and Rex's graduation in mid-June. Xi would call that romantic, maybe so would the cinnamon scent man.

Part of me wants him to come back this summer, too. If he and Xi and Rex are all here, I'll be too distracted to think about anything else.

How am I nineteen years old,
With too many lovers and too few?
A sailor has a girl in every port.
But a lady has many sailors too.
~~Fuck rhyming.~~ Could be worse.

[a section is missing, cut away by fabric shears]

The cinnamon scent man hasn't been here since two Octobers ago. I think he meant to see me again, but he might've been a truth-teller to me and a liar to himself.

A lot of people are.

PART TWO: THE NIGHT OF FOOLS

10. THE SÉANCE

Coming upon the beach at night meant entering an atmosphere of summer people—their drinking, their chatting, and their music blasting from beachfront summerhouse porches down the shore. They were strangers, at family homes or rentals, watching the ocean and the locals below.

Like Xi and Rex, two shadows building a small fire of dry driftwood on the sand. Coastal wind batted at its flames, fighting and feeding them.

The firelight glinted off nearby beer and soda cans. Xi never saw any of Cape Morning's homeless residents here, but Joan Fang said the town council blamed them for beach trash, bringing down the wrath of people like Cabrina's father and his fellow cops. Part of Viola Brite's beautification program, her way to *make it right*.

But from what Xi had seen since moving here, it was always tourists doing the dumping. In the offseason, a band of locals— Rex and his mothers among them—made efforts to clean up Cape Morning's lengthy beach, but with tourists in town, it would be a losing battle.

No cops ever forced *them* to leave. They were walking money. Most beach-cleaners would simply wait for the summer people's exodus in late August before tending to the aftermath.

Xi wouldn't see the post-season clean-up this year. She would be starting her first semester at Dartmouth by then.

Supposing she survived the summer.

A couple of other graduates from their class of 2018 drank hard lemonade nearby. They had nothing to do with this fire, or Xi's and Rex's purpose here. Their gathering offered a beach party façade.

Like that April night when Cabrina had nearly drowned.

Xi had blamed herself then. Still did. Cabrina had been venting quietly about her mother, but Xi had downed one drink too many and forgotten herself.

Viola's a swastika away from being those hare-brained goons who think we can get surgeries while burning hours in junior high, she'd said.

And that got Rex going. *Fuck, if only*, he'd said. *Send me to that school district.*

Only when Cabrina had slipped away had Xi recognized the unfairness in it. She had been on blockers for years before any of them could begin hormones proper. Rex had already started one puberty, but once he came out to his mothers, they had supported him through required therapy and appointments until he could start another.

Meanwhile, Cabrina had no choice but to find off-market spironolactone and estradiol. Her dealer had seemed a hero, before her hellish parents ripped that away.

When Cabrina started that game of dunking heads in the water, Xi had mistaken it for tipsy goofing off and not a cry for help. Only after she'd pointed out that Cabrina was under too long had Rex tackled her out of the water before she hurt herself. That had seemed like the end of it.

Until last week, when Cabrina finished the drowning.

Everyone called her death an accident. Xi and Rex kept their mouths shut, as if there hadn't been precedent for Cabrina to take her own life. Nightmares, depression, absence of meds, isolation by Viola's hand. Not to mention intimacy between Cabrina and Xi despite knowing Xi would be leaving town at August's end. Or maybe because of it.

But if she'd chosen to end her life, why drag herself back from the dead to Xi's duplex? Why had that woman—Ivory?—visited the graveyard with heavy questions?

What really happened to Cabrina Brite?

They would ask her tonight.

Rex's demeanor kept former classmates from intruding, his words clipped whenever they strolled by to feign interest over the wooden board he'd laid in the sand. His black fingernails tapped the edges as if waiting for the right moment to begin. Black stubble dotted his face. Xi predicted that in decades to come, Rex would age beautifully into eventual salt-and-pepper hair and a thicket-like beard. He would become the kind of hoary chaos wizard who lurked in the back of new age shops, except everything he dabbled in would carry threat incarnate.

Xi shouldn't have told him about last night. With Cabrina gone, he was her only close friend, but that didn't make him a good influence, and certainly not a paragon of good sense. He once refused to check out *The X-Files* with Xi, citing it as *a distortion of discovery,* and he'd likewise refused to elaborate.

Telling him about last night could never dredge up a dismissive *You just had a nightmare* or *You need more sleep.* The kinds of real-world reassurances Xi needed right now. Rex instead flung himself past sensible conclusions and toward—

"A ghost," he said. He rummaged through his canvas bag and flashed a lighter at the end of a tiny white paper roll. "How about calling her that until we know better?"

Xi didn't answer him. He sucked smoke and passed the joint to her, and she took it between her fingers and inhaled. They'd each taken a hit before arriving at the beach, but with the dark ocean spreading beside them, she needed more balm for her nerves.

Rex plucked the joint up again. "I'm brainstorming, that's all. Be nice if we'd give a name to what we're dealing with, wrap my head around it right."

It sounded haphazard, slapping a label on a box rather than opening it up to find out what was inside. To name someone or something was to define it. Xi, Rex, Cabrina, supposedly Ivory— everyone who gave themselves names knew that truth firsthand. A chosen and true name gave the mettle to fight back the dead. Power lived in names.

Xi hugged her chest. "We didn't consider everything."

"Why would we?" Rex asked. He pinched off the joint's burning end and then ran his palm across the wooden board at his knees, already griming with sand.

"Lack of forethought makes us sloppy," Xi said. Firelight glared in one lens of her glasses. "Like yesterday after the funeral, playing with the arcane."

"That was cultural, not arcane." Rex dug into his bag again, this time for candles. They seemed redundant against the beach fire, but this was his dangerous playground, not Xi's. "And we weren't fucking around. Sailors have been doing it for thousands of years."

"A burial at sea usually involves a body, not symbolism." Xi glanced at the dark tide. "Changing the rules might change the outcome. And now you want us to double-down with this Ouija junk."

Especially when she wasn't supposed to be playing with magic at all. Not because her mother would think she was out of her mind, or because her mother believed in the arcane. Josephine Munoz was very much the atheist, but as she had told Xi once, *I'm wise enough to know that I don't know everything.* Some stones were better left unturned. One reason neither Josephine nor Xi had gone poking at the internet for whereabouts of Xi's father, instead learning of his death through a phone call from relatives. Sometimes checking on the unwanted only drew its attention.

Josephine wanted to hold onto her disbelief in ghosts, not let the man she once feared prove her wrong. Xi shouldn't let Rex ruin her disbelief either. Yet here she was.

"It isn't Ouija," Rex said. He set the last candle and dug an arrowhead-shaped planchette from his bag. "That's a brand name. This is a spirit board."

Xi studied the white plastic in his hand. Rex was being pushy, nothing new there, but without Cabrina, who else would push back?

Rex lit the first candle. "Look, the best magic is personal. There's more power in a junior high school kid scrawling their crush's name all over a notebook than every spirit board in the northeast. Maybe in the world. Real magic is when it gets dangerous. But this?" He knocked on the spirit board. "I brought this cookie-cutter bullshit so you'd feel safe. I can't baby it down any worse than this and still act like we'll accomplish anything. Whatever happened to you last night, that was raw power. Maybe strong enough that 'Magic For Tweens' will do. Or maybe too strong for any of it to take notice of what we're doing tonight. Either way, I'm looking out for you, so cut me some slack."

He was railroading, and Xi was letting him. What else could she do? Everything seemed fragile in Cabrina's absence, even friendship.

"Maybe Cab will take to vanilla magic better," Xi said. "It's familiar."

Rex nodded, accepting the compromise. "If this doesn't work, we do things my way."

He could have babied the ceremony down another step by bringing a store-bought Ouija board, settling their efforts in the realm of bar codes and trademarks, but Xi nodded back. She doubted things would come to that, already certain something would happen here. The atmosphere felt swollen to bursting with another storm, as if Cape Morning were set on ruining the entire summer.

If that weren't enough, Xi assumed that Rex had cut this crude wooden slate himself off a hunk of driftwood. Things from the sea had power. Considering how she'd died, Cabrina could be the same.

Xi didn't have Rex's interest in the arcane to ward off any spirits, whether they were evil, sweet, or nostalgic. If any true magic lived in Xi's family, it was cut off when Josephine moved the two of them to Cape Morning and changed their names.

There had been no better time to come out of the closet. To Josephine, it must have seemed like cosmic convenience to have her child say, *I want a girl name*, right when they were doing everything in their power to bury their old life under a grandmother's maiden name. An old name became a deadname beneath Alyssa Xiomara Munoz, and then even that true name hid beneath the nickname Xi.

Her father would have never found them, at least not through her. He had believed in tough love, more tough than loving, that the world would show no mercy and neither should he. Doubtful he'd learned better before he died of a stroke at fifty-three.

But Xi had. When her mother moved them both to Cape Morning, she'd realized her father's way was a lie. Her mother said if the world would show no mercy, then she would be better than the world. Home had to be a haven. Xi could return there for shelter and to gather the strength she needed to face the merciless everything that waited outside their door.

Even a dead friend.

It didn't exactly thrill Xi to be doing this. The ghost hadn't acted like Cabrina, though maybe that's what death did to someone, leaving them cold and hungry for warmth. All the more reason not to play around with this shit.

But better to call her of Xi's and Rex's own volition than wait for her to crawl along Xi's windows again and find a way inside.

"That's it!" Rex cried, laughing. The candle flames danced at the four corners of the spirit board, and the planchette lay waiting. "You got yours?"

The candles were Rex's reagent for the séance. Xi had forgotten about her own, slipped into her purse when Ivory accosted them at the cemetery. The sandwich bag crinkled in the wind as Xi lifted it through zipper teeth, its plastic wrapped tight around clumps of black graveyard dirt, a fistful grabbed from Cabrina's grave. The earth was still chewed and soft from shovels, spongy enough that Xi could believe Cabrina might have crawled out and no one would have seen any difference upon visiting the grave the next day. Trekking to Xi's home would have been easy had Cabrina not been dead.

A long look down this beach might show Cabrina's pale figure walking the sand, clothed in Xi's hand-me-down hoodie and sweatpants.

Rex cleared his throat, and Xi handed over the graveyard dirt. Would it help? Cabrina's grave seemed a cursed place where a deadname glowered down on a dead young woman. Small wonder she might have crawled free.

In sophomore year, Viola had loaded Cabrina's lunch with protein to *man her up*, a phrase Xi had heard from her father a hundred times. Viola's plan made no sense, yet her wrongheaded paranoia had kept ever-sensitive Cabrina from eating for days.

Xi hadn't known how to help. It was Rex's idea to swap lunch portions between the three of them until everyone had even amounts of cafeteria food and Cabrina's packed lunch. They had both worried Cabrina would develop an eating disorder if left to her own judgment in defying Viola Brite.

Look, everybody's eating some of the school junk and some of your mom's junk, Rex had said, making both Cabrina and Xi laugh. *A gender-neutral, taste-neutral part of a balanced lunch.*

Xi had sat back and watched Rex solve the problem. He was good at solving, almost as much as causing.

Could Xi have done more? She'd stood by with gentle reassurances, but those felt like useless words as she watched Cabrina lose her pretty clothes and makeup beneath Viola's control. And then as an eating disorder developed anyway, gluing Cabrina's skin to her ribs and hips.

Rex could offer confidence, and Xi could take Cabrina shopping, but they couldn't have frozen Cabrina's hormones as they worked upon her body against her will. Especially after what happened to Germaine.

Xi had almost told Cabrina that not everyone got hormones or wanted them, but that would have sounded patronizing. Cabrina knew that. And she knew herself better. She didn't own the flesh and blood and bones she lived in, a town councilmember's trophy child, *mine, mine, mine*. No home anywhere, only a house and a body.

No amount of holding Cabrina, or crying on her, or kissing her could heal any of this. Maybe they had all failed her so badly as to break the laws of life and death.

If Cabrina had a vendetta against her mother, why had her ghost come rising up Xi's side of the duplex last night? That was no untouchable specter that left handprints on Xi's bedroom window glass. Something solid had crawled out of that storm, wearing Cabrina's face. Her desires.

"Quit blaming yourself," Rex said. "Keeps you from concentrating."

Xi shook her head. "I didn't say anything."

"You got on your guilty face. Neither of us did this to Cabrina, and she didn't do it either. We know who's to blame."

"I saw her," Xi said. "Before she died. I told her, *We got you.* But I didn't ask what was wrong."

"And?" Rex asked. "That wasn't a lie. We do have her, and we *know* who's to blame."

Xi shouldn't have felt this nervous anymore. "This weed's doing nothing for me."

"Germaine's locked up." Rex shrugged. "Got what I could."

Xi glanced from the fire and spirit board, down the beach. Porch music went on fighting the wind and tide, but it was losing. The sea was strong. It had beaten everyone who ever battled it since the beginning of time.

"Here she lay, our sweet Cab," Xi said, as if reciting one of her poems. "All those years of love, now lost to the mother of life."

She waited for Rex to call her weird, but he only set his attention on the bone-colored planchette. Its arrow slid over wood until it found the word HELLO, and then Rex guided it toward the spirit board's alphabetized center.

Xi joined her fingers with his. They had done this before, but without Cabrina to join in, their movements crawled frail and lacking.

And yet with her fingers on the planchette, and the music quivering above the beach, and the summer people milling here and there along the sand, Xi felt the cold sense of someone hunched in the shadows between flickering beach fires. Inches out of reach. Faintly out of sight.

As if Cabrina were here already.

11. AN OCEAN OF GHOSTS

For the right person, or the wrong one, humanity came with conditions. They might be imposed by strangers, but they could be imposed by the self, too, Ivory knew. Under surprise circumstances, certain choices of kindness, decency, or respect needed making, or else how could you call yourself human anymore?

The haunting would only end by showing Cabrina Brite the decency she deserved. These were conditions of the self.

And yet, Ivory had pushed Cabrina's truth away and let Viola Brite spin her into the family's post-mortem lie. It was a customer service routine, as if Ivory had worn her ugly café cap and apron to Fairview West Cemetery. Had Ivory curled her lip and sneered at Viola, that graveside scene wouldn't be plaguing her with what she could have done, should have done.

Small wonder Cabrina wasn't at rest. How could her spirit move on with her death a mystery, her resting place wearing the wrong name, and no one willing to do anything about it? The whole town was complacent.

Even Ivory. She stomped through her attic bedroom, tearing off her clothes and clawing at her skin. Her tank top snagged in her hair. The gaff caught at her legs mid-untucking. Every strip of fabric stretched away sticky with sweat and disappointment. Sick of clothes, sick of undeserved pleasantries, sick of that smile in the mirror.

"Fuck off," she whispered.

Who the hell was she whispering for though? Stella and Chelsea? They weren't coming back yet. No one was home to hear any commotion. Ivory could get loud.

Ivory could scream. "Fuck off, fuck off! Fuck. Off."

The vanity mirror across from the foot of her bed didn't deserve her curses. She should have directed them at Viola, and then said her daughter's name, corrected her at every turn, become a hellish whirlwind instead of sinking into the miasma of Viola's politician-perfected grief.

Ivory's pacing slowed. Her chest heaved, out of breath, but she felt better. Blowing off steam was preferable to bottling up her anguish. She should work it out of her system, find a summerhouse party, get hammered, get wasted. No one cared when townies joined the rowdy festivities. Tomorrow was her day off anyway. Skip sleep, skip the nightmares.

Anything but pacing here. To obsess over that graveyard confrontation was not the behavior for a creature of life.

Ivory turned to the mirror. "Fuck off," she whispered, once more for the road.

The scraping sound dragged airy claws over her ears and sent her shuddering back against the foot of her bed.

Was something in the house again? Had it ever been? She didn't know, and she was sick of not knowing.

"What?" Ivory snapped at her bedroom door. "What do you want? Your friends went to see you. *I* went to see you. Your awful fucking mother went to—"

The scraping cut her off. Distant now, a dry surface brushing against a door downstairs. Ivory parted her lips to curse again but caught herself. Acting like Cabrina should fuck off and be disregarded wasn't Ivory's way. That sounded more like Viola's job, except she would dress the cursing in niceties and practicality. The flawless mother in grief.

"It's her, isn't it?" Ivory asked. "That's why you can't rest. Because of Viola." She nodded at her reflection and spoke more firmly. "Okay then."

She threw on jeans, a blouse, and a robe, and then dug the driftwood angel out of her purse. It felt cold in her hand. She followed the banister downstairs to the front door and pulled it open.

A small animal vanished into the foliage bracing the driveway as a fresh breeze yanked at Ivory's blouse and hair. No Cabrina that she could see. Only the wind wanted her.

She'd messed up with the ghost of maybe-Cabrina at the beach, taking the death poem, ignoring the sensation at her back. She'd failed to follow outside Wolf's house that night, and again this morning. If Ivory messed up tonight too, she might not get another chance. To slip into her boots and follow the wind and whatever had vanished down the street toward the beach might look like a trap at worst, foolish wandering at best. But now might be a night for fools.

Lights dotted the sandy distance, where summerhouse porches attracted parties like clouds of gnats. Far-off beach fires whipped under coastal gusts. There were likely locals and summer people gathering around them, but they were only flickering lights from here. The nearby patch of shoreline lay black and empty, and it called to Ivory.

There was no elderly man at this visit, no call to authorities. No pale body in the surf, at least that Ivory could make out. Nighttime waves thrashed at the sand, the sea promising, *I'll take you there. To answers.*

Ivory shook the promises away. The sea couldn't give answers when it had taken Cabrina in the first place. It always wanted blood.

But to learn what happened to Cabrina—didn't she deserve at least that much respect?

Ivory's boots trudged down the dry sand. She slipped free and left them behind, fingers crossed they would be waiting for her when she came back. Same as Cabrina had left her death poem. Ivory's chest felt hollow, thinking of that poor, desperate girl, as if the Atlantic Ocean had sucked away all her organs and had no more purpose for her. Ivory sensed a similar threat waiting out there in her future. Was she right to head for it? There was a mistake on the wind, and it drifted from the shore with every salt-scented gust. But was the mistake to meet what lay ahead, or to flee from it?

"If you're going to do this, then do it," Ivory whispered.

She sank to her knees, spotting her jeans with sand, and clasped her hands around the driftwood angel. Its wings aimed her way, its featureless face watching the dark tide.

Now what? She couldn't be sure. Was it better to speak to Cabrina directly? Offer a prayer? Or should she treat the moment like a séance? An exorcism? She should have asked more questions at Marla's shop than, *Is it good?*

Ivory licked her lips and tasted the ocean on the air. "Cabrina," she said. *Or whoever's following me*, she thought but kept to herself. "Let this angel guide you wherever you meant to go. Into the sea. Out to Ghost Cat Island, if you never made it there." She chewed her lower lip before going on. "Forget this place. And forget everyone who didn't understand. You were a young girl with your whole life ahead of you, and now you're a dead girl, but maybe you have your whole death ahead of you too. Don't cling to me. I'm not worth it; I barely know what I want anymore."

Her arms felt limp, and she lowered the driftwood angel to her lap. Droning on about herself wouldn't help. Why would any ghost care? Especially Cabrina's.

The wind stilled as if the beach were holding its breath, and moist air stuck to Ivory's skin. A finger of cold traced her spine, and she glanced over her shoulder, expecting to find some tourist crouched grinning behind her. That was Ivory, one more summer attraction. Come see the fool talking to ghosts in the night.

Except there was no one behind her. Like outside Wolf's window, or her own this morning. Like last week when she left Cabrina's body on the beach.

Her fingers tensed around the driftwood angel and stroked its grooved surface. Was she sending a ghost away? Or showing a willingness to give it attention? Tonight might not be an appeasement—it might have been a summoning. Laying out the welcome mat.

The rush of frothing waves tore her attention to the sea. She felt that mistake on the wind again. A regretful ghost? Or something stranger?

"Cabrina?" Ivory whispered. "Whoever's there, get on with it. Please."

The tide rolled in, and something faint appeared from its froth. It walked toward Ivory, a living piece of four-legged flotsam.

Chasm Cat stood ghostlike in the surf. Her eyes glistened yellow from tawny half-faces around the black-furred stripe cutting her in two.

"You," Ivory said, the breath rushing out of her. "I saw you in my dream."

Chasm Cat paused on stiff legs, demanding Ivory step closer. Demanding she notice what dangled from these feline jaws.

The sea whispered tidal promises again. *I'll take you there.*

Ivory turned to the driftwood angel—Marla's nonsense. She then looked again at Chasm Cat and the tide behind her—real.

And maybe dangerous.

Ivory could still head home without answers. She could take off her robe, now spattered with saltwater droplets, and shower herself. Forget this day, this night. Abandon Cabrina in death, as others had in life. No one would call her wrong for climbing the grassy slope back to the house and her rented attic room, away from this ghost-choked ocean.

But tomorrow, she would have to look at herself in the mirror. She would question the conditions of her humanity, and she might not like the answers.

She crept on gentle steps, almost afraid she'd scare Chasm Cat away. Dreams liked to be chased, but Chasm Cat held firm and expectant.

Ivory slid to her knees in the surf, foamy tide spraying at her face, and held out her hands to take what this impossible dream-cat had brought, same as she'd seen in her nightmares.

A dark lump slid from feline teeth and plopped into Ivory's palms. Soft and warm, it leaked in a thick puddle over the sides of her hands, staining pale flesh with reddish blackness. She could scarcely tell the stains from the night itself.

It was another heart. Maybe a cat's heart, or maybe a treasure torn from dreams. Ivory couldn't guess where Chasm Cat would have found any such thing. But then, all signs suggested Chasm Cat was more than she appeared, as if this small creature were only a protrusion from elsewhere. A cat-shaped tip of the iceberg. Maybe in dreams, a cat cast a longer shadow, one who had shown Ivory what to place in her hollowing insides.

"This has something to do with Cabrina, right?" Ivory thought of petting the cat and then thought better of it. "The death poem, Ghost Cat Island, a cat in my dreams, outside Wolf's house, my house, here—it's not a coincidence. What's happening to Cabrina, you have something to do with it. Right?"

Chasm Cat licked her forepaw and then cocked her head at Ivory's hand.

Ivory squeezed a thumb against the lump the cat had given her, a once-thumping organ she could now slurp down like honey.

She'd been shown what to do in her Cape Shadow vision, but she sensed a warning in it. No takebacks; she had to mean it.

She raised the heart to her face and sniffed—a metallic tang, some sour stink. Anyone watching would think she was out of her mind.

But why did she always have to think about who was watching? Landladies, strangers, Joan, Marla, Wolf, Viola, the fucking mirror. Why did they get a say?

"Will this show me Cabrina?" Ivory asked. "The Brite girl. I want to understand."

Chasm Cat blinked slowly. She had brought an offering and that was answer enough. The sea had sent the cat somehow, and the sea wanted blood.

But it offered promises in return. *I'll take you.*

Ivory's lips parted by fractions of an inch, fighting to open around the dark heart. Warm dampness stroked her lips, teeth, tongue. The sour taste filled her mouth and pooled around her gums, but she sucked at the heart's narrow end, and the whole of it crawled from her hands little by little. Honey-like thickness drew it dripping down her throat.

She began to choke midway through, eyes watering, wishing she had spat the damn thing out, but her hands kept pressing against her lips, and her throat muscles rolled and fought and eased the heart inside her.

When she looked down, her stained hands were empty.

"I'm ready," Ivory said. Her voice came thick, the heart's blood sticky in her mouth. "Bring me to Cabrina."

Chasm Cat approached Ivory, whiskers tickling her wrist. A strange growl purred from deep inside. The cat raised one forepaw, glistening with bony knives, and then scratched Ivory's arm.

Each claw peeled her skin, as if she hid a secret underneath that the cat could yank out and throw onto the beach for the seagulls to devour.

Ivory watched redness swell, a ghost escaping these slits in her skin. Her robe slithered off her arms, smeared with dark stains, and the world swayed on ocean waves. Her ghost wouldn't leave her body—instead her flesh would drop away from her spirit.

Waves crashed at Chasm Cat's back, spattering fur and skin. Tidal foam laced itself into a circle against the dark sea and the black coastal sky. A darker coast and a brighter sky lay on the far side of this oceanic doorway, as wide and tall as Ivory, as the beach, as the night itself.

A hungry maw to devour every ghost it could catch.

To devour Ivory.

12. THE ANSWERING CRY

Every candle flame died as the planchette jerked beneath Xi's fingers. She licked drying lips against candle-snuffing wind and forced her limbs to be pliable, ready for movement. The planchette slid again.

"Cab, that better be you," Rex said, a warning in his tone.

Waves crashed against the shore, and a brutal gust slapped dark ringlets of hair across Xi's face. She rubbed her cheek against her shoulder to clear them without lifting her fingers. An unseasonal chill dug beneath her jacket. The wind no longer fed the fire but seemed to press it away, casting deeper shadows across the spirit board, as if the night itself now reached for the bone-white planchette.

"I don't want to fuck with this ghost nonsense anymore," Xi said.

Rex remained matter of fact. "This ghost nonsense is already fucking with you."

The fire behind him slanted beneath a stern gust. Xi could no longer make out his fingers or her own. She wondered if her glasses needing cleaning, but she was too nervous to reach for them.

Beneath her fingertips, the planchette slid unseen.

"Do you feel it?" Rex whispered. His front was a black blob wreathed by firelight.

"I do," Xi whispered back. "Is it you?"

Rex's silhouette shook a shadowy head. "Is this Cab?" he asked. "Cabrina Aphrodite Brite?"

The planchette quivered again. Were the clouds to abandon Cape Morning, the sky would offer its stars and moon to reveal the spirit board, but only a storm-coated night hovered around the beach. Xi had to rely on memory and feeling to tell where the planchette meant to go.

It paused at one corner. Xi couldn't see the words, but she knew it was where three letters carved the word YES.

Hungry waves licked at the coast. Their salt scent invaded Xi's nose, a blanket over the unwelcoming chill.

"How do we know it's Cab?" she asked.

The planchette drew back toward the spirit board's center. A chill wedged between Rex's skin and Xi's, the planchette turning to ice, and then it rushed back to the corner—YES—before pulling away and ramming forward again.

YES.

YES.

YES.

An echo of Cabrina in the past. *Yes, yes, yes*. A desperation, a prayer.

"Don't stall," Rex said. "Ask something. We don't know how long this'll last."

Xi opened her mouth and then stopped herself. She didn't want this moment to last. Cabrina had poisoned her grief with fear last night, and here she came again as a specter across the darkened spirit board.

But what if she had good reason? Back in the cemetery, Ivory had asked what really happened to Cabrina. Didn't her presence at the house, on this beach, suggest Ivory was right to wonder? Maybe Xi and Rex had been too weighed down in grief to question why Cabrina was gone. Back to work and college prep and futures, both of them chugging along in the great societal machine as if Cabrina's life hadn't left an emotional wound in their hearts. She had spent her final weeks in the same cogs, like she had a future too.

What a dismal way to live. If the dead could make sense out of life, Xi wanted to know, her terror be damned.

"Cab?" Rex leaned closer to the spirit board. "Did you kill yourself?"

The planchette retreated from its YES corner. If Rex would move out of the fire's way, it could light the spirit board again, but Xi was too petrified to say so, and the chill was getting worse.

The planchette slid into the opposite corner. NO.

Rex's silhouette looked up at Xi and then back to the board. "Cab, was it an accident?"

Xi felt the planchette retreat again. Her arms tensed, wishing to slide again to YES.

The planchette screeched back to where it had last pointed—NO.

A tremor ran up Xi's fingers. This didn't feel like the ghostly touch of cold air beside her. This was Rex on the spirit board's far side, his body quaking with sudden fury, like he might shatter the planchette. The beach howled with wolves in the wind.

Rex raised his voice against it. "What happened, then?"

The planchette twisted toward the board's center. This wasn't an easy yes-or-no question. The presence would have to spell things out for them. Why couldn't Xi see the board? Who had brought such deep shadows to Cape Morning?

"Slide aside," Xi said. "We need to see."

Rex fidgeted, digging sand across his jeans and letting the battered firelight grace the board again. Xi watched the planchette slide beneath their fingers, its arrow gliding quick from letter to letter.

L-E-T.

Xi's fingers twitched. They wanted to break from the planchette, but she couldn't let them.

M-E.

Rex whispered something under his breath that Xi couldn't catch. Even he couldn't pretend he'd expected what the firelight now revealed.

I-N.

Let me in.

Xi opened her mouth to answer. She wasn't sure what she meant to say. *We don't know how*, or *There's no coming back*.

But her voice died in a throaty creaking when she noticed the changed shape of the planchette. Its pale arrow now stretched to one side of the spirit board, forming softer shapes, too fleshy to be plastic.

Bone-white index fingers. Two hands. Two thin wrists, pressed together.

Xi and Rex froze in place. Both stared into the shadows to one edge of the spirit board. The fire danced one way and let in the darkness, and then it danced another way, illuminating sweatpants with the knees in the sand, the shoulder of a gray hoodie, a pale cheek, some colorless form playing séance with them on the beach.

Xi found her mouth dry. "Cab?" she asked.

A subtle hiss climbed a pale throat as the planchette slid screaming to its favorite corner—YES.

Xi's weight sank against a mattress edge, sheets tangled around her thighs. She became something of a snake halfway coiled around Cabrina's head in her lap, kissing her neck, shoulders.

Xi's sight returned to the fire, but she remembered this moment. She also remembered the scene outside her window, so dreamy and yet filled with nostalgia, an allure that had almost drawn her into ghostly arms. She'd sat at her bed's edge, cradling Cabrina as they touched. A sweet night between them.

But that was not this night, and Xi thrust her senses back to the salt-scented beach.

Firm fingers clutched Xi's wrist. Cabrina was rail-thin, same as last night, but too solid for a ghost. Every part of her snuggled against Xi as if only wanting warmth, but a desperation haunted Cabrina's gray-turned-golden eyes. Firelight twisted in her black pupils.

The planchette had only been pretense, a ritual to permit contact. Hadn't Cabrina talked about games like that before? She'd certainly written about them. People made a thousand excuses for closeness, calling them exercise, religion, anything you could think of so they wouldn't have to admit how badly they wanted affection.

Xi, Rex, and Cabrina had needed little excuse. They'd always been close, and in life, Xi had gladly let Cabrina press against her, and kiss, and beyond.

But in death, Cabrina felt like a panther on the brink of pouncing. Sweet memories camouflaged her hunger for warmth and maybe worse.

The wind roared down the beach and toward the ocean, a world-eating mouth sucking in a great breath. Another gust fought the spirit board and then ripped the planchette from beneath every finger. It tumbled over the beach, toward the tide. Rex started to rise, meaning to chase after, and Xi twitched to follow.

Cabrina clutched her in place with firm unspectral fingers.

Rex turned back and at last noticed the figure clinging to Xi's body. He lunged over the spirit board, mouth open to shout at them.

Only a hoarse cry shot out when Cabrina lunged back at him. She clung to him, jaw snapping open and shut, the desperation in her eyes now as deep as the ocean. He had to realize this wasn't any kind of ghost he'd imagined.

Xi shot to her feet and reached for Cabrina, but she didn't want to touch that cold skin again. Cabrina felt corpselike, even if she looked and acted like a starving animal.

Rex quit squirming against her, reeled back his arms, and shoved her down. She struck the sand and scuttled into the shadows. Rex grabbed a plank of driftwood from the beach fire and thrust it after her.

"Stop!" Xi cried.

But the patch of beach where Cabrina had retreated now lay empty. No sign of her, a presence borne on the wind and taken by it.

Xi staggered two steps from the spirit board and glanced in every direction. She panted, her skin hot and damp. The night surrounded her, pregnant with a monster.

"No, no, no—" Xi started. A hand seized her arm, and she almost screamed.

It was only Rex. "We can't go yet," he said. "We have to say goodbye."

"I have nothing good to say to whatever the hell that was," Xi snapped.

Rex snapped back. "We opened a door. You want to leave it that way?"

He tugged Xi toward the spirit board on wobbling legs and guided her hands to the center of the carvings. The planchette was long gone. They had to press their fingers together and glide them over the letters. GOODBYE awaited in another corner.

A cold grip encircled Xi's fingers, and she felt a presence touch her memories. Cabrina hadn't reached out in body again, but something of her lingered in the night wind.

Xi's fingers dragged toward a different corner than she wanted—NO.

She steered again toward GOODBYE, but the haze overtook her thoughts. Cabrina's kiss. Cabrina's need. Her fingertips scraped across the board again, and again, the rough wood cutting thin lacerations over her fingers. Red seeped into the letters.

NO.

NO.

NO.

NO.

NO.

Xi blinked; there were tears in her eyes. "I can't. I said goodbye yesterday. I can't do it again."

Rex pried his hands off the board, grabbed Xi's fingers tight, and slammed them down on the corner reading GOODBYE. They left a dark smear of two fingerprints.

The waves thrummed beside them. Some entrance had closed, but Xi wasn't sure it was the door Rex thought. The night stretched bigger than usual; she could feel it in the air. Grief might have become her internal puppeteer, but she imagined a more external force, old as the ocean.

"We're done," Rex said, plucking up the spirit board. He packed his bag in quick, jerky motions.

Xi understood. She didn't want to linger here either.

They stood together, and Rex stamped off. No one gathered at their own fires down the beach seemed to have noticed Xi's alarm, or the fight against an undead girl. Too many tourists liked to scream at the sea for anyone to have recognized genuine terror.

Xi passed the beach fire, leaving it to smolder beneath the wind, and then glanced again to the water. Firelight now flickered over the shoreline, where the tide rushed in and out.

Narrow grooves marred the damp sand, as if a hand had grasped the beach before the waves yanked a body out to sea.

And then the tide splashed over the beach again, smoothing the sand. When the water next retreated, there was no sign of anyone having clawed at the beach, no evidence anyone had drifted into the Atlantic.

Like tonight had never happened.

Who's coming into the house at night?

Nighttime was easier back when Angel was alive. I wasn't scared in the dark. Having a cat means you don't believe in monsters under the bed or people in the house at night. You just believe in cats. They're noisy and weird and they don't make sense, like me. If you have a cat, then anything you hear at night is probably the cat. Nothing to be scared of.

He probably went to Ghost Cat Island when he died. That's where I would go if I was a cat. That must be why I was dreaming about it until the noise woke me up. Kind of asleep, kind of awake. Sleepwalking? Dreaming? Can you do both at once?

I saw a dark ocean, and an island, and the creaking was like a ship fighting the water.

Everyone knows that when you fight the ocean, the ocean wins.

Dream sounds get mixed up with real sounds. The ship was creaking—the floorboards were creaking. The stairs, the banister. Cat noises without a cat.

<u>Nighttime Theories</u>
The house wants bad dreams to keep going
Her inside the house wants bad dreams to keep going

I went looking for someone else to add to the list of Nighttime People. The house was empty. The front door was shut, but the wind fought against it, and it seemed like it could have slipped a secret into the house through the keyhole. The air was salty and fishy. Beach smells.

But I haven't gone since that bad night with Xi and Rex, when we played the drowning game. If either of them were sneaking into my house so I wasn't alone anymore, it would make the place nicer, but it's neither of them, right?

Nighttime People
Sometimes Rex?

It's an alone feeling here. High school was bad, but no one tells you how lonely it gets when you don't have somewhere to be each day. The lonely tear the world down.

The things I could do to this awful house if I became the wind.

Maybe the ocean ghosts know that I feel alone here, and they've followed me from the beach to the house. Last evening led to one of those nights when every shadow has a heartbeat. I felt it in the walls—even though I couldn't hear it—a throbbing in my fingers when I touched the plaster, the staircase banister. It was like tracing the house's pulse everywhere I went. Was it me, creaking down the steps? I didn't think so.

But when I reached the bottom of the stairs, the sounds were gone except the rattling front door, like something had gone through it seconds before I got there. I stared at it for a long time, waiting for a knock. Something to scrape against it. Even a scratch. Nothing came. Whatever followed me must have already brought what it meant to bring.

I found out what it was when I went back to bed, like a dime from the tooth fairy.

Someone came to the house and sprinkled a trail of bad dreams telling me to follow them out to sea.

Out to Ghost Cat Island.

<u>Nighttime People</u>

Cabrina the Uncaged

Dad

Her

Sometimes Xi

Sometimes Rex

???

The Tooth Fairy

The Sandman

An emissary of Ghost Cat Island

A ghost

13. STAR OCEAN

Ivory recognized the bone-dotted black sand from her dreams. There was the great saber-toothed skull, its incisors long and terrible. Beyond it, a gentle fog rolled over Cape Shadow, its shore releasing a warm spectral breath.

Cape Morning's black curtain had fallen. Here, countless stars shined from every visible corner, only pausing around mountainous shapes in the distance. The rippling ocean reflected the brilliant sky, and every oncoming wave brought a tide of starlight, as if the universe had bred into the water.

Come, the waves whispered against the shore. *Come. And see.*

A clear invitation. Ivory would come. She would see. The thrusting and retreating waves would take her.

She ran against their frothing edges, feet splashing deeper and deeper until she dove into the star ocean. The tide churned around her, with her, against her. Each wave meant to erode her, a polished seaborn relic shaped for beauty and pain. Cold water waggled icy tongues up her knees, thighs, at private places. Nothing to be done but embrace the skin-deep chill and swim on.

Dark monuments towered from the water. To Ivory's left, white bone glistened where an island had formed from some long-dead leviathan. To her right, a spire of coiling rock stabbed at the sky, the horn of an enormous narwhal challenging the cosmos to a duel to the death. Gargantuan slabs of flat standing stone arose from distant waves. If Cape Morning had taken the domain of humanity, then Cape Shadow had devoured everything unwelcome at its sunlit sister.

Ivory swam through an empire of dreams and memories, home to a forgotten past both wild and dangerous.

Had Cabrina ever seen this place? Ivory would find her next.

The water ebbed and pulled, not only letting Ivory pass but urging her onward. Distances contracted, the ocean flexing its muscle. Her head dove underwater briefly, and when she emerged, the waves had finished sharpening her, and her destination towered ahead.

She had come to the mountainous island that blotted out the stars.

This couldn't be Ghost Cat Island. Even before the sea began to drink it, only a small outcrop of rock and foliage had jutted from the Atlantic Ocean off Cape Morning.

The island towering above Ivory was a titan rising from the sea, its vicious bulk climbing in an underbite of lengthy teeth formed by jagged sea-greened rock. White foam circled in a tide pool behind them, trapped and glistening in the starlight. Beyond that arose stone steps running with seawater, leading toward a black cavern. The waves' rhythm beckoned from deep in that tremendous stone mouth.

Come. And see.

It wasn't Ghost Cat Island off Cape Morning. That little scrap of rock was only the protrusion of this enormous shadow, with its own size, shape, and personality. Cabrina had gone swimming toward the iceberg's tip, but Ivory had gone deeper and found the whole of the iceberg, a spirit swollen into the skull of a colossal stone beast.

There was space for Ivory to squeeze between two teeth, but the sea-sharpened edges scraped at her palms and thighs as she clambered through. The shallow tide pool swallowed her feet and ankles. The island's mouth cast a shadow over its stone steps, but here the stars' radiance glimmered on the small circle of water, letting Ivory see the effects of her eroding swim.

Her clothes had been shucked away by the ocean's fingers. Stony patches gazed through her skin where she'd been cut by the island's teeth, her wounds glistening an eerie green of sea growth.

And her cock was gone.

Her testicles, too. Dark red curls instead encircled a slender vulva at the center of broadened hips, a starlit echo to the cavern above.

"It can't be." Ivory swallowed and tasted seawater. "That can't happen, can it?"

The words swirled in her mouth, unsure which part of tonight should be impossible. Her meal of a heart? Her drop into Cape Shadow? The islands upon the bloodthirsty sea? Or the reshaping?

No tattoo scrawled *I am a creature of life* down her thigh. Untouched pale flesh glistened in its place, as if no one had ever hurt her in a way she needed to hide under fresh conviction.

An exploratory finger slid along the new crevice between her legs. She found wetness, and warmth, and soft welcoming flesh. Her fingers sank through soft folds to find a channel dancing with tender nerves.

How could it be? *How*?

She couldn't trust it now, even seeing it, touching it. Was this a trick of the shadows and light, or was this ethereal island a shaping place? She wouldn't look or touch again, in case she blinked and everything went back. Better to carry on and simply believe.

"Don't let it be a dream," Ivory said.

The ocean whispered from within the island. *Come. And see.*

"I will."

Ivory clambered up the sea-sharpened steps beyond the tide pool. They were slick stone, likely to send her crashing down with torn skin and a cracked skull, where she could spill fresh humanity into the waves. The sea wanted blood. She made sure it wouldn't have hers as she ascended carefully and reached this Ghost Cat Island's maw.

Come. And see.

The ground inside the cavern was flat and cracked, biting at Ivory's feet. Gaping fissures along the ceiling let the stars peek inside to light her way, each wider and wider until the cavern broke open above and full starshine glowed down on a round chamber. A black gap opened the ground at the chamber's center, hinting at a winding subterranean staircase and crevices in the stone. Arched black openings marred the walls around the gap, each exhaling a light mist into the chamber that clouded Ivory's legs.

Something breathed within—many somethings, for each of the dozen or so doorways. One formed a ragged comma; another grimaced from stone as if carved into the snarl of an enormous lioness.

This was the core of Ghost Cat Island off Cape Shadow. A belly for beasts.

"Cabrina?" Ivory called. Her voice echoed down the caverns. "Cabrina Brite, are you here? I'm kind of a friend. Family, if you know what that means."

That didn't sound good enough. What did she know about this girl? What would Cabrina care about?

Ivory tried another approach. "Did this place make a dream come true for you, too?"

There was no answer beyond the sounds of breathing. Ivory would have to choose a path, either traveling down the steps at the chamber's center or aiming for one of the doorways here.

She glanced at the lioness-looking archway, and then the ragged comma. Another doorway seemed to curl at the sides, and she thought she glimpsed a figure in its blackness.

"Cabrina?" Ivory whispered.

Not Cabrina. There was a woman with long ringlets of hair, a lighter shade of red than Ivory's, tossing on a gentle wind, her body hidden by a tremendous veil. She stared with eyes like a violet storm on the horizon, long enough for Ivory to be certain she wasn't imagining this woman. Her jutting chin lifted as if challenging Ivory to approach.

And then she was gone. Beside that now-empty darkness, another doorway bore enormous pillars down either side, echoing the saber-toothed skull from the beach. The tidal rhythm croaked from the winding staircase, but it told Ivory nothing.

What did this place have to do with Cabrina?

She looked toward the saber-toothed doorway and thought again of Chasm Cat sliding from a similar skull on the beach. That had to be a sign. Ivory's feet scraped against the stone ground as she headed for the pillars and the black space between.

A rising laugh tickled her ear and froze her in place. Someone or something watched from another doorway.

I might like to be bitten, the waves hissed. Was that Ivory's voice? Had the sea been listening to her when she fucked Wolf last week?

The laugh came again, and Ivory jerked her head to catch where it had come from.

There—tucked into a blind spot from the chamber's entrance stood another doorway. No arch bowed at its top; instead it buckled at the center and curved at its corners like a mouth caught in laughter. Concave marks above the doorway echoed a pair of mirthful eyes. The carvings formed a theatrical comedy mask without its tragic counterpart.

Ivory slid toward the laughing doorway. Its darkness bubbled and stirred, a door-like pool ready to drink her in. She pointed a finger and stroked down the inky fluid, which rippled beneath her touch. A cackle raked her thoughts.

She doubled over, her guts grabbing her throat and twisting hard. Something inside her wanted out.

A dark red lump flowed past Ivory's tongue, her teeth, and then spattered onto the stone floor. It looked unchanged from when she'd slurped it out of her hands at dusk.

But she'd shown her willingness to eat, to give, and the sea wanted blood.

A claw-like wave sloshed from inside the laughing doorway and snatched the heart off the floor. It left a thin red puddle in its wake, as if a snake had been torn inside out.

Ivory felt the same, her insides gaping raw. The devoured heart had kept her warm and whole in her journey across Cape Morning, Cape Shadow, the sea, the island, and now her skin couldn't remember if it had ever felt the sun. She had come and seen, but what did she have to do next?

Go, the waves hissed. *And be*.

"Go?" Ivory asked. "Go back?"

Go. The ocean thrummed, and a whisper rang from deep within Ghost Cat Island. *Go, and become*.

An airy gust rippled around Ivory as if stealing the scent from her skin. She smelled herself in it, a musky human odor mixed with salt and blood. The wind then exhaled from the doorway, replacing Ivory's scent with a sweet, almost animal musk. It raised the hairs on her arms, the back of her neck, and she realized her mistake, a primal warning known deep in her blood.

This was not Cabrina Brite. Ivory had stumbled into the lair of a predator.

She spun on one heel and sprang out of the round chamber the way she'd come. Her feet slopped against stone as she darted through the cavern, its walls crashing with hidden waves.

A breathy moan followed her from that doorway of chiseled laughter. Unseen claws tested the floor of the stone chamber with playful scraping, and then they came stalking into the cavern.

Ivory burst from the cavern's mouth and ran for the stone steps. The ground was slicker here, and the steps remained slippery. One wrong move could crack her skull, but she had no choice; if she hesitated, her skull would crack between teeth instead.

She heard the beast snuffling as she descended the steps and plunged into the frothy tide pool, where white seafoam splashed at her thighs. Whatever she'd fed and released had to be nearing the island's mouth. Almost to the steps, the pool.

To her.

She jammed herself between the tall stone teeth surrounding the tide pool. Faster this time, clumsier. One tooth cut across her ribs and scraped one breast. She hissed, sucking in the taste of saltwater, but she couldn't slow, couldn't stop.

A dry chuckle climbed from a gruff throat behind her. The beast had reached the top of the steps and was watching. Laughing.

Ivory yanked her legs through—another cut across her knee—and dove again into the star ocean. The greenstone in her wounds must have crumbled when she vomited the heart. She was flesh and blood again, with all the frailty that entailed. Each fresh cut screamed saltwater shock.

Another rough laugh chased her onto the waves, and then something heavy splashed into the tide pool. Uproarious laughter beat at the sky, high-pitched and almost cruel. As if it might be more fun to watch Ivory struggle and flail than to catch her.

The beast was playing with her. The oldest game, with the oldest stakes.

Win and live. Lose and die.

Ivory thrust her arms one-two, one-two—fast as she could—chopping through the surf with every limb on fire. Waves smacked at her face, briefly blinding her. She was afraid to look at the sky in case the stars began to wink, and she was afraid to glance back in case only blackness awaited, the predator having swallowed all light to strand her in an unlit universe.

There was only ahead. Past the distant obelisks, the coiling spire, the skeletal island. There was only the black-sanded beach of bones.

Ivory kept swimming, seeing nothing, her stinging wounds going numb with the water's sharp chill, hearing laughter and snuffling and an empty-bellied moan. The sea always wanted blood. She'd given, and given, and she'd taken the heart and coughed it back still bloody, but it was never enough. The sea wanted and wanted. She might have come all this way only to fail.

Win and live, she thought. *Lose and die*.

Her limbs thrashed harder, but whatever power the heart had given her to swim from the shore to this shadowy vision of Ghost Cat Island was gone. A cramp squeezed her abdomen. Her legs begged her to go limp. Every part of her needed a break, and then they could get on with the same chase as always of trying to survive. She could never rest. One way or another, there was always a beast behind her.

Cruel laughter bounced across the waves, louder and sharper until thunder cracked through the sea. A scream lit over the sky. Ivory couldn't be sure it wasn't hers until she tasted water in her mouth while the scream carried on. She then heard bones crack, as if the beast had found replacement prey. The chewing of muscle, the tearing out of throats.

This was the crunching of worlds.

14. CAPE MORNING

Ivory emerged to find a familiar coastline staring at her from across the water. The sky was dark here, unlike Cape Shadow, but lights dotted the shore, cast by sparse beach fires and the porchlight glow of summerhouses. Cape Morning's luminous shimmer crept skyward behind them.

She was home. No leviathan skeletons or ancient spires haunted the ocean over her shoulder. No Ghost Cat Island she could see, either scrap of rock or gargantuan stone skull. No pursuing beast.

Her feet pressed against underwater sand. She would go walking onto the beach, drenched and aching beneath her chilled skin, but alive.

And in what shape?

She swallowed hard, knowing she had seawater in her mouth, not caring. The starless sky could not light her numb body, and she could hardly feel her skin. She could only cross her cold fingers as she strode toward shore and hope like hell to keep the changes she'd seen in Ghost Cat Island's tide pool. Even suffering the strips of greenstone gaping out of shadowy wounds would be worth it.

"Let me keep this," Ivory whispered to the rushing waves. "Don't let it be a trick of the light, and I'll put it all in the past. I'll make sure everyone's happy, I swear."

Impatient waves thrust hard at her back, forcing her down, and then up. The water wasn't interested in her promises. Hadn't she known the point of this since before she swallowed Chasm Cat's offering? Since she was a little girl? The sea did not want her to forgive, or forget, or to be nice or pretty or anything the rest of the world might like. It wanted blood.

The water sank from her neck, and then her shoulders and biceps. Her clothes sagged against her, as if she hadn't seen herself naked at Cape Shadow. Whatever magic had twisted shadow and light was gone, vomited up in some animal's cave. She was done being a naked creature of greenstone wounds and instead wore her blouse, jeans, underwear, everything. Her waist and hips emerged from the water, letting warmth into her flesh.

And she felt the weight between her thighs. Everything was the same as when she'd last left Cape Morning. A complete reset of Ivory Sloan.

She staggered out of the shallows and crumpled onto the wet sand. Her knees and legs pressed trenches for the tide to fill. Its next gentle wave splashed against her feet. She lowered her head into one hand, nose and mouth pressed against palm, desperate to slow her breath away from panic.

What now? The spectral otherworld hadn't helped her find Cabrina. Instead, it had dangled other offerings only to snatch them away, as fleeting as dreams.

A harsher wave crashed over her back, nearly knocking her forward. Her free hand clawed at the sand to steady herself, and a slow breath shuddered through her fingers.

Now she heard another sound against the waves. Not distant tourist commotion, or a ship's horn far from the beach, but footsteps splashing through the shallows. She'd reached Cape Morning, still pursued by the creature from Cape Shadow.

She crawled farther ashore, stumbled onto dry land, and made ready to run. Porchlights beckoned from far-off summerhouses. If she could reach one and make it inside, she could safely disappear into someone's living room, or a party, anywhere she'd find other people.

Another step splashed behind. Then another. Ivory realized that she couldn't hear that strange dry chuckling that had chased her toward Cape Shadow's shore.

She took another two steps up the sand and then spun around. Part of her expected a tremendous sea snake, or a mermaid, some new impossibility thrust from the sea.

White froth lapped at the legs of a nude figure emerging from the tide. Every inch of her rained saltwater. A mane of gold-and-black hair shot from her head and draped down her back in a scraggly mess. Same-colored hair formed a tangled patch between her legs and beneath her armpits, and it climbed in thin, salt-slick layers up her limbs and belly. She looked left and right as she approached the shore, baring her face to the light with her sharp nose, sharper cheekbones, and harsh jaw meant to crunch bones. Narrow honey-colored irises ringed her wide dark eyes.

Ivory's muscles jellied, and she grabbed her robe from the sand.

When she looked up again, the stranger stood closer to the beach. She was a little taller than Ivory, her muscles firm beneath sun-kissed skin. Dark spots shadowed the sides of her ribs and hips.

Ivory tugged her robe around her body. It was too much to hope, but she had to be certain. "You're from that other place, aren't you?"

The stranger stepped past the wet sand, walking on the balls of her feet. They left broad tracks, the toes sharpening to points. She leaned toward Ivory, and then she pressed her cheek against Ivory's brow and rubbed back and forth. A rich scent breathed from her skin, mixing thick musk with salt spray.

"You followed me," Ivory whispered.

The stranger withdrew a step, peering down at Ivory. Dark lips peeled from sharp teeth and gums in an open-mouthed fit of high-pitched laughter, the voice of a hyena in a woman's mouth.

Like a beast from Ghost Cat Island.

Ivory shook her head, dark red locks raining salty droplets every which way. Ridiculous thoughts; she should scatter them. She was supposed to pretend everything strange was a dream, like any sensible adult. You shouldn't believe in magic once you've grown up.

But she'd already tried to ignore the ghost last week, and that had only led to nightmares. Chasm Cat had come to tear her world open, a kind of wild feline magic. If such a gateway were possible, and Ivory could step from Cape Morning to Cape Shadow, why couldn't something unnatural, maybe impossible, follow her from Cape Shadow back to Cape Morning? Maybe finding and leading this woman had been the point from the start.

"Can you tell me your name?" Ivory asked.

The woman only grinned, and something in the gleam across her teeth made Ivory think she was older than names.

Ivory's robe brushed the stranger's chest. She should drape it around the nude woman's figure, clothe and hide her, but Ivory held still beneath the stranger's eyes of honey and darkness.

"Honey," Ivory said, tasting the word. "Maybe I'll call you that?"

A glimmer blinked in those eyes. Honey licked her lips.

Ivory reached for Honey's hand. "Have you come to help me? For Cabrina?"

Honey chinned at Ivory, and a giddy rumble climbed her throat. She pressed so close that her lips could kiss Ivory's neck.

"Okay," Ivory said, almost laughing again. "Okay, okay. Fuck it, if ghosts are real, why not that other world? Can it be that easy?"

Honey grew still, every firm muscle tensing down her body. Warm possibility thrummed through her skin like the humid promise of a coming storm. Her breath slid over Ivory's ear. She would break her silence now, offer a whispered secret, and then—

Sharp teeth sank through the skin of Ivory's neck.

The bite filled her head with darkness, glaring eyes, and the sense of verminous prey leaping down an all-consuming throat.

Ivory jerked backward and retreated up the beach. Sand slid underfoot, and a frail shriek leaped up her throat as she retreated, almost fell, kept stepping back. One hand swatted at her neck, and her fingers came away glistening with red.

"You—" Ivory winced. "I thought you'd help."

Honey grinned, her lengthy incisors flecked with Ivory's blood. A growl coiled in her throat and then broke into sharp laughter. When Ivory blinked, Honey stood a step closer. And then closer.

Ivory turned around and barreled toward the grassy slope and wooden walkways, toward houses and streets and the town. She couldn't stay here, had to get away.

But as hard as she ran, she kept hearing unhurried footsteps behind her. Laughter followed with them.

Most people don't want to hear about dreams, but I do. Sometimes. I stopped asking Rex about his when he told me about a nightmare where he was in a tall building, which kept growing shorter as he ran down the never-ending stairwell, like the ceiling was chasing him.

Xi has nightmares, too, I can tell, but she won't share. She'll only repeat the good dreams. Maybe she filters them for herself, but it might really be for me.

I should keep these ones to myself. Xi and Rex already have to deal with awake me. Dreaming me is another burden, and I love them too much to throw that Cabrina onto their shoulders.

Dreamtime
Ghost Cat Island is a pebble that dreams it's a mountain
Bobbing for apples in the sea, and I stole one that wasn't mine
Eating hearts for dinner and there's one inside that isn't mine

Is a storm waiting for me?
Or is the land calling,
And I am the storm?
But a storm has no legs,
And I can't make the swim.

Nighttime People
The wind
A dream
A devil

15. CREATURES OF THE NIGHT

Xi had been coming to Rex's house ever since they became friends in late middle school, the only one of Xi's friends that Josephine would let her visit back then. She used to chalk that up to Rex being the other trans kid, before they got to know Cabrina. Later she guessed Joan and Marla seemed more responsible than a lot of parents around this town.

Bulging at the seams and thin in structure, the house looked rickety in ways Xi had never cared about before. Its lack of sturdiness seemed worrisome now. Cabrina would have no trouble getting in.

But where else could Xi go? Her house, with her mother, who had no idea there were worse things to fear than a dead man neither Xi nor Josephine had seen in nearly a decade? Rex's house was the only place tonight. Xi needed someone who knew the world no longer made sense.

Rex eased the front door shut with a gentle hand, slid out of his shoes, and waved Xi left of the foyer, toward the stairs heading up. Besides the foyer, kitchen, and narrow excuse for a living room, the first floor largely belonged to Marla's shop, almost as if Rex's house were divided into a duplex, same as Xi's. She had one hand on the smooth wooden banister when her sneaker creaked against the lowest hardwood step.

Rex glanced down. "Hey, hey, don't go tracking sand in here, you know that."

Right, shoes off. Xi knew that; same at her house. But she was walking in a daze. The beach encounter had shaken every rule out of her head except to follow Rex wherever he went.

She retreated to the foyer and slid her sneakers off. They clacked against the floor, louder than when Rex had shut the door.

A lilting voice called from deep in the house. "Rex?"

Rex ushered Xi to hurry, but they had only climbed halfway up the creaking steps before Marla appeared from the foyer. Would Joan be far behind, or was she sleeping?

"How was the communing?" Marla asked. "Any spirits?"

"Yeah, yeah," Rex said. "Some ghost showed at the beach, said I was the last son of Krypton, then stuck up two thumbs and skittered off to the Arctic." He grabbed Xi's hand and then climbed another two steps.

"Wait a sec." Marla reached the stairs and gripped the banister. A gray residue stained the tips of her pinkish fingers. "I'm serious, how did it go? I'm a cool mom, you can tell me. Did the graveyard dirt help?"

"I don't know." Rex let go of Xi's hand. "Did it?"

"There was a visitor," Xi said, as if passing a secret.

Marla beamed. "Like what? Or who? Whom? Give me details."

Xi would have rather detailed her exhaustion, with a stanza for every muscle. How were she and Rex supposed to report on the supernatural as if recounting what they'd learned on some middle school field trip? Spiritual voyeurism had no place here; this was life and death.

And undeath.

Rex began telling it, and Xi watched Marla's excitement battle her skepticism and then melt into good humor. Her enthusiasm would lie rotting had she faced Cabrina out on the beach.

Xi was ready to leave herself rotting too. Cabrina might not be happy she'd been called and dismissed so readily. She might be gone now, but she could return on a furious tide.

"And then we told her goodbye," Rex said, finishing the story. There, Marla had her answer. Could they go now?

Marla looked them over. "Cabrina really loves you two."

"She wanted to get inside my house," Xi said, leaning over the banister. "You told us the graveyard dirt would help, but she's not a ghost. She can touch you." One hand slid from Xi's side and clapped onto Marla's soiled fingers. "Like this."

Marla stared at Xi's hand as if she were the ghost and Marla the summoner.

"Okay, and know that I say this without judgment," Marla said, taking a breath. "You two weren't drinking, right? Or high?"

Rex shook his head. "A little buzzed. Come on, we didn't imagine her."

"Not saying you did." Marla patted Xi's hand. "But you could have misinterpreted."

"No, no, this was clearer than crystals, and sure as shit scarier," Rex said. "Cab wanted something out of us. She was hungry, like back before I got her eating again."

"You mean, like a vampire?" Marla asked.

So calm. Like it was a normal thing to say. Xi didn't know how the hell Marla could speak with meadow-like serenity about ghosts and then keep an even keel when bringing up the even more ludicrous topic of vampires.

Rex scratched his stubble. "No way. Forget that. I don't believe in that *Blade* and *Tomb of Dracula* comic book bullshit."

Xi nearly balked. Now Rex sounded ridiculous in his sincerity. This guy believed in ghosts, psychics, mystics of varied cultures, North American lake monsters, occult rituals, extraterrestrial and possibly extradimensional abductions—but at vampires, he drew the line?

And maybe Xi was the same. She'd read her literary favorites like *Wuthering Heights*, *Rebecca*, *Her Body and Other Parties*, and various other ghostly texts both old and new, but she hadn't touched anything like *Dracula*, *Carmilla*, not even *Interview with the Vampire*. She knew of them but left them unread. As if her heart kept her distant from some distortion of discovery.

Marla flashed a patronizing smile. "Vampires are older than comics and movies. The folklore begins in different countries and cultures, with ghosts and sick people."

"Cabrina isn't sick," Xi said. "She's—she's gone." Except she wasn't.

"You've been through a heavy ordeal," Marla said. "It doesn't have to be me, talking to you about it. You can talk to your mother, too. She'd be there for you."

Xi shook her head. "I can talk to her, but she doesn't always listen."

If Xi told her mother about tonight or last night, Josephine would have dismissed the haunting outright—or worse, suspected Xi's father had found them at last from beyond the grave. No telling what Josephine would do then, and no sense panicking her without good cause.

"It's a lot to take," Rex said, raising his eyebrows in disbelief. "Creeping out of crypts, the big fangs, turned to ash by sunlight—"

Marla aimed a finger at Rex. "Now that part? That's the movies. They're supposed to be weak in the sun, but not killed by it. Some of those stories might have come from people with photosensitivity, or even odd phobias."

"Okay." Rex shrugged. "And turning into a bat?"

"Or wolf, or panther, things like that," Marla said. "A vampire could be a kind of ghost or spirit. And why should a ghost have to keep their old shape? A spirit could be anything. Death couldn't shape it to lie still, so why should flesh and bone make a difference? Memory keeps a ghost in human form, but what if a spirit forgets? What if a spirit was never human at all? It could pretend to be human, fooling everybody who saw it. Like a glamour."

Xi tried to absorb this. "But what was real?"

Marla chuckled. "I'm not *that* old. But best I can gather, early vampire myths would look like McCarthy hearings and witch trials. The kind of evil you could accuse your neighbor of being. The vampires inspired by those events would have been believably human. Shying from sunlight, maybe allergic. They wouldn't be combusting, and certainly not transforming into bats, cats, wolves, or anything else in the animal kingdom." She raised her hands in semblance of a defeated shrug. "But then, every superstition and scrap of folklore finds new transformations in retelling, region, medium. Yes, Rex, even movies. Beneath it all, you might find a little truth."

"And stakes?" Rex asked. "No way would I shove a stake through Cabrina's heart."

"She's already dead," Xi whispered. Like she wasn't supposed to say it or else risk breaking the spell of this mother-son nonsense conversation.

Marla didn't seem to hear. "Death by stake is another misconception. From what I know, it's a Western European bastardization. A stake's purpose was to pin the dead person in their casket so they couldn't climb out again. But we're talking Catholicism, the idea that every corpse waits for the end of days, heavenly judgment, blah, blah."

"Like an underground timeout?" Rex asked. He pantomimed banging a stake with a mallet. "*Now you stay here and wait for Jesus, young lady.*"

"It might bind the spirit, too," Marla said. "Hold their powers in place. I think some of them could influence the weather? And change shape? But staking them down would put a stop to that."

Rex lowered his hands. "No more powers, no more glamour? Nothing?"

Xi pictured herself and Rex standing in an emptied grave, with Cabrina lying at their feet, and shuddered with a sudden chill.

"Guess a staked vampire can't make trouble," Rex went on. "Sharp wood gives you time to decide what to do."

"Could be wood, sure," Marla said, and then she wiggled one finger to tap her wedding ring against the banister. *Click-click-click*. "Or silver."

"So they're still undead and wriggling, just—" Rex's face turned queasy. "—stuck in the ground?"

Marla shook her head. "I shouldn't be indulging. You're upset."

Xi shuddered against the stairway wall. "I'm not—I won't do that to Cab."

"Me neither," Rex said. "Hell no."

"We're way off track," Marla said, bemused. "I don't want you two to think your friend is really—I don't know."

She seemed to withdraw inside herself, like she realized she'd messed up in bringing this speculation to two grieving friends in the first place. Would she ask what really happened on the beach, as if Xi and Rex were lying? Maybe Marla thought Xi's visitor was a grief-summoned nightmare. She must have expected Xi and Rex to come home with a story of speaking to Cabrina through the spirit board, receiving a message of memory or love, anything to bring closure after losing a member of their trio after high school's end.

They had instead brought this story of a pale figure on the beach, and being grabbed, and hungered for. Of horrors in the wind and sea.

"I think you think you're humoring us," Xi said, plain as she could. "And you think we're inventing a story. We aren't."

Marla gave Xi's hand one last squeeze and then withdrew from the banister. "You should sleep. It'll feel different in the morning. And tell your mother you're staying here. She's called Joan three times already."

Xi hadn't thought to check her phone since returning to Rex's car. Josephine must have left a pile of text messages and voicemails. The same would carry on through college, and she would never think to ask if Xi had nightmares about a memory, a ghost, or something like a vampire.

Should they even be calling Cabrina that? Power lived in names, but that power could be tricky, too. Throwing one thing's name at another said you didn't understand it. You only wanted to slap a label on the box so it would quit being a mystery. Xi knew that from when her father used to tell her she'd be a man someday and needed to man up, over and over, as though repetition and statements would change the truth inside.

Anyone could name an apparition in the night, but calling it a ghost or a vampire did not enforce the apparition's behavior. It would do as it pleased.

Same went for giving it someone's name. This thing might wear Cabrina's features, but those resemblances did not make the thing Cabrina herself.

And hadn't Xi given last night's visitation a convenient name too? *Nightmare*, she'd said, like she could slap her imagination onto the presence and make it so, banishing handprints from the window come morning.

The handprints had remained until Xi opened the window and wiped the glass. No nightmare, only an unreal kind of reality. Tonight, too, seemed unreal.

"I don't believe in vampires," Rex said, starting upstairs again.

"Okay," Xi said. She wasn't sure what else to tell him.

Rex climbed another groaning step. "Look, eighteen and nineteen years old is a long damn time. If vampires were a real thing, we'd have known by now. Everybody would."

"Right." Xi lifted her glasses and rubbed the bridge of her nose. "But what if they make themselves seem like us? They're supposed to have hypnosis."

"The glamour," Rex said. "To look pretty instead of dead, laying illusions over themselves, moving shadows around, hiding in them. Make you like them, enjoy them. That'd mean what we met could look like Cab without being her, you know?"

"A trick of the light," Xi said. She needed time to digest this.

Rex led her into his bedroom. In early high school, Cabrina had cut him a skull and crossbones out of marker and construction paper to grace the bedroom door, but Marla had warned it would bring bad energy. Now it hung on the wall beside a pair of hooks holding a weathered machete, a gift from some local fisherman years ago. Red Sox paraphernalia and posters of comic book characters decorated the rest of his bedroom walls, and a print of an old Superman comic book cover hung over the bed.

"Do you believe what happened on the beach?" Xi asked, eyeing the windows.

"What choice is there?" Rex turned his back to her and began pulling off his shirt, revealing the black binder hugging his chest. A momentary stillness sank through him. "She wanted you. She was hungry for your warmth."

Xi pressed the door shut with a shudder. "She was naked when I first saw her."

"Probably tore out of the clothes she was buried in," Rex said. "She'd never want to wear a suit, whether she's a vampire or a ghost. Fuckin' Viola."

Xi nodded. *Fucking Viola.*

"Why come after us, though?" Xi asked. "What'd we do? We're her friends. She should go hunt her mother."

"Come on, Xi." Rex pulled off his binder and threw on an oversized black tee. "When has that woman ever been warm?"

Xi had not prepared for a night over. She would sleep in her blouse and jeans, maybe go home for new clothes tomorrow. Before that, she needed to call her mother.

"I can't hide in your house all summer," Xi said. "Especially not from Cab. She was more than hungry. She was desperate. And scared."

"Not our fault," Rex said, sitting heavily on his bed. "Cab wanted us, came to see us. We're nothing to fear. Had to be something else, something in the wind."

"Exactly. We're no threat." Xi sat on the bed beside Rex. "So, what does that say? What's out there that's so bad, even a dead girl is scared of the dark?"

16. PREY

Ivory's chest was a vice by the time she reached Wolf's asphalt driveway. Her heart pounded in her ears, drowning out the night sounds, and she kept looking this way and that in case she was failing to hear someone catching up behind her. A cramp squeezed her side, and her feet ached. She had left her boots on the beach with the driftwood angel, and though she had other shoes at home, she didn't want to lead her predator there. She had instead run up boarded walkways and sidewalks and streets to reach Wolf's doorstep.

She tore open the flimsy screen door, banging her fist against the solid wood beneath. Her hand groped for the knob—locked—and then she banged again, her hot breath panting in and out. Her robe and clothes hung damp with sweat and seawater.

And blood. She felt its warmth trickling down her neck and spine.

A tiny golden light flashed alive above Ivory's head. Locks clicked down the door, and then it opened onto the whites of two eyes staring from inner shadow.

"Wolf?" Ivory whispered, hopeful.

Darkness covered one eye—a hand rubbing a face. "Know what time it is?" Wolf asked.

Ivory exhaled through a relieved smile. "I don't know, I don't have my phone, but I needed to see you." She made to cross the threshold.

Wolf put out a hand, stopping her on the doorstep. "It isn't a good night, party animal."

Ivory retreated on reflex. The world held dark around Wolf's house. Honey might be hiding anywhere, between trees, behind neighboring houses, in the sound of the wind.

Wolf had no clue of tonight's impossibility and terror.

Ivory sucked in a harsh breath. "There's a girl. Cabrina Brite? They found her last week, drowned. I saw her body the day I asked you about ghosts, and I didn't tell you—" She bit her inner cheek. Wolf didn't need to know about the death poem. "I went to her grave, and she's a girl like—*like me*, understand? But her mother buried her wrong, and now she's some kind of disturbed spirit, and I went looking for her. To help her, I mean. And there was this cat, and it's like a doorway made of ocean stretched open, and I walked through to this other place, like a shadow of Cape Morning. I went there alone, and when I came back, I wasn't alone. It was—I don't have a name for it."

"A bad trip?" Wolf asked.

He cupped a warm palm to Ivory's cheek and turned her face to the driveway light, shining it in one eye, and then the other. She wanted to melt into this possessive grasp.

But he let her go and withdrew his hand. "What have you been taking?"

"Nothing, I'm not taking anything," Ivory said.

"You nicked yourself." Wolf pointed at her neck. A small metal object glimmered in his hand—a tiny cross, as if he'd grabbed it on his way to answer the door.

"I didn't nick myself; she tore a chunk out of me." Ivory pressed her hair up to better show her neck.

Wolf shook his head. "It's a little cut. Nothing worse."

Honey's bite felt ready to skin Ivory's throat, but she couldn't see for herself. Maybe it was negligible. Though if Honey caught up, her teeth would deepen the wound.

"None of this is coming out right," Ivory said. She was too tired to get her thoughts straight. Why couldn't Wolf make it simple and let her in? "I wanted to find Cabrina in that shadow place, and then I could find out what really happened to her, why she died, why she's haunting me. Maybe it's my fault, I didn't know it was dangerous."

"You need a good night's rest," Wolf said. The black space between door and doorframe narrowed an inch. "Not a night with me."

"I'm not here to fuck you." Ivory's voice turned desperate. "I just needed a place to go."

But Wolf's patience had slid away. He probably had work in the morning, or he'd been up with some religious activity, and Ivory wasn't being easy the way he liked, was she? Easy was the only Ivory he knew. Not his fault he knew no other kind—hers for failing to be easy tonight.

She let her robe open slightly. "Fine, I can be here to fuck you. If that's what it takes." Her damp blouse squeezed her belly and breasts.

But Wolf didn't eye her body. "This isn't healthy."

"What isn't healthy?" Ivory asked.

"You, projecting onto this dead girl," Wolf said.

The door gap narrowed another inch, blotting some of Wolf's face. He was again that special boy, brilliant boy, good little Catholic boy who only fucked trans women after dark, the everything-he-could-get-his-hands-on man. No one smarter, no one more reasonable. The kind of face that might smile gently over flames during a long-ago trick campfire.

Ivory bristled. "I'm not doing this for me."

"I didn't call you selfish," Wolf said, reassuring. "You care, I believe it. If I'd known where the ghost talk would go, I'd have shut it down last week."

Except he'd shut it down anyway. All the better when Ivory had slid her lips around his cock. She opened her mouth to speak now, have it out, shout him away so she could step inside.

Wolf cut her off. "She's dead, Ivory. The kindest choice might be letting her stay that way."

"I am!" Ivory snapped.

The wind whistled through crackling brush in the blackness beyond the house, catching Ivory's attention. Was that really just a breeze? Or something else? There might be laughter in the night. Ivory glanced to one side and the other, scanning for honey-colored eyes.

She almost missed the front door shutting in her face.

"Wait, damn you!" Ivory slammed both palms against the door, but the force of it made her arms tremble. She didn't have the muscle to fight this.

The door gap snapped wide, and Wolf stepped through. "What, Ivory?" he shouted. "Who's chasing you? It's a ghost town this time of night."

"Exactly." Tears pricked Ivory's eyes, but she wouldn't cry. Had to be pretty, be nice. "She's waiting."

"Good night, Ivory."

"I'm not making this up!" Ivory cried. She didn't want to beg, but she felt her knees slide toward the welcome mat. "I saw her ghost. I saw that other place. And I'm not on drugs."

Icy disbelief hardened Wolf's stare. He sensed something off about her and was mistaking it for intoxication. Maybe it was a ghostly touch, or a scent off the air of Cape Shadow. Honey's bite, no matter how shallow, might have tainted Ivory's flesh.

Whatever the difference, Wolf clearly had no plans to let her in. Ivory couldn't have anything, not sanctuary, not even the slightest peace of mind that she might be loved and protected here.

Hadn't she known better? She was a special kind of toy, but Wolf had no mind to play with her tonight. He'd held her, and fucked her, but that entitled her to nothing. She'd chosen to be inconvenient. Why should he give her sanctuary if she couldn't even be convenient?

Why should anyone see her as human?

Wolf's hand pressed against Ivory's chest. She tensed her legs, tried to hold firm, but the sea had beaten all resistance out of her. One foot stumbled back from the door. The other followed from the step.

"You need to figure life out for yourself, Ivory," Wolf said. "Whatever you think is supposed to happen here, it's not my problem to sort out. I don't own you. Clean yourself up, and maybe we can hang out. You're not mine, you're yours."

The door crashed shut, and the locks ticked along its inside. Wolf left the light on, his one little mercy, but that golden glow couldn't keep Ivory safe. It only told the night where she stood.

"But if you won't own me, someone else will," Ivory whispered.

She tugged her robe shut again and staggered down the driveway, back to the street, keeping her distance from the streetlights.

Where next? Too far to Joan and Marla. Sunshine & Chill? The library? Home?

The night wouldn't tell her the right place to hide. Honey was nowhere, and everywhere. Each time Ivory glanced over her shoulder, through tangles of drying red hair, she glimpsed that honey-gold gaze reflecting in streetlights or looming in the dark, its location always changing, ever closer.

She reached an unfamiliar residential street, somewhere deeper inland. Cape Morning was quiet here. Ivory had gone the wrong way, should have headed for Main Street, where people might still be gathering on sidewalks, eating and chatting and making plans to find a summerhouse party. They might not help Ivory, but she could hide among them.

This residential street offered only meager lights, parked cars, and thick-limbed maple trees that hid the nearby houses and bloomed against a black sky. Ivory meant to speed up, veer toward those houses, pound on their doors, but each glance away from the street sent her legs wobbling, as if the night were forcing her on this path.

The bite was slowing her down. Easy prey. Quick catch.

"Someone," Ivory said. "Please."

Her voice was frail. The bite had stolen its strength. She wanted to cry and shout and scream, but a nervous habit deeper than fear kept her quiet. No one would help her if she was panicky and ugly. Wolf had demonstrated that.

A throaty whine shot past Ivory's ear, and heat billowed at her back. She thrust one shaky leg into another step.

Honey chirped with laughter.

The noise tugged at Ivory's bite wound like she was hooked by a fishing line. Her steps slowed to a stagger. Wolf could say it looked thin and shallow, but a claw or tooth could still yank the slender cut wide open.

But Honey didn't touch yet. She didn't have to. Her will alone was enough to grasp Ivory by the neck and hold her, enthralled in the middle of the dark street. A growl thrummed through Ivory's bones, an almost pleasant tremor. It whispered promises of a night like no other if she would only turn around.

Ivory's beaten feet turned to face a house they couldn't reach, and then her head turned back the way she'd run.

A dark silhouette stood in the street, backlit by failing streetlights. Trick of the shadows, trick of the light.

Ivory stumbled toward Honey. Wasn't she so cold after her swim against water and wind? And wasn't Honey so warm? Didn't Ivory deserve a little warmth? Honey could become her beach fire.

Part of Ivory held back, didn't want this.

And yet a deeper part craved it. This warmth was a red heart-shaped box of Valentine's Day chocolate Ivory might have bought herself, not to be shared. The kind she might eat halfway through before swearing she wouldn't finish the box that same night. *I couldn't eat another bite*, she might say, except she could.

She wanted to. But she didn't. And yet she did.

Life would be easier if she could be blameless in her craving.

Honey crackled with heat where she stood nude on the asphalt. Saltwater still dripped from her gold-black mane, and her eyes glistened with a hunger of her own. She and Ivory could devour each other. Ivory only needed to step close and bare her neck.

The bite wound trickled sticky fluid down her spine. She shifted into a clumsy lope. Every limb sagged, and gravity swelled within Honey, and maybe Ivory could fly.

But it was easier to fall.

Honey placed one hand on Ivory's arm, the other on her shoulder, inches from the bite wound, and pressed her back, back, back until her spine struck hard against a firm wall. Was this someone's house? A boat shed? Ivory couldn't tell; her world was shadow and Honey.

Hot breath swept Ivory's neck as teeth grazed her tender skin. Honey sank down Ivory's front and nuzzled her thigh, where claws tore at soggy jeans and a long tongue licked at a tattoo-coated scar. She then climbed past groin and belly and breast, where that tongue lapped at a bead of blood.

A voice haunted this strange kiss, soaked by the rhythm of the tide. Ivory knew it from the beach.

Come. And see. A command, a promise.

Had it ever been the sea? Or was it always Honey, whispering across worlds, tides, and Chasm Cat for Ivory's attention? She had reached from Cape Shadow and stroked a claw through Ivory's mind.

She did the same to Ivory now. One claw-tipped finger pressed Ivory's chin and aimed her attention Honey's way. Ivory's head was a weathervane guided by honeyed wind, this claw digging through her neck wound and into her thoughts, offering new guidance and desires.

Ivory, look. Ivory, lick. Ivory, kiss.

And Ivory kissed. And she thought of devouring that whole box of Valentine's Day chocolates in a night, with prophecies of regret that she wouldn't feel good later. But it felt good in the moment, so she would do it anyway. Had her nights with Wolf really been so different?

Honey pressed her forehead to Ivory's temple, and another chirp flitted up her throat. Her warmth baked the sea from Ivory's skin, an almost-suffocating heat.

Ivory breathed hard and heavy as she tried to speak. "What can I do?"

Honey pressed her lips to Ivory's with the threat of another bite. Pointed teeth dotted the darkness within her maw. She was a beast in human skin, bloodthirsty, bone-crushing, curious, lethal. The sharp kiss leaked snakes of Honey's saliva into Ivory's mouth as one tongue caressed another. Yes, this beast had eyes of honey coloring, but she tasted of honey, too.

Ivory moaned in sweetness and self-denial—*I couldn't eat another bite*.

Except she could.

Honey's teeth slid to Ivory's neck. Last time had left a scratch, but this time, Honey would not flinch back.

Ivory sank trembling against the wall and clutched at Honey's torso. She should protest. She should slip away. The syrupy taste held thick on her tongue. *I couldn't help myself*. Except she could.

But she wouldn't.

Honey lapped at the narrow wound as if to clean it and then sank her teeth into Ivory's neck again, trapping Ivory in this place, this time. Radiant heat burst through her nerves, the bite full of sunshine and shadow. She clung to Honey through each sensation.

The night swirled between them, every moment dripping sweet, and for Ivory to sate Honey's hunger was to sate her own.

If anything hissed a warning against the wind, she pretended not to hear.

Rex said the weed would help me sleep, but I think it just makes me more afraid. Every substance has a different effect on every person. A pill that calms one person down can make another explode into a thousand pieces.

Nighttime People

Cabrina the Uncaged
Dad
Her
Sometimes Xi
Sometimes Rex
The Tooth Fairy
The Sandman
An emissary of Ghost Cat Island
A ghost
A dream
A devil

Nighttime Theories

I am dreaming
I am nightmaring
I am sleepwalking
I am being paranoid
I am being weed-paranoid
I am being watched
I am being followed

I am being possessed

I am being haunted

I am being haunted by devils who've flooded my head with dreams, they show me things

Bad as the dreams can get, sometimes they're easier than dealing with the house. Sometimes, I just pretend I'm dreaming.

A nightmare gets a lot worse when you realize you aren't asleep.

I was dreaming about the beach so vividly, I could smell the salt and sunblock, and then I smelled other things. The fabric softener in my sheets. The trees outside the house. Something with fur. I hadn't opened my eyes yet, and I didn't want to. It was like not wanting to open a door, knowing there was a crowd in the room behind it, and they would all look at you together if you stepped in.

The bedroom was full around me. They walked like people, I could *feel* their footsteps crossing the floor, creeping up to the bed. Too many of them to loom over me at once. Their heat mingled with the pre-summer, baking the air, urging me to throw off my sheets, but I couldn't do it. There's that little kid rule of how the sheets keep you safe from monsters, and I believed it then. If I kept my eyes shut, and my body under the sheets, the things that walked like people couldn't get to me. The devils. I didn't want to see them.

But somehow, I knew what their faces looked like. They each had different animal heads. Housecats like Angel. A lioness and a lion. Two tigers, the striped kind and the saber-toothed kind. There was a hyena, and a panther, and other things in the shadows behind them.

I held still, pretending to sleep, like it was all a dream. Maybe they weren't really here, but if I'd opened my eyes, they would have been. I don't even know if they were here for me or to leave me with more dreams.

They like dreams. A dream is wishy-washy and always changing, and the devils can relate. I think they come from a blurry place.

But they're real. They went away when I fell asleep and dreamed about them some more, but it isn't like I gave them what they want. Which means they'll be coming back. Maybe tonight. And will I hold still enough for them? Or will they want me to go with them to where they come from?

<u>Nighttime Theories</u>
I am being summoned
I am supposed to follow and bring back the heart I swallowed and stole, the cat-devils don't want to be here, they have to

But I don't want to be here either. I've thought about running up and down the states, but would the devils find me in Maine? Florida? New York? California?

Would *she*?

Oh yeah, she would hunt me. Town councilmember's daughter runs away from home? The campaign won't like it.

She wouldn't last one day in my skin.

<u>Nighttime Theories</u>
Wrong place, wrong girl
There is another Cabrina in California, I am a mistake, I was not supposed to be born, she is retaking the energy, I should give back what I stole, let her have the full good life

I tried to call Xi, and she says she'll make time to talk more, but I almost don't want her to. She's busy, she has classes and plans and college and a future. Talking to me is testing the universe, seeing if I can fuck up her life. What if this haunting is contagious?

Rex is busy too. Marla might know something, she's into creepy shit, but how to ask without sounding like I've been drinking seawater?

I tried to talk to Dad. A mistake. Everything is a nod and a shrug, end of conversation, because he thinks she'll know. I wish they'd divorce. It might not make anything better, but they could stop making me worse.

And when I gave up on him, I tried talking to her. Another mistake.

She told me I'm dreaming. Side effects of switching from meds that are good for me to meds that are good for her. She said I'm pretending to be important in my head because—I don't remember all the things she said, but she's probably right. Everyone tells us when we're little kids that we can be anything, but then we can't be ourselves. If we were important, our potential would come true instead of our failures. We should never think great things are coming our way.

And when we do? That's just a dream.

I think it's the same with any truly bad, end-of-the-world kind of problem. All dream, all fantasy. There's no comet coming to wipe me out. All I get is the slow decay in this house, and the world gets shittier. I read somewhere it takes a species generations to die off. People used to think the dinosaurs died out overnight, but really the extinction was so slow that most of them wouldn't have noticed. The ones who could have young that would become more like birds each generation, they kept going, and the ones who couldn't, they ended.

That's what my cells are like. The ones that can become worm food and seafoam will keep going, and the ones that can't, they'll die.

Maybe in a million years, everything will stop.

<u>Nighttime Theories</u>

I am wishing I was haunted because that is easier

I am waiting for the entropic death of all things because that is easier

I am pretending there are devils who want me to visit Ghost Cat Island because that is easier

But which Ghost Cat Island? There's the little speck off Cape Morning, but there's also its dream of a mountain rising out of the sea. That's another Ghost Cat Island.

Nighttime Theories
I am being punished for stealing

That's what I get for swallowing a piece of the sea. One little heart and I get delusions of grandeur that I'm smuggling a little of our world to that dream place. It's a dance between me and the devils, in and out, a door between the little Ghost Cat Island out here and the big one in my dreams, and that door needs a key.

They lead me to Ghost Cat Island. I leave what I swallowed. And then that door is open.

But then, what do I lead back here?

And what counts as here? The house, full of people with Brite names and dim souls? Or some other thing in that other place, the way Ghost Cat Island is different here from how it looks there? Our name could be different too. Small, dark place here. Shining there, like a lighthouse warning ships of danger.

Nighttime Theories
I am dreaming I'm a key to trick myself into thinking I'm important

PART THREE: PATIENT IS THE NIGHT

17. ALL MANNER OF BEASTS

Sunshine crept through the blinds, making the stuffy attic room pulse against Ivory's skin. Its meager light glinted off the vanity mirror and glimmered down the dead lava lamp, over tacky necklaces and bracelets dangling from the bed knobs.

Ivory scraped one hand against the headboard and dragged a soft blue-and-black tapestry of stars and crescent moons onto her head. Pleasant darkness guarded her. She silently thanked Joan for passing the unsold cloth from her wife's shop to Ivory.

Her eyes and skin soon adjusted to daylight. She still wore her robe, crusted with sand at the hem. Nothing underneath, as if Cape Shadow had again torn at her clothes, with permanence this time.

The bed shifted at Ivory's back as someone climbed from the mattress. An animal prowled her room, and then the second-floor hallway, and then the staircase and first floor. The front door creaked open, and Ivory slid through another few unremembered dreams.

She stirred awake again when she felt that animal returning to the bed.

How much time had passed? How many bugs had flitted into the house? The landladies would be furious whenever they got home.

Fabric crinkled at Ivory's neck. She was wearing a once-white scarf, knotted into a makeshift brownish-red bandage. She couldn't remember tying it there.

And she didn't remember slipping into bed with the presence beside her.

Honey lay tangled in the sheets. Her gold-and-black mane bristled from her back like a short spinal mohawk, and taut muscles formed hills around it as she rolled over. That golden gaze fell on Ivory, harsher than sunshine.

"Did we—" Ivory started, but her mouth was dry, and she let the question fall away.

Honey yawned with her full tongue flapping loose and then rolled back over, losing interest.

"No, then." Ivory must have undressed on her own. "Not that, at least."

But she and Honey must have done something. Ivory couldn't remember. It felt like someone had injected ink into her brain, filling her head with visions of a black sky.

She glanced over the room and found the light had shifted. Was it another hour, or another day entirely? She sat up and away from the blood-clotted pillow and sheet. Her neck wound would need disinfecting and a proper bandage.

One hand pawed past the nightstand lava lamp for her phone. Ten-thirty in the morning, which would be fine if she had a noon shift. Less fine was the date.

June 23rd. A lost day had passed since that night at the beach.

That was Ivory's day off. To black out through that time felt especially cruel during the summer months when every shift saw triple the customers. She should at least get to remember her meager time away from that shithole café.

Be nice, be pretty, she reminded herself. She untangled her body from the bed and reached to pop open the blinds.

Honey growled and then burrowed her head under the blankets. The sunshine seemed to annoy her, make her sluggish.

"The sun never rises on Cape Shadow, does it?" Ivory asked.

But the sun bothered her as if she, too, lived somewhere without that glaring demon eye. Sharp light gleamed through the second-floor bathroom's window, squeezing her flesh for weaknesses. She sped through showering and brushing teeth, passed an alcohol wipe over her stinging neck, and then taped a broad white bandage over the wound. The skin looked only scraped, as if Ivory had scratched too hard at a rash, but she didn't want people seeing the wound at work. They might make jokes about a hickey cover-up, but that was better than the truth.

Ivory soon made it downstairs, dressed for work, and found the living room wall ravaged beside the stereo system amplifiers and the bookcase where the Burke sisters kept family photos and memorabilia. Honey had clawed deep gashes across the pale blue drywall, in some places ripping black scratches through to the inside. Blue-and-white dust dotted the dark gray carpet, where small paw prints led away from the wall. Chasm Cat might have come and gone while Ivory slept in the attic.

What would the landladies say of this mess when they came home? Ivory could vacuum the carpet and try to smooth and repaint the drywall. And she would also have to look up online how to do those things. Would spackle work? Were there repair kits for drywall?

Honey might just carve into the wall again anyway. What the hell was Ivory supposed to do with her in the long term? Impossible creatures didn't come with care guides.

It was too much before a Saturday shift. Ivory grabbed her purse, stuffed a water bottle into her tote bag alongside her cap and apron, and hurried out the door. If she lost both this job and her low-rent attic bedroom, she would have nowhere to go.

The walk went briskly enough that Ivory arrived early. Tourists dotted the round glass tables set outside Sunshine & Chill, taking photos of each other and their drinks, pinging their Cape Morning locations on social media.

The only person Ivory recognized was Joan. She'd taken one of the outside tables and parked herself beneath its big umbrella. A book with a cracked spine rested in her hands. Ivory couldn't read the title from between Joan's fingers, but the simple art suggested the shapes of two women in ballgowns.

"Are you going to read here every day?" Ivory asked.

"That is my goal," Joan said, proud of herself. "This is how I enjoy my summer."

Ivory fitted her café cap over her hair. "This is how I enjoy mine."

"I've worn uglier outfits while teaching." Joan laughed. "Rex hated it, but he lost his say when he graduated."

Ivory needed to get inside, get her shift started, but now that Joan had brought up her son, to break away felt rude. Especially after what happened a day—no, *days* ago.

"I saw him," Ivory said. "He and his friend were at the cemetery. They had borrowed paint from Marla."

"Correcting a headstone?" Joan asked.

How did she know? Ivory almost smiled. "A grave marker. It was for the Brite girl, but her name wasn't right."

"I know." Joan ran her thumb down the pages of her book. "I feel sorry for that girl's mother, but she can be a piece of work too."

"I kind of met her." Ivory's breath rattled into the heat. "I mean, she was there. And poor Cabrina, with a mother who's nothing like you, the mother you are to Rex—"

"No need to praise me, Ives. I love my kid. End of story."

Ivory leaned into the table, palms flat on the glass. "I wish that for Cabrina. She deserved to know the peace of being herself. Even by herself. I think her friends wanted that too, and that's maybe why Rex can't let it go either."

"It's simpler than that, I think," Joan said. "I never lost a friend that young."

Ivory took a slow breath. "Before I understood what was different about me, I wanted to die. I made plans, Joan. And when I figured out the truth, I was angry. Life was so unfair, and then I figured, life would end someday." She pressed her palms together. "I told myself, *This won't last forever. What a relief.* And I decided I'd endure until then. But then—"

Sudden flames roared at the back of Ivory's thoughts. She swiped at her thigh as if batting away a mosquito, but the skin burned beneath the denim.

"Ives?" Joan asked, her tone pained, her eyes concerned.

"But then I started testing the waters," Ivory said, regaining her composure. "A little of me here, a little bit there, every lick of makeup or fashion or voice, and then the hormones. That really flipped things, you know? It would be different elsewhere, but I lucked out on a doctor who said, *Let's get you treated.* This wasn't a life choice; this was medicine. I was going to live, and I decided from then on to be a creature of life."

"I know." Joan placed one hand on Ivory's. "And you are."

"Rex has the love of two wonderful mothers," Ivory went on. The mood darkened beneath the table umbrella. "Cabrina clearly didn't have that and didn't live long enough to know better. Wolf says I'm projecting, but this matters."

"It does," Joan said. "To hell with Wolf."

Ivory scraped a shoe at the pavement. "I think I'm done with him."

Joan smiled. "Finally told him off. Good for you."

Ivory laughed to herself. She would let Joan believe she had that much fortitude. If Wolf came her way, she'd need to decide what she wanted, and fast.

The bite itched at her neck, and she wondered what that meant for their relationship. Especially after the other night. Her mind became a jumble of Cape Shadow beasts, and strange cat nightmares, and a pale body in the surf.

"Do you know if anyone else ever turned up like Cabrina?" Ivory asked. "Drowned on the shore, or—"

Her jaw snapped shut as she spotted a figure approaching from the curb. She wore a sunhat today, and her dark red nails looked freshly painted. A black dress hugged her figure.

Viola Brite.

"Joan," Viola said with a slight wave, the kind you gave your kid's teacher when crossing paths outside school.

Joan waved back and then looked hard at her book as if she hadn't been speaking to Ivory a moment ago. To Viola, it might not have looked like they knew each other.

"Ivory, right?" Viola asked, strangely chipper. "I don't think I thanked you for the other day." She forced a swift handshake that screamed *Vote for me*.

Ivory raised her eyebrows. What had she done for Viola the other day? She couldn't remember; too much had happened since. She'd been powerless at Cabrina's grave, and then she'd stamped around her bedroom, cursing herself for it. And then came Cape Shadow, and Honey, and—

"It was good to see someone at the cemetery." Viola leaned close. "I'm probably being paranoid, but it feels like everyone forgets once the ground is tilled over."

Ivory forced a smile. "Except vandals."

"Exactly," Viola said. "Thank God for you, Ivory."

"Serendipity," Ivory said. She was about to let Viola finish walking into the café, should have been standing inside behind the counter before Viola had even arrived.

But flames again licked at Ivory's thoughts. The heat of the day had kindled the trick campfire in memory, and it wouldn't leave, instead lighting malicious adolescent faces behind Ivory's eyes. She hurried from Joan's table to pass that heat to someone else, reached out one hand, and traced her fingers down Viola's wrist like Honey's claw digging into thought and mind.

Viola froze in place, a look of wonder in her eyes at Ivory's gentle touch. She was used to cushioning her awful thoughts in hollow niceties. Let her taste her own malice, but with its skin of polite façade flayed from the jagged bones.

"I mean, who do those two think they are?" Ivory asked in a conspiratorial whisper. "You knew your kid. You'd have known if you were raising some kind of freak, right?"

Viola paused, surprise creasing her features. "I would."

"Imagine you would've let that go on? Imagine you had a life like that?" Ivory clicked her tongue. "Everyone making your business their business. Asking if you're getting *the surgery*, wondering if you're a dangerous creep. Out to cut you, out to bleed you, accusing you of every sin under the sun until you run off or die or both. Or they kill you. And you're supposed to damn your child to that kind of life?"

Viola's eyes glittered with forming tears. "Exactly." She sounded stunned.

"You're no kind of mother to let your kid live that curse, right?" Ivory asked. "You got to look out for your own. No matter what. Who else will? Hell, you got to look out for the whole town, isn't that right?"

"I like to think so," Viola said.

"You *know* so." Ivory grinned. "*Viola Brite will make it right.* That's what you do on town council, and it's what you did for your kid. It's what you'll do for *all* kids, isn't it? Everyone? There's a whole town counting on you to keep everything in line. To make it *right*. Right? Well, you got my vote."

Viola set her teeth in an awkward smile.

Ivory squeezed Viola's wrist and leaned close enough to kiss her ear. "No, it's not me to thank. It's you who's blessed. Thank God for *you*, Viola."

She then dropped Viola's wrist and marched into the café. Clocking in took only seconds, and she was at the counter in her yellow apron by the time the next stream of customers snaked inside.

Viola was not among them.

18. THE HUNGER

By early afternoon, Ivory felt guilt-ridden over how she had spoken to Viola. Which didn't make sense to her. Viola was the terrible one. Not Ivory. What was she supposed to do, sleepwalk through every social encounter?

Maybe that was the café's effect on her. At mid-afternoon, another crowd flooded Sunshine & Chill's insides. Some were familiar faces, like Scarlet from a couple days ago, though she didn't seem to recognize Ivory. Others had piled off a tour bus stopping at various New England towns for a night here, a night there.

Locals. Summerhouse crowds. Everyone wanted special blends of their coffee or tea or protein-and-berry smoothie, and Ivory couldn't be sure which she'd gotten right.

Guilt melted to a gnawing hunger. There were plenty of things to eat around her, but the café's pastries glistened with an artificial sheen, as if management had given up serving real food and instead offered replicas from Walmart's toy aisle.

Ivory sipped water and crunched ice chips. Everything else overwhelmed her tongue or soured her gut.

She staggered home in the early evening, the waning sunlight relieving pressure from her skin and making the outdoors more bearable. The ease of it almost made her feel normal.

She found Honey prowling the sidewalk, strong again in the shadow of the house.

Any sense of normalcy dissolved as Ivory's bite wound tugged beneath its bandage, and in its place came a strange peacefulness. She could go to Honey. Offer herself. She made to head inside, thinking Honey might follow.

Honey didn't glance her way. Her gaze aimed east, toward the Atlantic Ocean, the wind brushing her long scraggly hair over her golden shoulders. Those locks echoed the tide, and she was the shore. Maybe she missed Cape Shadow.

Ivory became sure of it when she stepped into the dark house and crossed the foyer to the living room. The inner gloom stretched deeper than usual, even when she flicked on the light. She had to stare across the living room for some time before she realized what she was looking at.

No amount of drywall repair kits could mend this damage. The stereo system and bookcase stood dusty yet intact, but the wall that should have stood unblemished between them now bore a ragged-edged hole that was wide enough to drive a sedan through and stretched from the carpet to just over Ivory's height. No plywood, insulation, or wires crossed the torn-open gap. It didn't reveal the neighborhood either, where sunlight would still stroke yellowed grass split by the shadows of nearby trees.

The carpet instead broke onto a smattering of flat sea-beaten rock rising slightly from rhythmic waves. Curving columns of slate braced the other side of the hole, standing taller than the ceiling, like elephant ribs within a sunless netherworld cavern, its air breathing saltwater scents into the living room. It was briny and damp and dark, and the longer Ivory stared, the better she made out a black horizon. If she waited for the clouds within to clear, an ocean of stars might shine through the living room wall.

A doorway to Cape Shadow, carved out of Cape Morning.

Ivory stumbled backward into the foyer, her heart racing. "The hell, Honey?"

This was impossible. And yet, if a portal to Cape Shadow could open on the beach, why not in a house? Ivory had no idea of Honey's capabilities, her limits. What else was to come?

"I can't do this," Ivory said, laying her hand against her chest. "Can't deal with it right now."

Today's shift had been too long, and so had Thursday's, and she should have had the Friday in between off, should've remembered it, but she'd forgotten beneath a honeyed haze. An otherworldly opening in her living room wall was beyond the pale. Honey didn't need the shoreline to reach Cape Shadow now. She could do it right here because she didn't have to fucking worry about landladies, employment, maybe anything at all. Free to do as she pleased.

Heat slid under Ivory's skin, much like earlier when she'd grabbed Viola's wrist.

Why shouldn't Ivory do as she pleased too? Why should she have to stay? She couldn't deal with this, but more than that, she *shouldn't* have to deal with this. She was twenty-nine years old, and summerhouse parties were calling. None of those locations had gateways to netherworlds, she would bet.

Hunger gnawed at her as she hurried to the attic and out of her workday clothes. The impulse reminded her of craving takeout, but she couldn't imagine eating fast food tonight any more than Sunshine & Chill's pastries.

A claw traced the edges of thought. *Ivory, wander. Ivory, seek.*

She didn't have to deal with this, shouldn't have to deal with this, refused to deal with this. It would be tomorrow's problem.

Ivory, thrive. Ivory, live.

Time to get dolled up. Black top, bright sequined skirt, a darker edge to her makeup. She grabbed her purse and marched outside, daring Honey to stop her while conversely wondering if she might tag along.

But Honey was nowhere to be seen. The street lay darker now, welcoming the nocturnal stranger to stray from cover. Her claw ceased to carve at Ivory's mind, but she'd already tattooed another message in its place, same as *I am a creature of life* ran black down Ivory's thigh. She would escape this house, in mind and body alike.

Red sunset painted her way down the lane overlooking the beach. She could head for the boardwalk or the sand, but a thudding heartbeat drew her like a siren's bassline.

One of the larger summerhouses opened onto an outdoor pool party. Exactly what Ivory needed.

Tables lined with drinks and chips, easily a hundred people dancing, chatting, milling around, taking selfies, drinking, texting friends to hurry over. A dad-looking guy manned the grill, but there were no children in sight. The youngest Ivory spotted were maybe post-high schoolers, the same age as Xi and Rex. Maybe they were out partying somewhere too, but that was their business. Cabrina Brite was dead, and everyone needed to cope as best they could, whether by talking to ghosts, traveling between worlds, or never knowing she existed.

Or by getting hammered or wasted or both. Forget strange landscapes and daytime stress, Ivory was perfectly happy to become another summertime parasite on this little stretch of coastline, like she was supposed to be.

A creature of life. Always life.

She reached one of the tables and snapped up a red cup. Didn't matter what she found inside, so long as it was alcoholic. The taste of hard lemonade hit her tongue. She drank deep.

And sprayed it back into the cup.

Ivory clutched the plastic rim to her lips to hide her gagging, but even the smell now dizzied her head. She hurried toward a trash can as her gagging wound down and chucked the drink inside before wiping her forearm across her chin.

This was all wrong. She should be alluring right now, a lady of fun and mystery who could draw in some guy, some gal, somebody who wanted to party. They didn't have to come home with her, but she needed hands on her hips. A drink in her system. A dance.

Was it her imagination, or did people keep their heads turned from her, their attention elsewhere? No one looked at her, even in slipping past. She was almost nervous to force her way into someone's line of sight in case she found Wolf-like hostility.

She pawed at her neck bandage. Some drunk should have eyed it and made a vampire joke. That wasn't the kind of person she wanted to spend time with, but shouldn't some asshole be obligated to do it anyway? Give a lady a chance to roll her eyes, at least.

No one looked at her. She was a blank space in the air, a rundown tenement marked for demolition. Hadn't Wolf stared at her like she shouldn't exist the other night? Someone else had claimed ownership of the ruin, not his problem anymore.

An hour slid by, Ivory skulking the party's edges. Hunger wriggled in her gut. She stood in the middle of a poolside crowd, half of them dripping wet, all of them drunk or stoned.

What were they having such a good time for? Didn't they know they'd come to a sick place? Didn't they care a girl was dead? How would they feel if Honey came tearing through, cracking their necks open easy as beer bottles and slurping down their lives? The least they deserved for wasting time with a pool when the ocean was right there.

A few feet away, Ivory noticed another pale woman wedged between a college-aged guy and a familiar man in his mid-thirties. No black sunglasses hid the woman's face like Ivory had seen before, but black eyeshadow streaked to either side of the bridge of her tiny nose. A scarlet tint painted her lips. The man ahead of her—Ivory knew every inch of his looks. His touch.

Scarlet had come to this party. And Wolf stood beside her.

Ivory gaped. "Well, I'll be damned."

A clawlike sensation cut through Ivory's thoughts: *Yes, yes, be damned, yes.*

Had Scarlet been hiding in the dark corners of Wolf's house the other night? Lying on his bed, clueless that he'd pressed Ivory's face into that mattress when she was still an obedient effigy, no idea he was answering a late-night banging to cast that toy aside? Cape Shadow had marked Ivory as a bad dream, and Wolf had chosen to wake up. She wasn't worth helping.

But tonight could be better. Nothing about hers and Wolf's non-relationship forbade them from seeing other people. And that benefit went both ways.

Ivory went on watching until Scarlet pushed back from Wolf. He didn't look sorry to see her stagger away from the poolside, grass crunching under her feet. A gentleman might have offered his arm to walk her wherever she needed, but Ivory knew him better than that. He turned right back to the party without missing a beat. Maybe Scarlet would return in a moment.

Maybe she wouldn't.

Ivory walked the crowd's edge, outside Wolf's sight. She wouldn't crouch low, that would feel too much like a big cat stalking the outskirts of a herd, but his eyes were elsewhere. There were plenty of summer visitors. Would he be looking for women with dicks, thinking he could know by sight? He had that arrogance about him. But then, he might only be waiting for Scarlet.

The poolside gave way to flattened grass, where Scarlet had vanished into the darkness. The land here sloped toward the sea between houses, and a pedestrian could reach the sand without the help of wooden staircases or ramps. Someone had spread a line of gravel where the grass and sand met, as if that could keep back the Atlantic. Each year seemed to sacrifice a little more of the beach to the ocean. Looking northeast, Ivory made out porchlights shrinking where the cape's tip thinned like a road of light leading into the sea.

The sound of retching dragged Ivory's attention back to her patch of shore. She found Scarlet on hands and knees at the gravel line. She couldn't seem to vomit, but she wanted to. Something inside her needed out.

"It's like the world's falling to pieces," Ivory said. "Like it's always been in pieces."

Scarlet didn't respond. Her arms wobbled beneath her, and her head weaved side to side in an unsteady dance. She might have taken a party drug, and not the gentle kind. Ivory could relate—a little woozy, a lot confused. Gathering the ocean sounded easier than gathering her thoughts.

Small wonder Wolf had let both women go. He found all the thrill he wanted out of life on his own, and all the peace, too. Ivory could go back to him now, he would be open, available.

"Do you ever wonder what it would be like to wash up dead on the beach?" Ivory asked, glancing at the dark waves. "Why would our deaths ever matter? What were we doing that was so great? I can't even make a goddamn cup of coffee right."

Scarlet leaned onto her left arm and raised her trembling right hand as if to offer a consolatory greeting. Porchlight glistened down her sweat-dotted skin.

And the narrow red river leaking from a slender cut on her palm.

Ivory's gut clawed at her esophagus. She'd had nothing to eat but ice chips since two days ago, and her party drink had tasted wrong on her tongue. Wasn't she dehydrated? Wasn't she starving?

Her jaw slid open, teeth parting, but she fought down the rising hunger. Here came that other-night sensation of a heart-shaped Valentine's Day box, filled with sweets. She wanted it. But she didn't.

Except she did. The smell of blood climbed strong and sweet, less like metal and more like sugar or chocolate. Or maybe honey.

I couldn't eat another bite.

Ivory glanced up the shoreline and then back at the party. No one else close by. Only Ivory, Scarlet, and the blood.

How long until *I couldn't eat another bite* became *I couldn't help myself*? Ivory should walk away.

Her knees instead bent beside Scarlet and rubbed against grass and gravel. Scarlet turned her head, arm crooked at an awkward right angle. The blood now traveled her forearm, where its river forked as if chasing her blue veins. It knew where it belonged, but it couldn't find a way back inside.

"I cut it," Scarlet whispered. Her voice scarcely climbed over the crashing waves. "Oh, it's cut."

"It is," Ivory said. "Let me see."

She cupped one hand around Scarlet's thin forearm and let the coming blood darken her finger. They were both so pale. Scarlet must have struck a sharp rock among the gravel for so much blood to slither onto Ivory's skin. Enough to watch it pool. Sticky strands webbed between Scarlet's skin and Ivory's when she drew her finger back. They clung to her chin when she slipped the reddened finger into her mouth.

Thick and sweet. The hunger sucked greedily, a parasite in Ivory's throat, but at least it quit clawing at her insides. She'd tasted blood before and it had always been metallic and wrong.

Never this delightful syrup caressing her tongue.

She licked the insides of her mouth, spreading sweetness along her gums. When she drew her finger clean from her lips, she caught Scarlet staring. Her gaze drifted on uncertain tides, and her eyes were watery.

"Does it hurt?" Ivory asked, but her voice came weighted. She could lie down and sleep right here on the gravel if not for the hunger. It would claw again soon. She needed more. "I can help."

Both hands clasped Scarlet's forearm, and Ivory opened her mouth, latched her teeth onto Scarlet's hand, and ran her tongue along the bloody palm.

Scarlet gave a trembling gasp. Nerves lit beneath her skin, casting a prick of lightning each time Ivory licked. Did Scarlet feel the same kinetic rush? An echoing desire? Honey had bitten Ivory, and Ivory was biting Scarlet, and maybe the sweetness passed from blood to blood in a contagious ecstasy.

Everyone deserved a little pleasure. A little treat.

Scarlet's watery eyes slid shut as she turned to the sea, and she craned her neck in another kind of invitation. Warm life pulsed beneath her thin flesh. It would be so easy.

Another warmth breathed through the night, pressing along the coastal wind, and Ivory sat up. Porchlights watched from afar, but did another presence hide between light and shadow? Honey might be out prowling the town, deciding whether Cape Morning was enough or if she wanted to savage throats and claw at the thoughts of people in other parts of Massachusetts.

But she could also be lurking right here, right now, watchful for what Ivory might do. Never taking power, only enticing. If she were here, maybe Ivory couldn't be blamed for suffering a honey-sweet claw in her thoughts.

Or maybe Ivory's every action was her own choice.

She wrenched her mouth from Scarlet's skin in a sucking wet pop and flitted backward toward the summerhouse light. Her fingers wiped hard at her chin, and then she licked them near to clean.

Scarlet gasped like a lover abandoned in the act. Her attention returned to her hand, a *how did that get there?* look clinging to her eyes. Blood welled in crescent teeth marks along her palm. She needed a bandage.

But that couldn't be Ivory's problem. She needed to leave before she drank too deeply. Her hunger would nag, but she could fight it down through the graceless stagger toward home by herself. If she found Honey at the house again, she could take another turn drinking like last night, and then Ivory could let the choices run like dripping blood.

She almost made it. Or thought she did. Maybe choice was a joke that destiny liked to play on every living creature, and Ivory was tonight's punchline. She couldn't tell.

She only knew every part of her body tensed the moment she spotted Wolf again.

He was right where she'd left him and—no surprise—chatting with another woman. Seeing his muscles in a short-sleeve button-up, his dark eyes, his height. She always felt good in his grasp. Good enough to knock away the hunger?

I couldn't help myself.

The partygoers slid out of Ivory's way almost without noticing. They were tree limbs, and she was the coastal wind. Even the woman Wolf had been chatting with hardly seemed to notice when Ivory stepped between them, as if the sight of her made the other woman forget what she'd been doing.

Wolf was not the same. His eyes fell on Ivory the moment she stepped in front of him, and his gaze wandered her sequined skirt, her breasts, her face.

"You look good, party animal," he said, and then raised an eyebrow. "But are you?"

It was a question within a question: *Will you be easy? Will you be convenient? Are you on anything?* He was at last ready to receive her, so long as she behaved.

She offered a prim smile. "Should I be?"

Her hand settled on his chest. Another hand, not hers, rested on her shoulder, the fingers slick and warm. She glanced back to find Scarlet standing close behind. Her chest pressed Ivory's back, one arm ringing Ivory's waist. Scarlet exhaled sweet warmth as if she'd swallowed the summertime and needed to sweat it out.

"What you did—what you were doing," Scarlet said. "Do it more."

Ivory held still, caught between Wolf and Scarlet as if a hundred or so partiers didn't throb around them. Wolf was lucid. Scarlet hadn't been when Ivory licked at her, but fresh adrenaline now sharpened her eyes. What was that look she wore? The need to skydive, to jam a needle up a vein, the best drug being a night to die for, and Ivory held the keys and pulpit to some made-up church of ecstasy and oblivion.

She had been there, hadn't she? It looked like a mountain on a ghostly island, its insides full of holes, and it went down, down, down. Could Scarlet see it? A bite-based infection of vision might drive Cape Shadow and its Ghost Cat Island into her thoughts.

Ivory cocked her head. "How big a night do you want, big bad Wolf?"

The air thrummed hot between them. It would only keep warm for so long, and Wolf had little time to consider. Scarlet could never be his fetish, he might only have shown her attention for his ego's sake, but now he could have it all. Everyone could be happy.

Wolf at last grinned back. "Well, alright then."

The party faded around them. Scarlet clung to Ivory, and Ivory pressed to Wolf, and they started away from the poolside toward the street and his red Mercedes convertible. He made a half-funny joke, but Ivory laughed the way he liked in a rising titter.

And then they roared into the night.

19. LIE STILL IN THE DARK

Fingers stroked Xi's hair, and her eyelids fluttered open. Rex's bedroom spread dark around her, and an unseasonal chill crept through the air, but no one stood at the bedside.

Two nights had passed since the séance, and Xi had not yet gone home. Rex had instead given his bed to her and lay on a sleeping bag in T-shirt and shorts, lightly snoring. A fat candle burned atop the dresser, casting dancing light over a Dave McKean poster of *The Sandman*.

Nothing looked amiss. This was not Xi's hazardous bedroom with palm-streaked windows and the noises of another family traveling through walls and vents. She'd been safe here since the beach fire. Between Rex's presence, Marla's shop downstairs, and Xi's status as a guest, she had to be protected against any haunting. She let her eyes close.

Another finger touched her hair, and she looked around again. Still no one. But where could that chill be coming from?

Xi had flopped on her side in her sleep, and now one arm hung off the bedside. Her bones were heavy; she was too tired to roll over and drag her limbs back. She let the arm dangle and let the night seep in.

Calling her mother was last on the to-do list before collapsing here each evening. Josephine had sounded frantic two nights ago, as if she'd somehow known about the beach séance. Xi could imagine her mother with hair puffed out to either side in long curls, crimson robe flared, her skin gone bloodless with worry, as if she had transformed into an ill-fated Gothic heroine in the day her daughter was away. What would become of her when Xi went to college?

Josephine had been less frantic on the phone since after the séance night, but she clearly worried the same. *I only have this summer left before you go to Dartmouth*, she'd said this evening, voice tight, maybe holding back tears. *And you're still my daughter*.

Xi had promised that would always be the case, but she'd bitten her tongue against saying anything else. These old wounds never healed, did they? They only festered. And if paranoia could infect her mother, it could infect Xi.

She had been a freshman when she first plucked up Helen Oyeyemi's *White is for Witching* and read of the Silver family's malevolent house. From behind the eyes of that house. It cast a splinter from the page into her mind, how the house recalled doing good, and then chose to do harm. The splinter had turned to an icicle and chilled her blood. She'd read from animal characters' points of view as a child, but that was her first experience with a location's perspective, with the sense that *a place* could choose violence against its inhabitants at any time. Only later did she learn this was a longstanding tradition in ghost and Gothic stories, and she had to wonder if inspiration for the idea bled from real life, as most ideas did.

And sometimes she wondered if Cape Morning might be the same.

A coldness ached into her dangling arm, and at last she felt warm air brush her skin like hot breath—a summer breeze.

Someone had pushed one of the windows open. The air smelled of salt.

"Rex?" Xi whispered.

Rex burned hot in summer and must have opened the window while Xi slept. Wouldn't Joan or Marla be pissed to find them wasting the AC? Someone would have to shut it. Xi sucked in a protesting breath and then began the hard work of rolling onto her back.

Her arm went taut over the side of the bed.

The dark room quieted around her, wind dying, the sounds of Rex fading beneath an oppressive silence in Xi's ears. If she held still, she wouldn't have to find out whether or not she'd imagined resistance when she tried to move her arm. Anything could be blamed on the imagination if you quit poking around, if you were smart enough to never find the truth.

Xi couldn't feel her hand. The chill had seeped so absolutely into her fingers that everything below the elbow had gone numb.

She licked her lips and wriggled her other arm from beneath her body. The angle was strange, but she managed to paw at the nightstand. Fingers sought glasses and beside them found her phone. With its flashlight feature.

She shoved her glasses on and stared at the blurry darkness, letting her eyes adjust better to the shoved-open window, the Red Sox decorations rendered black in the gloom, the useless dresser candle, the suggestion of Rex's sleeping bag on the floor. It lay too far from the bed for him to have grasped Xi's hand while they slept. If she turned on her phone's flashlight, she would get a better idea what had become of her stray arm and numb hand in the dark.

Be nothing, she wished in her thoughts. *Be caught between the mattress and bedframe.*

That wouldn't explain the window, but she could blame that on Rex. She could rationalize anything, given the chance.

Her phone screen lit up, and her thumb slid over digital displays, activating the flashlight. A bright beam spread from the back of the phone, bathing the nightstand in white. She steered the light toward the bedside's edge, where her bicep pressed against the mattress. The light then ran along her elbow, where it vanished down the mattress's side, toward the bed's underside. Her forearm thinned at her wrist and then splayed into her hand.

Where another hand held hers.

Chalk-white fingers laced between Xi's olive digits. They seized with cold, as if she'd plunged her bare fist into a snowdrift.

Her body trembled with a summertime winter. She had to clench her teeth to keep them from chattering. Her phone's light wavered toward an empty stretch of floor, looking for the source of those pale fingers, but there was no one waiting beside the bed.

Only under it.

Xi tried to breathe, but her lungs were shrinking into raisins. Quick breaths came and went, and her heartbeat thumped in her ears. She tugged again. Her arm held fast. She dropped the phone and tried to pry herself free, but she couldn't unlace undead fingers from her icy hand. They would not let go.

Xi drew in a stinging breath and exhaled a soft-spoken name. "Cab?"

The fingers flexed around her hand in answer. *You already had all the good things*, it seemed to say. *Now I get the freedom, the loving mother, the life. It's my turn.*

A memory floated cloudlike over Xi's thoughts. She didn't want to reminisce right now, but she couldn't help knowing this touch. This was not a thing with Cabrina's face.

This was true Cabrina. Sweet Cab.

Who else could slip into Rex's bedroom? Xi didn't know if vampires genuinely needed an invite to enter someone's home, but if so, Cabrina was always welcome here, same as Xi's house. Cabrina had been waiting for Xi to wake up and take notice. There was a question in this touch, nothing Xi could have answered in her sleep.

Do you still love me? the ghost seemed to ask. *Do you remember?*

"Yes," Xi muttered. "I do. Yes."

A pale figure unfolded over the bed like a great alabaster butterfly, and she breathed another cloud of memory across Xi's thoughts.

Cabrina, in a different room. Xi sat at the foot of another bed, and Cabrina sat on her lap, legs spread around Xi's waist.

The pale figure leaned close. Yes, she was Xi's Cabrina. She always had been, outside Xi's house, on the beach. The life Cabrina had known was gone, but nothing else had really changed.

Except the hunger. It sucked at the bottom of Cabrina's soul, a pain that a true friend could ease.

Remember, Xi, the pale figure breathed. *You love me, don't you?*

"Yes, Cab," Xi said. "It's okay. Yes."

The pale figure slid her legs from Xi's waist, the way Cabrina had shifted off Xi's lap that night in her bedroom. Onto the floor. Cabrina on her knees, between Xi's legs, head toward Xi's lap.

Teeth came too cold for pain. Xi only felt the barest sensation of a cut across her inner thigh before—

A special kiss, Cabrina had called it, because she could be silly in her sweetness when distant from her house. Xi had cradled Cabrina's head in her lap, kissing her hair and holding tight, and feeling Cabrina's lips and tongue run deep and sweet to her core.

This new sensation was warmth and life. It was death, too, letting the world seep away behind Cabrina's lips.

Xi's memories ran soppy. That day with Cabrina vanished in the curve of Xi's remembered posture until her shadow formed a black archway, letting night hang ringlike over the past.

And if Xi peered through that ring, she saw places beyond Rex's bedroom. Here was Cape Morning, with its familiar beaten sand, gray Atlantic, and unsteady sunshine.

But when the sun sank beneath purple-red skies and gave way to starlight, the world broke open, leading past memory and into a new vision.

White bones dotted a coastline of black sand and dark water.
Constellations shined brighter than Xi had ever seen, but they were
unfamiliar, the stars of some other world. Immense shapes blotted
them from the horizon, rising from the sea. A tremendous skeleton,
a towering horn, gargantuan slabs.

And beyond them all, a shape lay where Ghost Cat Island should
have poked offshore from Cape Morning. But this was no measly
scrap of rock; it had been replaced by some impossible mountain, a
Ghost Cat Island of prehistoric times. Of another world.

The pleasant sensation of Cabrina's mouth against Xi's thigh
cut out as Cabrina flinched to the foot of the bed, hissing Xi awake
from the vision.

Xi sat up too fast, and the rush made her head spin. "Were you
swimming to the island?" she asked, sounding groggy. "Cab, what
happened to you?"

A dark stain leaked down Cabrina's chin and formed a valley
over the chest of her borrowed hoodie. She tensed over the piled
sheets, where a similar stain echoed. She had been sloppy with Xi's
blood. These were animal movements, an instinct rooted up from
deep in her head. Was it the hunger? Or was this what death had
done to her?

"Cab?" Xi slid toward the bed's edge on shaky legs. "Cab, wait."

"Haaah," Cabrina breathed. "Heart."

Xi shook her head, not understanding, but her next question died
as darkness shifted beyond the foot of the bed. She and Cabrina
weren't the only ones awake in the bedroom.

Rex stood from his sleeping bag, muttering panicked curses
under his breath.

Xi tried to stand. "Rex, don't." She reached for him, but her
first footstep sent her falling.

Rex caught her arm and steered her around the bed, through
the door, into the hall and down the stairs.

"Where are we going?" Xi asked, fainter now. How much blood had Cabrina taken?

Rex hurried them through the foyer, unlocked and thrust open the front door, and pulled Xi into the night air. The AC slipped away, and the summer night blew hot breath across Xi's skin.

She flinched from Rex's grasp as if retreating from an open flame. He was hot, too. The air hung soupy around them, its humidity stifling. Xi could have handled it at other times, but the sudden swerve from chilly to overheated left her reeling.

Her eyes fell on Rex, panting beside her. "Rex?"

"Don't know," Rex said between breaths. "Had to get you the hell away from her. You were so fucking cold. Wasn't right. Didn't really think."

He was only a short, muscular blob in the faint outdoor light of neighboring houses, but Xi made out the growing blackness of his car as they reached it. Its inner light flared when Rex tugged open the driver's door, and then he shoved Xi inside to crawl over the shift stick. He slipped in behind her. The door shut, and the light quickly doused itself.

Xi caught a white blur slink down the side of Rex's house and disappear into thick shadows beyond.

She pawed at her thigh. Her fingers came away slick. "She bit me."

"While you were sleeping?" Rex asked, catching his breath.

"No, she waited," Xi said. "I think Cab wanted to show me something. She wanted to show me—" She rubbed her face, feeling light-headed. "Maybe I'd have seen the vision better if I was dreaming. Or she wanted to know if I still loved her. But she wanted me to have a say."

"You *let* her bite you?" Rex snapped. "The hell would you do that for? What if she turned you? You want to ditch me like that?"

Xi watched him without blinking, without speaking. She let him have a moment to hear himself and take in the vastness of their situation. How a dead friend had scaled Rex's creaky little house and climbed in the window—the dream and the nightmare of it all. How Cabrina could be gone and yet linger in their lives. They might be stuck in this car until daylight, pressing hands to Xi's thigh to staunch the blood flow. And they could face worse before then.

Rex let out a long sigh, turned from Xi to the windshield, and settled against his seat. "Sorry," he said, quick. He took another breath before speaking again. "Was it really Cab?"

The figure that had unfolded over Xi had looked like Cabrina, and she carried an undefinable Cabrina-ness to her. Did that still make her Cabrina at this point? Xi remembered Marla's warning: An inhuman spirit could pretend to be human, fooling everybody who saw it. Some vampiric glamour coating the dead.

But what about when the ghost quit pretending? What devil would haunt the world then?

"I think it was Cab," Xi said. "It had to be."

"But she hurt you," Rex said.

"She's cold, and I was warm." Xi wiped at her thigh. "I think she's starving, too."

And lonely, she wanted to add. *And scared. And she wants to know if she's still loved.*

"And what'll happen to you?" Rex asked.

Xi had no answer for that. She could only think of Cabrina's face as she sank her teeth into Xi's thigh, and how good it had felt.

How she'd do it again.

20. THE SHAPING PLACE

Ivory flicked on the foyer light and dropped her keys on the scant patch of linoleum surrounding the indoor welcome mat. Wolf and Scarlet stumbled in behind her, and the door clacked firmly behind them, trying to seal out the night.

As if the night didn't lurk on the far side of the living room.

"Roommates?" Wolf asked. His chest pressed to Ivory's back, and raw heat seeped down her spine.

"Landladies," Ivory said. "Out of town." She wasn't used to his curiosity.

Wolf broke from Ivory's skin. "Too much to drink. Need to drain the snake." He disappeared into the half-bath beneath the staircase.

Scarlet offered a smirk and backstepped into the black living room. Wolf had wrapped her wound in napkins snatched from his glovebox, and they formed a tempting crimson clot.

"I can be a snake," she said, dropping the napkins. "Will you drain me?"

An obvious need burned in her eyes, her scarlet lips, a longing for Ivory's mouth. They slid together into the living room, where the tide whispered through the walls.

Ivory grasped Scarlet's arm and ran her tongue along sticky skin. "What's your name?"

"Do we still have names?" Scarlet asked, sounding dazed. She nearly lost her balance, but she never tore her gaze from Ivory. "It's Tiffany."

Ivory kissed that candy-blood forearm. "Can I call you Scarlet instead?"

Scarlet lifted her arm toward her head, drawing Ivory with it, until they faced each other, and then she dove in for a kiss. She had to taste her own blood on Ivory's lips. Did it taste like syrup and dreams? Ivory hoped so.

"I can *be* Scarlet if you want." A red ring blotted the skin around Scarlet's mouth. Her lipstick was smeared, traces of it dotting Ivory's face.

They slipped deeper into the dark. No lights, no Wolf, and Ivory paid no attention to the passing shadows of the coffee table, couch, or stereo system. There were only hers and Scarlet's steps leading toward the sound of crashing waves, and beneath them, a bizarre chuckle.

The living room's blackness gave way to faint natural light ebbing through the Cape Shadow gap across from the foyer. Ivory smelled salt on the air, felt her feet move from carpet to cold stone, pounded smooth by oceanic erosion. Scarlet clung to her arm, unbothered and undeterred. Door hinges warned Wolf might be coming, too.

Had Ivory brought them here because she wanted them? Or was it the will of someone else?

Ivory, drink. Ivory, call.

Stars glimmered distantly where Cape Morning's lit-up businesses and summerhouses should have polluted the sky against them. But these were the constellations of Cape Shadow. Beneath them lay the rocks spreading from the edge of the living room carpet, onto Cape Shadow's ocean. Its foam splashed Ivory's legs.

Scarlet pressed her wounded hand to Ivory's mouth, and her eyes begged for feeding. Ivory knew the sensation. She longed to be fed upon too, and to feed, torn between worlds with no relief from either urge. They sank to the sea-beaten rocks, where Scarlet ripped her wound wide open with sharp fingernails and gasped with delight as Ivory fed again.

She only broke away when Wolf cleared his throat behind her.

"Is this some kind of projector room?" he asked, looking around the room for the source of the image.

He stood bowlegged at the hole leading to the living room, his gaze dancing between Ivory and Scarlet. They could drink of him, too. Ivory slipped one arm from Scarlet and reached for him.

"Yeah, blood play isn't my scene," Wolf said. "Easy diseases."

"This is different," Ivory said, and her finger curled inward.

"Play with us," Scarlet said through a pleased sigh.

Wolf made to answer, but another rippling chuckle cut him off. He glanced from Ivory and Scarlet to the impossible shadow shore around them, like he'd refused to notice until an alien sound thrust the knowledge into him. His eyes widened, the realization that this was no trick crossing his face.

"Who else is there?" he asked, balling one fist. "How the hell can there even be a there?"

"No, no, don't start to care now," Ivory said, wagging her once-inviting finger. "You never cared about the details before. Aren't I still your plaything?"

"My plaything?" Wolf blinked hard. "Ivory, that's not how it was." His attention jerked left, then right, as if the opening to Cape Shadow might snap at him. "That can't be what you want to talk about right now when this is—look at it."

"Play with us," Scarlet said again, in sing-song this time, and then she broke into laughter and dropped her head to Ivory's chest.

"How can you be so easygoing about this?" Wolf asked. He reached out to touch the wall bridging the worlds and then thought better of it.

"If I wasn't easy, I wasn't worth having," Ivory said. "You didn't want me. Someone else did."

Now Wolf laughed, tearing his attention from the surrounding strangeness. "What are you looking for, an apology?"

Not if he had to ask like that. An irritated drum pounded in Ivory's ears, the sound of her heart, Scarlet's heart, and maybe Wolf's heart too. Would his blood taste like candy?

Cape Shadow tensed its black stone silhouettes. The stars shined so bright as to blur the lines between the sky and the darkness, and then a shadow climbed from the stone, first all dark, and then two halves of tawny light, a figure Ivory hadn't seen since the beach.

Chasm Cat.

She sauntered down the stone, past the spot where Ivory and Scarlet cuddled in a heap, and twisted around Wolf's legs. He smiled and bent to scratch her ear. She let him for a moment and then slipped past him as if headed toward the front door and Cape Morning.

"Good idea, kitty," Wolf said, and he thumbed over his shoulder. "This shit's not right, Ivory. It's unholy."

Ivory pulled herself over Scarlet. "I can give you head. Right here. Like you like. Isn't that all I was good for?"

"Like *you* like." Wolf took a step back. "You're thinking too much of everyone else. Taking things personally."

"Funny you never put it that way when you were inside me," Ivory said. "When you were telling me your bed is where I belong."

"Sure," Wolf said. "When I want it like that."

The want was gone from his eyes. He might have toyed with Scarlet until he felt she wasn't right, and then chased Ivory thinking he could have her after his dismissal the other night, exactly as they used to be, no consequences, no strings, lusting for his effigy.

But the blood had profaned her. He couldn't handle what she'd become, or the worlds she could now inhabit. Likely he had never cared that much from the start.

He wanted her despite all her awkward talk and angles and thoughts, but only when convenient. When easy.

Conditional humanity. How human would he find her when she wasn't certain herself?

The living room curled behind him in a black fog, and its darkness suggested humanity was more optional than conditional. Discardable by others, as loose as torn skin.

Chasm Cat's feline silhouette stretched behind Wolf's legs. Her shape climbed his back until two long legs planted behind him. Ivory could only make out the changes as they rose past his shoulders, a shadow puppet show where the hands realized the fingers could split apart, grow new joints, and bewilder everyone who set eyes on the performance.

Wolf shuddered at the change in the air. He glanced over his shoulder, maybe expecting the front door to have opened and another visitor to stand in the foyer, but a giggling figure loomed behind him. He stumbled with a surprised grunt into the pocket world of stone and sea, nearly trampling Scarlet's ankles. She drew tighter against Ivory. They all looked to the living room, where the shadow slid from the house.

Honey stood in place of Wolf, her eyes gleaming with starlit gold.

A headache beat behind Ivory's eyes. Had Honey been Chasm Cat from the start? Maybe that smaller creature was an aspect of the whole woman, tip of the iceberg, the way Ghost Cat Island protruded as a pathetic scrap of rock off Cape Morning when it was really the great mountainous Ghost Cat Island off Cape Shadow.

Or maybe these cross-worldly shapes defied Ivory's understanding, with the change a scribble on cosmic paper beyond her grasp. She blinked hard twice, and the headache faded.

Wolf looked every which way, mouth gaping in confusion. He didn't understand. He was never meant for understanding.

Honey-slick claws cut at Ivory's thoughts. *Ivory, think. Ivory, be. Ivory, choose.*

Ivory had begged Wolf to take control the other night. Be her keeper, her protector. Honey had taken Ivory's charge instead, and she'd used that position to insist Ivory decide for herself. She could do it again, with a different life in her hands.

Wolf glanced sideways at her. "I don't like this game."

Ivory wanted to tell him she didn't like the games he played either. That he should be straightforward, that she didn't like the way he'd thrown her aside when she came begging for help, all because he wasn't in the mood to fuck her and that was all she was good for. Maybe they should find a way to hate each other like two mature adults.

But Ivory said none of it. She only blinked, and then Honey was standing inches from Wolf, yet perfectly still, like she'd always been right in his face.

He flinched back. "Don't do that," he said, raising a warning hand.

Scarlet crushed herself against Ivory's chest. Maybe they could both feel the trouble brewing in the air.

Honey and Wolf looked ready to spar. She pursed her lips, and her throat clicked with strange laughter. The sound had to remind him of a hyena, Ivory thought. Not the way you'd think if you never heard one before, but Wolf might've caught the noise in a zoo or while watching a documentary. Hyenas had an eerie laugh, as if predators could be ghosts.

Honey's cackle could shake bones. Wolf had to be feeling the same as Ivory when she'd faced that hollow darkness at the mountainous Ghost Cat Island—the sense she was about to be hunted. Wrong place, wrong night.

"This is ridiculous," Wolf said with a nervous chuckle. He had to feign bravado to feel the slightest comfort. "You're nothing but some strung-out junkie psycho."

Honey snapped at Wolf's face, her teeth clacking an inch short of his chin. Lengthy canines braced a row of sharp front teeth.

Wolf stumbled away from her, slipped on smooth stone, and landed on his back.

Every part of Honey went stiff with corded muscle, eager for a neck she could practically taste. Ivory could taste it too. Oh yes, Wolf's blood would run like a creamy milkshake, thick and frothing and sweet.

Cruel laughter again filled this pocket world of sea-slick stone. Not *like* a hyena—exactly a hyena's laugh, as if Honey's form as Chasm Cat let her tap into the depths of feline ancestral legacy.

But her teeth were her own, gleaming sharp as her lips peeled back from her gums. Wolf wouldn't be thinking of hyenas now. He should be thinking of monsters.

Scarlet whispered something, her mouth buried in Ivory's hair. Ivory didn't catch it.

But Honey did. She turned from Wolf, her eyes fixing on Ivory and Scarlet. In a blink, she towered over them, a vision of loveliness and terror. Her sharp teeth scraped down her own forearm, unleashing a thin trickle of blood.

Ivory opened her mouth, ready to receive this new treat like a baby bird accepting a worm. This blood had to taste the sweetest yet.

But Honey guided her arm toward Scarlet instead. Red sweetness spattered her chin and nose before the trickle leaked into her mouth, and she lapped greedily at Honey's arm.

Why not me? Ivory thought.

Honey's claw scraped Ivory's mind, as if she could hear the question. *Ivory, no. Ivory, him.*

Wolf groaned, sitting up and rummaging in his pockets. His keys jangled against the stone, but he didn't make to fetch them. They had become unimportant in the face of predation, and whatever he'd gone digging for would decide whether keys mattered beyond this moment.

Ivory blinked again. Honey had moved another step deeper into the room. Wolf tore his hand loose from his jeans and raised a triumphant fist.

A chain wound around his fingers, dangling a silvery cross that gleamed with starlight.

Ivory's brow furrowed. She had glimpsed this cross in Wolf's fist the other night, eyed crucifixes in passing when she walked through his home, but she'd never known he carried one with him.

"Get back," Wolf said, his voice stern. He placed his free hand against the stone beneath him and began to stand, his cross-wielding arm firm and outstretched. "Lord Christ wills it."

Honey tilted her head, her gaze fixed on the bright silver. Her spine curled as if she might scuttle toward the hole in uncertainty, maybe fear.

But then her golden eyes glimmered, and her sharp teeth ran slick, and they told Ivory, Scarlet, Wolf, and all the stars that watched above that whatever lurked in Honey was older than this cross, older than Christ, than the idea of crucifixion itself. That she had broken the bones of extinct animals and tasted the marrow of men from the earliest days of the human race.

And she would taste of this man here.

She lunged at last, hands striking Wolf's chest. He crashed to the ground. The cross flew from his fist, clanked against his keys, and vanished between slabs of stone. Thin drool slithered from Honey's lips and dampened Wolf's shirt. He strained against her, but she slammed an open palm to his face and jerked his head sideways, exposing his neck.

Her eyes flickered to Ivory, and then Scarlet. Time to choose. Every moment was an invitation, one world making way for another, from dream to life, tooth to thought, an island to Ivory's neck and dreams. Her future. Her hunger.

I couldn't help myself.

Ivory sank into the ease of Honey's commands. *Ivory, shape. Ivory, lick. Ivory, kiss.*

She found herself leaning over this thrashing body, Scarlet gasping at Ivory's side, Wolf's warmth beating at her hand, his neck throbbing beneath her teeth.

Ivory, good. And then Honey carved out a new desire. *Ivory, kill.*

And beneath Honey's golden gaze, Ivory killed.

From the Diary of Cabrina Brite,
May 27, 2018

I think there are dead things in the waves. The ocean is the world's biggest graveyard, and it watched me and Rex together by this weekend's beach fire.

<u>Dreamtime</u>
Bobbing for hearts in the Atlantic Ocean
Bobbing for hearts in the Atlantic chest cavity, a dream full of meat and blood

<u>Nighttime People</u>
My dreams that come from me
My dreams that come from somebody else
The cinnamon scent man

That can't be right. He hasn't been back to Cape Morning since that October. Never came to see me last summer, and now another summer's on the way. I don't think I'll ever see him again.

But I smell him in the wind. Something knows I like the way he smelled, that I wanted him inside me. And it wants to be inside me too, but not the same way. It's making promises I don't want it to keep, and it's asking for things I shouldn't give.

I could offer it all the seashells and every poem and my last breath, and I don't think that would be enough.

It would be nice to talk about it, but when Rex met up with me at the beach, I couldn't tell him the things I wanted to. Sneaking off felt electric, and I didn't want to ruin it by bringing up the bad dreams. We didn't even really talk; I nestled against him, and he let me. He's a rock that way.

Neither of us meant for anything to happen.

I told him what Xi and I did in her room. I didn't want secrets between us.

But I think I made us have secrets anyway. I'm good at confusing people without meaning to.

What happened was nothing I thought through beforehand, and Rex probably didn't either. We were there together by the fire, and then we were there, *together*, by the fire.

I won't tear out diary pages like flower petals this time. I've learned better, and Rex made his feelings clear.

Am I incapable of loving someone without falling in love with them? It's okay if we crush on each other, but it doesn't need to turn into sex every time, and I don't want to start problems. High school's almost over for everyone but me, and if I ever finish my GED, that will be a miracle.

And what about Xi? And Rex?

I tell myself I need to take them into me, like we could all be a special kind of together inside my body. There's nothing wrong with that, and everything right. They're whole people, and I'm as empty as a pretty conical shell, but I could be different with them. Better.

Daytime People
Cabrina the Lonely
Cabrina's Excuses
Cabrina the Touch-Starved
Cabrina Who Can't Stop Fucking Her Friends
Cabrina Who Can't Stop Lying About It
Cabrina Who Can't Stop Loving Them

Dreamtime

The devils tear me apart, they know how I want my friends to climb inside and fill me up, but they want to fill me up instead, nestle in my flesh-shell, cuddle with my insides, so there's no room for the people I love

Xi and Rex are wiser than me. They went to that beach on spring break to have fun, and I went to be melodramatic, and something noticed me.

Shouldn't I know already?

Devils and organs make perfect lovers.

They play them in the church.

They play them inside me.

Why couldn't I have been like Xi or Rex that night in April? Why did I have to kiss the sea? Both of them were too smart to swallow a piece of that other place.

Nighttime Theories

I am being punished for stealing

I am being summoned to Ghost Cat Island to give back what I stole

I am being summoned to Ghost Cat Island to bring something back, and it will twist my heart into a devil shape, offering a new shape instead, one more like itself and less like me

If these devils chose me, they had to have a reason. They can make excuses about what ritual I've started and left unfinished, but it's all justification for something they're hinting at in the dreams. I see them clustered behind a grand door, their eyes gumming up a keyhole, and I'm just the right size for it.

Come and see, Cabrina. We're lonely, and you're empty. Let

us make you the right shape to open our door. Their poetry, not mine. I could let it all happen.

The lonely tear the world down. How am I any different?

One of Rex's moms once told me that when she was younger, she would get her friends to practice kissing each other so that when they had boyfriends, they'd be really good at it. The friends went along with that. But it was really something unsaid in her, which she wouldn't know until she left her ex-husband and came here with Rex.

This outsider feeling could be inside everybody, and they've all figured out how to hide or forget it.

Practice, marriage, unity inside me—everything's an excuse for us when we don't want to go untouched and alone. We invent rituals to approve our desires.

Like our desires aren't good enough on their own.

Like we're not good enough, and maybe we aren't.

We are sad creatures. I don't know how we'll ever be better.

21. TWILIGHT

The only thing worse than crying now was wishing to cry and yet nothing would come. The urge pounded inside Rex, his heart a grasshopper in his chest, but he could only curl up on the bathroom floor and squeeze his fists against his head.

He had brought Xi back inside, helped bandage her thigh, locked the bedroom windows, and waited for her to fall asleep. It didn't take long; she was exhausted after Cabrina's leeching visit. The sound of even breaths told Rex that he could step away. He meant to guard Xi, and he would do it, but he doubted Cabrina would come back tonight. Already fed, and the Earth would soon turn Cape Morning to face the sun. Maybe its light didn't kill vampires like in the movies, but Rex had to believe it would make them suffer.

Even if this one used to be a friend.

Now he sat seething on cold tiles, wishing he hadn't been a coward at the wake. He hated himself for obeying his mother's order to stay away from the funeral unless he could promise not to bite Viola Brite's head off. Had he been stronger, he could've seen Cabrina, maybe noticed something was off. He should've lied to Joan.

Now he didn't know how to ask her his questions. *Ma, when you saw the body, did Cab look like she might come back? Like she wanted to take Xi away too, leave me on my own? You hear any scratching in the casket before they put it in the ground?*

Pre-dawn twilight crept through the bathroom window. Rex eventually forced himself to stand. He'd barely gotten any sleep, but summer being tourist season left little chance for late mornings. Marla would need him at the shop. It was a job anyone could do, but he wanted to get paid. Customers of Secret Spell never knew what they were looking for; they just needed Rex or Marla to plunk something into their hands and promise, *Whatever the problem, this'll make you feel better*.

On good days, Rex even believed it.

He was quiet in leaving the bathroom and heading for the stairs, didn't want to wake Xi as he passed. His foot was about to thump onto the steps when he heard murmuring from the living room. He descended carefully. No one should be up yet. Was he wrong, and Cabrina had come back after all? She had an open invitation to this house.

Only when he reached a few steps down and could peer over the banister into the living room did he see two familiar silhouettes and recognize the notes of his mothers' voices.

He couldn't make out what they were saying, and Joan's face was a dark sheet in the dim light. He could only tell Marla held her, and Joan held back, and they must have been up for at least a few minutes to have two mugs of coffee steaming on the end table nearby. Had they heard the racket in the middle of the night and needed to discuss Xi's continued presence in the house? Rex's behavior? Had Marla told Joan about the séance a couple nights ago, knowing that was a bad idea?

A minute passed, and Marla giggled something into Joan's ear. They then picked up their coffee mugs and turned to the picture window. Joan opened the blinds and laid her hand on the small of Marla's back. After another minute, the dim light turned a faint purple shade.

They had woken up early to watch the sunrise together. Simple as that.

Rex settled back onto the step for a long moment, watching them against the changing sky. He wanted to go to them, share in the affection.

But more than that, he wanted to let them have this moment. Let them exist together in their own lives. He could wait for the sunrise to reach some glittery milestone, the right shade of purple-red over the Atlantic, and then he would join them. Tell them he loved them.

And he would hope their moment together would last a long while. Enough sunshiny brightness to forget vampires.

Maybe enough to last for when the sun again abandoned them to their nighttime fates.

22. REAL AND DANGEROUS

Sometime after feeding on Wolf, Honey chewed open her arm and pressed the fresh wound to Scarlet's mouth.

Ivory became a bystander, still licking her blood-gloved hands. If Honey's bite turned ordinary blood into a delicious treat, Ivory couldn't imagine what ecstasy Honey's special blood would bring to Scarlet.

But Scarlet's breath slowed as morning crawled closer. Ivory watched her chest struggle to rise, fall with shuddering suddenness, then a glacial pause before creaking into life again.

At dawn, Scarlet stopped breathing. Ivory pawed at her chest and wrists, but Scarlet had no pulse, and the heat had rushed out of her as if Cape Shadow were drinking it in, linking her with its mountainous Ghost Cat Island.

Ivory retreated from the hole in the wall to the living room couch. The stronger the daylight shined around the house, the sharper its shadow stretched from the picture window and over the yard and driveway. Ivory could almost forget the depths in the wall where Honey lurked among the bodies.

Wolf's death made sense. Scarlet's didn't. Had Honey's blood poisoned her?

Ivory should've had a feeling about that. An opinion. Anything.

These were deaths; they mattered. If she could twist herself in a knot over Cabrina Brite, she could certainly give a damn about her dead sort-of boyfriend, no matter how he'd treated her, or about Scarlet. Ivory hadn't known her, hadn't really liked her, but a mutual appetite had drawn them together, and now she was gone.

Ivory pinched the doughy flesh of her bicep and twisted hard. Stinging pain needled across her skin—okay, she could feel that much.

Maybe that claw in Ivory's head had transformed into a scalpel and amputated guilt, grief, and everything morose.

Or maybe the real problem was that death felt unreal. Like it might not be a goodbye anymore, not now that Ivory knew of a world beyond the flesh.

The day dragged by in crude sunny inches, measured by the sliding shadows of the house and the afternoon glare through the picture window. Ivory managed to shower, but she wasn't going to work, and she wasn't hungry. She half-expected to vomit up Wolf's blood, or Scarlet's, but nothing came.

An accidental nap invited evening into Ivory's life. She was only awake for a few minutes before Honey crawled from the cavernous gate torn into the wall, her hands pawing at the stony slabs bracing its sides before it gave way to drywall. Seawater slithered to the living room carpet from the mane running down her spine.

"You killed her," Ivory said.

She didn't mean to blurt it out like that, but seeing Honey in the waning light seemed to drag it out, as if that claw had marked her mind with new commands. *Be honest. Be forthcoming.*

Except this was Ivory's choice. "Did you know she'd die?"

Honey stretched from the carpet in a full-body yawn and strode toward the broad window. Evening reds and purples dripped down her collar, breasts, and the spots along her sides. She flashed Ivory a grin over her shoulder and then started for the front door.

"Are you going to be a cat again?" Ivory asked. "If not, I think you need some clothes, or we won't make it far."

Honey's ear twitched at the word *we*. She slinked toward the couch and fixed Ivory with an expectant stare. The sunset clung to her eyes.

Ivory grabbed a shawl and cloth belt from her attic bedroom, and a silk robe from Chelsea's closet. The sleek texture seemed a better fit for Honey's attitude than Ivory's robe.

The awkward assortment should have looked terrible—*would* have looked terrible on Ivory—but Honey burned with natural grace, her elegance shining through the draping clothes. She offered Ivory a questioning chirp.

"Yeah," Ivory said. "We can go. Let me grab one more thing."

Wolf's keys jangled from Ivory's fingers as she approached the driveway. Sweltering heat breathed off the pavement into the cooling night air. The outdoors felt sobering after the long night and day inside the house, and likely it would do her and Honey good to get away from the mouth of Cape Shadow.

Creamy white trim formed a bony appendage wrapped around Wolf's Mercedes, and its sleek red paint became taut muscle in the waning light, as if the car used to have a skin that Wolf had stripped away. Its engine purred at Ivory's touch, a rumble in her chest and between her legs. The same quake worked through Honey. They were riding a flayed beast, and Honey flashed Ivory another grin as they peeled out of the driveway and onto the roads of Cape Morning.

The open windows sent the night screaming through the car's inside. Honey bayed through the passenger side window, shining with the divine thrill of riding a dead man's stolen car. Anything was possible behind this wheel. Ivory could rip down every avenue in town, lights blurring past, people throbbing with life, each heartbeat a dinner bell. She could take Honey into greater

Massachusetts, and neither of them would have to think of the people they'd killed in that house, the deaths that summoned no sadness in Ivory.

A panther wouldn't worry over a hunt while lazing in digestion. No lion ever stressed about a day job or making the rent. Not one hyena in history had mourned over crunched zebra bones and strips of marrow.

Ivory turned onto Main Street, drove a block, turned off, listened to Honey, listened to the heartbeats—*eat me, eat me, eat me*—was she a cat or a woman? Honey could be both.

Could Ivory?

The ritual of mourning is what matters, Marla had said.

The ritual was key, and Ivory could go through those motions. Elephants and other animals might grieve, but only humans faked it. If she could do that, then that might be enough to prove she was still human in the roiling tunnels of her bloodstream, no matter what else Honey might have made of her.

But first, they were both hungry, and that mattered too. Hunger was eternal. Every animal on Earth would agree.

They parked at a curb not far from Sunshine & Chill, closed for the night. Restaurants gleamed in a cluster off Main Street, the usual Red Lobster and Popeye's, but also a few local establishments. Nothing Honey would want. Nothing Ivory wanted anymore, either.

She spotted the man leaning against a brick corner only seconds before he spoke. Aged in that nebulous range between thirty and forty, he wore a five-o'clock shadow beneath his harsh eyes, pink cheeks, and reddened nose. His denim jacket hung around a yellow shirt with *Had a helluva night at Cape Morning!* spoken by a dull-eyed fish. His thin hand clutched a brown bottle.

"Tourist," Ivory said, about to pull away. She didn't want to deal with tourists tonight.

But then came the other two—a tall girl with dark hair, and an older man with a beard and glasses, maybe her father. They crossed the street ahead of the Mercedes and turned at the sidewalk, where they fell into Helluva Night's line of sight.

"Nice-looking daughter you got there," he said as if handing out pearls.

Ivory clutched the steering wheel. She watched the girl and her father keep walking, maybe heading for a nearby restaurant.

Helluva Night raised his voice. "I said, nice-looking daughter you got there."

A few steps away, the father hunched his shoulders, annoyed but trying to live with it.

The girl called back over her shoulder, "Okay!" in the tone of answering a mother's warning that she'd need a jacket on a chilly night.

Helluva Night mumbled sarcasm, "*Okay*," and then tipped his bottle toward his lips.

A fresh pulse dug into Ivory's thigh. She felt the movement before she saw it—Honey turning her head ever so slowly, a cat creeping through tall grass, until she leered with yellow-hate glee.

What was that look? Encouragement? Seeking good luck? Asking permission?

Ivory pressed her hand over Honey's and leaned past the gear shift to kiss her cheek.

That was everything Honey needed. She gripped the passenger door and slid through the window with snakelike ease, hitting the sidewalk on all fours. Her robe and shawl wafted around her as she stood.

Helluva Night was looking. Why wouldn't he? She was a revelation, she was too good for this town. He was right where he belonged, the weakest of his herd, some water buffalo beaten down by sunstroke or disease. Too inhibited to notice the coming threat. Too brainless to even consider the possibility that he might become a meal.

He tipped his bottle to Honey as she stalked closer. "Hey there, sweetie."

Ivory watched from the corner of her eye as Honey laid a hand on the man's shoulder. She couldn't hear what he said, his catcalls melting into a slurring rumble now that he'd caught the attention of a real cat. He'd never met anyone like Honey before. No one had.

"Hey," Ivory said, leaning over the passenger seat. "Honey likes you."

"Fond of her myself," Helluva Night said, eyeing Honey up and down.

But there was a quake in his voice, his nerves turning to butter. He couldn't suspect what she was already, could he? Some people were sensitive, Ivory had no doubt, but not this bipedal slug.

"Come with us, we're—" Ivory faltered, hunting for inspiration. "We're heading to the beach."

Honey tittered agreement and then made graceful steps backward toward the car, her robe shushing around her legs. She could lure this man to follow them with an entrancing bite, but it was more fun to watch him step willingly toward the car, pool into the back seat, and tangle with Honey's limbs as if the Mercedes had grown golden tongues.

"To the beach," Ivory said, starting the car.

Helluva Night cleared his throat. "You know, maybe this isn't such a good idea," he said, fighting to sound tough against a squeaky tightness in his throat. "Kind of waiting for my friends. Not right to ditch your friends."

Ivory bristled. It was a little late for Helluva Night to decide he had principles.

And a little late to back out of Honey's embrace. She straightened with rattlesnake quickness behind him, eyes aflame with dual sunshine, and her lips peeled back from sharp teeth in a feral hiss. Muscle and fervor burned beneath her loose robe and shawl, and her eyes sharpened to a predator's curious gaze. She was interested, so damn interested, the way a cat might study every inch of a small bird before turning that fascination into a clawed pounce.

Ivory couldn't let Honey feed here. Too many locals and tourists alike trod the sidewalks and streets, or sat by the restaurant windows. They would create an unforgettable crimson scene.

"We'll be your friends," Ivory said, adjusting the rearview mirror to focus on Helluva Night. She shot him a smile in the dark. "You wouldn't ditch us, would you? Don't you want a hell of a night?"

Helluva Night's skin shined with nervous sweat, but an urge swarmed behind his eyes. He was hard already. Honey could feel it in her hands, and the same pulse shoved at Ivory's palms.

"Yeah," he said at last. "Sure. It'll be a good night."

"You wait," Ivory said, starting the car to the sound of Honey's giggling. "We'll be so friendly, you won't think about those other friends anymore. You won't think about anything."

23. HEIGHTENED SENSES

Helluva Night tried to tell them his name once they parked above the beach, but Ivory covered her ears and hummed with her mouth shut, filling her head with a protective drone. She didn't want to know his name, and she wouldn't share her own.

He didn't notice, his attention wrapped around Honey's finger as they left the car and headed down the wooden steps to the sand. She teased at his hair and tugged his clothes, made him kick off his shoes and abandon his beer to wander the beach's damp edge. Her bare foot stroked the dim tide, the sea her true lover.

The ocean breeze sent Ivory shivering. Or was that her heart again? Every part of her thrummed with anticipation. Wasn't it the dream of every local in a tourist town to devour at least one rude tourist?

Maybe that explained the lack of guilt. Too busy making dreams come true.

Unless Honey meant to change Helluva Night, the way she'd changed Ivory. No, she couldn't want that, but her thoughts were unknowable except when she poured them out.

Ivory had to tell her, but she didn't have any mental claw. Only real teeth.

She slipped to Honey's side and nipped at her arm. Her flesh was tough between Ivory's teeth, but her bite grabbed Honey's attention. She brightened, expectation shining in her eyes.

Honey, kill, Ivory thought, hard as she could, and then she let go. If a dark spot beaded over Honey's skin, Ivory didn't see it. She couldn't taste anything sweet on her tongue.

Honey's expression hid in the shadow of summerhouse lights, but her body became a fleshy tremor, purring into the wind. She and Ivory were joined, the two of them. Each demanded the other kill, and each listened, a mutual need akin to understanding.

Helluva Night snickered, watching them. "You ladies are kind of freaky, huh?"

"Kind of," Ivory said.

Honey's answering chuckle silenced Helluva Night. She took his arm and urged him onward, putting a short distance between them and Ivory.

That was fine. Ivory could hang back, watch, wait. This wasn't like last night with Wolf; no sensuality worked its fingers through her. Nothing stirred between her legs, in her skin, only this chest-deep quake, the drawing out of the moment.

Honey wanted to play with her food. She wanted Helluva Night to know his place, but not too soon.

He grew restless and handsy as the beach turned quiet, and Honey had to bite him to keep him servile. Wolf had been resistant, but not this guy. Ivory wasn't sure what that said about herself and Scarlet, having given in at touches and tongues. She, Scarlet, and Helluva Night had wanted it, but Wolf hadn't? Was that because of his faith or his stubbornness? Ivory had no idea.

She let every sensation ease into the tidal rhythm and watched the beach turn black as summerhouse lights winked out in advance of the coming dawn. The stars made a brief bright appearance overhead. There were so many, Ivory could imagine she'd drifted to Cape Shadow.

When all the summerhouse lights were gone, and only the stars lit the beach, Honey led Helluva Night into the water. The sea wanted blood, and she wasn't too greedy to share.

The sky clouded over, taking a breath before the night's end, and a long darkness followed. Honey was in no rush, always the patient predator.

Expectations swirled in a hurricane of Ivory's thoughts. She waited for a watery scream to rake up the sand, or a moan and then a splash. She imagined Helluva Night would piss himself as Honey peeled back the skin of seduction from her true vicious nature and then drove her teeth into his neck, snapping the tension with one orgasmic bite.

The moment fizzled as a tingling slipped into Ivory's teeth and jaw. Her muscles twitched as if clenching, and then her breath quickened.

That claw had returned inside her mind, not a scalpel anymore but a dripping member plunging into Ivory's thoughts. Fiery sensations rained down her head and body, dragging her knees to the sand. She could feel Honey biting hard into tendons and blood vessels like Ivory was biting that tourist herself, living the same thrill of tearing his flesh. A powerline connection burned between them, Ivory losing herself, no longer herself. A piece of Honey's incomprehensible whole.

And she gave a damn about killing this man. Morose sensations kept clear, but a Honey-like laugh wafted with ventriloquist finesse from Ivory's throat.

Helluva Night deserved this. Every animal would agree had they the chance to feast on him.

"Honey," Ivory whispered and then gasped with delight. "It's another treat."

The influence—Ivory understood. Honey hadn't dulled Ivory's feelings into some pre-transition depression, had instead brightened Ivory's sense of justice until a sunshiny retribution whited out any sympathy for those who'd wronged her. Wronged anyone. It made perfect sense.

Another peel of Honey's laughter belted out from Ivory's throat. Why was Scarlet dead? Because she'd been rude. Why was Wolf dead? Because he liked to make women walk on eggshells around him, to cow them, to never let them be fully human, and he'd left Ivory to die on his doorstep out of inconvenience.

And why was Helluva Night going to die now? For his disgusting nature and his misfortune to have a thumping heart, one in all the hearts to be eaten.

Ivory approached a starlit spot of damp sand. The tide beat wrathful across Helluva Night's prone body and Honey's hunched form, where the heat of him practically steamed from her skin. He was putting up a meager fight, but she kept him pinned.

"I want to try his heart," Ivory said. She didn't have a hunger for it, only a sense of being left out from Honey's experience. "Let me."

She bent over Honey's shoulders, but one robed arm nudged Ivory away. Her legs went wobbly, and she buckled laughing to the sand. She then crawled closer, splaying a teasing hand toward the body.

Honey sprang off Helluva Night's chest and pounced onto Ivory, knocking her on her back. The same intense interest radiated from her eyes and skin as the last time they were on the beach together, when Ivory had mistaken herself for prey. She might have become prey in the end had she made different choices, had different desires, but something in her must've spoken her dreams to Honey.

"We're united," Ivory said. "The same."

Honey growled out a laugh, grasped Ivory's cheeks in both hands, and tugged her into a deep, open-mouthed kiss.

Her rough tongue pressed Ivory's against the bottom of her mouth. Ivory tried to fight it, as if they were playing, but then liquid sugar dribbled onto her tongue.

They weren't playing. Honey was feeding, like a bird to her hatchling.

Warm blood slid across Ivory's lips in a gentle stream, and her throat narrowed and flexed to gulp down every syrupy mouthful. There was sustenance in this, and justice, but there was Honey, too. She could have beckoned Ivory to follow, to join in tonight's hunt like she'd helped kill Wolf, but instead Honey had pulled this lifeforce into herself and now offered it to Ivory in a flesh-and-tooth chalice overflowing with a crimson heartbeat.

Give me your blood, Ivory thought, sucking it down. *Give me your love*.

She hardly noticed the sounds of slopping against the tide, where Helluva Night fought first to sit up, crawl, and then stagger. He shouldn't get away, Ivory knew it, but she couldn't pry herself from beneath Honey and didn't want to. Besides, Helluva Night had left too much of his blood behind. Maybe he would collapse into the sea and drown. Or maybe he would escape the beach and make it to a hospital. He'd learn to keep to himself if he didn't want to be devoured whole.

When the blood ran out, or Honey didn't want to give anymore, the feeding became a gnawing kiss, Honey scraping her teeth at Ivory's neck, Ivory clawing into Honey's robe. A sense of bristling light crackled off Honey's fingertips, her toes, and then the place in Ivory's mind where Honey thrust deep. They might have kept like this for another stretch of night.

But a molten eye peeked across the reddening waves.

Honey broke from Ivory and sat hard in the sand, her face turned from the rising sun. The sky had been lightening without either of them noticing. How long had they been feeding and feeling each other?

"It's hard for you in the day," Ivory said, almost a question.

Honey rubbed at her head, and a harsh breath sighed through her nose.

Ivory stood wobbly from the stand and then drew Honey up beside her. "I'll get you home. I'll look after you."

Honey's face went placid. She cocked her head sideways, and her pupils became swelling black pools, drinking Ivory in with strangely forlorn affection. At least, that was how Ivory read the look. She couldn't be sure she'd ever know what Honey was thinking or feeling.

They ambled to the car in a half-lope, half-stagger. Ivory wasn't too fond of the sun right now either, especially after a sleepless night, but she bit the inside of her cheek each time she felt drowsy behind the wheel along the short drive from the beach to her home.

A presence had followed her along this path the day she found Cabrina's body. Chasm Cat, the piece of Honey that could leave Cape Shadow on her own. And now she rode at Ivory's side, almost weak and yet her full self.

As far as Ivory knew.

Past the front door, Honey pushed her way from Ivory's arms and stumbled through the living room, into the forever starlight of Cape Shadow. Ivory didn't want to lie there again, but she curled up with a blanket on the living room carpet and reached a hand through the gap in the wall.

Honey's fingers closed around it, and then her nose and forehead nuzzled Ivory's palm. A warmth washed through the door between worlds. Ivory wanted to put a name to it, but her thoughts melted as sunlight pounded the outsides of the house.

Another day trickled past with fitful dreams. Ivory's senses blurred together, watching the reverberations of Honey's laughter and listening to the grandiose rhythm of Cape Shadow, and its Ghost Cat Island, however far away it might be, and smelling the ferocity of life waiting at its core.

Honey's touch dragged Ivory's senses back to themselves. Evening bathed the outer world in violet, and she had left Cape

Shadow to crawl over the living room carpet at Cape Morning. A salty scent clouded around her as she groped lazily down Ivory's body. Was she hungry? Restless?

Her lips grazed Ivory's, a testing kiss. Teeth scraped Ivory's chin, and curious fingers played in her thick hair. Down her sides. To her thigh.

"Honey," Ivory said, a bemused whine.

Golden eyes shined over her, questioning and needful.

Ivory looked away. "What you want from me—a lover, another like you, something else—I'll try to be it. But I don't know if I can be everything."

She slid out of her clothes, one nervous limb at a time. Honey watched every movement, her expression a changeless eagerness, and once Ivory was nude, her warm fingers traveled pale skin. Ivory slid one thigh over the other, hiding part of her behind crossed limbs and reddish curls.

Honey licked at her belly and studied Ivory's face. There was a promise in her eyes that Ivory couldn't decipher.

"Why can't I figure you out?" Ivory asked.

Honey didn't answer, and Ivory didn't mind as she sank into that gaze.

They glistened together, an oceanic layer sliding between them while a golden thrusting pierced Ivory's mind, again and again. She tried to keep quiet like it mattered anymore, but Honey was laughing, and Ivory moaned as if trying and failing to join in. Her thoughts became naked sunlight, too sharp to stare at, forcing her to look away and become only her senses and the tactile world around them.

Except for Honey's presence in her head. All-becoming, all-consuming, an ecstasy in being fucked by this beauty, outside and in.

"Keep me," Ivory whispered. "Always. Please."

A lukewarm hand settled on Ivory's back. She almost didn't notice it amid Honey's other touches before realizing Honey's hands grasped Ivory's neck and cock. She twisted in Honey's grip to glance behind her.

Once-red lips smirked beneath wild eyes. Ivory had seen them cloaked in shades. She'd seen blood and lipstick smearing that mouth.

"Scarlet?" Ivory gasped.

A furtive hiss slid through Scarlet's teeth as she bared a sharp grin. She pressed her body close to the floor and crept against Honey, nuzzling her breast, kissing her belly and then her thighs. Ivory made to pull away.

Ivory, wait, Honey's claw carved into Ivory's mind. *Ivory, stay*.

And she did. The night slithered around them in a tangled threesome of pounding hearts and flowing warmth and Honey's raucous laughter. Was she overwhelmed with joy?

Or was she laughing at a joke that Ivory just couldn't get?

From the Diary of Cabrina Brite,
May 29, 2018

See me waiting tables,
And lying to the customers.
"I want to be an actress," I say,
And they tell me I can do it.
And I don't care.
I take every shortcut in town,
And I take every drug in L.A.,
And I take a thousand lovers.
And I take them to radioactive beaches,
And I don't care.
There are phone calls from home,
And the beaches I left behind,
"The Atlantic misses you,
Get a foundation, a career, a plan,"
And I don't care, I don't care, I don't care.

PART FOUR: THE DROWNING PLACE

24. SYMPTOMS

Xi raised the binoculars to her face a tenth time, careful not to let them clink against her glasses, and watched Ghost Cat Island from across the water. Midday sunshine flashed at her eyes, playing a game with her sight.

The tiny dot of mostly submerged rock lingered as always. Ghost Cat Island seemed a tranquil place, kissed by melancholy, exactly the blend of sweetness and sadness that might have lured Cabrina. An island of stories; an island disappearing. Maybe its shadow's presence in Xi's vision had nothing to do with death and everything to do with the kind of person Cabrina Brite used to be.

Except there wasn't only the Ghost Cat Island caught in borrowed binoculars. There was another, lost in nightmare. Hidden beneath the waves.

"Spot any ghost cats?" Rex asked.

He sat in the sand at Xi's feet, watching her from behind black shades. Neither of them were dressed for the beach. Oblivious tourists in bathing suits traipsed around them, laughing, shouting, complaining. One day the ocean would swallow this beach and scatter them back where they came from. Or maybe they'd run when they learned that Cape Morning was haunted.

If only Xi could figure that out herself. She had spent another couple of nights at Rex's house, sneaking home in the daylight to grab outfits, meds, and other necessities while Josephine was at work, offering hollow replies to her mother's calls and texts each evening. Rex's room was not an absolute sanctuary, but continuing to share it at least offered a buddy system, far preferable to Xi sleeping in her bedroom alone.

But that hadn't stopped the twisted-up knot inside her. Whatever damage Cabrina could do, she might have already done it.

Xi had tried catching up on her literary gaps since that encounter, but the Stoker and Le Fanu novels had their own ideas, and an unfinished viewing of *The Lost Boys* had only given her nightmares of flying devils.

She'd have eaten the movie up before all this. Now she only thought of Cabrina's fingerprints on her window glass, and nothing she read or watched explained why Cabrina acted different now than when she'd lived, as if she were the limb of some great cosmic hunger.

Xi used to believe that confining a thing to fiction meant it couldn't be real. But actually, she couldn't mistake fiction for research. They were on their own.

"I see sunshine, nothing else," Xi said. She lowered the binoculars and thumped beside Rex. "I want to help her."

Rex tapped at his phone without a word. He'd been furiously searching and texting since they arrived nearly an hour ago, likely with Marla. They might be concocting a plan together.

Xi had to be sure they stayed on the same page. "I can open up for her. Feed her, if she's hungry."

Rex's thumbs paused. Without tearing his gaze from the phone, he grabbed a thermos from beside him and passed it to Xi.

She raised an open palm. "No, thank you."

"Afraid of a little coffee?" Rex asked.

"We've been out here a while, and coffee is dehydrating. It messes up my stomach."

"Maybe they changed your meds to give you monthly cramps."

Xi smacked his arm and took the thermos. She knew what came next, but some part of her hoped for better, like testing a leg that had fallen asleep to see if it had stopped hurting.

The sip of coffee turned to sunbaked garbage in her mouth. She spat it to the sand and coughed, ragged and hoarse with an earthquake in her chest. The coffee left a hideous aftertaste.

Anything stronger than water sent Xi hacking and choking. Food tasted like sweaty clothes, and beverages became pond scum. The world meant to poison her. She hadn't swallowed anything but water, meds, and a vitamin C tablet since Cabrina's nocturnal bite.

"She got you, girl." Rex snatched the thermos back. "You're her servant, a walking buffet, one of those—there's a word for it."

"A thrall," Xi said, her tone empty. She'd spent time on her phone too, but she didn't believe Rex. She couldn't.

"That's you," Rex said. "A thrall."

"Can you knock it off?" Xi rubbed her forehead. "My brain has the consistency of a strawberry smoothie."

"That's you, one sweet blood smoothie." Rex gestured down Xi's body, his black nails gleaming in the sun. "You might even be turning. I'll be the guy in Cape Morning whose only friends went—" He lowered his voice, catching himself. "Went vampire."

Xi glanced toward the glimmering Atlantic waves. The same sun they reflected bore hot on her skin, yet never burning enough to leave a skeleton draped on the sand.

"Marla told us death-by-sunlight was made up in the movies," she said. "But Cab's only visited at night. If I'm turning, shouldn't I only come out at night too? Maybe feeding only infected me with a craving, and a—I don't know, a temporary allergy to kinds of food and drink. Or a phobia? Like a type of rabies. Or I can stand the sun easier because I have more melanin."

"Or none of that matters, and it's too early to tell," Rex said. "We don't know a damn thing."

"We should've watched *The X-Files* like I said." Xi tried to smile. "Research."

Rex ignored her, hunching deeper over his phone. "You're talking allergies and bodily substances. We left biology in a ditch the moment Cab showed up after her funeral."

"She came to me for help!" Xi snapped, more desperate now. "And neither of us want her to suffer. If she's fed, she might become more like herself. And it's my choice."

My blood, she almost added.

"Yeah, bet it fucking feels like a choice now," Rex said. "But no way I'd hear talk like that if the you from a few nights back could see you today. Remember how scared you were?" His thumbs tapped his phone again, answering another text. "How's the bite doing?"

"Fading." Xi couldn't be sure whether that was a good sign or a bad one. "If it goes away, maybe I can eat properly again."

"Maybe it's like getting sick." Rex adjusted his shades. "Symptoms could come in stages. She bit you a couple nights back, now you have early onset vampirism. Like a first stage. Bitten, bloodlust, this hunger. Second stage could be more like the Cabrina we saw on the beach."

"Stage one, hungry but still alive," Xi said. "Stage two, a hungry ghost."

Beach sounds swelled around them. Seagulls made war, children barked playful commands, and a nearby seventy-something man wolf-whistled at his same-aged wife as she strode in her maroon one-piece. Waves crashed, and the wind whipped Xi's hair. Cape Morning got on as if nothing strange were happening.

Xi and Rex had been the same leading up to Cabrina's death.

What the hell could have happened to her in those final weeks of life? She had been disturbed, no doubt, but with Viola keeping her daughter caged tighter than braces against teeth, it was impossible to discern the struggle of everyday abuse from a supernatural haunting.

"I think I'm not okay," Xi said, almost begrudging. "Neither is Cab."

"If she keeps feeding, what then?" Rex asked, shifting in the sand. "You think there's something worse she'll become?"

Xi turned to him. "Like what? Turning into a bat? Or a panther?"

"We should be so unlucky." Rex waggled his phone. "Been doing searches while you scan the horizon. Relaying with Ma."

"Does Marla understand now?" Xi asked.

Rex glanced between his screen and Xi's face. "Ma, not Mom. She's good at digging into things." Reason enough for him to have avoided getting online profiles and accounts.

Xi lowered her voice to a whisper. "You didn't tell her about the vampires, right?"

"Would've been hilarious," Rex said, grinning. "No, Ma's not into Mom's weirdness. She would have ignored me. I told her it's about Cab; that's good enough." An unspoken thought sank through him, shifting his weight. "Cab wasn't the first. People have washed ashore a bunch of damn times over the years."

Xi scooted closer and leaned over his shoulder. A green-and-blue series of text blobs hid beneath her reflection. Her hair was a mess.

"That's not so unusual, is it?" Xi asked. "It's a beach. People drown."

"But right here, at this stretch," Rex went on. "Like they were trying to hit Ghost Cat Island and didn't survive the return swim. There've been disappearances, too, going way back. Obviously nobody knows if they vanished from this part of the beach, but it's hard not to be suspicious. Especially if the undertow took them. Right by that island."

Xi wondered which Ghost Cat Island—the scrap of rock beyond this beach, or the mammoth of stone Cabrina had shared in a vision while latched to Xi's thigh.

"Could be coincidence." Rex made to shrug again and then rolled his shoulders. "Not all of them can be connected." He sounded wistful, more to say but unwilling to say it.

"This is a good place for disappearing," Xi said. She glanced over the beach, the running kids, the elderly couple. "A local goes missing, someone has to notice. A tourist goes missing, that's harder to tell."

A pattern of disappearances had left people-shaped holes across Cape Morning's past few decades, and again earlier this month, when it caught Cabrina in its claws. Had she seen a vision of Ghost Cat Island like she'd shown Xi? Cabrina must have thought the place was important enough to swim out there the night of June 14th, maybe thinking she would journey toward the scrap of rock and find herself in that other place.

Or had she been trying to escape those visions? She'd been so quiet those last few weeks. She might have felt a death reaching for her and decided to meet it.

"If only we could see inside her head," Xi said.

"Can't ask again," Rex said. "Not after that séance."

Not a séance, Xi thought. She had a much worse idea, and she turned to Rex to share it and hear how bad an idea it was.

But Rex was already climbing from the sand. "I need rest. Busy night ahead."

"Why?" Xi asked. "Are you going to a summerhouse party?"

"Need to keep vigilant," Rex said. "Meanwhile, you head somewhere Cab's never been invited."

"Do you think the vampire invitation rule matters?" Xi watched Rex shrug. "What about flying?"

"You said Cab kind of glided up to your bedroom. Didn't see that at mine."

"But at the beach." Xi glanced over the sand. "Like the wind was blowing her out to sea."

Rex let out a hard sigh. "Just steer clear of my place, your place, Mom's shop. And the beach. Head somewhere indoors where she wouldn't feel welcome."

"Like her house?" Xi asked.

Rex got a faraway look in his eyes. Like he was thinking what it would be like for Xi to ask Viola for help.

Xi had her own thoughts involving Viola. A path into Cabrina's head. If Rex meant to keep Xi out of danger, there was no way he would agree to help with her impulsive new plan. Neither would his mothers, for different reasons. And Josephine? She would sooner lock Xi in her bedroom than let her do anything illegal. Ditching potential studious paths beneath the STEM umbrella for Xi to focus on an English major had already been a leap over a thousand-foot parental ravine, especially with the student loan debt to come. Anything that risked her freedom, her place at Dartmouth—Josephine was out. Xi needed a near-stranger.

Who, then?

"That friend of your mother's," Xi said. "Ivory, from the cemetery? I could stay with her. She never even met Cab, right? Not while Cab was alive."

Rex scratched his chin. "That might work. You'd have to ask."

"I will." Xi fished her phone from her purse.

"I'll check the address with Ma and text it to you." Rex tapped at his phone screen.

Maybe Ivory could help Xi with her bad idea and not try to stop her.

"And what's keeping you busy tonight?" Xi asked.

"Checking the beaches with Mom. There's a storm coming tonight, but can't let that stop us." Rex finished his text, stuffed his phone in his jacket pocket, and slung it over one arm. "Got a vampire to catch before it gets worse."

Xi's gut rolled. He was going to hunt Cabrina like a wild dog. The quicker this ended, the better.

"Before it gets worse," Xi echoed.

"Right," Rex said. "We can't let Cab turn out that way. Can't let her kill anyone either."

The wind rushed between them, as if to cut Rex off before he could add, *If she hasn't killed anyone already*. He started away from the sand, toward the wooden steps leading to the grassy slope above.

Xi lingered, her thoughts cycling over the moment she'd let Cabrina drink her blood. The sooner she understood what Cabrina was going through, the better.

Her phone buzzed in her purse. A text from Rex, with the address for Ivory Sloan.

25. THE PLAN

The house looked to be waiting for visitors. Xi found it after a brief walk from the beach, and her first inclination was to think the house had likewise recently left the immediate seaside. Its face stood firm, but the glaring sun made its edges blur and sag as if waterlogged. The house seemed to breathe, and Xi had caught its last exhalation.

Two floors with a split-level attic. Prime real estate near the tourist-chocked shoreline. Tire marks crossed the lawn as if someone had clumsily driven vehicles toward the house, hiding a couple beside it while parking two others in the driveway. Xi didn't know much about car models, but the top of the red Mercedes had been drawn down to reveal pale leather seats, a retro feel she'd always associated with rich people's cars.

Xi passed the driveway, reached the front door, and rang the doorbell twice.

A minute passed before the door whined open. Ivory's face prodded the meager gap, with shadows obscuring her features. The way she blinked and craned her neck suggested the doorbell had woken her up, but deep in the house, a speaker system boomed some pop song from muffled amplifiers and down the halls. Ivory couldn't have been sleeping through that racket.

"I didn't mean to disturb you," Xi said, clearing her throat. "Do you remember me?"

Ivory blinked again, and her dark blue eyes glinted with sunshine. She quietly hummed along to the music. *Honey, Honey*. Thick darkness bristled behind her, where the inner house teemed with impatient shadows.

"We crossed paths." Xi paused. "In the cemetery. I'm Xi Munoz."

Ivory quit humming. "Cabrina's grave," she said, each word slow, as if dredged from memory.

"Exactly, yes," Xi said. "That's why I'm here. You talked about Cab, when I was with Rex there. And you asked if we'd seen her, or if she had a diary. It sounded like you could've cared about her, if you ever knew her."

Ivory twitched as if she'd heard a dish shatter deep in the house. Xi might have interrupted more than sleep. The house sagged again, another calm breath. That had to be the air conditioning sliding out the front door, or drawing the summer heat inward.

"Do you want to turn the music down, talk inside?" Xi asked, trying to be polite.

"Honey likes the music," Ivory said, her tone sleepy.

Xi was about to ask, *Who's Honey?*, realized it wasn't her business, and then wanted to apologize. She didn't know who else lived here, or if Ivory had guests.

The words clotted up in Xi's mouth as Ivory's stance turned pensive, sizing up the world outside her door with almost animalistic wariness.

Much like Cabrina.

Xi's muscles tensed. She stood exposed, peeled open, a stranger's fingernails tracing her skin, guts, and organs, and every touch demanded she give a good reason for her existence.

She should run from this house. This woman. The place was alive, impatient from looming, ready to strike, its front door now a salivating mouth. A draft slid around Ivory, but it didn't smell like freon.

It smelled like the sea.

"I need your help," Xi blurted out. "For Cabrina. I need to take her diary. From her house."

"Diary," Ivory whispered, bizarrely awestruck. The grogginess seeped from her voice, and she blinked hard as if fighting to wake up. "She had a diary after all."

Her face climbed the doorway. She must have been hunching, but now she stood straight. The house stood the same. Its front no longer sagged with breath but towered unwavering.

"You asked what really happened to Cabrina," Xi said. "If it wasn't an accident, then we deserve to know the truth. Maybe what she wrote when she was alive can help put her to rest now."

"Help her." Ivory sounded more coherent each time she spoke. "And what would I do?"

"You met Cab's mom," Xi said. "Viola Brite hates me, hates Rex. She must have hated Cab, too, even if she never said it. But you two looked kind of chummy."

"We weren't." That animal look returned to Ivory's eyes.

Xi went quiet. She preferred not to judge Ivory, certainly didn't want to assume she was some truscum befriending people like Viola and stabbing other trans folk in the back, but between the cars and the house, Ivory screamed money. Either hers, or some lover's.

Her world was comfortable. She might lack the conviction to break its rules.

"Sorry for assuming," Xi said. She took a breath and tried to explain her plan again. "You could show up at Viola's place by surprise. Be a sympathizer. Keep her distracted, and she won't turn up in Cab's room when I go through the window and hunt down the diary."

"Through her window." Ivory sounded impressed.

"I've done it before. I can do it again." Xi wiped sweat from her lip. "Though it might be locked now. It'd be easier if you left the door unlocked on your way in."

"When?"

"Today," Xi said. "Really, tonight."

Ivory scoffed with laughter. "No hurry, huh?"

The darkness shuffled inside the house. Someone else moved deep in the foyer, obscured by Ivory as she filled the narrow gap between door and doorframe. The muffled music warped around shifting shapes with another pop song.

"Have you seen Cab since you came to her grave?" Xi asked, losing her patience. "Because I have. She isn't better for it. I need her to find peace. And I need to survive this summer and go to college and get the hell away from this damn town."

She shuddered as her lips closed. She'd never said as much aloud at hearing the news of her friend's death, or attending the funeral, but the thought had been forming somewhere deep inside—her future was no more certain than Cabrina's. She could lose it to a hungry sea, or a hungrier undead friend.

Beyond helping Cabrina, Xi needed to help herself.

"Why didn't Cabrina leave?" Ivory cleared her throat, and some of the dry roughness shed away. "If her mother hated her."

"Where could she have gone?" Xi asked. "Nowheresville, New Hampshire? The world doesn't work that way, there's no sanctuary for people like Cab. Like us."

"Not your place?" Ivory asked.

Xi almost laughed. "In our half of a duplex, where my mother won't trust anyone? With Joan and Marla, getting by only because Rex helps at the shop and he works for cheap? Besides, her mother wouldn't have allowed it. For Cab, it was either her parents' house or the street, and she tried to run. The cops took her back to her parents."

Ivory scraped a fingernail down the doorframe. It left a thin scratch in the rubber sealant. Xi could've conjured up that same fingernail across her mind, a frustration and a need. This town was hungry, but so was she.

"I'll help," Ivory said. "But I need to see the diary too."

Xi recoiled. "Why?"

Ivory stared ahead. Her fingernail again scratched at the doorframe, and the air tensed like a big cat quaking before it pounced.

"Okay, fine, I'll let you see Cab's diary." Xi sighed hard. "But you can't keep it."

Ivory gave a nod.

"Nine tonight, okay?" Xi retreated from the door. "Did Viola give the address?"

Another nod.

Xi opened her mouth to give further instructions, but then she thought better of it and turned toward the street. Ivory seemed unwell, but any distraction would work, and maybe someone who wasn't exactly okay right now could keep Viola busier than a careful performance. Enough time to find the diary.

Which Xi had no plans of surrendering. Ivory had to be a decade Xi's senior; what did she know about Cabrina? Nothing.

When Xi had introduced her friend to her mother, Cabrina had wrung her nervous hands, but all Xi needed to tell Josephine was, *She's like me*. Cabrina had spent so much time and energy fighting her mother, she'd almost burst into tears at Josephine's ease and acceptance.

Funny—no Ivory there that day.

Or when Cabrina had been hanging out with that creep the summer before last? Xi and Rex had kept an eye on her without saying a word—no Ivory then either.

The Halloween when Rex had convinced the girls to be two Brides to his green-skinned monster of Frankenstein, hiding from every passing cop car in case Cabrina's father was prowling. Junior prom night, when they'd absconded to the beach with stolen beer and sat discussing whether God was real and how many dicks such an entity might have, which segued into desired surgeries and each of their certainties and uncertainties toward the future. Xi helping Cabrina to write her first poem. Rex showing them how to fish even though they hated it. Cabrina holding Xi after a nightmare made her certain that her father had found Cape Morning.

These memories belonged to Xi, Rex, and Cabrina. They haunted Xi like they haunted the sea and sand, and no one else had a right to them. The tourists could take of this place, but they couldn't take of these personal specters draped through Xi's thoughts. Cape Morning wasn't a ghost town by any stretch of the imagination.

But it was a town of ghosts.

26. PURPOSE

It took every ounce of Ivory's restraint to keep from lunging out the door, dragging Xi inside, and splitting her open like a wine box.

She'd done nothing wrong to justify it. The bloodlust was Ivory's hunger talking. Her gut sucked against her spine, her circulatory system clenching into an angry fist, veiny fingers pressing beneath skin. Even her brain rebelled in a hungry fog. Put feeding off too long and she'd abandon her choices, leaving her consciousness to be devoured by the mindless animal in her skull.

"Sober up," she whispered.

She nudged the door shut and pressed her forehead against it. Music thumped through the cool wood, the house having grown a heartbeat since Scarlet began messing with the stereo system.

For Honey, she'd said.

She was annoying, but she made sense. There was no music at Cape Shadow, and over the past couple of days, Honey had fallen in love with the amplifiers and the tunes like someone who hadn't heard a song in centuries. Scarlet didn't always play Ivory's choices of music, but she didn't want to complain.

She wanted sustenance.

We deserve to know the truth. Xi's words. A demand where Ivory had been asking a question. *What really happened to Cabrina*

Brite? Cabrina was the reason Ivory had started any of this. Wouldn't she have been surprised to see how it all turned out?

Ivory sank from the door and let the house's inner world and all its residents open to her.

The shadow of Chelsea Burke hunched over a prone figure at the foyer's edge. She and Stella had returned from their trip early this morning—or was it yesterday morning? Ivory had lost track of time again.

Meanwhile, Chelsea had lost track of her entire world. Doubtful she'd thought of asking Ivory about rent when Honey came pouncing from the Cape Shadow hole in the wall.

Home in their fancy car, with their fancy blood. Did Chelsea realize she'd chosen to feed on her own sister? Or had she ceased to care once Honey sank her teeth and claws in? Blood-sucking landlady, blood-sucking town.

At least Ivory wasn't the meal for a change. She no longer needed to cover Thursday night's neck bite; it had closed and healed to a dull blemish.

The foyer's depths welcomed her toward the living room, where a UPS deliveryman in a khaki button-down and matching shorts hunched beside Scarlet, and they fed upon a mailman in a pale blue uniform. Ivory had been forced to move both their trucks closer to the beach.

Her deception wouldn't work forever. Someone would eventually notice at what points these people had gone missing on their routes. Cops would show up. More deaths.

Ivory was trying hard to care, but hunger washed away her thoughts. She imagined the same was true for every animal.

The mailman's chest gaped open with broken-ribbed teeth. Human blood had been wine of the gods for the UPS deliveryman until Honey let him drink from her. After that, he'd died like Scarlet, come back today, and now blood wasn't enough. He and

Scarlet needed flesh, innards, muscles as warm as the heart. Human blood, Honey's blood, death, revival, human flesh—Honey moved each newcomer through the cycle. Some took longer to return than others. The deliveryman had laid dormant in the back corner for two days before rising again this morning, while Scarlet had died one dawn and come back the next evening. Ivory wasn't sure what caused the difference.

And she had no idea why she would get different treatment. No matter how many times she opened her mouth for Honey's gift, Honey had not spared a drop for the woman who'd led her into this world.

She and Scarlet had gone off the night of Scarlet's return to hunt down Helluva Night, leaving Ivory as an afterthought. Even when they dragged him home, blood-starved and raving and terrified, Honey wouldn't feed Ivory mouth-to-mouth again. She had lost her appetite then, and she wouldn't eat now, leaving her stomach empty in protest. If Honey really cared, she would have turned Ivory like the others, wouldn't she?

Scarlet wrenched off her dead meal's arm. "I dream hungry," she said, almost afraid.

"I know," Ivory said. She petted Scarlet's hair. "What else do you dream?"

"Honey showed me an island and a wasteland." Scarlet's eyes turned dark. "We ravaged the world. It could've been our cornucopia forever, endless good food and water, but instead we'll lick the soil, and we'll cry tears of ash, and everything we eat, drink, and breathe will taste of plastic until our poison becomes us and the smoke blots out the sun." Her voice came grizzled then, as if too much talking had damaged her throat. "And then all the sleeping things will wake up. And they'll realize it's their time. Only the hungry will be saved."

Ivory glanced at the dark hole in the wall, forever aglimmer with starlight. Honey had snapped her teeth to Scarlet first, and then the others in her collection, and there were visions in her bite.

Sights to convince each to do as Honey needed. None of them seemed to see the same thing, but by fear or allure or other prospects, Honey brought them into her fold.

Even Ivory had faced as much, only her inclinations had come shallow. First to run and give Honey prey to chase, and then darkness and heat. Simple sensations, nothing like Scarlet's complex and threatening premonition.

"But that's a dream, right?" Scarlet asked, clawing a desperate hand up Ivory's chest and parting her robe. "Just a bad dream?"

"Everything is," Ivory said, despondent.

She strayed from Scarlet, left her to her feeding beside the deliveryman, and headed for the sea-scented cavern broken from the living room. The stereo slid to another song beside her, but she didn't recognize the tune. Didn't care much, either.

Wolf's corpse bobbed in the ocean beyond the carpet. His death wasn't special; humanity carried a long history of people dying. Ivory had seen that herself when she spotted Cabrina's remains swept against the shore. Remains that might have clawed their way out of a grave a few nights later. The sea wanted blood, and now it had Wolf's. He had rejected Honey's companionship, and Scarlet had taken to it.

Unknowable predilections might have decided which was worth good company and which would make good slaughter, but Honey liked to force her targets into making choices. It was a contradictory concept, but while Ivory might buckle under Honey's influence, she was not under Honey's control. Honey expected choices. Demanded them.

At least after death, Wolf couldn't feel Honey's claws on his brain, or her teeth plucking open his ribs like a wild dog chewing at chicken-wire fencing. The stars had watched with voyeuristic glee as Honey gnawed dark muscle between her teeth.

Now she languished over the damp sea rock. Another newcomer

stumbled from the Cape Shadow opening with blood on her face, dismissed to the living room. She passed Ivory without a glance, red with Honey's gifts. Some strange pheromone must've told her charges when to come or go, a scent unique for each new friend. Or maybe she was magic, a wizardly Mickey Mouse playing with his bucket-wielding broomsticks.

Worse than that—Scarlet and the others were almost limbs. New facets to Honey, like the little tawny cat. Her appearance as Chasm Cat had seemed a protrusion jutting from Cape Morning, an iceberg's tip while the rest lay in Cape Shadow. She could fit some semblance of self through a keyhole in the door between worlds, but it had taken Ivory's bloody invitation to bring her through.

And what if this beautiful woman was not Honey's entirety? How far did her presence spread beyond this body? She might be growing with every piece of meat she fed to her fleshy acolytes. Honey might be enormous at Cape Shadow. A titanic creature, one body the size of a mountain, or enough limb-like bodies that she could fill a world.

But I'm not one of them, Ivory thought. Why was she being left out?

Honey didn't look at her. Shallow bite marks dotted her limbs, either where she had bitten herself or let the others bite her. An otherworldly eucharist for Honey's collection of hearts.

"You took them," Ivory said. "Bit them, drank their blood, let them drink yours. You showed them what would scare them, or seduce them, let them cross worlds, and then you changed them."

She stepped onto the sea-slick rocks of Cape Shadow. Honey lay still, her bare skin exposed to the sky as if she were sunning herself beneath the stars.

Ivory hunched beside her. "But you don't make me drink your blood. You won't kill me and change me. Out on the street that first night, you wanted me to choose. And you keep waiting for me to choose." She reached out a cupped hand as if it were a wine goblet. "I could bite and drink from your body, couldn't I? Sink into that intoxicating fog and quit being myself, turn into another beating heart of yours. You won't force me, and you won't stop me."

Honey at last turned to Ivory. A pensive stillness clung to her skin.

"But that's not what you want, is it?" Ivory asked. "There's something else I can become. Bigger than a kept heart. Something with a purpose."

A smirk tugged the corner of Honey's lips, and her throat rumbled out a hyena's chuckle. She cocked her head down, gesturing for Ivory to come closer. Always closer, a predator with a lover's gaze.

Ivory scooted down and laid her head against Honey's thigh. The gentle sea wind ran cool, but a minor sun burned through Honey's sweet skin, melting Ivory's hunger to the bottom of her thoughts.

And then the trick campfire lashed up from those depths. It came sharp, as if Honey had lapped it out of Ivory's mind and now breathed it into her skin.

That night had started with innocence. Or at least, the high school junior year equivalent. Orange and red leaves reflected the backyard fire as if the night blazed around sixteen-year-old Ivory. She remembered Shannon lamenting to Carrie over how she and her boyfriend might be split between colleges. Lana playing romantic Sherlock as if they were still in middle school. Trevor and Casey were debating which *Kill Bill* movie was superior, and then arguing over which Quentin Tarantino movie was best, and that broke down to them getting in each other's faces and calling each other all manner of slurs.

The other girls thought they were funny. Ivory had to remind herself again and again to relax, enjoy the evening. They were dumb straight boys, having a pointless disagreement, and neither of them had venom for her.

Until later, when they did. When they all did.

Ivory tucked her head deeper into Honey's lap. If she drank of Honey's blood, became a limb like the others, the vicious memories might slink away, same as any guilt she should have felt for what happened to Wolf. She could forget that the blood and death and feeding ever bothered her.

But she wanted to be herself, too. Cozied up to Honey, not a heart or limb obeying Honey's instinct. Ivory might need an enabler or a commander, to be owned and kept. Deep down, she enjoyed playing the housecat to the true predator.

A helpful claw scratched across her mind. *Ivory, look. Ivory, here.*

She turned to face Honey, whose head wore a halo of twinkling starlight, blessed by the unending night.

The claw slid again. *Ivory, stay. Ivory kiss.*

Ivory stretched toward Honey's lips and tasted syrup on her tongue. Her hunger roiled again in a sudden tempest and then calmed to the nearby sea's gentleness. Honey had been holding someone else's savory blood inside, and now she fed it to Ivory, the way Chasm Cat—no, the way Honey's protrusion from Cape Shadow had first fed a dream-heart down Ivory's dream-throat, and later upon Cape Morning's beach. The way they'd shared Helluva Night's blood.

Wet fingertips found Ivory's leg, just above the knee, and then crept in careful inches up her thigh. Honey's grasp was firm but gentle, and her tongue stroked the inside of Ivory's mouth in time to fingers stroking between her legs. Every touch came in a blurry mix of dozing, dreaming, and stark wakefulness.

Ivory, sigh. Ivory, come. Ivory, scream.

Ivory was still quivering when Honey came licking her fingers and then lapping Ivory's soft member. Did her meager ejaculate taste as sweet as blood? She thought of the soothing warmth and pressure of wrapping lips and tongue around Wolf's cock, and then remembered she would never have the chance to find out if he tasted like liquid candy that way, too. He wasn't hers anymore.

Never really had been.

None of these people were hers, either. They answered Honey's enchanted call. None of them loved Ivory. They had lost whoever they used to be and were too changed to notice their new loneliness, or how it stole people from their lives. Chelsea would not know her sister again, and Ivory had lost Wolf forever. Death would not be undone, only changed by Honey.

Except when it came to Cabrina Brite. Was that spectral resurrection a gift or a punishment? The poor girl had been through enough when she was alive; she shouldn't have to haunt Cape Morning ever on.

Xi meant to do something about that.

And what did Ivory mean to do? She patted her face, fighting out of the haze and back into the world.

"Sober up now," she said. "Get your head on straight."

Honey's menace and adoration had torn Ivory from Cabrina's troubles. What right did she have to get involved again? Or hell, to get involved for the first time? That hadn't been Cabrina's ghost outside Wolf's house, only Honey projecting a cat onto Cape Morning. Not outside this house, either. No Cabrina presence had followed Ivory off the beach.

Aside from spotting the body, what did a confused barista and a dead teenager have to do with each other?

Ivory crawled from the hole in the wall, back into the house, and staggered upstairs. No blood here, no intrusive sea and stone. She could almost pretend the world was ordinary and unchanged as she dug through her purse and snatched out Cabrina's crumpled death poem.

Don't call me a suicide. I want to live.
I've simply chosen one death over another
After I've been robbed of life.
—*Cabrina Aphrodite Brite*

Only a scrap of pink-tinted page, wreathed in a flower pattern. Torn from a diary. Xi's plan offered a chance to find the rest of that book. Maybe Ivory would only uncover poems, but there was a chance the full diary could tell her what Cabrina had meant to do off the coast the night of June 14th.

It could tell what kinds of trick campfires had haunted Cabrina in the end. Ivory had only faced the one. Cabrina had lived with Viola, and her mistreatment burned long after her demise. Ivory and Cabrina came bound in the same trouble, only on different sides of the door between life and death.

Or was Ivory standing in the doorway? She ran a palm down her damp thigh as if the tattoo could hold her hand.

I am a creature of life.

Ivory wished she could have told Xi to focus less on death. This town didn't have to be the end of her, or that boy Rex. They were grown now, and they could leave.

But their friend was dead. Ivory had no right telling them where to put their minds and hearts, and no business feeling sorry for them over the varied hells they might someday face. Had already faced. The past was hungry, and the future had no mind for easing up. There would always be more people, and more futures, and the collisions between them, and nothing anyone said or did or felt could ever change that. Not even Ivory.

But she did have a right to see this through.

Ivory had made the most of these past few years, but there was unkindness at the edges, in the past. What if she hadn't been alone? What if there had been someone when she was young, someone older who could've helped?

And what if that person had chosen to stay out of it? Nothing of the end result would've changed, but their presence meant nothing was set in stone. That trick campfire—Ivory might have never fallen for it.

She couldn't fix her own past. Maybe she could influence Cabrina's future. In some small way, she needed to be for Cabrina what no one was for Ivory when she was young.

Even though Cabrina was dead. Ivory couldn't change that, but she could help fetch this diary.

And if nothing else, she could at last find out what really happened to Cabrina.

Viola Brite Will Make It Right. That's too long-winded! How couldn't she see it? I told her my idea—*Brite Makes Right.*

BRITE MAKES RIGHT.

I can't stop laughing.

She hates it. I told her to run it by Campaign Claude, but she doesn't like the implications. *It's like might makes right, is that what you think of me?* She shouted at me! SHOUTED!

But for the first time, I didn't care. It's the most I've laughed in the longest time. Doesn't she want a snappy slogan? Doesn't she want to win her reelection? And every moment she shouted at me, I couldn't think about the devils or the dreams. Even now, with my head ringing, I

I forget what I was writing. I had to tell her.

When I'm old enough, I won't vote for you.

Whoever's against you, I'm for them.

Whatever you want, I'm against it.

The laughter kind of died when I went to the garage to tell Dad. He wasn't going to find it funny, I could see it in his face. But that's okay.

Caged up in the house, deviled in the night, I think I figured out what happened.

She waited until the wedding day to do it to Dad. They must have kissed a hundred times before then, but she wouldn't have risked doing it early or else he couldn't have said, "I do." She waited.

She's like the cavemen. Back in eleventh grade bio, or maybe it was an anthropology elective, hard to remember, I learned that our ancestors didn't have it fair compared to the wolves and saber-toothed tigers. Those hunters had sharp teeth or claws for taking down prey, advantages we never evolved. Blades could only do so much against a few tons of angry mammoth, and guns hadn't been invented yet.

But we had our legs and stamina, and we could keep walking, endless walking, behind the mammoths. They would get tired, but we wouldn't, and we would wait until they got so tired, they couldn't fight back. It's a special kind of hunting, I forget the name.

She's like that, and back then, Dad was her mammoth.

She waited until the wedding day when she'd caught him, and then she did it. She sealed her lips tight and sucked the voice out of him. Every little bit.

So now he's quiet in the house. The only loud parts of him are his music in the garage and the sirens on top of his cop car. When he looks at me, his eyes have got so much to say, but he keeps that grimace on and goes "Mm" or "Mm-hmm" or "Mm-mm" and that's about it. That's why he can't say boo to her. She took his boo-speaking, and his screaming, and his hollering. There's no voice in him now. No wonder he took a job that follows orders in the worst way.

He still tells me things. He doesn't write or say them, but I look in his eyes.

I see how he blames me.

That's why he won't stand up to her, won't call me Cabrina, won't protect me, can only ignore me and dislike me. Yeah, his voice is stuck inside her.

But so was I.

Eight and half months is a long time to sit growing in her womb. A long time of doing nothing. Dad's voice was right there inside her with me, like a baby sibling, or a tapeworm, something that should have been born when I came out. I should have grabbed his voice in my tiny blob fist before I fell out of her in the hospital and they called me the wrong things. He blames me for failing as a fetus, and a baby. It isn't fair, but he's right. It's my fault. That's why he can't love me.

I bet if I had grabbed his voice then, he would have told them not to call me that. He would have told them I was a girl, and I was Cabrina.

Nighttime Theories

I am being punished for being a bad daughter

I am being punished for failing to steal a voice and for stealing a heart

If I could be pregnant, I would have the cinnamon scent man's baby, and the baby could grab the thing I swallowed on the way out. They would be a better newborn than I was.

But nothing works that way, and nobody can help me, so I don't know who to be mad at.

Except myself.

27. IN THE BELLY OF THE BRITE

A discarded moniker rang thunderous bells in Ivory's ears. She heard them every time Viola said that name, and the knell thrummed down Ivory's bones. She must have swallowed a seaborn poison at Cape Shadow, one to stun her each time she heard Cabrina's deadname.

Ivory's teeth pinched her tongue. *Quit saying it*, she almost said. *Quit hurting me.*

She swallowed every word. Viola had invited her in, and a guest had no say over her host, especially when she had to play the distraction for Xi's upstairs intrusion. Be nice, be pretty, make good conversation. That was Ivory's job, caught in Viola's hollow politician smile.

Ivory had showered, put on makeup, and dressed in a long dark blouse and white jeans before taking Wolf's Mercedes for another roar across Cape Morning. She only realized wearing white was a mistake when she spotted the pale-painted two-story colonial.

"The Brite family in their too-bright house," she'd whispered.

She'd crunched over the gravel walkway, climbed the steps between two bony columns, and knocked on the front door. Broad awnings reached out from the house's face like dark shingled cheekbones. One of the windows above might have opened on Cabrina's bedroom.

Ivory hadn't had time to assess the structure. Seconds after the knocking, Viola answered the door with a surprised smile. Her fidgety tone and overenthusiastic welcome suggested no one had visited since the funeral. A dead teenager made everyone uncomfortable.

Or maybe it was Viola, and her insistence on that bell-ringing name.

Ivory pretended to sip coffee at a countertop island while Viola apologized again and again for the messy kitchen, as if Ivory hadn't shown up by surprise. A need for usefulness twitched in her skin. She wanted to offer comfort almost on reflex—*your child is gone, who cares about your house?* To stand here silently while kissing a coffee mug's rim seemed cruel.

But Viola could be a monster, and someone should tell her.

"Thank you for having me," Ivory said, swallowing again what she really wanted to say. "It's been a weird few days."

"I feel like I've forced your visit," Viola said, shifting one plastic container and then another over the countertops. "That's how lonely you get in a big house. Gary's usually either at the station, on patrol, or in the garage, tortoise in his shell. My campaign manager has been absent too, meaning to give me space. You get desperate for company."

Even a stranger is company when no one wants to stick around, Ivory wanted to say.

Another swallow, another smile, nice and pretty. She almost complimented the coffee she hadn't been drinking, but she didn't want to come across as someone who never drank good coffee.

"In any case, thanks for taking me up on it." Viola's smile shrank. "It's been a bizarre few days for me, too. I should've known what to expect at the cemetery. They haven't been back, but still. Those are the kinds of people who orbit a troubled kid like—"

Bells again clanged. Ivory clutched one hand around her other wrist to keep from spilling the coffee. Her neck muscles tensed in a fleshy choke chain.

Xi must have crept in through the front door by now. Ivory had made sure she and Viola left it unlocked. Xi might even be upstairs already, in Cabrina's room. That was the hope.

"I'm sorry about the other day at the café," Ivory said. She tried to mean it. "And for taking so long to come by on short notice. And for the cemetery. Again."

Viola waved a dismissive hand. "The plastic marker at Fairview West is only temporary anyway. The real headstone will be solid granite with a two-inch deep inscription, coated with an inch-thick shatterproof shell. I talked to the mason this morning. It's a larger construction, but between the local influences and the outsiders trashing our town to have their fun, it will keep anyone else from defacing my son's grave."

"A lot of expense to control that memory." Ivory said it in a quick breath. Her stomach was too full of venom to ingest any more words this evening.

"Is it?" Political nicety slid away as Viola's expression stole every shadow from the room. "Memory is all I have now."

"Right," Ivory said. She stared hard at her coffee.

Viola's smile returned to full power. "It isn't like I'm left with anything else. No matter what I accomplish going forward, it'll be in the shadow of his death. I should have the freedom to see his grave and his name without worrying a couple of bored townies have defaced that memory."

"But. The name." Ivory had to drag the words out. Diplomacy came so much harder than frustration. "Cabrina. Is that not what she called herself?" She expected the smile to shrink again.

But Viola went on beaming with debate-winning confidence. "Do you have any children, Ivory?"

"Yes," Ivory blurted out.

The lie surprised her. She could've excused it to herself as referring to the nest of feeders in her house, but they belonged to

Honey. No, Ivory meant the lie the way it sounded. It came as smooth and silky as pulling a colorful handkerchief from a magician's sleeve, tied to its fellow handkerchiefs in a furious rainbow. And like any great magic act, distraction was the key. The more Viola focused on Ivory, the less likely she might hear a floorboard or footstep upstairs, especially if Xi needed to tear Cabrina's room apart.

More of the lie spilled out as Ivory went on. "I have a daughter," she said. "At college."

"College?" Viola balked. "You look too young for it."

"I get that a lot." Between Ivory's hormone injections and her true age of twenty-nine, she looked several years short of what Viola might expect for a college freshman's mother. The lie went on weaving anyway. "She's a funny young woman, whip smart. She works hard, and that doesn't always make her the best company, but she still talks to me, thankfully. You can't always get that out of kids."

Viola nodded, shifted some magazines from one counter to another, placed her phone to one side, raised another steaming mug of coffee. She looked uncomfortable. She might end this visit soon.

Hurry up, Xi, Ivory thought.

She scraped the next lie off her tongue. "She doesn't talk to her father, though. He still expects her to be his son."

"Is that why I found you at my son's grave?" Viola snapped. "You think he's like her?"

Ivory pretended to drink again. She could go for a lick of blood right now, but no matter how Ivory gazed, Viola looked no more appetizing than slurping up kelp-strewn seawater. Did she say *her* for Ivory's imaginary daughter out of hostess respectability, or was it fine for others to be trans, but not the real-life daughter of Viola Brite, up for reelection to Cape Morning town council with ambitions to go further?

Xi had better be finding the diary upstairs to make it worth putting Ivory through this.

"I'm sorry," Viola said, sighing through another hollow smile. "That was rude."

Yes, Ivory wanted to say. She couldn't make anything else come out right. "It wasn't—" she started. "At the cemetery, I was trying to—"

"My son wasn't like your child," Viola said at last. "He was confused. Mentally unwell. That made him susceptible to influences that had nothing to do with him, and his peers at school weren't helping. Even after I pulled him out, the influence never went away. They would show up at the house, call him that nickname, like they were making fun of him. Like any kid with problems. You know how it is."

"Hearing the name you don't want kind of drives you mad, doesn't it?" Ivory asked.

Viola didn't seem to notice Ivory's jab. "Don't get me started. It's like *Psycho*, right? Hitchcock? We all go a little mad sometimes. We're not supposed to be okay with movies like that anymore, with how it ends, but it's the same problem. Mental illness. And if you encourage it, they turn into predators."

Ivory listened for the creak of footsteps above, but there was nothing. Either Xi was truly stealthy, or entirely absent, abandoning Ivory to handle Cabrina's house alone.

"But when they called your kid Cabrina," Ivory said. "That didn't mean anything else?"

Viola's tone turned brusque. "Are you a journalist? Going to write a hit piece on me? Say that Viola Brite flipflops so much, you'd think she was Mayor Haversham's zoning stance? Maybe say we women aren't cut out for power and leadership positions?"

Ivory blinked. "I don't know anything about that."

"Let me be crystal clear," Viola said. "Maybe you don't remember high school, but I do. We all get nicknames, like it or not. They used to call me Vivi, and I hated it." She flopped her hand in a bizarre shrug. "But what can you do? Shout at them to stop, and they only do it more. It was the same for my son and his friends. I'm sure you had a nickname back in your high school days, too."

Faggot, Ivory thought.

She stuck the mug to her lips and bit down against the rank flavor. The word had trailed her through late elementary school, then middle school, and finally high school in snarls and taunts and adjoined brutality, and even with polite tones as if it were Ivory's genuine name. She'd first struggled in trying to figure out what it meant or how it applied to her. To pretend she'd had any control was almost teenage superstition.

Especially on the night of the trick campfire.

"You're remembering it now," Viola said. "Can you understand what they were doing to my boy?"

"Can you understand—" Ivory started.

Finish it, she told herself. *Can you understand what you were doing to her? Can you understand wanting to tear your skin and muscle off? You can't, I should bite you, I should drain you, I should—*

Ivory shuddered through another swallow and wished Honey was here.

"Do you remember the little rules of love we'd make up back in those days?" Ivory asked. "The moments when your heart teetered on a crush, and you'd promise yourself, if he turns this way now, that means he likes me, and I'll tell him I like him too. And if he didn't turn, you'd be heartbroken. And if he did, you'd say to yourself, that doesn't count, or he has to do it three times. Like there was a magic rule we couldn't control. It's a hard age all around. You're realizing, one day after another, that there's no magic in the world except what you choose."

A stillness crept over Viola. "I doubt I was ever that kind of girl." Another thoughtful pause followed. "In fact, I'm sure of it."

Ivory was starting to wonder if Viola had been the kind of girl with a soul. Never mind that Ivory had no place caring what Viola thought. Viola certainly wasn't about to give a damn the other way around.

I knew people like you, Ivory wanted to say. Another tongue bite. *They pretended to be my friends.*

No, she wouldn't tell about the trick campfire, especially not in this awful house with this grim damn woman.

"You're bleeding," Viola said, almost monotone.

Ivory glanced at her coffee mug, where a rock-hard fist curled around the grip. She'd dug her thumbnail into one finger, slitting it open down the side.

She quickly set the mug down and curled up the bleeding digit. What a waste of good sweetness. Scarlet would have longed to wrap her lips around this wound. The red sent Ivory's gut aching.

Viola hurried to the counter and tore off a sheet of paper towel. Ivory tucked the wadded paper into her fist.

Her phone began to buzz in her purse. Too many troubles were coming at once. Time to get out of this house, whether Xi had found the diary or not. A few minutes more, and even Viola Brite might be tempting to drink.

"You should check that," Viola said, nodding at the trembling purse. "You never know when it's an emergency. I learned that the hard way when they found my boy."

Ivory gritted her teeth, clenched the paper towel, and fished out her phone.

It was a text from Joan Fang: *If you see my son, please call me.*

"It's my friend," Ivory said. "Looking for her kid, but I'm sure he's fine." She was glad Rex had nothing to do with Xi's plan. Joan's presence would only complicate the night.

"Friend." Viola sniffed. "You find out your real friends when you lose your child."

Ivory didn't know what else to say. She held up the bloody wad of paper towel. "I'm going to rinse this. Can you tell me where to find the restroom?"

"Here, I'll take you." Viola reached for Ivory's bicep.

Ivory raised a hand. "That's okay, I can find it."

Viola opened her mouth, probably to insist, when another little earthquake rumbled over the kitchen island. She backpedaled close enough to grab a glowing phone.

Her upper lip became a tense red snake above her teeth. "Claude." She then swerved into a vote-for-me smile and flashed it at Ivory. "I have to take this. One restroom's at the bottom of the stairs. And if Gary's in there, we have another at the top. He hides inside sometimes. I don't know why."

"Okay," Ivory said again, retreating.

Viola swiped at the phone and jammed it against her head. "It's late, Claude," she said, and then paused to listen. "What do you mean? We shook hands on the rezoning three weeks ago. It's done."

Ivory decided the moment she left the kitchen that Gary would be occupying the downstairs bathroom. An easier excuse to head upstairs and check on Xi.

A sigh swept through the kitchen. "Haversham can't have second thoughts," Viola said. "He hardly has first thoughts."

The air hung desolate and cryptlike as Ivory crossed a high-ceilinged living room dressed in cream-colored furniture and shelves of wooden knickknacks. A pair of plaques said *Home, Sweet Home*, and *Family Makes the House a Home*, and a legion of framed photographs draped the walls. Cabrina's old school and family photos were slathered here like middle fingers behind glass.

The breadth of the rooms, Viola's demeanor, and her fancy plans for Cabrina's headstone—a façade of a whole house. These people were too heart-poor to fill this upper middle-class emptiness with genuine love.

Ivory fought down bitter thoughts as she set foot on the carpeted stairway. She wasn't being fair. The only people who lived here anymore were two grieving parents.

Grieving, Ivory told herself. Even if Viola didn't sound like it. What was she supposed to do, put on a skit as the mourning mother for every conversation? Maybe her political rivals would judge her for too little sadness, or call her weak if she showed too much feeling, but not Ivory.

What Ivory couldn't forgive was the unnecessity of it all. The Brites could have avoided grief altogether with an alive kid. If they'd treated her better. Ivory couldn't know for certain, but this place, these parents—they had to be connected to what had happened to their daughter.

Despite the insistent plaques, this house had not been Cabrina's home for a long time. This was a fortress against the world, meant to clutch and manipulate and fantasize boyish futures for a teenage girl. No choices for a princess trapped inside her mother's castle.

And in the end, her mother had won.

28. THE HUNTERS

The beach seemed best for hunting. Rex gathered that wherever you would find clusters of people at Cape Morning, you might find a hunter. Xi might be hiding, but for all any of them knew, Cabrina had been feeding on others before she chose a house with a blood source closer to heart.

Fires, dancers, and drinkers dotted the open sand. Music blasted from summerhouse parties, and no one would be checking who was coming or going. Cabrina's strange behavior might raise eyebrows, but judging by the way she swept ghostlike from shadow to shadow, Rex guessed no one would see her coming, and he doubted they'd catch her when she fled.

He could only hope she hadn't killed anyone yet.

Sand kicked his heels where Marla trudged behind him, swinging Rex's shoulder-strapped canvas bag at her side. The zipper gaped open where a hole-poked plastic container breathed a metallic aroma. Rex had dripped his own blood inside, against Marla's wishes. The bag also held an oversized T-shirt and jeans in case Cabrina wanted to change into anything clean of Xi's blood.

Rex wished they had the dresses Cabrina liked. Her old makeup. Set her dealer Germaine loose from prison, with meds as bait. He'd vanished into the grasp of Cabrina's father and other cops, and then away to some penitentiary for daring to bring his trade to a tourist town, as if half the summer people didn't haul their own stewpots of powders and pills to Cape Morning. But damn anyone who gave a girl her medication.

Marla left the canvas bag gaping open in case Rex needed to stash the machete he clutched in his right hand. The late Roy Long had been a sharp-eyed local fisherman who thought a dull machete made the right manly gift for the scrappy weird boy who'd just come out of the closet. Joan had let it remain as decoration, but Rex had learned how to sharpen it.

He never thought he would need it like this. And maybe old Mr. Long had known there was something funny about this town when he had passed along the machete. Like he'd suspected Rex would need it.

"Please, Cab," Rex whispered. "Don't make me use it."

Cabrina's state wasn't her fault. Something had done this to her. And her mother had put her in that position first, a woman too scornful to let anything into her head.

The trouble was a lack of empathetic perspective. Viola Brite had never once bothered to walk in someone else's shoes, see through their eyes, as if her way was the only way.

There was a Superman comic by Grant Morrison, *All-Star Superman*, that Rex always wished he could make come true. Near the end, Lex Luthor finally quit being an evil bastard when Superman let him see the world through Kryptonian eyes and feel the aliveness of all things, constantly.

What Rex wouldn't give to stuff that perspective into Viola's head. And maybe his own, if he thought it would help. That absolute, contagious empathy could have done everyone a world of good.

Instead, Viola Brite had remained her terrible self, and Cabrina was dead, and now Rex might stand at a fork in the road between his two best friends. One didn't have a future. The other did. If he had to choose—

Flickering blue light washed his thoughts away, stealing his attention toward the Atlantic. He caught the briefest glimpse of Ghost Cat Island in the lightning, a tiny scrap of rock among unruly waves. Thunder growled across the ocean and sky.

"This won't be worse than a squall according to the weather," Marla said, glancing at her phone. "Still, maybe we should put the vampire hunt off to another night? I told your Ma you weren't with me. You'll have hell to pay if she doesn't get hold of you soon."

Rex marched onward, scrutinizing every beach shadow as they parted, joined, danced, drank, made out, bled cigarette butts and beer cans. No sign of Cabrina baring her teeth from a bloodstained hoodie, but the light played tricks when she came around. Whatever aspects of vampirism were cinematic inventions, the glamour had to be real. Cabrina's presence could distort the senses, induce visions, and add or omit darkness for her purposes.

She could be hiding three steps ahead. Would Rex even know?

"Everyone's at summerhouse parties," Marla said. Lightning heralded another thunderous growl, louder now, and she raised her voice against it. "If we don't find Cabrina here, might be we'll have to dig up her grave, stake her down, until we can think of anything better."

Machete in hand, Rex envisioned himself like Blade, only without a titanium sword or half-vampire protection. But he could set down this weapon, take up a mallet and wooden spike, and act as some trans Van Helsing. Hell, maybe the famous vampire-hunting professor *was* trans. Not like Rex had read that book. Didn't matter. He could dig, and descend, and aim a wooden point at Cabrina's chest if he absolutely had to. The mallet would nail the stake through skin, breastbone, heart, and pin a twitching vampire into the earth.

Vampire hunter Rex, staking his undead best friend. *Slam, slam, slam.*

He shuddered, nearly dropping his machete to the sand. To stake Cabrina in her grave, the one marked and curated by Viola Brite—the sight of it would haunt him forever, same as if he had to cut her with the machete.

"Not sure she's in her grave," Rex said. "Can't be sure of anything."

Clustered silhouettes crept from the beach fires, but most visitors remained. They had come from near and far to partake of Cape Morning, day and night, and they would cling to their nocturnal joy until the storm blew them away.

Rex wedged the machete under one arm and dug into his jacket pockets for a joint and a light. His hands trembled as he thumbed the lighter.

Marla raised an eyebrow, concerned.

"Takes the edge off," Rex said. "Aren't you a cool mom?"

He puffed twice and then offered it to Marla. She glanced over it, accepted the offer, inhaled once, and then pinched it out.

"You're a good kid, Rex," she said, blowing smoke into the surging wind.

Rex watched another beach fire lose half its gatherers. "Ma says every now and then, someone dies here, or goes missing in some weird way. Cab might've been aiming for Ghost Cat Island. Maybe the others were trying for it too."

Marla swiped hair out of her face. "Maybe."

"Don't know if we'll ever figure that part out," Rex said. "But that island—guessing we shouldn't fuck with it, should we?"

"No," Marla said. "I have a feeling it fucks back."

"It wants my friends." Rex squeezed the flat of the machete to his thigh as he crossed dancing firelight. "Like they're sacrifices to some ancient priestess weird shit, you know? Can't let it happen to Xi. Even if I got to stop Cab."

Marla's boots were nearly silent in the sand. "Rex? Do you have feelings for Xi?"

"Jesus." Rex rolled his eyes. "What next? *Do you like-like her?* Please."

"Wait a second, guy—" Marla started.

"Mom," Rex snapped. The tone made him sound younger, petulant, but he couldn't take it back, only try to sound calmer as he explained. "Yes, and she's had feelings for me, and we both have for Cab, and Cab for us, and it's gone around and around. That was high school, and we're beyond it. Left it with the homework and bullying and standardized tests. She's going to Dartmouth, end of summer. I'm just making sure she lives that long." He took another two steps and looked at Marla. "You get it?"

"I do," Marla said.

They walked onward. Rex wished there was gravel in the sand. Their footsteps were too quiet for comfort, and if someone else walked behind them, they wouldn't know until it was too late. The sky's rumbling didn't help, and neither did the eternal tide crashing against the shore. Cape Morning was too loud, and Rex felt too quiet. Maybe Cabrina had the right idea that night in April when she encouraged them all to scream and shout at the sea.

Marla gave him a soft look. "Do you remember my dad? Axel?"

Rex didn't answer. He remembered attending the funeral but not the man himself.

"He was like you," Marla said. "Curious and brave. He wore his heart on his sleeve. Do you know the fistfights he would get into when he was your age? He was a scrapper, plenty of stories, and his tongue got dog-eared telling them. And he loved just as hard. Same as you." She nudged her hip against Rex's side. "You want your friend to be okay. I know that."

What Rex wanted and what he could do were not always the same. Especially not with Cab's death haunting him, or Cab herself.

He only knew he'd do right for Xi, same as she would do right for him.

She couldn't turn out like Cab. Never.

Thunder rumbled, and the rain fell at last. Beach fires hissed and sputtered, and those who had built them hurried off the sand, laughing and loping drunkenly back to their summerhouses. Muffled music blasted louder to fight the storm and try to scare it back to sea.

"Counts to be prepared." Marla plucked two frail purse umbrellas from the canvas bag. "But we should think about heading in, guy."

"Why don't they?" Rex asked, chinning ahead.

Ten yards up the beach, at the edge of dying firelight, a dark lump lay across the sand, and a figure hunched over it. Rex couldn't make out what either was doing, and maybe the lump was a chunk of driftwood eased onto land ahead of the storm, but why didn't the figure run from the rain? Why not call for help if there was trouble? In the dim, Rex couldn't tell if the hunching figure was Cabrina.

But he couldn't be sure it wasn't, either. He needed to step closer. Needed to see.

29. THE CLEAN ROOM

Floral wallpaper cast the upstairs walls in pale cream and off-color blues. The first doorway stood right of the stairway, and it led to the bathroom, as Viola had said. Ivory reached inside, flipped on the light and fan, and shut the door. Hopefully if Viola came looking, the semblance of an occupied bathroom would send her back downstairs for a time.

The next door was a linen closet, and the next was shut and locked. Ivory supposed it might be a storage room, but she didn't think so. A small circle dotted the doorknob's center, the hole for a wire-thin key. Ivory patted atop the doorframe until she found an iron rod half the length of her index finger, ending in a right-angle hook. She tried it in the door, and the knob clicked loose.

Dishes clanked downstairs. Viola had taken to busying herself in the kitchen. How long would she remain patient before wondering if Ivory needed help? No time to stall. Quick and quiet, in and out.

Ivory pressed the door open by steady inches, wary of creaky hinges, only far enough to squeeze inside before she shut it behind her.

The room hung thick and dark. Meager porchlight seeped through the windows from a house across the street, but Ivory wouldn't risk flipping a wall switch and letting it fill the crack under the door. She plucked out her phone and hit the flashlight.

What despair had driven Cabrina to the sea? Ivory had a feeling she'd been speaking to part of it minutes ago, and she stood in the rest of it now.

A small desk ahead of the door carried a jumble of school notebooks, a gray laptop, and a tall black cup stuffed with pencils, pens, and a lengthy pair of scissors with a blue grip. In one desk corner sat a cardboard box that read SCRAPBOOKING on the side in black sharpie. Ivory glanced inside, but the box was empty. Only the inky scent of magazine and newspaper pages lingered.

The closet hung open with a hoodie, sweatshirts, and dress pants. A pair of sneakers hid on the floor, partway buried under plastic bags of assorted belongings. The walls bore no posters, nothing framed, no signs of the person Cabrina used to be, as if she'd tucked her personality away before death.

Or someone had hosed down the room. The wrongs of this house turned the air suffocating. There was no sign that a teenage girl ever lived here. Ivory couldn't articulate what she'd expected to find, but she would have known it had she stepped inside Xi's house. Teenagers breathed influence into their spaces.

Every room and hall of Cabrina's house instead wore Viola's hollow smile. The walls themselves had to feign happiness. She must have taken it upon herself to cleanse Cabrina's room. She'd probably done it over and over, throwing away anything she perceived as too feminine. Given time, she would arrange the room to careful perfection, a temple full of altars to suit the child she'd really wanted, same as her plan for the headstone.

Only one trace of Cabrina remained—Xi, lying on Cabrina's bed. Her eyes were closed, and her mouth hung open, while long dark hair splayed across her face. Her glasses had slid off and lay open beside her.

Ivory took a deep breath and stepped away from the door. The house was muffled now that she'd shut herself inside Cabrina's room. Viola could be anywhere. Quick and quiet.

The blood-dotted paper towel fell from Ivory's hand as she reached for Xi's shoulder.

"Wake up," Ivory whispered. "Xi, you can't sleep here."

Xi murmured something. She was a loose doll draped sideways across the dark blue bedspread, both arms clutched to her chest as if cuddling a stuffed animal.

Nothing soft lingered here for her to grasp. Viola would have made sure no such thing could be found in Cabrina's room. Xi instead clutched a small thin book, the kind you might grab from an art store at checkout. Its meadowy green cover bound a slim set of pink pages.

The diary of Cabrina Brite.

Traces of dust and hair clung to the spine, as if Xi had plucked it from a vent somewhere Viola wouldn't think to look. She had been thorough but careful, leaving the room looking undisturbed.

Ivory lifted one of Xi's arms and slid the diary free. She could stuff it in her purse—it was small enough—and then shake Xi until she woke up. One of the windows hung partway open. Viola might have left it that way to air out the room, or Xi had wisely opened it herself as a risky escape route in case anyone caught her. She could descend the front of the house, and Ivory could hurry downstairs, and they would drive off in Wolf's car without Viola ever knowing. She would have already destroyed the diary had she known about it. Best to get away before she learned better.

But Ivory couldn't help cracking it open beneath her phone's light. Here was a window into Cabrina's thoughts, the origin paper for the death poem, everything that had led to that poor girl's demise.

I tried to stop writing my thoughts, but then it was like I swallowed a scream—

Ivory almost clapped the diary shut. The honest outpouring of Cabrina's feelings dug nails beneath her skin.

But she had to keep reading, had to try. What else had she come here for?

Perusing the diary and clutching her phone became a juggling act, but Ivory managed to skim a dream here, a theory there, drawing in a vague understanding of Cabrina's final days. The name *Ghost Cat Island* sprang out, and *devils*, and other problems. Home problems. Cabrina had been desperate to make her life work no matter how poorly its pieces fit together, as if one nineteen-year-old girl with an ocean of troubles could figure out and fix her world, her life, her mother.

Always pretty, always nice. If only Ivory had known this teenager before, she could have become an anchor to keep Cabrina from drifting off in a Cape Morning storm. This soft, desperate girl.

A scuffling noise tore Ivory's attention from the pink diary pages, and she turned to the window in time to see a pale figure blotting the frame. Auburn hair swept across a shadowed face.

"Cabrina?" Ivory whispered.

The pale figure bolted from sight, and Ivory chased to the open window.

"Cabrina, wait!"

The screen had been torn ragged. With the bedroom locked, Cabrina might have hidden here undisturbed, coming and going as she pleased. Viola's daughter, haunting the house without her mother knowing. But then, a lack of understanding and care sounded exactly like Viola when her daughter was alive, too.

Ivory could do better than that now. She'd seen for herself there was life after death. Honey had given that gift to Scarlet, Chelsea, and the rest at the house.

Maybe Cabrina's resurrection wasn't exactly the same, but there was a similarity. Honey or something like her could've given

Cabrina that gift. She might have found her way through another of Cape Shadow's entrances.

But unlike Ivory and the others, Cabrina was alone. If she would come back to the house, maybe Honey could help. Introduce her to the others. Let her find a new family in their communal undeath.

Ivory leaned her head over the sill. "Cabrina, I can help," she said. "*We* can help. Honey can't make you live again, but you can be one of us. You have choices. Just like me. You don't have to be alone."

But was that true? Did Cabrina have choices? Could Ivory be of any good to anyone, especially a dead girl? For as much as Cabrina had tried to escape, she'd still ended up crawling toward this house in the dark. What good was being dead when every moment craved life?

Another noise pricked Ivory's ears—creaking footsteps. Someone was coming.

Ivory hurried to stuff the diary in her purse, but pulling out her phone had shuffled her wallet, her keys, Wolf's keys, receipts, the myriad junk. There wasn't room to jam the diary in quickly.

Another creak. Footsteps in the hall.

Ivory slid a hand through the torn gap in the window screen and flicked her wrist, sending the diary sailing toward the front lawn. She had to hope the fall wouldn't tear out any pages. She twisted back to the bed to shake Xi again, get her up and moving.

They were out of time. The bedroom door creaked open, a wall switch ticked, and bright light flared from the ceiling lamp.

Viola filled the doorway.

30. OUT

Ivory's hand slid from Xi's shoulder. The light would surely wake her now. Even someone dead tired had to feel the glow against her eyelids and the bristling anger in the air.

"What are you two doing in here?" Viola snapped, and she jiggled the doorknob. "This room is private."

Ivory tensed her throat muscles, squeezing out her voice. "Mrs. Brite—"

"Get out." Viola stormed into the room and pointed at the doorway. "And don't come back."

Ivory hesitated. She couldn't be sure if the trouble was the invasion of privacy into a dead girl's room, or that an outsider had seen the barrenness left in Viola's wake.

"She won't wake up," Ivory said, tilting her head toward sleeping Xi. "Something's wrong with her. We have to call someone."

"I intend to." Viola looked over her shoulder, through the doorway. "Gary! Get up here!" She turned again to Ivory, grimacing. "You've never met my husband, have you? *Officer* Gary Brite."

Ivory's jaw dropped. "You're kidding me."

Viola blinked. "Gary? Do you hear me? Up here. Now."

Ivory whirled toward the bed again and grabbed Xi with both hands. She didn't care if she got blood on the girl's jacket. Time to wake up, to run, faster than she'd fled the cemetery, and maybe farther too. Ivory certainly couldn't stay, couldn't get caught.

Not after everything she'd done with Honey. She abandoned the bed and Xi, turning to face the rest of the room.

Viola glanced over the furniture as if wondering whether Ivory or Xi had stolen anything. Far as she knew, what was left to take? She'd pushed everything about her daughter away until this little chamber became the void of outer space. This room itself was the intruder in Viola's house.

Ivory dodged past Viola, heading for the door. "Are you sure you were never a girl in love? Or did you just never know how?"

Viola's lip curled.

"Go on," Ivory said. "Tell me to fuck off. But I know what I'm talking about better than you do, and Xi—she loves Cabrina. Actually loves her for herself. Can you have a heart for once in your life? She's just a kid."

"That is an adult," Viola said, gesturing at the bed. "Do you understand? That is a nineteen-year-old who knows better, and this is my house. My dead boy's room. Where do you get the nerve?"

"God blessed it to me," Ivory said, a sourness on her tongue. "Remember?"

Wide-eyed realization crossed Viola's face. "You don't have a child, do you?"

Ivory's nerves faltered, and she tried for the doorway. She'd long overstayed her welcome, and her desire to help Cabrina could only make her so brave.

Viola grabbed Ivory's shoulder. "That story you concocted downstairs—that was you." A fire ripped through Viola's eyes, and she shoved Ivory against the door-side desk. "You're one of them."

The desk's edge bit into the small of Ivory's back. She winced, but Honey had taught her to be stronger than giving in to this woman, hadn't she?

"You think that scares me?" Ivory asked, her voice steady. "That you know? Do you think your daughter's one of a kind?"

"I don't know you," Viola said. "And you didn't know my son."

Uncertainty clawed at Ivory's heart. What right did she have to get involved? See a wrong, stop it? This was not her family. Honey's influence alone could not pull rank, and Honey herself wasn't here.

Ivory bristled. Not her family, no, but Cabrina was *family*.

"If I'd been Cabrina," Ivory went on, stalking close again, "I'd have marched down those steps into your pretty goddamn living room and slit my throat all over your home. You'd be cleaning trans bitch out of the carpet and wallpaper for years and years. And even when the sight of me went away, you'd sit down to watch TV, and you'd smell me in the fibers and the air. You'd never get the blood out. No matter what, a part of me would haunt you to your death. Just like Cabrina will."

Viola's open palm struck snake-quick across Ivory's face. She faltered a step, but Viola wasn't done. She came tearing closer, and one hand stretched past Ivory, toward the desk.

"Real women don't threaten," Viola snapped. "We act."

Ivory clenched her teeth to shut up, be nice, be pretty, but she couldn't do it. "Is that how you put it to Cabrina when you killed her?"

Viola slammed into Ivory's chest, knocking her back against the door. Her other hand whipped loose from the desk, spilling its cup of pens and pencils. Large gleaming scissors stretched from her fingers.

Ivory struggled to stand against the door, but she wasn't like Honey or the others. They had climbed to some supernatural pinnacle. Ivory wasn't any stronger than she used to be.

Certainly not stronger than Viola, and nowhere as vicious.

The point of a sharp blade pressed against Ivory's neck, and her arms went stiff at her sides. She held her breath, afraid to inhale against Viola's steel, afraid to swallow. The blade scraped at skin and pressed down.

"You don't have a child," Viola said, tasting each word as if they were sugar-coated victory. "Never did. Never will. You could never know what I'm going through, you freak."

Ivory wanted to say she'd been called worse, but the scissor blade locked the words in her throat. She held them there, choking on them, until the scissors descended to her chest and let her swallow.

"Could never," she muttered.

"That's right," Viola said.

"What are you so afraid of? Your life's so simple, you could never understand real fear. You had to invent monsters." Ivory sucked in a shaky breath as the scissors slid down and down. "But I could show you real monsters. People like you would see how bad it can get, and then you would fantasize over how good you had it when the worst thing you could think of was me, and a couple of teenagers, and your own daughter. Then you'd have something to be afraid of."

Viola shoved a forceful hand between Ivory's legs, clutching where Ivory had tucked herself into a gaff before sliding into these white jeans. An ache rocked up her spine, and her gut swirled.

The bravery dribbled down Ivory's throat. "Please," she whispered.

The scissors snapped open at Viola's other hand, and one blade traced Ivory's inner thigh, right where her tattoo hid beneath her clothes. If Viola pressed too hard, she'd bleed a new wound there. A new scar, like on the night of the trick campfire. As if Ivory had learned nothing in over a decade since she'd been that sixteen-year-old kid surrounded by wolves wearing pretend friends' faces.

Don't think about that, think about right now, she told herself. *I am a creature of life, a creature of life, I am a creature who wants to live.*

"This is part of your trouble, yes?" Viola hissed. One scissor blade climbed beside her clutching hand. "The part where you can't understand my boy was nothing like you. He wasn't a freak, or a monster. He was unwell in a different way. But I can cut your trouble out. Say the word. It's your choice."

A sharp prick stung Ivory's thigh. She didn't want to look, couldn't stop herself—one pointed blade had jabbed through her jeans and into her flesh. A maroon patch darkened the denim.

Ivory's eyes burned with tears. She was being taken apart by this hateful touch, every inch measured and found wanting. And yet she wished to ask if Viola had ever done anything like this to Cabrina. Wished to see what kind of reaction that might have, whether it would wake Viola up or make her worse. If only Honey were here.

A tired moan shook Viola back from Ivory, and they both turned to the bed.

Xi rolled onto her back and covered her eyes with one arm. Her hair splayed across the bedspread and would likely leave strands behind, evidence of her presence. One hand pawed for her glasses.

Viola let go of Ivory and aimed herself at the bed, readying the scissors.

Ivory wouldn't get another chance—she scrambled past Viola's back, out the bedroom door, and hurried down the stairs, turning at the landing, her purse clacking the banister at every step. Her thigh stung at each movement, but she brushed it off. It was a shallow wound, and stopping for it might be the end of her.

"Gary!" Viola shouted from behind, stamping from the bedroom. "Gary, goddammit, there's someone in the house!"

Ivory cut across the living room and ducked into the foyer. A doorknob clicked somewhere in the house, and she froze in the shadows cast by the second floor.

A man with auburn hair and a thick beard emerged from the opposite side of the living room from the stairs. He walked with a heavy lurch, his sleeves rolled up, as if he'd been hunched over a car hood before he heard Viola shouting from upstairs. Without glancing up, he started for the stairs and disappeared halfway to the landing.

Ivory didn't wait—she crossed the rest of the foyer, wrenched open the front door, and fled down the steps, past the columns. Her shoes crunched over the gravel. She only paused to hit the lawn, where she grabbed up the diary as raindrops struck her head. A sea-driven storm must have reached this side of town.

She slipped into Wolf's Mercedes, fought with the keys, and slammed the gas, sending gravel chunks shooting across the driveway. No slowing, no stopping. Rain spit across the windshield, blurring the headlights. Ivory flipped on the wipers before turning at the driveway's end onto Harper Lane, away from this house from hell.

"Sorry, Xi," she whispered.

She took one last glance through the driver side window at the columns, the awnings, the front door left gaping to the rain. Light shined from every room, the house turning bright. Not with the warm welcome of sunshine—this was cold radiance, a lighthouse warning ships of jagged rocks and hopeless tragedy.

The light told Ivory to stay away. She would find only death here.

31. THE HUNTED

The hunched shadow grew at Rex's every step, but it offered little definition through the windswept rain. He could make out one figure kneeling, another lying in the sand, and a rhythm of movement between them.

Rex cleared his throat. "Hey there. You good?"

No answer. The hunched figure pressed closer to the one lying in front of it.

A wet chill dribbled down Rex's spine. He could walk away right now. He could turn back to Marla, shove his machete into the open canvas bag, and call it a night. No need to find out this was Cabrina hunching over a dead body. No need to confirm it wasn't. Maybe someone had almost drowned, and someone else was listening for a heartbeat, or maybe it was some public sex kink, or maybe these two were performing a seaside occult ritual, like the one Rex and Xi had performed the night of Cabrina's funeral. Everyone had a ghost to call.

Rex could walk away and, in time, forget all about it.

Lightning flickered across a pale face as it turned his way—not Cabrina. Someone a few years older, with slighter features.

But similar dark stains matted this stranger's chest, and a scarlet smear coated every inch of her face beneath her eyes, as if she wore a mask of blood. It rained in thick drops from her chin. The same color ran down her arms, toward her hands, where they sank into a prone body.

"Is she hurt?" Marla asked, stuffing the purse umbrellas back into her bag. Without waiting for an answer, she stepped closer. "It's going to be okay, you hear?"

Rex doubted that. The body in the sand had been wearing a tank top, the upper part torn and stretched to cover their face. Now the rain piled on, and lightning let Rex glimpse the fabric glued against a nose, cheeks, lips, and unblinking eyes.

He also glimpsed a partway-exposed chest, where a hole gaped open on the left side, toothed by broken ribs, as if a needful ex-lover had come tearing out a still-beating heart.

"Can you tell us your name?" Marla asked.

"Scar," a rasping voice said. "Scarlet. Now." Thunder rumbled over the beach, muffling whatever she said next.

"Scarlet. Okay." Marla took another step past Rex.

"Mom, she's not right. Cab—" Rex didn't know how to say it. Cabrina might have bit this woman. Turned her.

"Leave it to me," Marla said. She reached out one hand as if trying to calm a feral cat. "Scarlet? Did you meet a girl named Cabrina? Did she do something to you?"

Scarlet's eyes gleamed in a lightning flash. Her tongue ran over her upper lip.

Marla tried again. "Scarlet?"

"It was Honey," Scarlet said, and thunder rang after the name. "She had us all."

Not Cabrina. *Honey. She had us all.* Who the hell was Honey? How many damn vampires were lurking in Cape Morning?

Rex grabbed for Marla's arm to pull her back.

She took another step anyway. "Scarlet, it's okay," Marla said. "This Honey, what did she do to—"

Her words pinched to a breathy gasp as Scarlet snapped off the body and lunged. Marla hopped back, crashing against Rex. Thunder muffled whatever she said next, and Rex almost warned her not to panic. That made no sense; they both had every right to panic. Especially as Scarlet snatched at Marla's arm.

Rex raised his machete and slashed through open air. "Stay back!"

Raindrops bounded off the blade as Scarlet twisted away, hissing through the wind, before swinging both fists down on Rex's right shoulder and knocking him to one side. He slashed again before crashing into the sand.

"This isn't right." Marla retreated in slow steps, and Scarlet stalked toward her. "We should commune with the unsettled spirit. Find her path to peace." She rummaged through the canvas bag, spilling the T-shirt meant for Cabrina. "I didn't bring the right crystals for this."

Rex squeezed the machete's grip as Marla retreated and Scarlet advanced. They were getting away from him.

"Hell with it," Marla said. "I'm sorry!"

Her hand rushed from the bag and jammed a fistful of drenched herbs and leaves into Scarlet's face.

Scarlet paused to shake her head, as if someone had thrown pepper at her nose. Bits of leaf clung briefly to her bloody cheeks and then slid off in the rain. Her lips stretched into a grin, and then she grabbed at Marla.

Rex rushed close, machete raised. The vampire and his mother were grappling, and he couldn't get a clean strike, wasn't sure he wanted to feel the quake of his blade cleaving into flesh. But he couldn't watch Marla crumple under a vampire bite either. He had to be Blade, be Van Helsing, be some kind of hero if he could.

Heat poured from Scarlet's skin as the world slowed. The rain fell in cautious plump drops, uncertain they wanted to touch this moment.

Something cracked ahead, and Rex at first mistook it for thunder somehow drifting down to the sand before realizing bones had broken and shifted down Scarlet's spine. Across her shoulders. Down her legs.

She was stretching, growing taller, her form climbing beyond Rex's head, past Marla's.

Her face lengthened with her torso, the jaw reaching into the beginnings of a snout. Each hand splayed at her sides, where knives jutted from cracking fingernails. Wild golden light burned behind Scarlet's eyes, and a thunderous moan tore up her throat as her lengthening grin bared a mouth full of sharkish teeth.

This was a glamour. She was pretending to be a monster, Rex had to believe that, couldn't accept this transformation as real.

Or worse, Scarlet had pretended to be alive and human, fooling Rex and Marla here on the beach. Now the pretending was done, and the nightmare beneath could haunt real life, dredged from the darkness by the storm itself.

Rex couldn't watch her finish changing. Couldn't watch the nightmare come true.

He raised his machete and swung its blade into Scarlet's neck.

A miserable hiss shot up her throat, and she yowled in fresh agony. Rex thought he'd heard this noise from a cat once, struck by a car back in Boston, and he didn't want to think about that. He tore the machete loose and hacked again. Claws slashed at his jacket, and the pained yowling came louder, and he hacked again and again until blood spattered his face, and a lump fell to the sand.

The noise finally stopped. He didn't realize he'd been screaming through gritted teeth until Marla grabbed him and hugged him to her chest.

"It's okay, guy," she said, hushing him. "It's over now. It's done."

He trembled in her arms. The rain had soaked into his skin, and so had the blood, but also something else both unnamable and much harder to wipe away, deep in his bones and soul. Had Scarlet not been so focused on Marla, she could have smashed Rex into the beach. Crushed him, murdered him. It would be his body lying bloody in the sand instead of the vampire's corpse and her last victim.

"Why's she still lying there?" Rex pried his face from Marla and kicked at Scarlet's shoulder. "She should be ash. Vampires turn to ash and dirt when they die."

"Sweetie." Marla's words came slow and gentle, as if afraid to startle a small animal. "I think that's the movies again."

"For fucking real?" Rex snapped. He kicked again and stormed away from the body. "Christ, you can't count on anything in this goddamn town anymore. Jesus!"

"Rex. Rex!" Marla chased after him, grabbed the machete, and then wiped the blade on the inside of the canvas bag. "We can't get caught, you hear me, young man?"

The rain began to ebb, and Rex forced himself to face it. He ran his hands down his drenched hair, his cheeks, his chest. Something moved in the lightning's next flicker. He crossed his fingers against another vampire, but there was only a tawny cat watching from the dying beach fire's edge. Its eyes glistened, and then it sank again into shadow.

It almost seemed an omen.

"Trying to figure if there are different ways into vampirism," Rex said. "Why Cabrina's one way and this thing's another. And that Honey? Maybe she's something else entirely?"

Marla jammed the machete into the canvas bag. "None of it has to make sense if it doesn't want to."

Rex hated that she was right. All life branched and varied, and the world had tried to hide it here. Undeath could be the same. People had to have known about vampires in the past, but society had swept them into myths and legends and silly TV shows. Maybe out of malice. Maybe out of fear from something they couldn't understand and didn't want to truly remember.

"Don't know," Rex said.

"Don't know what?" Marla asked, standing beside him.

Rex turned to her, his eyes warm with tears. "Don't know how I can do this to Cab."

Marla held him again. "We're not going to start with her. Because it didn't start with her either, you know? We're going to find out what happened to Cabrina, and then we'll do anything we can to help her."

She moved to pick up the spilled T-shirt and anything else she'd dropped.

Rex looked past her, at the still-stormy sea. Unruly waves thrashed against the shore, barely visible but for the frail summerhouse porchlights. Stronger than wind came the sense that something terrible would soon wash onto Cape Morning's shore. Worse than a headless woman lying on the beach, or the broken-open body of the person she'd killed, or the storm now seeping inland.

And unlike any frail vampire feeding on the beach, Rex didn't think he'd have the choice to walk away from it. There would be nowhere to go.

I think the devils want to make a deal, and I don't want to make it. They've come often enough these last couple months that I get it. They aren't subtle.

<u>The Devil Dance</u>
Step One: I swallowed the sea's heart and it wasn't mine.
Step Two: The devils brought the dreams.
Step Three: I'm supposed to go to Ghost Cat Island.
Step Four: I'm supposed to go from there to the dream of Ghost Cat Island.
Step Five: Leave the heart.
Step Six: Go home.
Step Seven: Something follows.
Step Eight: It will teach me to shine.
Step Nine: I become the key.
Step Ten: I open the door.

But after the door is open, what then? What happens to the key?
Something big and mean. If I make the deal, maybe I can have everything I want. Cinnamon scent man, friends, freedom. All I have to do is consent.
But the devils want blood. I don't think that's who I am.

<u>Nighttime Theories</u>
I am sleepwalking ✓✓✓

Cops found me on the beach. They didn't need to cuff me, stuff me in their squad car, but they wanted to. They liked it. What a thrill to take Officer Brite's kid in. I asked Dad not to tell her, but he told. And she wanted to talk, so we talked.

She knew about what Xi and I did. I don't know how, maybe Xi told her mother and Ms. Munoz told mine. Or maybe this diary isn't secret enough.

But it's exactly like I worried. She thinks if I was with a girl, then I can't be one. If I kissed Xi, I can't be who I am. Forget about Rex's moms. Forget about anyone else. Nothing has to make sense in the world if she decides it.

Brite Makes Right.

I snapped at her—what does liking dick decide? Does it matter who it's attached to? Does that give me some kind of special treatment?

Brite Makes Right. Well, I'm a Brite too. From my lips to her ears, I told her all the true things and I made up a bunch of other shit too. Things about the cinnamon scent man. That he did the things I wished he'd have done but never did.

She was stammering, crocodile eyes, crocodile tears. My mother is a reptile and I STILL FEEL SORRY FOR HER. What is wrong with me? She's twisted up at the pain of ideas, concepts too big for her, making her burst, and

I wish it could be better. That's all I want.

But it won't happen. She's like the devils. She wants blood, and Brite Makes Right, and a needle made of clay has a better chance of getting through to her than anything I say. Contradiction doesn't matter so long as love loses.

She could've chosen to have my back. So could Dad. They could have helped me, even if it was hard for all of us. Names, medicine, love. It's about feeling like my body is a home instead of a cage.

I want what Xi and Rex have. That sense of the self and the only, and of parents who don't hate their child.

But what's the point of me if I'm not suffering? Happy girls don't write diaries like this, and no one wants to read their poetry. Blood makes for good reading. The world would want me for the sake of enjoying the suffering. Nothing else.

I can't be what the devils want.

And I can't be what she wants either.

But she won't let me go. So now we're here. I'm stuck, and the devils will come to the house at night with the deal they want to make.

I had to pretend I ran away, and then lie that I won't do it again. If I keep sleepwalking, she'll set up an alarm system, and then I can't sneak out to see Xi and Rex. I barely get to do that as it is.

~~I wish for one day I could stuff her in too-tight skin so everything feels wrong for her~~

That isn't true. I think I wish that—I wish I could wish that—but really I don't want anyone to feel the way she's made me feel.

Not even her.

The devils have answers. They pour like ghosts inside the house, leaving the dreams, telling me where to go.

First, our little Ghost Cat Island. Then the grand Ghost Cat Island in the other place.

If I let them change me, then what will I be? I can come in and out through a keyhole, but they need a key to open their grand door.

They need an invitation.

Step Eleven: Invite the devils to dinner.

At least it's different than the empty promise I've had hammered into me a million times.

It gets better, it gets better.

But what is IT?

And what is BETTER?

And when, when, when?

Eventually, you get sick of disappointment.

What good is being alive when every moment feels like death? At least the devils offer blood and teeth. Tactile sensations, the real carnal stuff. I could give up and be a devil like them. She couldn't cage me anymore. She would feel bad for once, and I couldn't be a disappointment anymore. If I'd just let the devils win.

But then I couldn't be all the things I want to be, or all the things I am. There's so much I want to do. I want to kiss Xi again. And Rex. And the cinnamon scent man. I want to wander, not be stuck in this evil little town.

Give me the world. Let me see everything that isn't Dad, or her, or this house. I'm not a girl for blood and teeth. I feel like I'm supposed to love.

But I'm not allowed to do that, and doing nothing is killing me.

32. A DANCE WITH DEVILS

Cover to cover, the diary was a horror story. Over a dozen entries left a chunk of blank pages for a life unwritten, and past the last entry, Ivory found a half-torn page. She could have slid the death poem from her purse and taped it into place, but she didn't think it would fit perfectly.

There had apparently been two poems for two possible futures. Cabrina had written versions of them in her final entry, and then she must have written copies, torn them out, and planted them on the beach. Ivory had found the death poem. The other was a life poem. Either the tide had taken its scrap of paper, or the erasure of its future had torn it out of existence. All that remained of the life poem was the version in the diary, sharing a page with a copy of the death poem.

And she'd signed them both *Cabrina Aphrodite Brite*.

Damn that Viola.

Ivory was home again, but she should drive back to Cabrina's house, stand between Viola and Xi, and force Viola to read the diary. She'd finally see—

Nothing. She would see nothing, because she would grab the contradictory pages and snip them to shreds with the same scissors she'd dug between Ivory's legs. Or she'd burn the pages in the oven, and maybe throw Ivory in for good measure. A resurrection of the trick campfire, and no personal sense of justice would change that.

Ivory thought of sending the diary to a newspaper, but to which one? And how? She could plaster the pages online, but she had no reach, and what good would it do? Viola had apparently found an online diary predating this one, and she could easily call the book a forgery, cooked up by a political rival to smear her campaign with some family-hating agenda to posthumously convince her she had a daughter.

Which was all Cabrina had wanted. She'd been hell-bent on it before the end. This was not a girl who'd wanted to die, or else why write the life poem at all? She'd been like Ivory, another creature of life. They were the same.

Except Ivory was alive, and Cabrina was dead.

Ivory hugged the diary to her chest and sank into the couch. "I'm sorry, Cabrina."

The tide splashed against smooth stone and soggy carpet, and Ivory turned to the hole in the wall. Cape Shadow glowed with moonlight. It was always night on that side of the worlds, no sign that it even had a sun, and yet the moon there somehow glowed. Maybe it stole sunlight from Cape Morning. Or maybe it was too dreamlike a place to make sense for Ivory.

She preferred its impossibility to the house's reality. Bloodstains mapped the walls and carpet where bodies once lay. Honey's brood had made slow work of feeding, leaving only gristle-coated bone before they went out into the town to feed themselves anew. Every bird had to leave the nest sometime. Honey had been dragging the used-up bodies through the hole in the wall to Cape Shadow, as if oceanic disposal alone could clean the house, but she was an eater of bones.

Only feelings were left to rot here, the small meats of regret and injustice.

Ivory looked to the diary again. Had Xi read from beginning to end before she fell unconscious on Cabrina's bed? The toll might have winded her. All those feelings, observations, deductions. She might have been the brains of their outfit, and Rex the courage, but Cabrina was the heart, and she had been dying of sadness and desire, and a sense of unlove.

And in her despair, she had swallowed a heart from the sea. It hadn't been the same for Ivory, who had been fed by Honey in her Chasm Cat protrusion, and Cabrina had never carried that heart to Cape Shadow or guided a beast back to Cape Morning. Instead, she'd let the nightmares eat at her life. Viola's house had smothered that poor girl, and the people who should have cared for and listened to her had instead isolated her. She'd drowned off the coast of Cape Morning when she tried to give back the heart.

Maybe she'd been too delicate to become Honey's key.

"I'm sorry," Ivory said again, gazing at the diary's green cover. "I didn't know as early as you, but I knew something was off about me. A feeling. There've been others who thought they were aliens abandoned by UFOs, or imaginary friends come to life. We're all princesses stuck with evil stepparents, waiting for the real deal to make it right. Except sometimes the real deal is terrible. The world knows how to ruin us, and sometimes it's shaped like your mother. I'm so sorry, Cabrina."

Ivory read the life poem one last time and then set the diary down. It couldn't help anyone anymore. Viola must've caught Xi, and she'd certainly proven Ivory useless, and who could say what hell might come next?

Of course everything had gone wrong. Ivory had set her own course, intending to do right by a trans girl of all people. She'd practically gone looking for trouble, and consequence came baked into that deviation, layer by layer. Was that why no one had helped her when she was a teen? There had to be some unspoken rule which decided that any person who dared do a trans girl a good turn, in life or in death, would be damned.

To the world, Ivory deserved this and worse. Was that justice?

"This goddamn world," she whispered, rubbing the maroon patch on her jeans.

A familiar numbness settled inside her, soothing the stinging pain in her thigh. It was almost automatic. She could be too nice to bother everyone with her feelings. Too pretty to ruin this face with tears. Nice enough and pretty enough so no one would hurt her.

If she let this thick glob of sound climb her throat into a sob—what the hell kind of noise would that be? Not a pretty noise. Ugly, croaking, toadlike. She would disappoint everyone. Her world demanded a picturesque statue of clean misery. Could she give it that much?

She tugged open the cut in her jeans, stretching clotted blood between her scissor wound and the denim, and gazed across her leg, where her tattoo seemed to deepen against ever-paling skin.

I am a creature of life.

She should have been a creature of rage.

One hand clawed at her tattoo as the other covered her face and dug brutal nails across her scalp. These fingernails had worn blood. She could dress them in it again. A broken heart should cut throats and gouge out its unbroken kin.

Eyes lingered on Ivory, and she let her hand drop. Back to niceness and prettiness. Cleanliness and godliness. She glanced up, expecting one of the feeders to have come home.

But there stood Honey.

Her gold-and-black hair trembled in Cape Shadow's breeze, and her gleaming eyes awaited some future Ivory could neither see nor feel. Was it her responsibility to bring it? Cabrina's diary suggested another road had reached out to her, offering an alternative to death.

What would Ivory do when that same road opened to her? Cabrina had met so-called devils. Ivory had met the real thing. She could refuse them.

But why should she?

Wolf thought he was choosing to be better when he rejected Honey, and now he was dead. Couldn't Ivory choose to be worse? If she was to exist as one damned, then she should be damned in glory.

"Why should anyone else have it easy?" Ivory asked. "When do we get a turn to be strong?"

Rage slid hot down Ivory's spine. She sprang off the couch, head aflare, feet burning, every part of her shaking and eager for— what? She needed to run, thrash, break herself apart. If only Honey's claw would scratch fresh commands in Ivory's mind, but there was nothing intruding on her thoughts now.

Except her own words. *There's something else I can become. Bigger than a kept heart. Something with a purpose.*

There was a decision to be made. Become that something else, take up that purpose, or don't. Simple as that, right? Ivory only needed to give her consent.

Honey approached one side of the hole to Cape Shadow and ran her fingers down the aging stereo set. Ivory was about to protest that Stella wouldn't want Honey playing with it, but Stella was dead, her flesh eaten by her sister, the bones devoured by Ivory's lover.

So why not let Honey mess with the stereo? She liked the music, thrumming onto Cape Shadow's waves.

The amplifiers crackled and hissed, and then a song seeped into the living room. Its melody ran tinny and strange. A deep-throated horn played in the distance, slowly joined by other brass, their notes warped by travel across a great sea. There was an ambience to it, and Ivory struggled to recognize the instruments, as if Honey had spun the radio dial to another time, maybe back to whenever her beast-kin first roamed the land. Everything in Cape Morning seemed to echo the past. Maybe Cape Shadow was the same.

The music had a rhythm, though. Honey stepped to it as she neared the couch and took Ivory's hands.

Ivory guffawed. "Are you trying to cheer me up?"

The rhythm rippled and moaned as the horns grew louder, and the wind played games with their notes in a grand ululation.

"Dancing," Ivory said, looking up at Honey. "Do you dance in Cape Shadow?"

Honey slipped close and placed her hands on Ivory's sides. Ivory let her eyes close against the world, invited the smooth rhythm to guide her hips, slide her arms, press her head from side to side. Honey wanted to take Ivory and keep her.

"Alright," she said. "I'll dance with you, devil."

Honey flashed a lovely grin. Ivory had always liked the look of a smile that showed gums along with teeth. She couldn't say why. Something about the rich and carefree fullness of such a smile made her heart tremble in delight. Honey's teeth gleamed, and Ivory wanted to slide her tongue across them.

She swayed closer to Honey, one cautious step at a time. Honey swayed too, less Ivory's mirror than her shadow, distorting every movement to something weightless and agile across the carpet. She brushed her arm, breasts, and hip against Ivory's side.

Sinking into these charms came easier than thinking of the diary of pain or the house where Ivory had stolen it. She reached one hand to Honey's hip, the other to Honey's long neck. Her skin was fiery, as if she had stepped indoors from sunbathing on a bright summer day. Ivory could almost taste the heat as she nestled her cheek to Honey's neck, nuzzling against her slender ear and shaggy hair.

"How long until you stop pretending to be human?" Ivory asked. "And will you still haunt me? My devil who makes me do terrible things."

A wild laugh shrieked out between Honey's teeth. Ivory realized her words sounded almost accusatory, and she shook her head to take it back. Honey had guided, but Ivory made choices. Deep down, she had wanted to do everything she'd done.

And she could do worse. Every heartbeat across Cape Morning sang to her, tempting as chocolate, sweet as honey. The night wind was here, and the spirit of the tide. A beast's firm hands grasped Ivory's hips, the two of them dancers, wanderers, and world-crossers.

When Ivory leaned back, a sandpaper tongue caressed her throat. She returned the touch, stroking lips and tongue across Honey's neck.

"I'll never understand you all the way, will I?" Ivory asked. She shut her eyes and sank into an embracing darkness. "This isn't your full shape, your full *you*. You've been waiting for me to figure it out. I think I have."

That coarse tongue laid harsh strokes across the back of her neck, and Honey's teeth scraped the skin.

"You're not magic, are you?" Ivory asked. "You're not going to help me be anything they want." She leaned back from Honey's mouth and stared into those wide black eyes with their slim golden rings. "You're a revenge in flesh and blood. I mean, you're more than that, too. But that's why you're here. Revenge for the nice ones, the good ones. Girls like Cabrina, who couldn't become keys or spill blood."

Honey smirked with open lips, a laugh caught in her grin. Like she wanted to play.

"I never did anything to anyone, you know?" Ivory ran gentle fingers through Honey's hair. "But they acted like I did. Like they wanted revenge for seeing me, being around me. The offense of my existence. Worst thing I ever did was try to help a dead girl. And she never did anything either. Maybe that was the trouble. If they're going to *act* like we wronged them, then maybe we should give it a try."

Honey chinned at Ivory, urging her on.

Ivory could let go if she wanted. Let this gold-dark star fade from Cape Morning. The dead would stay dead, and the victors would rip more victories from the world. Viola would never face consequences for what she'd done. She would squeeze out pity and use it to fuel the bright visage of her political career, propped up on the headstone of a daughter she'd spurned.

Every time Ivory's heart pounded, it would drum a song of regret.

"I can't let it go," Ivory whispered, burying her face against Honey's chest. Faint fuzz brushed her cheeks. "It's an inked tattoo. And a burn scar."

Honey nuzzled the top of Ivory's head. Her heart offered steady thunder, and the stereo billowed with horns. Their tune curled a beckoning finger at Ivory, same as the ocean waves.

Come, they whispered. *And see.*

"Viola needs a world of people like her," Ivory said. "But I can't be that person."

Honey purred encouragement. Her tremor spread into Ivory's bones and blurred the sounds of the amplifiers.

"And I don't want to be a creature like me anymore, either."

The music hung in the living room air with humid stillness, and the waves of Cape Shadow went silent as if the ocean were tensing with anticipation.

"Make me—" Ivory stared into Honey's eyes, deep as the sea and just as needful. "Make me a devil, too. Make me your key."

Honey took Ivory's chin in two fingers and licked Ivory's lips. She then slipped back, still clutching Ivory, and aimed for the moonlit hole in the wall.

Ivory opened her mouth to ask a question, but Honey tugged harder. The music swelled around them, embraced them, and drew them tight toward the dark stone and sloshing waves. Cool air pricked Ivory's skin with goosebumps. She kept her lips pursed, and she let her world become the growing horns and strange sea.

And Honey's grasp, too. That mattered more than anything.

She led Ivory across the line where the living room carpet lay damp against Cape Shadow's flat stones. Ivory slowed at the edge and took a steadying breath. Then she crossed at Honey's heels, sinking into the cool air. She had a feeling she would never return to this house, and she didn't mind it.

Behind her, she now saw the entirety of the path Honey had carved between worlds. The opening from Cape Morning was a strange cave set in black stone, Ivory had seen that before. Only now did she notice it was part of a much greater landmass climbing in mounds of dark earth and tremendous slabs of rock. She should have taken in its enormity before, but her head had been foggy, and Honey hadn't guided her to look around and better understand where the path from the living room truly led.

A mountain stretched up from the sea, reaching for the stars in the enormous skull of a great stone beast. Green growth dotted the black rock, and foam splashed at the edges.

Around the cavern climbed stone steps gleaming with pale moonlight. Ivory had seen similar steps rising from jagged toothlike rock when she first came to Cape Shadow and entered the glowing tide pool. She knew this gaping maw and its hollow geography. Not the scrap of nothing she'd seen off the coast of Cape Morning ever since she moved there.

Honey had returned her to the mammoth truth of Ghost Cat Island.

33. THE KEY

Shadows filled the mouth of a dripping cavern. Everything Ivory touched was fog. Nothing felt solid—not even herself—until Honey's silhouette bled from the blackness and into the growing moonlight.

Ivory recognized this place. A gap in the ceiling let the stars peer inside, where arches above the doorways formed fangs or eyes. Ivory had called for Cabrina here, expecting to find a ghost. She'd chosen a laughing doorway and found Honey instead. Each opening exhaled scents of animal musk and salt.

"Back at the start," Ivory said. She squeezed Honey's hand. "But it's different this time. I know Cabrina isn't here."

Honey led her toward the chamber's center, where one more opening stared like a black eye in the stone floor. Their pensive feet braced its edges as if awaiting invitation, but Honey chinned toward the hollow and then slid one leg into the subterranean darkness. A flat step braced her below, followed by another, and another, leading down from the cavern of beasts to some unknown place beneath Ghost Cat Island.

Unknown to Ivory, at least. Honey knew. She tugged Ivory's hand and grinned up at her. Waves beat within the earth. *Come. And see.*

But Ivory wasn't certain anymore that it was the ocean she heard speaking. Something else lingered below, and it knew the water and its desires well, could echo and whisper like it. The whisper had always been a beast deep down.

"I'll have to come and see," Ivory said, forcing a laugh. The choice was hers. Always hers.

Honey tugged again, and Ivory followed.

Impossible moonlight curved through the opening as if to guide the way, revealing the once-black chasm to Ivory. Flat stone steps lined the walls in a broad descending spiral. They ended in a round sloshing pool below, the island caught in the sea's rhythm.

And across every surface above the water, bodies plastered the chasm.

The milky light caressed their skin with radiant fingers, painting a collage of varied flesh tones that writhed and slept and breathed a dream of understanding into Ivory's thoughts. Their surety struck as unflinching as any dark vision from Honey's teeth.

There were never any ghost cats on Ghost Cat Island. Only protrusions from the other side, be they feline or a scrap of rock. Whatever the visitors or locals of Cape Morning thought they had seen over the years, the truth had always been these sleepers beneath the island, casting visions through a hole in the worlds.

Come, they inhaled. *And see*, they exhaled.

And Ivory saw.

Spirits roamed beastlike across an ancient Earth. They were animals, and they were people, and they were so much more across the spectrum between. In the night they devoured mankind, and in the day they crept into subterranean chambers, beneath water, anywhere to escape the sunshine that weakened them enough for prey to overtake them.

But light found its way into the nighttime too. It blinked from flint and tinder, from wood and oil. The sun had chosen the prey, and the blood-sweet beasts found their moon and stars polluted with fire and lightning.

When the world had no more room for them, they clawed themselves a corner outside of it, where they sank into a shadow of forever night. Here they shattered into pieces, growing fearsome as they fed on darkness. Before, they had only been blood-drinkers and flesh-eaters in the shape of beasts. Now they grew ripe on their moon and stars, their wind and sea, waiting for the true world to turn to poison.

But their light-polluted home saw them as strangers. Hungry as they became, they could not go back.

Not without an invitation. A key to let them in the door.

A beastlike shard had gone looking along the water, the beach, for someone to open the way. Like Cabrina, who had dreamed of devils. There were others before, failures all.

Until Ivory.

She could almost see the last before her—the too-thin figure of Cabrina Brite, there and gone on the gloomy steps. Reluctance made her hands shake, the way Ivory had felt when she first visited Cape Shadow and the soul of Ghost Cat Island.

But the vision of Cabrina fled from Ivory's sight, the way she must have fled from this road. Ivory could see that fate too—poor Cabrina, flitting back into the world, panicking on the waves, and drowning off Cape Morning. Her splashing and fighting for breath stabbed a deathly percussion through Ivory's thoughts.

Even when the impossible had extended a hand, the world was cruel to Cabrina.

But Ivory was different. She had seized Cabrina's memory, her death, and kept herself strong despite every trial and tribulation. She'd led Honey home, and she'd shown Ivory what the world could be.

Not the same, a whisper sang inside her. *Ivory, changed. Ivory, right. Ivory, ours.*

Ivory felt her heart race as she descended the throat of bodies. She had mistakenly believed Honey only fed on blood, but Honey drained other things, too. Ivory couldn't put her finger on exactly what they were, but unlike blood, she had a feeling they were things you couldn't grow back.

To choose this road was to walk it until the end of time. Any attempt to turn around and become who she used to be would only reveal someone had changed the locks on her soul.

She could become Honey's key, or remain her own. Not both.

The chasm filled with a dry cacophony as sleeping flesh rubbed against stone. Bodies jerked from their matted resting places and began a slinking descent toward the dim water below, eyes shut, faces serene, their reverie unbroken as they pooled beneath Ivory and Honey.

"Are they still sleeping?" Ivory asked. "Do they know what they're doing?"

Honey's palm flattened against Ivory's lips, and she cupped her free hand to Ivory's throat. Ivory melted into Honey's grasp as the fleshy tide lapped around them, and they fell from the steps into the encircling throng, the bodies forming a warm spiderweb below. Honey held on, and Ivory didn't resist.

The sleepers buoyed them deeper into the chasm on a bed of tender limbs. They clambered toward sloshing water on a dreamlike cloud, and the moonlight shrank to a glistening white eye above. Their touch was strange yet pleasant; not greedy like Scarlet or apathetic like Wolf, but it wasn't Honey's overpowering intensity either.

Even Honey seemed to soften. Her now-gentle fingers stroked Ivory's hair, and her careful teeth teased at Ivory's neck.

Ivory had never known such sympathetic hands, with their empathetic dreams. A communal slumber of the blessed damned could only thrive outside the solid world she knew, its contradiction alive in Cape Shadow. Here, they invited her as friend, lover, sister, priestess. Starved for blood but swollen with belief.

She could offer hallowed revelation. A creature of life, of lives.

Their lives. This dream might find new purchase in the world beyond, and from a merging of Cape Morning and Cape Shadow, they might breed a waking sunless paradise.

The sleepers thrummed as one. Below, beside, everywhere, they formed a nest for lovers. Limbs of a greater hunger, facets to an unseen beautiful enigma. The many who were one.

Honey crushed down against Ivory, and Ivory spread her legs around that burning torso. Music again filled her ears, the horns now throat-like, the wind moaning down the island's every channel and into its depths, infected by Cape Shadow.

The tangle of bodies rippled against Ivory's spine. She pawed at Honey's chest, her legs, but someone pressed Ivory's arm away, and then a clamor of hands dug and tore into her clothing. Fingers hooked her waistline; others drove nails into her thigh. They tore her jeans, and then Honey ripped Ivory's underwear down off her waist in one slick motion.

Ragged shadows flashed past the moonlight. A black mass blocked Ivory's sight as Honey's mouth found the crevice between Ivory's breasts, snagged cloth between unrelenting teeth, and savaged the remains of Ivory's bra in a harsh twist.

That rough tongue again stroked her throat and then sank down, down, lapping molten saliva around one nipple, across Ivory's belly, and then along her inner thigh. Its tip found her tender cock and teased the head, exploring and tasting and wanting. A firm hand cupped one breast in the dark, as gentle as the tongue was coarse, and other hands pressed at Ivory's hip, jaw, lips.

Which touches were Honey? Which were the sleepers? Ivory couldn't tell, couldn't care.

Teeth scraped her inner thigh. She hadn't realized that place was sensitive anymore until this moment, but lightning shot down her leg, and she pressed her foot against Honey's calf. Were they still underground? The sea might have taken them now for all Ivory knew.

Hard fire climbed Ivory's thighs, the tip of her cock pressing deeper into Honey's tongue. Teeth nudged the round flesh, all tender organs held beneath a predator's breath.

Honey paused from licking. Ivory could hardly see in the dark, but she felt eyes watching below her waist. The sleepers expected nothing, but Honey waited on one more exchange, a swallowing.

This was the making of a key. Honey's bite would cut Ivory into the key's teeth, and she had to sacrifice pieces to become that shape. Honey was asking permission again, one last choice for Ivory, waiting on her invitation. No coming back. This bite would herald a forever change.

"Do it, take it, all of me," Ivory said in a short-breathed whisper. "I like to be bitten."

A deep hum sang up Honey's throat. Her jaws widened to cavernous depths before she wrapped her lips and tongue around Ivory's cock and testicles, taking the whole of this flesh into her mouth.

And then her sharp teeth sank tearing through Ivory's groin.

Ivory's scream clawed up the dark chasm as slow pain crushed between her thighs.

Honey dug her teeth in harder, catching skin, muscle, veins. Her rough tongue carved through the bloody crevice forming where she slowly tore away Ivory's genitals.

Ivory sucked at harsh air, screamed hard enough to hurt, gasped in pain, screamed yet again, hoping somewhere between one breath and the next that the ripping would end, that she might black out and let agony's memory vanish, that she could die and end it. Her nerves burned down her hips, confused at one moment's near orgasm and the next moment's glass-sharp agony.

Sweetness and pain danced together as the stretching sinew ripped free from its foundation in a surging heaven-hell ejaculation of blood.

I'm going to die, Ivory tried to say, but another shriek belted out.

Honey's swallow rumbled down the length of her, and the surrounding bodies quaked as if the chasm had swallowed part of Ivory, too. Then, Honey plowed her head again between Ivory's legs. Her coarse tongue swept like a soft dream between her brutal teeth, and she lapped furiously at the blood-caked mess she'd made of Ivory's body. Flesh seemed to curl and twist beneath her damp touch.

Heat surged through Ivory's blood. It pricked her fingers and toes, wormed through her limbs, head, and chest. Her shifting groin became a wellspring of nerve-wracked fire. There was a boiling ocean here. There was nightmare.

Ivory tried craning her head to see the wound, but Honey's jaws covered her lap. A new tremor chased up Ivory's spine. How could she feel anything between her legs anymore? She didn't know, but Honey's lips and tongue turned now to the labor of altered flesh, and her jaw worked up and down with feverish determination. Ivory's toes curled against Honey's lower legs, the bed of limbs and torsos, the air, everything, her body spreading under Honey's and ready to burst.

A fresh merry scream trembled from Ivory's mouth, the sound rising and crashing in frothy, delighted waves. It was new pleasure, born of dream-flesh and the supreme agony of transformation.

She had forgotten Ghost Cat Island was a shaping place.

Honey crawled over Ivory's waist in a blanket of hairy heat. Her weight eased onto and then past Ivory's heaving chest. Ivory licked her lips, about to ask a question, but she hadn't figured out the words when a soppy cavern settled over her face. Light flared from the hole in the ceiling, and Ivory glimpsed distant gleaming eyes, and spotted thighs, and the space between them, where a patch of golden hair curled into *come hither* fingers.

Somewhere between Ivory's and Honey's panting, a rush of ocean wind howled through the sleepers' conjoined breath, as rhythmic as the tide.

Come, they whispered. *Your turn to drink. Birth your vengeance.*

The words might have been wind and waves, or they might have been spoken by the surrounding sleepers, murmured from their dreams. Ivory could only be certain she wanted to taste Honey in every deep way. She'd been longing for it since Honey first spilled blood into Scarlet's mouth.

My turn, Ivory thought hungrily. *My Honey, my love.*

Golden hair caressed Ivory's cheeks as she kissed deeply into Honey's groin, where her tongue coated an erect hill of tender nerves. A damp musky scent clouded the air before Ivory's breath slid away.

She couldn't be sure it ever returned. She only tasted of Honey, and smelled of her, and felt her soft folds and firm hips and the great swelling edges of her before quaking thighs let their dam burst. A burning ocean swept down Ivory's face, tongue, and throat as Honey erupted head to toe with an abyss-deep moan.

Radiance flared above as if called by Honey's delighted howling. The collage of bodies writhed against Ivory's spine again, and her gaze traveled the dark shape above her. A sigh chased Honey's orgasmic shriek, and when she tossed her head back, a new shape crossed the moonlight.

The black silhouette of an open snout now stretched from her head. Sharp teeth shone clear against the white brilliance, their points dripping raw fluid.

Laughter roared across the chasm as a familiar claw scraped Ivory's thoughts. *Ivory, lick. Ivory, kiss. Ivory, change.*

Twisted dream-flesh pulsed between her legs, and Honey cackled in the shadows between light and dark. Ivory glanced down her body, where her skin glowed with moonlight. A patch of sea-slick stone curled thick and oceanic between her legs, torn beyond flesh. Exactly as the sleepers needed.

A vessel of Cape Shadow. An invitation. A key.

"Yes, I'm ready." Ivory leaned her head back into a nest of

hands and stared into the eye of the gleaming moon. "Finish it."

The sleepers curled close to Ivory, and then they drove their fingers into her.

Layers of skin curled beneath fingernails. Grasping hands tugged at Ivory's shoulder blades, across her hips. Her flesh came to life as they opened it, and licked it like the ocean smoothing out stones. Her skin held too tight now, and the pain was necessary to undo this fleshy deception, breaking doorways for the caged spirit. A canyon opened down her ribcage and exhaled the depths of the sea across her waist, into waiting mouths.

Becoming them, becoming her, blood to blood. She was too late to be an anchor for Cabrina Brite, but Ivory could be a key for the sleepers beneath Ghost Cat Island.

Except they were done sleeping.

Their fingers slipped away, and Ivory looked again to her lover. Honey's shadow maw glistened in the milky light, and her silhouette's toothy snout spread to gorge on the island, the stars, everything. Her tongue teased at Ivory's changed flesh.

Sea-beaten greenstone and black ocean depths swelled from the gaps dug into Ivory's body, where her shadowy spirit reached up the chasm and toward the sky. This island could no longer contain the truth of her. Soon the flimsy half-world of Cape Shadow would fail her too. It had never been the sleepers' true home.

Claws of night sky reached for a firmer precipice, chased by another quake of Honey's monstrous laughter. Ivory's small form slid from the nest of arms, and her massive spirit surged up the throat of bodies and shattered the stony cage of Ghost Cat Island.

The mountain cracked open. The worlds remembered each other. It was time.

The sleepers' eyes shot open, and they began to rise from the chasm on the roaring night wind. Naked forms twisted between human and beast, each a storm of teeth and hair and claws. There were more of them than Ivory and Honey had laid upon. More than Ivory had dreamed.

Their rising stream of bodies turned cloudlike as they billowed out of and over the island, cutting corpse-shapes against the stars. A quake rocked the constellations in a fit of celestial glee, as if the night itself might be having the time of its life. The sleepers spiraled laughing through the sky, their bodies encircling the eye of a flesh-made hurricane. They were a nightmare storm like the world beyond had not seen in forgotten eons.

Cabrina had it wrong. They weren't devils, Ivory realized. They were angels, forming a beautiful sky. She could listen to them laugh forever. Their music was the prelude to a new world bathed in old predators.

At last Ivory joined the bout of raucous laughter. Couldn't help it anymore; she had to laugh with the sleepers, with Honey, the sound contagious across shattered Ghost Cat Island. She'd wasted a lifetime on appeasement and tears when these shadows had been waiting to break it all down. And now their time had come.

To hell with being nice. And to hell with being pretty. There was only joy to be had, amid the beasts, and the blood, and the dream to blot out the sun. The days of mankind were done.

Now came the endless night of beasts.

34. THE NIGHT WIND

A damp lawn squished underfoot a few steps from where Xi crawled through Harper Lane's underbrush. Damp leaves clung to her hair and scraped her face, but she froze where she crouched between a thick bush and a maple tree's trunk. She couldn't risk being seen or heard. Likely the footsteps were only some Harper Lane homeowner looking for their cat or tossing an apple core to squirrels.

But they might have been Viola.

Safer to stay hidden in the underbrush than peek out and check. Xi didn't need hell on her heels again tonight.

The gentle break-in had gone smoothly to a point. Ivory had left the front door unlocked as planned and then kept Viola distracted in the kitchen. Xi had then crept inside. Careful through the living room, careful up the stairs. Once she'd found the diary in Cabrina's bedroom, taking it should have been an in-and-out affair. It hadn't taken her long to discover it tucked in a vent behind and under the bed.

But her curiosity had been restless. It demanded she see the first diary page, and once those words dug their hooks in, she had to at least skim the next page, and the next. Cabrina's thoughts had poured into Xi, more words than Cabrina herself had offered in the two months before she died. It was the closest the two of them had been since that one gentle night.

Xi hadn't meant to fall asleep tonight in Cabrina's room. Too dizzy with lack of food, or maybe vampiric turning if Rex's theory held weight. The diary was gone when she woke up. It must have fallen off the bed, and she was too busy shoving on her glasses and escaping Cabrina's house to think of grabbing it.

Viola likely had the diary now. She would read it herself, and then probably burn it.

Ivory had run like hell, and that was the only reason Xi had gotten away. Had Ivory meant to act as a distraction, or had she ditched her partner in crime? Xi couldn't read that moment clearly with the bedroom light glaring above and Viola waving around lengthy fabric shears like she meant to slice out a pair of intrusive tongues.

Better for Xi to dash out the window while she had the chance. Cabrina must have torn the hole in the screen, either before she died or after, and though its mesh had scraped at Xi's clothes and scratched her midriff, she'd made it through.

Moments ahead of Viola Brite.

Shouting for her husband, screaming for Ivory to come back, Viola had come tearing into Cabrina's bedroom with the scissors flailing, a demon in her throat, and her eyes had fallen to Xi. Rex had pissed that woman off in the past, but never like this. Ivory had a talent.

A tirade of obscenities chased Xi out the window, where she'd scuttled over the shingled awning and hang-dropped to the front lawn.

She'd escaped without scissor wounds. Viola must have known better than to stab a teenage girl, at least in an election year. Of course, she could've said Xi attacked first. She and Ivory were the intruders, and who would believe a nobody teenager versus an upper middle-class town councilmember and cop's wife who had buried her only child mere days ago?

Xi couldn't risk getting caught again. She landed on the lawn, bending her knees to absorb the impact. Running down the driveway and chasing Harper Lane to Main Street seemed an obvious route to being snatched up by Gary Brite. Xi had instead dodged to one side of the house and ducked into the neighborhood underbrush, where dense trees separated Harper Lane houses from having to see each other with a forested grid of hedges, ferns, and bushes. An easy place for Xi to disappear so long as she moved slowly and kept her mouth shut.

Not like she had anyone to speak with—she realized too late that she'd left her purse on Cabrina's bed in her frantic escape. No phone, no money, no way to call for a ride. She would have to crawl through the dark foliage, unseen and unheard, until she reached another street.

Now an hour or two had gone by. Viola had come tromping into the brush directly behind the Brites' place, but Xi had already moved on from there, and Viola wasn't the type to storm into her neighbors' yards. She'd sent her husband to go looking instead.

Golden headlights flared through the foliage, followed by blinking red and blue, casting every leaf and limb as black silhouettes glistening with fresh rainfall.

Xi ducked low and kept still. Gary had made this pass six times since Xi first disappeared into the trees, but he hadn't stepped out to search for her on foot. He might have been patrolling Harper Lane solely to pacify Viola's rage. Or to avoid her.

Was she still fondling Cabrina's fabric shears somewhere, or was she rifling through Xi's purse? Or maybe she, like Xi, had cracked open the diary, its secrets irresistible after Cabrina's death.

Xi didn't want to know. She needed to put distance between herself and that house, and then her heart could finally quit racing.

The red-and-blue lights flickered down the street, pulling an uneasy exhalation through Xi's lips. She was used to holding still between movements now, but brief rainfall had soaked her clothes, and she was feeling faint again. Rex was right; she should have stayed somewhere safe tonight.

A bushy branch scraped her cheek as she crawled behind another house. Someone had left their first-floor window open, and they were humming loudly to themselves. Xi moved behind the next house and heard car tires and a truck's engine through the trees ahead.

If she kept to her steady journey, she might reach the brush-coated roadside of Main Street, maybe near Peyton's Ice Cream. There would come an end to this neighborhood. She could fade into Cape Morning, eventually reaching safe havens and home.

And then away entirely. She thought of the books in her room and the hauntings within them—*White is for Witching*'s Silver family house, the Earnshaw land of *Wuthering Heights*, Hill House. All those haunted places kept victims, but there were also survivors. People who chose to walk away. Xi could be like one, or she could be like the other.

Except a town was not a house. There were exit routes, but there was a greater ground to escape, and Cape Morning had the sea as its ally and lover, too. It did not have to let anyone go.

Red-and-blue lights swept by again, this time from beyond the nearby yard and house. There was almost zero chance that Gary would spot anyone hiding within the foliage from this distance, but Xi held still again anyway.

The lights didn't fade as they moved on this time—they winked out. Gary had shut them off, and through the neighborhood came the growl of his cruiser revving up. He was either going home or heading out. Either way, he would quit being Xi's problem, at least until he or Viola plucked the driver's license from Xi's purse. They would have her eventually.

But not tonight. She sighed through an open grin and pressed on toward the sounds of traffic and Main Street.

Where another mouth sighed through the undergrowth ahead.

Xi stalled in place, almost falling backward. Her breath caught in her throat, and she bit her tongue not to scream.

The figure crept closer and knocked a bush's branch, sending a damp leaf fluttering toward Xi's jacket. Streaks of light broke through the greenery, revealing a stained hoodie and sweatpants. Bare feet clutched at the patchy grass and soil.

Xi pressed a hand to her thudding chest. "Cabrina?"

Once-gray eyes flashed yellow against the nearby house's backyard light. A catlike hiss climbed Cabrina's throat, and she peeled her lips back from a row of sharp teeth.

She meant to feed again. What visions would pour into Xi's head this time? She had seen the island the other night, but she hadn't understood its gravity until the diary offered its own horrors of devils and bad dreams. Of a teenage girl trying to make things right and suffering for it.

Leaves slid against tree roots as Cabrina inched over the soil. She was a victim in all this, Xi reminded herself. It felt wrong to have ever been afraid of her.

And yet, Xi trembled as Cabrina neared.

"I'm sorry," Xi whispered. "For what happened. We should've been there."

Cabrina tilted her head to one side like a curious bird and then reached a hand for Xi's cheek. Her skin was ice, and her gaze winced with distant pain. She looked ready to say goodbye.

Xi touched Cabrina's cheek in return. "Something bad's coming, isn't it? And you knew that before any of us. It wanted your help, but you wouldn't give it. So what happened? You never wrote it down."

Cabrina leaned past Xi's outstretched arm, drawing their faces together. Her cold nose brushed Xi's, and then she pressed her lips into a soft kiss. Cabrina had been a jittery wire that first time, months ago, and worse when that kiss had led to other intimate touches.

Tonight she thrust against Xi with a bestial hunger. Xi was not surprised when those sharp feline teeth scraped at her lower lip and nipped at her tongue, or when Cabrina went drinking and kissing as blood trickled down Xi's chin. Xi tasted iron and hot saliva. She could almost believe Cabrina was warm again.

Like that night of their first kiss.

Off-gold wallpaper embraced them while Xi sat at the edge of her soft bed, Cabrina straddling her lap, the two of them caught in a tender, trembling kiss, and then harder, hungrier kisses, and then Cabrina sank to the floor, before shedding their clothes.

An eternity ago, when they seemed young and ridiculous. Maybe hopeful, too. Weren't they allowed to be hopeful back then, before funerals and undeath?

The warm vision snapped away as Cabrina broke from Xi's lips and slid back. Leafy fern limbs folded around her like a shutting green mouth. She was fading from Xi's touch and sight.

"Wait. Wait!" Xi charged after her on hands and knees, not caring which pieces of underbrush scratched her hands or her blood-dotted face. "Can't you talk to me?"

Cabrina slowed her retreat. "Haaah, haaah," she exhaled, almost a mocking, whispered laugh. "Haaah. Hurts."

Strange thunder boomed overhead, the sky answering with a genuine full-belly laugh. It sent a shivering jolt down Xi's spine. She looked up as if she could see the night sky through the tangled black tree limbs, and she almost missed Cabrina's continued retreat from the undergrowth, out in the direction Xi had been heading. She followed now, first on all fours, and then standing and jogging as the foliage thinned.

They reached the side of Main Street. Orange-gold lights glowed down the four-lane thoroughfare. Traffic ran gentle at this time of night, with most tourists having found whatever bars and restaurants they meant to hole up in until two in the morning, if they weren't off drinking and partying at summerhouses or the beach itself. Cape Morning businesses stayed open late in the summer. Peyton's Ice Cream glowed to the left, and beyond it, the

Cape Morning Police Department. To the right was Burger King, and the dark-windowed library, and distantly Xi made out the café Sunshine & Chill. Familiar places on the busiest street in town.

The sky hung dark and sounded alien. Another laughing thunderclap shot across Cape Morning, as if the town were a big joke.

"Cab?" Xi looked beside her. "Do you know what that sound—"

Her words cut away when she caught the change in Cabrina's expression. Solemnity and affection had sunken into the black pools of her pupils, and now she only offered an empty-eyed stare. As if she'd fallen under a hypnotist's trance.

Xi waved an open palm. "Cab, are you there?" She wiped a sleeve across her mouth and then planted both hands on Cabrina's shoulders. "Cabrina? You're scaring me."

The warning almost sounded funny after Cabrina had terrified Xi outside her bedroom and at the beach séance. She had shown brief consciousness in Rex's room, but now that animal-ghost from the funeral night had returned, as if her lucid moments of feeding were a brief reprieve toward living Cabrina. She stood hollowed out, almost like this was her true fate, more monster than woman.

More ghost than friend.

Xi crashed against Cabrina, folding her arms around her shoulders and chest to clutch her tight. "It's Xi," she whispered. "Cab, you know me. It's Xiomara, it's Alyssa. You remember, right? You have to, even if everything else disappears. I don't know what death does to someone, but you knew who I was a minute ago, you—you did this."

Xi pressed her lips to Cabrina's. They still tasted of blood, and maybe Xi had a particular flavor that could wake Cabrina like a favorite coffee blend, or a lover's tender touch.

But Cabrina did not kiss back. She only hissed in Xi's face. Her eyes remained empty.

"Please, Cab." Xi hugged her tighter. "Snap out of it."

Cabrina jerked beneath Xi's grasp, and Xi stumbled forward trying to keep hold of her. The tug was too strong, and Xi's limbs slid loose.

Main Street's lights shined brighter around Cabrina as she drifted toward the asphalt. Passing cars didn't seem to notice the pale figure sliding close.

Xi followed on clumsy steps. She wanted time to ask another question, make another demand. She wanted more than hissing and hunger. The sky laughed again, and she shouted for it to shut the fuck up. Its booming percussion sounded less like thunder this time, more a cruel sitcom audience pointing and snickering at Xi's desperation. A terrible wind raked through the foliage behind her in a rushing cry.

Cabrina's baggy clothes whipped up from her limbs and torso in the fresh gust. She stood straight for a lingering moment as the wind tore into her, and then she rose up on her toes.

And then her toes broke from the earth, and Cabrina slid inches into the air.

Xi wanted to laugh. She should have figured it out when Cabrina had come half-gliding, half-climbing outside her bedroom window. That night, too, had brought a miserable storm to Cape Morning.

Now it would take Cabrina. Pale and weightless as paper, her body climbed the wind.

Xi dashed for the roadside and grabbed Cabrina's forearms. "Hold onto me, Cab! Don't let it take you!"

She managed to pull Cabrina a few inches closer to the ground, and then another gust tore into them. Cabrina lifted; Xi did not. She squeezed hard as Cabrina drifted from the earth. As Xi's arms stretched out, she begged Cabrina to stop, not yet, to stay, please, but the only thing that would end was the touch between them.

"Cab!" Xi shouted. "How do I help you? How do I save you?"

Stormy air rippled between them like a fist of wind punching

Xi away. Her hands slid loose from Cabrina's forearms, and she went sprawling back into the soil and grass.

Cabrina broke away in a slow, steady ascent.

Xi sprang off the ground and leaped after her. She grabbed at Cabrina's wrist, her hand, anything.

Her fingers swept through empty air, inches out of Cabrina's reach. She fell empty-handed onto the side of the road, still peering up, still reaching out.

And then the night wind gusted Cabrina into the sky.

A scream tore up Xi's throat. "CABRINA!" She staggered to her feet.

Storm clouds hung low over Cape Morning, hiding whatever lurked above, laughing at the world.

"No, no," Xi whispered to herself in a whimpering chant. "No, no, Cabrina, no."

Hot tears rushed down her cheeks. She kept staring at the sky like the storm might break into teenaged raindrops, giving Cabrina back to Cape Morning where she belonged.

Xi swallowed against the hot sensation in the back of her throat and let anger pool inside her. Whatever had come to Cape Morning, it couldn't have Cabrina. It had been trying to get her, and it had failed, and damn it all if Xi was going to let it win even after Cabrina's death.

She was about to step onto the sidewalk and then the street. Chase the wind. Find Cabrina.

Headlights shined across pavement, and Xi thought of a prowling cop cruiser moments before an aged station wagon skidded to the roadside. It almost jumped the curb, its front tire screeching against the asphalt. The passenger door popped open.

Xi didn't hesitate—she saw Rex and collapsed into his arms.

"Cabrina," she whispered. "It took her."

After that summer with the cinnamon scent man, I asked Xi what she thought it would be like to live somewhere important.

What do you mean? she asked.

I rattled off names of important-sounding cities: New York, Chicago, Los Angeles. Watery places, too. The Great Lakes. Probably others I can't think of right now.

What would be different there? Xi asked. I started to tell her about the things I'd do, but she stopped me and clarified. *I don't mean like a dream. I mean if you were living in those places the way you are now. Same parents. Same you.*

I didn't have answers. It sounded evil for my life to follow me into the hypothetical.

But I understand now. They say it gets better, but it can get worse too, and when it does, you just want everything to stop. You want stillness. A day doesn't have to have highs and lows if it can just be pleasant and never end. I could see a day like that with Xi and Rex, all of us watching the sea, playing in it, drying beside it, splashing again. A day that's always at that perfect moment before evening, when the shadows stretch east, into the tide.

Dreamtime

Sitting on the beach in the bright sunshine, cooking my skin while the water laps at my feet and everything is easy

Sitting on the beach and there is a whole world out past that ocean

Sitting on a beach of bones and all of humanity is a picked-clean garden, swarmed by the eaters. They came for our hearts, and then they told us we could have back the world they'd ravaged while they waited for the garden to grow fruitful again

[a section is missing, cut away by fabric shears]

Waking up from that last dream didn't feel like the other times, with the devils in my room waiting for me to fuck up. This time, it was like I'd seen too much, and the sheets were holding me down. They didn't trust me not to throw them off and open my eyes. I had to fight against them. A snake's prey must feel like I did when it's caught in a throat. Do snakes eat their prey alive? Maybe not.

But the devils do. Each dream is nipping away a tiny part of me, and I'm not going to get any of it back.

I gritted my teeth and started calling for Xi. And then Rex. I knew they could save me if I could get them here. Or would I get them killed? Was I wrong to keep wishing I was closer to them? If they were part of me, wouldn't the devils eat them, too?

I woke up again. The sheets weren't fighting me anymore, maybe never had been. There aren't shadows looming over the bed.

But it feels like someone just ran out of the room. The air is displaced, somebody's tailwind, and the stairs are creaking again like someone's tiptoeing down, pretending they don't want to get caught. If I go out there right now, it might run again. Trying to get me to chase, maybe out of the house, maybe all the way to Ghost Cat Island.

Nighttime People
The runner

What does that last dream mean? Hungry devils in a garden? The greedy harvesting us?

One time, Rex said the ones who eat culture will sell manufactured culture to replace it, but he got quiet when Xi asked if that included his superheroes.

Is that the dream's meaning? Xi and Rex would tell me what they think if I could be brave enough to say it all. Or show them these pages.

It's useless. Genocide or warning, you can fish whatever symbols you like from a dream. Anything can mean anything if you twist it right.

Dreamtime
I imagine I am important

And I wake up believing it. For a whole second.

The dreams will never stop. Not until I do something.

I miss my Rex, my Xi. And I miss the world. I haven't gotten to see it yet, but I miss it.

Sometimes I'm not sure what real things feel like anymore. The dreams are realer than my bedposts, the drywall, every drink of water. Whatever's inside me is eating me.

I am the picked-clean garden.

I am the chest cavity.

Drink from my sea of blood.

Dine on my world of meat.

I want my friends' help, but I'm alone, and now there's a choice to make.

Pros of letting the devils have me
The dreams will stop
I can be important
The devils will be happy they have their key
She will be unhappy

<u>Cons of letting the devils have me</u>
The world might not be there to see
I might not be there to see it

I could let the ocean of ghosts take me a different way, into the cold depths. Make me a beach of a woman, not land, not sea, not alive or dead. Forever between states, like them. Driftwood souls. Shattered wrecks of forever hungry people.

Like I'm not already a wreck here.

Brite Makes Right.

The truths of who and what I am mean nothing because she will twist logic until she breaks its spine to keep me in a cage. I can't be what she wants.

But I can't be what the devils want either. Maybe I'm selfish, only wanting to preserve the world so I can see it. Maybe I'm selfish because if I become their key, I might stop being myself. Cabrina Aphrodite Brite—this name is me, means the world to me.

I've failed everything I'm supposed to do for the devils since I drank that heart out of the sea, and I can keep on failing them. They show me the way, but I never go to Ghost Cat Island, never cross from its real pebble to its mountainous dream.

<u>Dreamtime</u>
Blood shapes the key

But I don't want blood. I don't have it in me. ~~I can't even hate my m~~

I can't even hate her when she shatters me over and over.

No blood, no key. No key, no open door. No open door, no devils. I can't be the woman who carries them on her back and soul.

I'm going to make a different deal. Not with them.

With her.

The Future

Step One: Handle the devil problem another way (brainstorm later).

Step Two: Start anti-depressants again.

Step Three: Shut up about the nightmares.

Step Four: Get my GED.

Step Five: Don't talk back, be good, behave.

Step Six: Convince her to let me see my friends.

Step Seven: Convince her to take me to therapy.

Step Eight: Convince her to let me see a doctor about hormones.

Step Nine: Convince her that she loves me.

Step Ten: Convince her I'm her daughter.

PART FIVE: THE NIGHT OF BEASTS

35. THOSE WHO REMAIN

Xi rode in the back of Marla's station wagon for just half a block before Marla turned around and parked in the lot beside Peyton's Ice Cream. She then escorted Rex and Xi to the front, where umbrella-topped tables dotted the asphalt outside the shop's windows, offering patrons a place to eat their ice cream in the shade during the day. Those broad umbrellas had failed to protect the outdoor seating against the evening rain. Xi sat on one of the tables, her sneakers resting on a pulled-out chair, while Marla paced between the other tables with a phone to her ear, talking to Joan in a low voice.

"Yeah, they're both with me now." Marla paused. "No, not before, but I found one on the beach and the other on Main. Kids out here popping up from sidewalk cracks." She winked at Xi and then turned away. "Right, I know."

A tinny bell jingled above Rex as he pushed open a glass door and left the ice cream shop. Over a dozen people stared at him through the door and windows from the shop's salmon pink insides, but he didn't seem to notice. He clutched a clump of napkins and a band-aid.

"You wouldn't believe me, promise," Marla said, pacing closer again. "Yeah, but still."

Rex leaned over the table and began to wipe at Xi's chin. Two of the napkins were damp at the center and helped to clear the flakes of dried blood.

"Don't think I can slap the band-aid on your lip," Rex said. He was trying for humor.

Xi wasn't in the mood. Her voice came stilted. "It took her."

"So you said." Rex kept his focus on Xi's chin. "What did? Took who?"

"Cabrina," Xi said, gripping the open flaps of Rex's jacket. "The sky took her. Like she was nothing. Like that's how the world's always seen her, and now it's treating her that way too." Her hands slid to her lap, letting Rex's jacket dangle loose. "Why is there blood on you?"

"Not mine." Rex finished wiping the crusted blood from Xi's jaw and then pincered her chin between his thumb and forefinger to turn her head left and right. "What the hell have you been through?"

Xi sifted through possible explanations. Where to begin? She tried to speak and out came a rough cough. She covered her mouth with her arm.

Marla strolled from the table again, one hand now pressed to the side of her head. "Hang on two secs, love. I need to step away from the kids so I can hear."

"Not kids," Rex said, gesturing to the bloodstains on his jacket, as if that proved anything.

"Right, the young man and the young lady," Marla said.

She rounded the ice cream shop's corner, laughing at something Joan must have said from the phone.

Xi turned to Rex again. "How did you find me?"

"Couldn't get ahold of you," Rex said. "We were on the way to your house and saw you over here. Made a U-turn, doubled back."

"I lost my phone," Xi said. She looked to the road, hopeful she might spot a girl in a bloodstained hoodie, but there was no one. "Did you see Cabrina with me?"

"Was she there? Seriously, what happened?"

Xi took a shrill breath. Best to try starting from the start. "I went to Ivory's house like we talked about, but not to hide there. She was going to help me find Cab's diary. At Cab's house. It would've worked if Viola hadn't caught us. We got away, but she sent her husband after me. I had to crawl through the brush to keep out of sight."

"Sounds like cops, alright," Rex said. "They're so touch-starved, they choose a pat-down at airport security for fun." He leaned beside Xi's head, his mouth near her hair. "Didn't tell them anything, right?"

"The Brites?" Xi asked, incredulous. "About what? Ghosts? Vampires? What would I say?"

Rex snickered. "The world was like that when I got here?"

Xi wanted to laugh too, but tears slid down her cheeks. She couldn't swallow them this time, and she fell sobbing into Rex's shoulder, an ugly sound she couldn't stop. The sky grumbled, and Xi waited for it to laugh again. Rex offered a napkin for her to wipe her eyes and blow her nose. Her lip was bleeding again.

Rex clicked his tongue. "Told you to hide. Didn't I tell you?"

"I know," Xi said, clearing her throat and humming a note to even out her voice. "But I found Cab's diary."

Rex looked her over, searching for any sign of that thin green-and-pink tome.

"It's gone." Xi swept a hand over her lap as if scattering pages. "Viola got it."

"You saw her with it?" Rex asked.

"No, but it was gone, and she was there. Had to be her. Or Ivory. I don't know. But I had a chance to skim it first." Xi hung her head. "Cab thought a devil was coming to her while she slept, up to her room, trying to make a deal. Anything she wanted if she'd be its key. It didn't all make sense, maybe it would have if I'd had more time. But I don't think she gave in. Like she knew that, no matter the promises, this thing had its own agenda. She didn't want to hurt anyone. And now it's taken her."

Rex wiped Xi's lip again and wadded up the reddened napkins. "She did this to you?"

Xi shook her head. "It's not like that."

"Not like I'm saying, or not Cab?" Rex asked. "You saw another vampire too?"

"It was Cab, but not like you're thinking." Xi glanced again over Rex's jacket and its stains. "What do you mean, *too?*"

Rex lowered his voice to a whisper again. "We cut down a different one tonight. Someone I thought Cabrina had turned, but she said someone else. *Honey. She had us all.*"

"Honey," Xi echoed. Where else had she heard that word referring to someone today?

"Yeah, Honey. Don't know who that is, but I'm thinking we have meaner visitors than ever before." Rex had tired eyes. He might've aged a decade tonight. "This woman was eating someone in front of us, a dead body on the beach. And then her body started changing. Some kind of animal, or a monster. Didn't look any different from Cab at first, but after—I think the hunger drives them feral. Messes with their bodies, their minds."

"Cab isn't a monster," Xi said, more defensive than she liked. "Not yet. And she wouldn't have turned anybody but us."

"Like you have any clue," Rex snapped. "You don't know her better just because she kissed your princess wand."

Xi sat up straight, stunned. "You—did you read her diary too?"

"She told me. Wanted me to know before we—"A tremble worked through Rex's hands, and he dumped the wadded napkins onto the table beside Xi. "Didn't she tell you she was with both of us?"

"She did," Xi said. "But I thought it happened earlier than that, too. That you were her first."

"She made it sound like you were," Rex said. "Guess we'll never know." He looked away and touched his cheek, as if remembering a gentle kiss. "Wasn't about sex for her, not specifically. She wanted affection. Any touch, any kind word, needed it, whichever way, giving and receiving. Same for me, except I never starved for it."

They both went quiet. Xi kept her eyes on him, but he wouldn't look at her. He had more to say and seemed afraid to say it. She wanted to squeeze his hand, but the last time she'd shown affection to a friend, the wind had swept that friend away.

"I wish I knew how to make everything okay," Xi said.

"Yeah." Rex studied the street, busy with occasional vehicles. "Me too."

To hell with it. Xi reached out and took Rex's hand. She couldn't pretend it would make any difference. Cabrina had buried herself in her friends' lives, bodies, and hearts, but that comfort and affection hadn't been enough to save her.

The sky banged another bout of thunderous laughter. It had been mostly quiet since taking Cabrina, as if waiting for permission to start again. Waiting for Xi's hilarious hopefulness.

"The hell's going on up there?" Rex asked, letting go of Xi's hand. His gaze wandered the blackness above. "Never heard a storm like this."

A harsh gust sprayed raindrops from the table umbrella, and then the wind cut out. Car tires and engines grew muffled, and a quiet spread across the sky, and then down Main Street, as if the whole of Cape Morning had ceased to breathe. With the wind dead, Cabrina might float back to earth.

But what would she bring with her?

"I think we assumed too much today at the beach," Xi said. "We thought of a vampire's glamour like an illusion covering our eyes, but that's not the case. The world is thin as paper, and maybe Cabrina's devils can sketch new pictures on it where they stand. They can even tear through it and hide on the shadow side of the page. I think they change what's real about themselves. Sketch whatever they want. Become what they want."

"You're talking transformation?" Rex asked, and he swiped a hand down his stained jacket. "Or transmogrification?"

The metallic screech of a car crash echoed in the distance, and Xi slid off the table to glance up Main Street. No sign of an accident here, but other noises clamored over the echo. Laughter again, not thunderous this time, but scattered across many sources, and cruel. So cruel.

And beneath it, the sound of screaming.

Streetlights and glowing windows merged into a haze far up Main Street, but overhead, Xi thought she could make out something moving against the storm-blackened sky. Many somethings. A flock of large birds coming from the sea. Or a flock of some worse kind of creature, and with them, a widespread chorus of screams.

Tears again pricked Xi's eyes. "We don't know how any of this works. It's ghosts, and vampires, and devils. And they wanted Cabrina as their key. To open a doorway to this side of the paper."

Rex leaned close to her. "You thinking it'll get worse?"

"Rex," Xi said, voice quavering as she turned to him. "I think it already has."

36. THE SEA TAKES BLOOD

Cape Shadow's starlight gave way to Cape Morning's blackened sky. It had rained while Ivory was gone, and though that storm had settled, the wind moaned across the water, joyous in carrying what she'd brought from the other world. She used to think that, if you were watching from the sky on a cloudless night, the cape's houses might twinkle into the dark ocean like fairy lights against black paint. She'd never seen anything so lovely here, but the sleepers might find wonder and beauty as they soared free.

Ivory emerged from the sea in a sloshing white-foamed tide. Anyone looking from their summerhouse porch down the dark coast might at first mistake her for pale driftwood, or a corpse like Cabrina. They would not see her fissures of bone, turned to greenstone, until it was too late. They could not understand what rode ashore tonight.

A woman in one way, the sea in another, and a sea-stone key for beasts beneath.

The people here might have thought themselves bystanders to Cabrina's tragedy, if they thought of her at all, but they would be wrong. Viola had washed down Cabrina's bedroom, erased her name, drowned the daughter to call her son.

Sure, Viola owned most of the blame, but everyone at Cape Morning had let her do it. Like Cabrina had no right to herself, alive or dead. Even Ivory had been oblivious and useless.

Everyone had stood by for this atrocity, and they could fall by it, too. Giving them nothing would be a kindness when they had ignored Cabrina. They had let her pain drag on when she'd only wanted to live, nothing more harmful than that. Nothing harmful at all.

Since nothing was not enough to rouse the people of Cape Morning, Ivory would give them something. They wouldn't want it though. And once they had it, they would never want anything again.

Grief was antithetical to a summer of joy. These people had no idea what true laughter sounded like. Absolute laughter knew pain in its merriment. True laughter rang from the gallows, and the bloody places, intimate with inequality and wrongness.

Ivory could give that laughter to them. Honey would help, climbing from the sea.

She looked nothing like the woman who'd first followed Ivory onto the shore several nights ago. Golden fur coated her changed body, large as an ox. Black fur smeared her spine and snout, and dark spots dotted her flanks. She stepped ashore on clawed feet and muscly haunches, her clawed hands tensing at her sides.

Ivory straddled her mountainous shoulders. Sea-like darkness teemed between her legs and lapped at the hair of Honey's neck. Both their bodies quaked, eager for summerhouse lights and the blood beyond, and Honey stalked deeper onto the sand, toward the town proper.

Heralds to the great unseen brood who'd abandoned this world long ago. Who'd patiently waited long after they were ready to return.

And from the night, the wind, and the sea, the beasts spread across the sky of Cape Morning.

They wore human torsos and inhuman snouts, human muscle

draped over feline skeletons, the horde a mash-up of hands and claws and slitted cat eyes. Their swarm draped summerhouse rooftops, porches, and walkways like enormous locusts. They smashed awnings, windows, doors. Anything that stood between their bestial hunger and their blood-rich prey splintered and shattered beneath them as they crashed into parties. Into bedrooms.

A high-pitched cry echoed from one house. And then another. And then the screams and shouts swelled up and down the shoreline.

The sleepers quickly emerged from houses, caked in blood. They had been hungry for so long, and now that they'd fed, they could move on. At the next coastal breeze, they swept again to the sky on the loving night wind.

"Deeper," Ivory said with a pleasant sigh. "Harder. In we go."

Honey's chuckle quaked through Ivory's core as she charged onto the nearest street. Pedestrians stood frozen on the sidewalks, maybe thinking a large dog had escaped her home. They didn't understand hyenas were part of the cat family. Couldn't imagine how much more dangerous Honey was than a housecat or a hyena.

Not until she tore through them. Her snout dove into bellies, and her teeth cracked ribcages apart. Red gore splashed the asphalt and wooden walkways.

A small cluster of familiar figures approached—Chelsea Burke and the others Honey had turned. Unlike Ivory, they had swallowed Honey's blood outside of Cape Shadow rituals, had died and returned. Ivory had become the key, and they had become like the sleepers. They belonged in the sky.

"Go," Ivory said, waving an arm. "It's yours. It's all yours!"

A powerful gust tore through Chelsea's dark hair, and then she and the others flung off the street, forgotten by gravity, to join the bloodthirsty storm. They would flit away to see the world. Humanity had clung to its conditions, and so Ivory and the sleepers had ceased to be human. Simple as that. Their kind knew wildness and play and calm. They had cruelty, care, hunger, and they had fucking and pleasure, blood and bone—so many aspects that left no room for simple humanity and morals.

Ivory almost wished she could fly away with them. The world would belong to them, one night after another.

But Ivory was the key. A creature of life, but also a creature of sea and stone. She had another purpose tonight.

Revenge was a holiness beyond good and evil.

Especially revenge for the Brite girl. Cabrina had never been much more than a ghost clinging to the edges of life. That was fine—not everyone had to be strong. The innocent should be allowed their softness.

"I'll do right by you," Ivory whispered. "And those who did wrong will get what they deserve."

Viola Brite. Ivory would find her, and she would wield more fearsome weapons than scissors. Blades that lined Honey's gums, grown within a monstrous hyena-like maw.

Gunshots shouted from beyond the trees. The cops had noticed the figures overhead. How long until they noticed that shooting them was like shooting the ocean? They would only briefly disturb uncaring surfaces before the flying beasts vanished like waves.

Honey was another story. She was here, and she was hungry.

It's the head and heart, little piggies, Ivory thought, cackling. *You wouldn't know. You've never used yours.*

Honey lunged through brush and undergrowth. She had worked so hard over the past few days, leading Ivory to the other world, following her back, priming her to become the key, showing what this world could become. She deserved a little fun, too.

The cops turned their guns from the sky to the street, at last spotting Honey barreling down on them. Too late to make a difference before she opened her prey with tooth and claw.

Ivory didn't watch the unmaking of the blue-uniformed

officers. She leaned far over Honey's side and vomited a black-red stream. It didn't hurt coming up, only looked and felt strange, like the spit-up blood wasn't hers.

Nothing to fret about. There was too much else to focus on tonight.

The sky began to thin of sleepers, little by little. They wouldn't all flit away at once, but by morning the cape town could expect an empty sky. The sleepers wouldn't risk being trapped in the netherworld off this coast again. Cape Morning could keep its shadow; they had elsewhere to explore and feed.

Like the rest of the world.

Ivory felt one among them in particular, drawn up by the wind as the horde approached this world for the first time in untold centuries. A lost girl, unfit to become Honey's key, her love unbound from the earth.

Ivory leaned toward Honey's ear. "Do you feel Cabrina on the wind? Do you smell her mother?" She sniffed the air. "I do. Through the trees, I see that awful house and its awful people."

Honey's throat rumbled with slurped-down innards. She had her eyes up Main Street, where cruiser lights dared threaten her. Soon there would be more cops, more bullets digging into her flesh, more ribcages to crack open across the street in a wreckage of clot-filled eggshells.

"You don't have to come with me," Ivory said. "This is your fun, and that's my justice. I opened the door to make you strong again and free the others, and I'm different now. I can do this myself. You can fly away. I won't hate you for it. I'll always love what you've done for me."

Honey bent forward, sliding Ivory down her neck and over her head. Ivory let it happen, trusting Honey's enormous claws to catch hold, scraping the stone-like bones within her wounds. A massive pink tongue lapped between Ivory's legs, half-hungry, half-playful, and then crushed the enormity of her skull against Ivory's chest. Honey's small laugh haunted her throat.

A bigger laugh shot from Ivory's mouth. "Together then," she said.

She kissed Honey's snout, coated in cop gore, and then clambered up her face, onto her shoulders, where she began to hum as they waded onward. *Honey, Honey.*

Main Street stretched toward blurring lights, but a turn-off ducked past maples and birches onto Harper Lane. Ivory guided, and Honey chased the turn in the road. They had done their work as harbinger and key, and now came time for holy vengeance.

"This way." Ivory's hand slipped between Honey's eyes. "Almost there."

Every step brought them closer to Viola. Close enough to taste. Only Viola Brite mattered now, and the fate coming her way. She thought Ivory and Cabrina were monsters? Let her. She was half-wrong.

Her daughter was too gentle to be a monster. Ivory might have shared that frailty once, but she had proven on Ghost Cat Island that she could change.

And now she would ravage those who had broken Cabrina Brite. "Ivory?"

The hum split from Ivory's mouth as she jerked her head toward the roadside.

Marla stumbled from a corner parking lot where Main Street met the Harper Lane turn-off, about five feet from Ivory and Honey. Cars had stalled elsewhere amid the lanes and cluttered the lot, people were running panicked from the sleepers in the sky, but here was Joan's wife, stepping into Honey's path with a cellphone in one hand and a gleaming machete in the other.

"Are you high?" Ivory snapped, and then hated how she sounded like Wolf. "Get out of her way." She ran her fingers through Honey's fur, hoping to coax her toward a momentary calm.

But Marla stepped closer. "God, is that what they turn into?" she asked, gawking up and down.

"Nothing to do with you." Ivory chinned to the right. "Go back to Joan. Forget me."

Marla didn't seem to hear. "Ivory, you look awful. What did this thing do to you?" She shook her machete as if making a threat. Or maybe she was trembling. Ivory couldn't tell.

Neither could Honey—she reared up on her thick hind legs, shaggy golden hair dripping down her chest, limbs, and maw. Her head cocked to one side. Studying prey.

Ivory leaned toward her pointed ear. "Not this one."

Marla had done nothing to justify hurting her. There were better places to be, Brite places, and stalling here would only give the cops more time to stall them further.

"Stay out of it," Ivory said. "This is between us and Viola Brite." She felt Honey shudder with an impatient groan, and then they stepped to weave past.

Marla studied Ivory and Honey, a calculation creasing her forehead, and then she thrust herself into Honey's way again.

"You can't," Marla said.

"Don't start with what we can or can't do," Ivory said. She and Honey bristled together. "You don't even know what we are."

"Do *you* know what this thing is?" Marla's teeth chattered until she clenched them. "I'm trying to save you."

Ivory leaned over Honey's snout. "*I'm* trying to save *you*. Your useless driftwood angel couldn't help me, but she has." The world dimmed around Marla, as if she were momentarily the only living thing, and Ivory wondered if this was how Honey felt when she set eyes on her prey. "Run home to your family and your nonsense trinkets. This is us, and we're real and dangerous."

Marla eyed Honey and then Ivory, and then she raised her machete. "I can be dangerous too."

She had to be out of her mind right now, panicking into a fight the way most people panicked into running away or curling into a ball. Sirens wailed in the distance. Any more delay, and Honey would quit caring about Viola, giving in to the long-unmet need for wild carnage inside her, the kind unfelt since mankind's most primitive days.

Ivory kissed between her ears and urged her onward.

She was about to hum a sweet melody to Honey when her leg seized up. Marla had reached out and latched on, and her fingers stroked a sea-stone fissure before hooking onto the tender lip of its wound. Skin snagged, and ribbons of pain wound themselves around Ivory's leg. She'd had no idea she was still weak anywhere.

Honey's fur stiffened beneath Ivory and down her entire body. She wheeled around, a roar like a tidal wave booming inside her chest.

At last Marla's eyes widened, taking in the big picture and her smallness beneath it.

"Not her!" Ivory cried out, but the pain had withered her voice to a thin rasp.

And Honey was quick. Ivory could only shut her eyes.

Even then, the darkness wouldn't excuse her place in this moment. Honey lashed out, mouth open, claw swimming, and Ivory couldn't escape the violent tremor, or the wet sound of teeth puncturing flesh, or the force of a body swatted toward a nearby parking lot. The machete's steel clanged against the pavement.

Sensations rained through Ivory's mind—pressure in her jaws as if she herself was latching onto tendons and muscle. Churning rage at being interrupted from giving a lover a gift. Indignation at having that lover grabbed like a token this other creature could take. Disgust at flinging the meat away, at having more important deaths to bring tonight.

And worse, Ivory tasted Marla on her tongue, and her blood sang of sweet honey.

She kept her eyes closed as the wind swept through her hair. Honey was on the move again. Nothing would stop her now.

"Didn't deserve it, didn't deserve it," Ivory whispered, almost a chant. "Didn't deserve it, didn't deserve, didn't, didn't."

She shook her head, desperate to toss this memory aside and focus only on her sense of being wronged. On retribution.

"Take me, Honey," she whispered.

Her mind spread open to a golden influence, and it filled her head with possession and power and love. There was no room for thoughts or memory. Only this moment, right now, of the hairy sun beneath Ivory's body and the tremorous heart within.

Much better. All better. Ivory pursed her lips in a grim smile and hummed again for Honey.

37. THE DEAD

The sound of gunfire shot Rex's heart into his throat. His eyes flashed to the big windows and glass door of Peyton's Ice Cream as he stepped back, expecting some gun-wielding maniac to loom against the pink walls. He'd been prepping for this inevitability since childhood, with a lifetime of school shooting drills penetrating his nerves.

But the ice cream shop patrons looked around perplexed, same as him. Something over Main Street caught a small girl's attention, and then everyone else inside, all turning Rex's way but looking above him, as if some gunship in the sky were firing rather than any random shooter on the ground.

Xi left the table, face tilted up. Rex turned to stare above town, too.

There were people in the sky. Not flying like Clark Kent, Kong Kenan, nor anyone else in the Superman crew. More like dried leaves blown off tree limbs as autumn ebbed toward winter. A season of death had brought windswept corpses to the summertime.

Gunfire crackled again, and this time Rex caught muzzle flares blinking down Main Street.

Bodies dripped from the black clouds. Rex thought at first that they'd been shot, a dead rain falling over Cape Morning, but in their last moments before impact, they glided on the wind, toward the muzzle flares, and then gunfire gave way to screaming. Tires screeched at a nearby intersection, and headlights swirled at the sound of crunching metal.

Xi gripped Rex's arm, making him jolt. Her eyes were wide and black.

"It's like Cabrina," she said, a quake in her voice.

Rex remembered. "The sky took her," he said.

He might not have believed it before, but he believed now. The sky had taken Cabrina and was giving back hell. A night storm of vampires, their cloud giving shape to the wind that carried them. They looked guided by an absence between them, as hollow and hungry as an empty stomach. Its hunger was spreading, dispersing the bodies as far as they would reach.

Xi wrenched Rex's arm and tugged him past the outdoor tables, aiming for the parking lot on Peyton's far side.

Rex made to follow her, but the front door of the ice cream shop crashed open, pouring out a wave of patrons and cutting Rex and Xi off from the side parking lot.

Xi lunged for the far side of the building, opposite the parking lot, towing Rex behind her. The ice cream shop's bell went on jangling bloody murder. More people trying to escape Peyton's, weave around the tables, head for their cars, only to be cut off by gaunt monstrosities.

Marla had gone to that parking lot, on her cell with Joan. Rex wanted to head her way, but Xi dragged him into the roadside foliage. It made a grim sort of sense. She'd been hiding in the brush for a long time tonight and must've associated its dark greenery with safety. These woods were only thick enough to keep businesses and suburban neighborhoods from seeing each other while this cape town pretended to own a forest, but at least the trees somewhat blocked out the sky.

The bodies weren't descending in a bee-like swarm. Their numbers looked to be breaking farther apart, the flock too big for its own good. They might scatter across town.

Or maybe the world.

Beneath the panicked screams, revving engines, and distant gunshots, a cry sang from the far side of Peyton's Ice Cream. From the parking lot. Rex's heart thudded against his ribcage—that wasn't Marla. Couldn't be Marla. He must have misheard beneath the night's cacophony. Especially when the descending bodies kept flitting back up into the sky. Heading west, out of town, sating their vicious appetites along the way.

Xi brushed his shoulder. "Text my mom."

"They're leaving," Rex said. "Why come here just to leave?"

"Rex," Xi snapped. "My phone's gone. Text my mom, tell her Alyssa says, *It's him, he's here.*"

Rex looked at her. "Him?"

"She'll understand." Xi's head sank against his arm.

Rex didn't argue with her further. He hurried out a text to Josephine Munoz.

Was that all? Shouldn't he text his mothers? What about the people he used to know at school? There were assholes, sure, but good people too. He didn't have their contacts, had deleted his social media. What could he do?

And why no sign of Marla? She must've seen the blood-colored writing on the wall, forewarned of vampires after the beach.

She's got to be safe, Rex told himself.

Xi shrieked into one hand. The other pointed through the foliage, into the trees. What now?

Rex peered through the underbrush, where something the size of a bull skulked down Harper Lane, its black-and-yellow fur glistening. He'd never seen anything like it.

But he knew the figure mounted on its shoulders—Ivory Sloan.

She wasn't the same as he'd known before. Her nude white shape curled atop the gold-black creature's neck and rubbed its snout. Open wounds gaped down her body like wet black mouths, and streetlights glinted off hard green surfaces within, as if her bones had transformed into sea glass. Red-black bile trickled down her neck and disappeared into a cavern at her chest.

There was a moment's pause, as if she and her mount were catching a scent, and then they disappeared deeper behind the maple trees guarding Harper Lane from Main Street.

Xi sprang to her feet. "She's going back to Cab's house."

"Wait!" Rex whispered, grabbing for her arm. "What're you rambling about?"

"Honey, Honey," Xi said, almost a chant. "It was her, at Ivory's house."

"You're not making sense." Rex let his hand drop away. "You think *that's* Honey?"

"Goddamn it, she knew about the vampires all along," Xi went on, like Rex wasn't there. "She did it. Took Cab's place, and that's how the sky took her, too."

Rex could only stare. He needed bigger puzzle pieces to make it all make sense, but Xi was talking in fragments.

"I'll explain on the way to Cab's house." Xi crashed through the underbrush, ferns and bushes swatting her limbs.

Rex held still, and Xi didn't show she noticed as she disappeared into the dark. What would following Ivory and that monster to Cabrina's house do for anyone? Even with cover from the sky, the moment Xi flipped on houselights, the vampires would see. Rex doubted they had any problem smashing through windows to catch prey.

And if the thing Ivory rode was the mysterious Honey that Scarlet had mentioned? Following might only add to the plots at Fairview West Cemetery.

So what then, let her go alone? Rex asked himself.

Never. Not the kind of man he was. But he couldn't follow Xi until he made sure Marla was safe.

He trailed the underbrush behind Peyton's Ice Cream, past its back door and green dumpster coated in white seagull streaks, until he reached the side lot's edge, not far from the turn-off to Harper Lane. Marla's past-its-prime station wagon with the wood-paneled doors sat parked in the second row of cars, right where they'd all left it when bringing Xi to the shop's front.

Ivory would have passed here, Rex realized. *And her monster*.

He squatted on bent knees and ducked behind other cars as he headed for the station wagon's trunk. His shadow was a black ball chasing him down the pavement.

He was three feet from the car when he spotted other shadows stretching from its passenger side. The back door hung open. Rex shuffled around the trunk, teeth clenched and fists balled at his sides, and leaned around the car's back corner. Marla couldn't be dead. He could not get on his phone and tell his Ma that her sweet clueless wife was dead.

There—Marla lay on her back against the pavement beneath the station wagon's open back door.

Rex planted his knee beside her. "Mom?"

"Thought I could take it," Marla whispered. "We stopped one on the beach. Don't know what I was thinking. This one—so big."

The enormous frame of golden-furred Honey stamped through Rex's thoughts. Against his will, he imagined that mammoth hyena maw clamping over Marla.

He wanted to shout at her for putting herself in danger. He wanted to save her. His useless hands hovered over her body—what was he supposed to do? Vicious teeth had flayed Marla's neck in a ragged weeping strip, and a crescent bitemark bled a dark puddle into the side of her torso and across her belly. If Rex hadn't seen that monster, he'd have thought Marla had wrestled with a mountain lion.

He pressed both hands against her gut to staunch the bleeding, and then he reached for her neck, and then he looked to her side. Too many places needed tending. None of Marla's crystals could undo this curse.

"Meant a lot." Marla swallowed. "Calling me Mom."

Why the hell did she have to bring that up now? Rex had never given the names any thought. He'd gone from calling Joan *Mommy* to *Ma*, with the title of *Mom* sitting unused until Marla became a permanent part of their lives.

And now that permanence was ebbing away.

"Don't," Marla rasped. One blood-stained hand squeezed the machete grip.

"Don't?" Rex asked. He didn't know what she was saying.

"Don't let me come back like that," Marla said, gasping.

Rex gritted his teeth and squeezed her shoulders. "What are you saying?"

A red stream leaked from Marla's lips and trickled down her paling cheek. She didn't look like herself. Why did she have to look like someone else when Rex might never see her again?

He leaned close. "Mom?"

"If it got in me," Marla said, "don't let me come back like one of them. Promise me, guy. I want to come back as a mountain hare. And maple trees." Her free hand aimed a trembling finger up at the car. "Love her. She needs it, like every—"

She cut off as her jaw trembled, and then her body jerked taut, stretching her neck wound wide open. Her eyelids squeezed shut in a sudden grimace.

And then she went limp.

Something else limpened in Rex's chest, and he moaned through clenched teeth. Everything was collapsing in on itself, a yawning black hole where his heart should pound, its event horizon wreathed in futility. This was wrong. Everything was wrong.

"Can't just walk into somebody's life and then walk out of it," Rex said, choking back tears.

The wrong thing to say to Marla, but part of him wanted to blame her. He went to hold her hand. One still gripped the machete, so he grabbed the other, where an extended finger pointed at the car.

Love her, Marla had said. *She needs it.*

Rex looked over Marla for a long moment, blinking back tears. He then glanced up at the car.

A pale figure perched atop the station wagon, wearing gray sweatpants that puddled over her bare feet. Dried rust-brown blood stained the chest of her gray hoodie. The hood encircled tufts of auburn hair and once-gray eyes turned golden. Her cheeks had gone sunken and gaunt, but the rest of her features were unmistakable. Unforgettable.

Rex sank against the pavement. "Cab?"

Cabrina hugged the hoodie around her. She had always been the cold type. Her teeth used to chatter wildly on cooler beach nights, and she would sit so close to the fire that Xi worried she'd burn her hands, and even then the fire wouldn't help. That much hadn't changed.

But other things had. Old Cabrina would have rushed to hug Rex where he knelt in the parking lot, with Marla underneath him. Cabrina had always brimmed with affection.

Not anymore. Chills and hunger had stolen her heart.

She stared with vacant animal eyes. Placid, unaware. At least the young woman who'd crept into Rex's bedroom had shown traces of her old self.

But since then, something had stolen that self away, or buried it deep inside.

Rex wanted to hug her. Joan had kept him from Cabrina's funeral, but he still cared. He had led Xi in that ridiculous beach ritual afterward, genuinely believing it would help.

Though he knew better now than to think he'd caused Cabrina to rise from the dead, she was undead just the same. Her body thrummed with barely restrained hunger. Still, the longer Rex watched her, the longer he could pretend Marla didn't lie dead beneath them. And he needed to watch Cabrina right now. Absorb her reality in all its horror.

Another scream rang out beyond the parking lot. Futile gunshots popped off from elsewhere in town, and the corpse-dotted sky churned with giddy laughter.

Cabrina twitched like she might bolt from the roof of the car. She'd fled from Xi's home, Rex's house, the beach, a dead girl running through Cape Morning from sunset to sunrise.

How long had she been running? Since the night her parents put her in the ground? Rex hadn't seen them do it; how could he be sure she'd ever gone that far? He'd attended the wake, and while he hadn't been able to bring himself to glance inside the casket, see what the mortician might've done to Cabrina's body at her mother's request, he could tell there was a body by others' reactions. She'd never been staked down in her grave.

Free to roam. Free to find warm blood on windy nights.

Was this Cabrina in front of him the same body, having clambered out of the grave? That didn't seem possible after embalming, but the same transformation that had given her wild hair, sharp teeth, and golden irises could have cleared post-mortem abominations from her body.

Rex had seen worse tonight. Like Xi had said, these vampires treated the world like paper, drawing new shapes for themselves on it as they pleased. One part of Cabrina might have floated ashore while another remained on the shadow side of the page, taking on new flesh, new shapes, her soul stricken by a curse. Spirits could form solid bodies, and the dead could move. Was there really much difference then between a ghost and a vampire?

Or maybe, deep down, Xi was right, and none of them knew anything at all.

Glass shattered somewhere down the street. If Rex delayed for too long, some sky fiend might sniff him out and decide to make him its going-away meal. Easy-to-find prey would eventually grow scarce.

Rex turned to Marla, her skin painted in glistening red splatter. The last thing he'd said to her was in blame. Would she despise him for that? If she was turning, he could find out how she felt. Let her rise from the dead, and then her son could tell her that he loved her, and that she really was a cool mom, and how it mattered that she trusted him.

But she didn't want to come back like that.

The machete's blade stretched gleaming from her fist, where sharp steel peeked from beneath thick blood. Her own? Or had she given Honey a wound to remember her by?

Harsh wind rushed over the car, and Rex almost thought he heard a cry atop it.

The station wagon frame creaked as Cabrina went springing off its roof, a gust tossing her body toward the trees behind Peyton's Ice Cream. Toward her home.

Rex watched her disappear into the woods. He couldn't blame her for rushing away. Likely the only thing she had wanted to do from the beginning was run from this nightmare and never touch it again.

"You go," Rex whispered, sliding beside Marla's body. "I can't yet. Too much to do."

He pried the machete from Marla's grasp and tucked his legs under himself where he sat beside her chest. Her skin was already going cold where he touched her throat.

A familiar gleam caught his eye, and he glanced at Main Street. Several cars had skewed to one side or another, their occupants watching the sky or cowering in their seats at the dissipating vampire flock above, but at least one was trying to worm its way through the traffic clog.

Rex recognized Joan's black Toyota. Whenever her phone call had ended, she must have torn across town, and he hoped she hadn't heard Marla take the killing blow.

Joan's car crawled partway onto the curb around a derelict

SUV. Her eyes locked with Rex's as she glanced at the ice cream shop parking lot.

"Rex," she said, calling across the lanes.

He didn't know how to answer her, only kept on staring while he readied for an impossible task.

Joan glanced ahead and then back across the lanes. "Stay put. I'm coming to fetch you."

Her car slugged behind other parked and idling cars, past the corner of the ice cream shop. She couldn't possibly see what her son was doing or the face of the body lying beneath him, but if she managed a U-turn at the next light and pulled onto the lot, she would see everything. Grief-stricken and ignorant, she would stop Rex from helping Marla. She would keep him from running off to help Xi.

Or worse, she would join in. And then that monster Honey might take both of Rex's mothers tonight.

His head ached with tears as he wiped the flat of the machete's blade over his sleeve and studied its sharp edge. The vampires might be decayed beneath the glamour. They might be tough, and Marla had hopefully gotten a lucky strike against the monster that killed her. Rex might not get so lucky.

But he would try. For everyone.

Cabrina, Xi, and himself—they had all loved each other. Joan and Marla had loved them, too. Rex hadn't known how to lose one mother, and he sure as hell didn't know how to lose another if he let Joan get too close or follow him into the woods. One loss was too much already. The same went for friends. Couldn't allow it.

"Can't abandon Xi," he said. "Let me finish this, and then I promise, I'll finish the whole thing." He wasn't sure who he was talking to. Maybe Joan, or Cabrina, or even Marla.

Or maybe himself.

He took a steady breath, tensed his arm, and then raised the machete. The world darkened around him as he set to work.

38. SISTER NIGHT

Viola Brite tried to ignore the thumping noise. Tried to pretend it was one dream intruding on another, because if everything was her imagination, she wouldn't have to come back to the world of other people. All would be quiet and dark here.

But the walls thudded with busy drums, as if the house had grown a frantic heartbeat.

She forced her head up from the desk, where she'd laid it on her crossed arms beside a box for scrapbook cuttings. Light glowed from the ceiling. The large scissors lay at the desk corner, blades open. Strands of blond hair clung to one stiff cheek, and Viola rubbed them free of her dried tears. She must have cried herself to sleep here after sending Gary hunting for those intruders. Ivory and—was it Alyssa or Xiomara? She could never keep the friends' names straight, and she wasn't about to go looking through the purse left behind for ID. She had to be better than her intruders.

Gary had run the license plate on that car Ivory had driven away. Too nice for a barista, and sure enough, it came back as owned by one Wilfred Thompson. Reported missing by his assistant yesterday. Who the hell had Viola let step inside her house this evening?

The bedroom door hung open, the way she'd left it. She wandered into the second-floor hallway, where the music boomed from downstairs. The living room house didn't have any kind of stereo or amplifiers, but Gary kept a small radio with a collapsible antenna in the garage to listen to while he worked on the cars or hid from his family.

Viola reached the top of the stairs. "Gary?"

The house lay dark below, except where red-and-blue lights flashed through the windows. He couldn't be back from arresting that kid already. Maybe he had given up.

Except the music didn't sound like his preferred station, playing bands like Korn or Rage Against the Machine. Thrashing guitars, sonic voices, Freddie Mercury—Viola recognized some Queen song that hadn't been licensed to death, early work, like she used to listen from her older brother's albums in childhood. She couldn't remember the name, but she knew the tune, like déjà vu or a ghost in her ear.

Sirens wailed in the distance, briefly joining the soundscape. Many sirens. There could be bigger trouble in Cape Morning tonight than Ivory and the girl. Gary might have to head right back out again.

Doubtful it mattered. Even when he was home, he wasn't here.

The music thudded louder as Viola descended the carpeted stairs to the landing and then to the living room. Her hand raised on instinct to flip a light switch, but the first-floor darkness encircled a standing rectangle of light, emphasizing it for her to better see clearly inside.

Past the couch and recliner, across the house, the side door to the garage hung open beneath the *Home, Sweet Home* plaque. The garage's bare golden bulb gleamed off Gary's workbench, his tools. Some lay scattered on the garage floor.

Viola gritted her teeth at the mess. Always the same story. Mr. Important Policeman couldn't be expected to clean up after himself or play his music at a respectable volume.

There was a time when she had found his incompetence charming. She was needed because of it, she had a place, in the annoying yet amiable way of litter training their old cat Angel. Aggravating for him to piss on the floor, but still, kittens were cute.

Gary had shucked off his sloppy charm at an imperceptible crawl. Viola hadn't noticed for the longest time, too distracted with her ambitions, with motherhood, especially when their son had been such a good boy. *He* was the dependable one around the house. Mommy's helper.

Until the world decided to confuse him. Being Mommy's helper wasn't good enough then; he wanted to be like Mommy. She had tried to explain there was nothing wrong with becoming a domesticated man who preferred tending house over engines, but he'd said it was deeper than that. Like she didn't know her own child when she'd grown those very cells inside her.

Calm explanations turned to arguments, and arguments turned to fights, and he wouldn't see her side, and she'd seen his and it was terrifying, a landscape of drugs and sterilization and dying young. She'd tried homeschooling to save him, but cause and effect fought harder, and they won. Her child became an emotional fortress.

Neither of the men in her life understood. She'd never had anything of her own, always lifting interests and desires from her brother, her father, her husband, her fellow town councilmembers, the town itself. A son was supposed to be hers, grown within. He wasn't supposed to become his own. And he certainly was not supposed to become a daughter.

That was the point. Viola knew the world of teenage girls, and she sure as hell wasn't raising one. That was her past, belonging to no one else in the family, understood by her alone. No one could take that, not even her baby. And yet that sentiment had made her the household tyrant.

Especially after the death.

She wouldn't have to worry about sterilization anymore. There would never be grandchildren either way. But she had kept herself composed through losses past, present, and future. She could be a fortress too, unyielding to challenges from the outside or the screaming in her head. The reliable mother, even when putting her child in the ground.

Viola stepped deeper into the dark living room. Gary's cruiser had to be parked cattycorner in the driveway, the lights swirling on its roof. They cast Viola's shadow in strange gaunt shapes up the living room wall. If Gary left his lights on, he couldn't mean to be home for more than a minute. But then, why turn on the radio?

A hiss pricked Viola's ears—someone whispering to someone else.

She tried calling out. "Gary? Who's with you? I need you to turn that down."

A muffled voice answered, obscured by the radio. "Honey likes the music." That couldn't be right. *Money spikes the music? But he likes the music?*

"Gary," Viola snapped. "Turn it down. Now."

The voice answered again. Louder now. Alien. "We're not Gary."

A shadow coated the scattered tools on the garage floor, and the light began to sway as if something had struck the bare hanging bulb. Something tall. Heading for the garage door, with only a living room between the doorway and Viola.

She retreated two steps and bumped her heel against the bottom of the stairs. Another intruder. Gary would know what to do this time, except Gary wasn't here. Only his car blinked outside, and now someone else was in the house.

"My husband's with the CMPD," Viola said, but her voice came almost whispery, and the music grew louder. "The police can be here in a finger snap. I'm warning you."

"Honey likes the music," the voice answered again, clearer now.

Viola thought of the wall phone hanging in the kitchen, and her cell phone—where had she left it? On the kitchen island? In the bedroom?

A wooden crack rang from the kitchen beneath the stairs, shooting a tremor through Viola's limbs. She gripped the stairway banister to steady herself. That sound had to be the back door. Which meant more than one intruder had come to her home. Same as earlier today.

"Xiomara?" Viola coughed out. "Ivory Sloan?"

That raspy voice answered, calling from the back door. "He's in here."

The next flash of red-and-blue lights cast a stranger's thin shadow up the living room wall.

Viola averted her eyes, looking hard at the steps as she ascended backward. If she thought of either intruder watching her in the dark, she could never sleep here again. And this was her house, damn them.

"I'm calling the police," she said. "I want you to leave now, understand?"

The music faded as she reached the landing, the song ending, only for another to take its place. Strange how the new tune began with a moan of destruction—no, that part wasn't the radio. A brute of a silhouette had thrashed into her living room and chucked an end table through the picture window.

"I see him," the voice said. Less raspy this time, more certain of itself. More familiar.

"Ivory?" Viola asked. She stumbled backward across the landing, one hand groping for guidance, and then she turned and dashed up the remaining staircase.

The first floor stretched dark below her, as if murky water now flooded the living room. Only the flashing cruiser lights broke the mirage into clearer shapes—the couch, the TV, the family photos on the wall, Viola's shelves of tchotchkes.

The shadowy figure crossing the carpet in slow, deliberate steps.

"Ivory, is that you?" Viola asked. She forced her breath to ease and set an imperative tone in her voice. "You had better leave. I'm still armed." At least, she would be armed again soon.

"Ivory?" the voice asked. "Oh. You think I'm Ivory Sloan." The voice sounded almost playful, riding a mirthful sing-song up from the dark living room. "No, no, you had your chance with her. Now there's the sea and the island, the nightmare and the dream. There's no Ivory anymore. *We've* come instead, and we are sister night, and the ghost cat queen, and the laughing beast."

A black eyelid shut over the garage doorway. Hints of light peeked around golden edges, but a massive figure blocked the way, hiding the garage's glowing bulb before it shattered to black.

Viola bit her tongue to keep down a surprised shriek and hurried past the upstairs bathroom. That thing couldn't be Ivory. Couldn't even be human.

Music blasted behind Viola, a soundtrack to her escape, making the radio speakers crackle. Furniture crashed below as she darted into the small bedroom. The large scissors gleamed from the desk where she'd left them, and she grabbed them up and aimed them ahead of her. Gary kept a spare pistol in the safe beneath their bed, but there wasn't time to fetch it.

"I smell him," Ivory's voice said, and the stairway creaked.

Viola slapped the light switch, darkening the bedroom, and ducked into the closet. She slid the door closed slower than she liked, but she couldn't risk the sharp *clack* of a shutting door now that whatever was coming had reached the stairs.

No, farther—the next creak said it had reached the stairway landing.

"God, please," Viola whispered. It was the beginning to a prayer. She'd never been too religious, but now seemed a good time to start.

She didn't know what to say, and any inspiration vanished at the sound of another creak, this time at the top of the steps.

Viola was not alone on the second floor. She should have flipped on the upstairs bathroom light and shut the door, the same trick Ivory had played earlier in the evening. Too late now.

Viola's fingers intertwined where both hands squeezed the scissors. Would they be enough? They were all she had. She huddled against the floor in a painful crouch, ready to drive the blades up into a cheek, a throat, if anyone dared open this door.

Soft footsteps padded into the small bedroom. The floor went on creaking beyond the doorway, where something massive paced the upstairs hall.

Ivory's voice hissed through the room. "He's in this place."

Viola aimed the scissor blades at the shut closet door. "There's no one with me. You're looking for someone else. Go away, my husband's a police officer."

"I hear him," Ivory's voice said, closer to the closet now.

"No, you don't," Viola said. "He's at the station. I'm the only one here!"

Her voice cracked at the last word, and she hated herself for it. This was her house. Hers. She shouldn't ever feel frightened here. Powerless, frustrated, unappreciated, but not afraid.

Something thumped the other side of the closet door. "He's talking to us."

"Me?" Viola cocked her head in confusion. "You're looking for someone else. I'm a woman, and I'm the only one here."

The closet doorknob clinked beneath an unseen hand, and then the door wrenched open.

No looking, pure instinct, Viola lunged forward and up, hoping to ram the large scissor blades into a gut, under a ribcage, into a neck. This would be far more satisfying than any gun. She would cut Ivory open, on purpose this time, for the last time, to defend herself and her home with blood on her hands to show for it. And most importantly, to live.

The blades drove into the figure standing in the closet doorway, but there was no soft pulpy resistance. Steel scraped off a hard rounded surface as if Viola had tried to impale a slick stone, and the unexpected impact knocked the scissors out of her grasp. She fell back into the depths of the closet, onto discarded shoes and sweaters.

Standing above her, Ivory was nude, and she was not herself. A mysterious green midnight haunted between her legs, as if there she held the gateway to dream and nightmare. It was phallic, and vulval, and some oceanic *other* filled with hunger and rage. Her flesh danced like kelp beneath the waves, the pale skin cracked open by murky underwater fissures. Green bone shined through the gaps.

Her canines stretched against a backdrop of sharp teeth, and a brief catlike hiss erupted before twisting into a fit of cruel laughter.

"*I'm a woman*," Ivory echoed, almost giddy. "Now you know how your daughter felt."

Viola's jaw quivered, her teeth chattering, she had no words, no thoughts, all her understanding had slipped away.

Ivory's shadow twitched—her fist rocketing toward Viola's face. Pain exploded across her temple.

And then everything went black.

From the Diary of Cabrina Brite,
June 12, 2018

They asked me: What do you think happens when we die?
And I told them: I think, therefore I am.
And they said: A penny for your thoughts.
And I asked them: What do you think happens when we die?

39. THE LAUGHING BEAST

There it was—Cabrina's house. Xi had spent hours crawling through underbrush away from it, evading Cabrina's father, but the return had only taken minutes. Likely too late to head off Ivory and Honey, but at least Xi didn't have to worry about being handcuffed and stuffed in the back of Gary Brite's cruiser. He had worse troubles to deal with in town than harassing the locals, if he wasn't dead already.

A chorus of screams, sirens, and gunshots spread from Main Street and across Cape Morning. Rex had interpreted the vampires' westward movement as them leaving town, but that didn't mean they would leave it unscathed. Xi could hear the echoes down Harper Lane, where neighboring houses felt the coming onslaught crash through their lit windows.

And yet this house stood quiet.

Xi emerged onto the backyard, its grass still wet from the earlier rain. A gravel patch scarred the ground beneath a rusted swing set, its chains dangling seatless. The house's windows had been lit up when she escaped earlier, but now the glass stood dark. Flashing red-and-blue lights at the front cast the house in silhouette.

If only Xi had her phone and its flashlight. She could find it upstairs in her purse were she to wander that far, but she would have to step inside first.

Nothing barred her way—the screen door looked to have been torn off its hinges and abandoned in the grass. The back door hung ajar, its outer wooden edge broken around the knob. Xi tried to tell herself anyone from high school could've done that damage with the right boots and thigh muscles.

But a former classmate hadn't kicked this door in. Shallow grooves striped the frame, suggesting sizable claws. Evidence of Honey? Or had Ivory changed when she became the vampires' key?

Xi tiptoed around the fallen screen door and hunched close to the black open gap. A subtle breeze slid around her, into the house and through. Maybe another door stood open, allowing for a draft, but the airy movement felt more like the house was breathing her in. Like it could smell her.

She'd felt the same outside Ivory's home, and now she knew why. Ivory had been part of this nightmare since before Xi found Cabrina's diary, certainly before Xi had stopped by earlier today. Maybe even back in the cemetery when Xi and Rex had painted the grave marker, thinking Cabrina still lay in the ground. Ivory must've had her own agenda to come asking what had happened to Cabrina, and in coming to the house tonight, and oblivious Xi had gone to Ivory asking for help. She must've been absolutely thrilled. Hadn't she asked about the diary at the cemetery? Odds were good that she, rather than Viola, had taken it from the bedroom after Xi passed out.

Her heart raced too fast for her to black out again. Someone like Viola might faint, or crack up mentally. Not Xi.

"I love you, Cab," Xi whispered, with the faintest hope that Cabrina would somehow know it, wherever the sky had taken her.

Xi crossed the splintered wood and kitchen tiles, then passed the countertops and island. Her open palm found a light switch, but she stopped herself from hitting it. Light might draw eyes from the sky, while darkness would pretend there was no prey here to find. It could also hide Ivory and her pet monster.

What would Xi say when she found them? Beg Ivory to cut Cabrina loose from the horde? Xi had only the faintest grasp of how tonight affected Cabrina. Ivory might not understand what she'd done at all. That shadow of Ghost Cat Island was the source, but had it released a flock of individual prisoners? Or did some great cosmic hunger link the vampires like smartphones to a cloud service, and the infectious instinct had Cabrina in its grip?

They could be many throats with one stomach, couldn't they? Ivory was their key, had opened their door, but that didn't mean she had control, or that she cared what happened to this town.

This house, these people, Cabrina—they were what Ivory had come for. Convincing her to abandon her intent might be fruitless.

Xi had to try anyway. She crept toward the kitchen's edge and peered into the living room. A black rectangle formed the side door to the garage. Red-and-blue lights from atop a police cruiser flashed across the darkness from the picture window at the front of the house.

Illuminating the silhouettes of hunched figures throughout the living room.

Xi flinched back, stifling a yelp. A few of the vampires must have followed Honey here.

Except nothing came creeping from the living room, at least that Xi could hear. She waited a breath before peeking half her face around the kitchen doorway again.

Light again flashed from the cop cruiser outside, sharpening the figures' shapes—they were overturned furniture. The couch, a recliner, the coffee table with its papers and coasters scattered. One of the end tables was missing. Each passing light made the shadows twitch and come alive, but there were no vampires here that Xi could see. No living people either.

She slinked onto the living room carpet, her eyes on the picture window. The curtains and their rod had fallen, and lengthy shards jutted from the window's borders in a row of glassy teeth.

Beyond the window, the cop cruiser blinked its lights from an odd angle in the driveway, its driver having parked fast and sloppy. Xi guessed it had been Cabrina's father. The driver side door hung open, suggesting the driver had tried stepping out. The red spatter on the door's edge said he hadn't made it far. Something must've forced its way inside, pushing the driver deeper. Had he fought back, or instead tried to slide over the gear shift and passenger seat to escape? Xi had no idea.

She could only tell the attacker had painted the inner windshield with a shredded blue uniform and the cop's insides.

Honey, Honey.

Only a few shards of glass crunched underfoot as Xi backed away. The window looked to have been smashed outward, its fragments glittering red and blue over the bushes and the lawn. Everywhere disaster touched gave hints of a predator's territory.

We left biology in a ditch the moment Cab showed up after her funeral, Rex had said at the beach.

He had a point. These vampires weren't simple animals with rules of territory and aggression, especially if some great united instinct bound them together in the wind. But had something remained inside the house after dealing with Gary Brite?

Xi turned around and approached the wall. To her left, the stairway to the second floor climbed over the first-floor bathroom door and kitchen. Any other day she should have found framed photographs on this wall, but tonight they dotted the carpet instead, cracked and broken by an angry hand.

In their place, thick gouges opened the plaster, carved by massive claws. A wound taller than Xi opened the living room to what should have been insulation and wiring, or even the backyard, but Xi saw none of that on the other side.

Instead, she faced the sea.

Unsteady waters lapped at the living room carpet, running off rhythmic tides. They beat at slabs of black rock spreading inches beneath the oceanic surface, forming a broad trail away from the house, and then they climbed toward a dark mountain rising from the sea. Where black clouds smothered Cape Morning's sky tonight, stars painted the world beyond the otherworldly gateway, their light cold and loveless.

Xi knew this place. Cabrina had passed it through a vision-filled feeding, some shadow to Cape Morning, a kind of Cape Shadow. Someplace Cabrina had seen and written about.

A place where vampires might have slept while their spirits haunted an innocent girl on the far side of two worlds. Wanting to make her their key. Taking someone else when she refused.

This was where it began.

The living room floor groaned behind Xi and to her right, as if something were stepping from the side door connecting the garage to the house. Gruff breathing filled the living room.

Xi fixed her eyes hard on the opening to Cape Shadow. Her thoughts skittered to that night in Rex's bed, her hand caught in Cabrina's unseen grasp. Something far more fearsome lurked in the house tonight. She would relish turning to see Cabrina now.

But harsh breath suggested a larger beast, some big bad wolf come to blow the house down along with the fool who'd wandered inside. Maybe the whole of Cape Morning would scatter like small-town confetti.

Or the beast might be a cat, playing with its food. Waiting for Xi to turn around before carving into her with the same claws that had broken through reality to reach Cape Shadow.

Xi's neck twitched. She didn't want to look but couldn't stop herself.

Two yellow eyes burned above her shoulder like evil suns. Shadows shifted around them, where the upturned living room furniture seemed to strain at this presence, pulled by a violent wind. Winking lights outlined an ox-sized mass of gold and black fur standing on two legs. A hyena-like head stretched forward, its snout caked in red and black.

Xi fell backward screaming. She landed on a shattered photo frame, tried to get up, and slashed one palm on cracked glass. Her painful hesitation let the beast slide over her, cutting off any escape.

It didn't look right. Not like a real animal, more like a thousand sleepers had conjured the beast together and then awoken so abruptly that they'd dragged their conjuration from dream into reality. Xi couldn't guess whose blood coated the muzzle, couldn't guess anything, could only exhale another shrill scream until it scraped her throat raw. Her limbs and insides were going limp. Her organs would unravel themselves and die before accepting this abomination, and Xi wished for that bodily collapse.

Anything not to feel the hot breath, like a ghost house catching her scent.

Honey, Honey. Yes, Xi recognized this thing from Main Street.

She let out a shaky whisper. "Honey?"

The monster's chest swelled and sank with excited breath, and thick slobber dripped from her smirking muzzle, like no one had properly fed her in a thousand years. Why did Honey have to smile like that?

Xi turned to the eyes and immediately regretted it. Each iris formed a halo of sunshine around a black ocean, where Xi's reflection twisted in the waves at each flashing light. Eyes wide, lips peeled back from teeth, every part of her expression distorted in terror. She didn't look like herself in that reflection. She looked like a girl screaming without sound as she sank to the bottom of the sea.

Honey's shadow drank in the world. She dipped her head to Xi's side, and a coarse tongue lapped the blood from Xi's palm.

"Please, please," Xi muttered. She couldn't squeeze her desperation into a proper sentence. Only begging.

Honey let out a breathy two-note laugh—*heeee-heeee*, as if mocking Xi's plea—and then her jaws cracked wide open over Xi's head.

Humidity fogged her glasses. Hot slobber ran syrupy into her hair and down her neck, and the world above Xi's head turned into a dripping carnivorous sky. Glistening rows of sharp teeth rounded undulating muscles over a bottomless black throat. This hunger had no end.

Xi squeezed her eyes shut. She hugged her knees to her chest, curling into a tight ball. Small prey would be easier to devour, she knew that, but she couldn't fight the childlike instinct to become tiny, and then hide and hope the predator would ignore her like any decent monster from stories.

Think of something, she told herself. *A poem, a plan. Anything but this.*

If she filled her head with enough thoughts, maybe she could turn her skull into a rock-hard jawbreaker, and that would be the end of Honey's hunger. She would vanish, and her brood would vanish too, and this night would be nothing but a bad dream.

But instead an intrusive memory yanked Xi down into childhood, when her arms were thin as pencils and her father squeezed her wrist in his meaty hand, demanding she *take it like a man*, as if he could wring out her soul in purpling bruises.

The world stilled, its outside noises muffled as Honey's mouth closed against both sides of Xi's head. She stopped feeling her bent-up legs, or the sting in her lacerated palm. The only sensation became the harsh points around her ears where sharp teeth readied to drive through her flesh and skull. Tears slithered down her cheeks.

And then footsteps stomped across the living room, and Honey recoiled from Xi to face a blurry shadow rushing out of the night, and a steel blade glowing with red and blue reflections.

Rex told himself Marla's spirit had coiled around the machete. She could be animals and trees when tonight was over, but first her blood had gone to the blade, and he needed her strength right now. And Joan's. And his dad's, too, down in Boston. All of Rex's parents should surge through him, watch over him, see they'd raised the kind of son who stood by his friends with only the frailest hope against the monsters that had haunted Cabrina.

And turned her. Split her apart in ways Rex didn't understand, likely never would.

But he could split Honey in a way he knew. Same as he'd done to Scarlet, and Marla in the end, if only to keep a promise. A greater kindness than this fucked-up vampire deserved.

Across the flickering living room, Honey hunched with Xi's head in her jaws, a deep chuckle aching from her monstrous chest.

Rex could stop her now, while she only had eyes for Xi.

He tensed his sweat-soaked fingers tight around the machete's grip, stormed across the carpet, over the upturned couch, and swung the blade into the thick meat of Honey's neck.

Her deep chuckle snapped into a wet shriek. Tendons split with a crimson spray as Rex tore the machete free, leaving a deep gash in Honey's flesh. Her outstretched limbs jerked in reflex, letting Xi wriggle loose as neck blood poured down her face and clothes.

"Shouldn't have happened!" Rex shouted, a growl in his voice. "Should've been the three of us forever!"

He didn't know if he meant himself and his friends or himself and his mothers. Every possible trio, a life too complex for the undead. His machete slashed Honey's neck again.

She thrashed a claw as he dodged back, and she snapped her jaws at him moments after he'd strafed to one side, keeping to her shoulder. Right in the crook where a beast couldn't easily reach.

He swung again, and the blade kissed bone. A canyon drooled crimson down Honey's golden fur. Her tissue was thick, but she wasn't tougher than steel.

She stretched her jaws wide open in another scream, almost as if dislocated, and then she twisted around and crunched down on Rex's free arm.

Teeth sank through flesh, through mind. The house melted from sight, its cream-colored plaster shedding its skin.

A swirl of pinkish tubes glistened and writhed where there used to be walls. Nightmare faces peeked between them, their unblinking eyes glaring at Rex, through Rex, and their mouths chattered out discordant laughter.

Cab wanted to show me something, Xi had said the other night. *The vision.*

Illusions. Hallucinations. Another kind of glamour. This wasn't real.

Rex jolted under knifelike teeth, and his bones caved in their grip. He wasn't in a nest of tubes and eyes—he was in Cabrina's house. Honey had him by the arm, eager to tear him limb from limb.

He tilted his head back in a screech, hauled his machete up, and hacked again, again. Vertebrae snapped apart, tendons splitting in a hot river.

And yet Honey clung on, teeth sinking deeper. Another claw swiped through empty air.

Rex dodged left. His chopping turned manic, spattering his clothes and skin with blood and sinew, anything to get this monstrous head off his arm.

Honey's eyes had lost their glaring suns, the irises decaying to an off-yellow pus with gray shapes wriggling in the pupils. Something in her was dying, or already dead. These were corpse-creatures, only pretending to live. How much of her proud beastly form was an illusion? Rex couldn't know, but she had a head and a body. Separating these parts would have to be enough to kill her.

Xi lurched from the floor and kicked at Honey's chest. She was gasping for breath, for sight, her glasses caked in blood.

Rex could barely manage a coherent thought. Pain spat black spots across his sight. He wanted to shout for Xi to run, but only a wordless roar scratched up from his throat.

Honey's head bubbled around his arm. Semblance to an overgrown hyena wasn't enough anymore; fresh rows of teeth burst from her gums and through her snout in spiny fields of raw red muscle. One eye bulged, its decayed sun collapsing into a black, worming ocean. Her long pink tongue slithered out and jabbed Rex's caught forearm with needly teeth.

The same rippling power tore at Honey's body. Sharp points jutted along her spine, and her gut sagged with fresh teeth as if it might split into a new maw. She might soon explode into a bodiless cloud of fangs and claws, the vampire becoming an organic garbage disposal, ready to stew everything it touched into meaty pulp.

Xi wrapped her arms around the jittering head and tugged away from Rex. Vicious pain stabbed up his arm and into his shoulder.

"Now!" Xi shrieked. "Do it now!"

Rex wanted to cry again, scream again, let the black spots take over. He raised the machete as high as he could and gave another strike, deepening the canyon through Honey's neck.

White barbs pricked up from the canyon's depths as if Honey's spine had grown a crown. Fresh teeth twitched back and forth like a pair of jaws reaching from the redness.

She was trying to form a new head before she lost the first. Not hyena at all this time, not like any animal on Earth, but a nightmare face of saber teeth and tusks and horns.

Rex slashed again, and now the tendons reached for him like a twisting red serpent, its tip splitting open in a nest of fangs. This snake would devour the sun. Honey's flesh was a story of her making, and she could give it the end she pleased before she ripped everyone in this room apart.

On the far side of the nightmare, Xi ducked toward the neck in a high-pitched cry. Mouth open, head swinging down, her teeth ripped into the flesh of Honey's serpentine muscles.

Honey twisted, snapping tendons within herself. The darkness clouded in her eyes, as if she'd quit seeing Rex, the living room, anything, her mind overtaken by Xi's sudden bite.

It was enough of a distraction. Honey's jaws loosened slightly from Rex's left arm, and he tensed his right as it climbed overhead. The machete slashed again in one hard swing, severing the last tendons from Honey's neck.

Her body jolted with a sharp quake and then collapsed in a tangled pile, limbs splaying in every direction. A puddle oozed from her fresh neck stump, glowing with red-and-blue light.

The head turned to dead weight on Rex's arm. It dragged him sideways for an instant, and then the teeth scraped from his bicep and forearm as the head dropped to the floor.

He forced himself back a step. Every movement shot pain up his nerves, and his mangled arm hung limp at his side. The jacket sleeve was a chewed mess, the flesh beneath likely worse. Honey must have broken a bone. Torn important tissue. Rex had never felt blades in his muscle before. Would he go into shock now?

Xi scuttled from the severed head and wiped blood off her glasses. "Holy hell, Rex."

Hell, Rex thought. Yes, that sounded right.

A soul-sucking thought told him he should bleed out right here. If he lived, he would eventually have to go back into town and find out if his Ma was alive. What if she wasn't?

And what if she was? Rex would have to tell her about Marla, if she didn't already know. He could make up a nice lie about what he'd had to do to her body, but that wouldn't change that she was dead, and Joan would have to know it. To see her face then—he would wish Honey had killed him.

He was halfway there already. With every breath, his arm hurt a little worse.

Something wet dragged against the carpet. Had Honey torn Rex's arm from his body instead of breaking it? He felt the pain and weight too keenly for that relief, and a glance to his left showed it hanging there, miserable yet intact.

He swallowed hard. Didn't want to look down. Forced himself to look anyway.

Honey's head twitched at his feet. Glistening fingers of muscle clawed from its ragged wound, and lines of sinew reached from the body's stumpy neck nearby.

Her severed parts were groping for each other like lovers in the dark.

Rex began hacking at the floor in sloppy strikes. The machete cut ragged lines in the carpet, but the crimson worms retreated from the blade and sought new paths between the head and neck. He kept chopping at them, again and again, his teeth set in fury.

Honey's jaws snapped open and shut, and the head wriggled toward Rex's ankles. He kicked and scrambled backward, swinging the machete at another muscly strand. They were getting thicker, the head growing bold. A phlegmy chuckle tore from Honey's open throat.

Rex veered from the connecting tissue and swung at the head itself, splitting open a putrid eye. The pupil cracked egglike, and long maggoty things wriggled free from the skull.

Laughter screamed through Honey's teeth, and her surviving sulfuric eye blazed wild at the ceiling.

Xi launched past the pulsating body and grabbed for the head. Its lower jaw hung open, eye pus and bloody drool mixing as they dripped over Xi's arms. Honey snapped twice, but Xi hugged the head tight against her chest. Honey's laughter quieted behind clenched teeth.

The body thumped toward Xi in clumsy spasms. Without the head, it didn't seem to know how to use its limbs, but every muscle jerked and thrashed to fix that, like Honey could taste herself in the air. Her toothy gut gave a sucking wet gulp.

Everything hurt, and Rex wanted to stop, but this monster wouldn't give them a break.

Xi darted from the body and toward the living room wall. A dark mouth opened in the plaster, maybe four feet around, and she ducked through to the other side. Her sneakers should have crushed backyard grass, but instead they slopped through shallow water.

"In here!" Xi shouted.

Rex hesitated—there shouldn't be an *in there*, only an *out there*.

Honey's body slapped at the floor beside him, still blindly chasing its head toward the *in there*. He loped past it, the machete dripping in his grasp. The strange hole in the wall was not the kind of escape he'd have chosen, but Xi was there, and he didn't know where else to go.

The air shifted around him as he stepped over the lip. Calm wind slid through his short hair, and a coolness sank into his skin.

Ocean scents coated the smell of animal musk and the metallic taste in his mouth. Even his arm ached less.

Xi hurried from the hole, still clutching the head in her arms. Slabs of rock lingered inches beneath the water's surface, leading toward a stretch of black land rising from the waves.

Rex followed her, but he couldn't help glancing over his shoulder.

Honey's body pounded the floor like a fish out of water, smacking ragdoll limbs against furniture and fallen photo frames. It looked to have lost whatever compass directed it toward the head, broken by this impossible rift from Cape Morning to wherever Xi had led them. Or maybe it could only move so much after decapitation, and they just needed to wait it out.

Or was the body frightened of crossing through the hole?

Rex eyed the dark world around him, its unfamiliar ocean and glimmering stars of alien constellations, and then he chased Xi toward the rising land.

With a feeling he should be frightened, too.

41. CAPE SHADOW

In visions, when Cabrina bit into her, Xi had seen the wrong Ghost Cat Island. The one she'd read about in the pages of Cabrina's diary.

And she saw it now, leading away from Cabrina's house. Cape Morning's scrap of rock had vanished, and in this shadow place swelled a mountainous land against a twinkling night sky. The diary had answered some of what happened to Cabrina—she'd swallowed something from the sea, been plagued by visions and visitors, had hoped to put everything right—but there was no entry to tell of her fate that final night. Why hadn't Cabrina come home?

Ghost Cat Island. Everything began and ended here. Maybe for everyone.

Some of the geography differed from the vision. The once-solid mountain had cracked open like a titanic stone cocoon, and Xi could guess what nightmarish butterflies had flown from that open door. She hadn't seen this path of scarcely submerged stones branching off the island either. A small nub of rock jutted from the sea, its face marred by a cave of red and blue lights—the way back to Cabrina's house.

Cape Shadow seemed a permeable shore. Openings on the other side of the worlds might dictate which parts formed and crumbled here, as shifting as the sands. As dreams.

Honey's claws had gouged the way here from Cabrina's house. Would they make another?

Xi and Rex put some distance between themselves and the hole, in case Honey's body came crawling through to grab its head. The snouted bulk fought in Xi's arms, but weaker now. Either the distance from her torso had drained Honey's strength, or Cape Shadow's frailness had infected her remains.

The rupture back to the house was a tiny dot by the time Rex plunked down on the island's shore and cradled his injured arm in his lap.

"Is it bad?" Xi asked, lugging Honey's head toward him. "Can I see?"

Rex said nothing. He only gazed out at the choppy gray sea and the sky awash in cold starlight. The skeleton of some long-dead sea monster formed another island a little ways from shore, and near it towered a curving bony spire, while gargantuan stone monoliths climbed from the waves and reached for unknown constellations.

Beyond them stretched a separate black-sanded shoreline, but Xi didn't think there was much land beyond. It was only an edge to this ocean.

"I stood there in Cab's vision," Xi said, stepping beside Rex. "I looked out on the ocean's dead things, and old things, off to the shadow of Ghost Cat Island. Cab didn't have me look back, but if she had, there wasn't going to be a shadow town. This feels like a cramped world." She hefted the severed head tight to her chest. "A place where devils sleep."

Rex remained quiet. The waves hushed as they struck the shore, looking dimmer than Xi's vision, too. Moonlight ebbed; it might have stolen its light from Cape Morning and was now running dry. Cape Shadow seemed the less real of the two, one rude awakening away from melting into fog.

"It's like with their bodies," Xi said. "We left biology behind.

Physics, too. They're more like poetry. They write over their forms, write everything they want into the world. I don't know if they found this place or made it, but Cab dreamed about it."

Rex let out a hard sigh. "Fuckin' vampires."

Xi coughed into a blunt laugh. "Yeah," she said. "Fucking vampires."

She laughed again, harder this time, and kept on laughing. Nothing to be done but let it out. If she didn't laugh, she would sob again, and they had more hardship ahead tonight before she was allowed to collapse and cry like she deserved.

Rex turned to her, his voice hollow. "The hell we doing here, Xi? Waiting out the dead?"

Xi's last laugh died away. She cleared her throat. "Viola threatened Ivory. I saw it, and it only made sense when she was riding Honey toward Harper Lane that they were headed back to Cab's house. I didn't know about this place, but Ivory wasn't in the house with Honey. She could've come this way."

"So, Ivory started this?" Rex asked, a knife in his tone.

"I think it started way before any of us were born," Xi said, clutching the severed head. "Cabrina wrote about being a key for the devils on Ghost Cat Island. She was trying to figure them out with the scraps she had. When she died, they must've turned to Ivory." She shook her head, sticking together thoughts of diary pages and glimpses of nightmare. "It's like with a real key. You can't shove clean metal into a hole; you have to cut its teeth. Cabrina wouldn't do it, but Ivory must've been—I don't know, more cooperative."

Rex nodded, taking this in. "She was willing."

Xi supposed so. "It's like the rule about vampires having to be invited in, but for our entire world. Now they're in, and like you said, it looks like they're moving on."

"If I were them, I wouldn't risk getting trapped here again," Rex said.

That made sense to Xi. "What'll happen to the town?"

"I don't care anymore." Rex sounded like he meant it.

"And everywhere else?" Xi asked.

Rex squeezed his eyes shut. "Same as here. Death."

Xi could picture it—a spreading threat too slow to notice at first, and then unavoidable once everyone gave up on denying it. "They'll be everywhere. Alleyways, back porches, farmhouses, other beaches—"

"Ice cream place parking lots," Rex said blankly.

Xi stiffened. What did he mean by that?

Except she knew, didn't she? In her fervor to beat Ivory and Honey to Cabrina's house, Xi had forgotten Marla. At best, some subconscious basement thought might've assumed she was safe in the car. But not now.

"Rex, is Marla—"

"Gone," Rex cut in. "She's gone." He kicked a pebble into the water. "Nothing I could do."

Xi set Honey's head down and then crashed against Rex's back, her arms around his shoulders. She squeezed him tight, bloody face against his hair, letting him sink against her gore-coated chest.

They were overwhelmed and exhausted. The night should be over, with both of them victorious, but it ran on and on, and people were dead. Marla was dead.

"I love you," Xi whispered.

It seemed better than telling Rex she was sorry. And it was true. Same as she loved Cabrina.

"Cutting off the head killed the one I met before." Rex raised his uninjured arm and wiped the flat of his machete blade against his jeans. Dark blood stained the denim. "Why not her?"

He didn't look back, but Xi turned toward Honey's head. She had no idea why she'd set it down gently. Some part of her didn't want to throw a moving creature on the ground, even undead, no matter how terrible.

Had Rex arrived a moment later, Xi might have seen a new vision beneath Honey's bite, same as with Cab. An education in horror before death.

And what about Xi's bite? She'd tasted blood when she sank her teeth into Honey's neck, but Honey had reacted like a drug had struck her system.

"When I bit her, it felt like part of me reached into her head," Xi said. "Not just my teeth. Cab's bite showed me visions of this place, her feelings, anything she wanted me to see."

Rex finished cleaning the machete. He must have seen something when Honey bit him, but he didn't look up for sharing.

"Honey must have seen something when I bit her, too," Xi went on. "I didn't mean to show her anything. I was scared out of my mind. But it's like you said at the beach—I might be turning. Going vampire. At least enough to crave blood and slip a thought into someone's mind."

Rex turned back toward Honey's still-living head with a starry glint of murder in his eyes.

Xi hugged him again. She wouldn't have thought it possible before, but now she was grateful for Cabrina showing up like a ghost outside her window after the funeral. Tonight would have snapped her brain in two otherwise. The days and nights of hauntings, vampires, and weird shit that followed had built a foundation before she had to watch a severed hyena-woman head wriggle on a rocky island in this shadowy netherworld.

Then again, fear of her dead father had haunted both Xi and her mother for years. Maybe she'd always been ready for some dreadful eventuality.

Her father felt trite in the wake of a monster like Honey. Had Josephine ever genuinely feared him after death? Or had Xi projected her own fears onto her mother? Her father's ghost now seemed a childlike explanation for Josephine's trauma, an empty cup Xi had kept sipping from that she could now toss aside. Silver lining to the night's dark vampiric presence.

"Those things," Rex said. "They've been trying to come back for a long time, haven't they? Why pick on Cab?"

"She crossed their path," Xi said. "That's as much as she knew."

"Nothing special to it, right?" Rex forced a one-shouldered shrug, as if his were the smallest problems in the world. "She didn't want to be a key. Just a girl, last to say *No*. And Ivory's nothing special either. Just the first to say *Yes*."

Xi thought of Cabrina's empty eyes, how she'd drifted away without any say of her own. Drones to a unified craving, one overlord stomach guiding their conjoined cosmic hunger first to Cape Morning and then away. It had given them the strength to punch a hole in the world.

It had let them take Cabrina. Her choices in life and death alike were only pretend things. Honey and the others had wanted her, and that was her fate. She could have lived and let herself be molded into Honey's key. She'd died instead and become a phantom. Decay in her house, undead washed ashore, vampire priestess at sea—doom down Cabrina's every road.

Unless Xi and Rex changed her future.

He chinned over his shoulder. "What about that thing?"

Honey's head strained inch by inch to get away. Xi paced over to it, squatted on her haunches, and reached out to pick it up. It snapped at her hand, but she scooped under its lower jaw and hugged it hard against her chest, clamping Honey's teeth together.

"Show me," Xi said. "Where's the key?"

Honey fussed another moment, and then her nostrils flared and her hyena snout tensed. She leaned to one side and drooled over

Xi's arms. There was a taste in the air leading up the shore, around the base of the cracked-open mountain. Something Honey knew.

Xi started along the mountain's foot, and Rex followed. She had no idea what they were going to do when they found Ivory or what kind of monster she had become.

But finding her was their only chance to help Cabrina.

42. HER SMILE

Rex.

The voice was a claw in his mind. He was trying to think of Marla, but a new sensation itched through every thought. He looked to Xi at his side, carrying the head against her chest like a squirming kitten she couldn't let escape, its mouth full of knives. An emptied eye socket gazed at the sky.

Rex, wake. Dream ends. All dark.

He shook his head too hard, and the movement tugged at his shoulder and aching arm. Should've known better than to do that, but he wasn't used to this voice scratching inside him, creeping up his likely cracked bones. Hearing voices that until now had been locked in his marrow. Maybe brought out by this gray dreamland.

Come. And see. Make right. Your pain.

"You hear that?" Rex asked.

Xi gave the slightest headshake. Talking out what had happened and piecing together the arrangement of nightmare had taken its toll. She was a worn-out girl, needing rest. Carrying that head was a heavy task to bear.

It shifted in her arms, turning to Rex, and it offered a new smile.

He gritted his teeth and faced the path ahead. Up the stony shore, around the curve of this mountainous island. One step in front of the other.

Rex, come. Rex, be.

But wherever he put his attention, the voice kept clawing.

From the Diary of Cabrina Brite,
June 14, 2018

This entry is not for me. I write it for Xi and Rex, who I love most, in case the devils have their way. In case they cut their losses and leave me a ghost in the water.

> ~~I didn't let you kill me.~~
> ~~Can't be what they want, even if it kills me~~
> ~~Everything's killing me~~

No, it's too harsh. And obvious. Come on, kill, kill, kill, all three lines? Xi taught me better, try again.

Rex came by this afternoon. Maybe he used one of his talismans and sensed a wrong feeling in the air. He might've got inside if Dad had been here to answer the door.

But there was only her. She sent Rex away. I heard her chastising him in that perfect political way, and I didn't realize who she was talking to until I heard him cursing up the driveway. I wish I could've seen him, even hugged him.

But it was better for him to go away. He was never going to be my only visitor today. Just the one who tried to use the door.

There's something else outside the house this evening. It isn't hard to guess what it is.

The devils have lost their patience. They're coming up the walls, toward the windows, not even waiting for me to fall asleep. I want to finish this poem before they take me, but they're right on the other side of the sill while I write this, tapping at the screen. There's even a voice, whispering for me. They

It was Xi. Not devils. Just Xi, standing on the front lawn, throwing bits of backyard gravel she must have got from under the swing set.

I started laughing so hard, I had to bite my wrist to keep quiet. She just stood there waiting for me to straighten up before I could open the glass and screen to talk to her. I told her she was nuts, throwing stones at the house.

She ignored me. *We know something's wrong*, she said, meaning her and Rex, but it's pretty obvious they don't know much of anything.

And Xi didn't ask. I even mentioned I was writing in the diary when she surprised me, but she didn't want to know what I was writing. Instead, she started telling me how special this summer was going to be. How she and Rex wouldn't let me be captive here. No more Cabrina the Caged. Xi didn't put it that way, but it's what she meant. She said they were going to pool their money and get me a phone of my own so we can text, and I just have to keep it hidden.

We got you, she said. *You know that, right?*

I know she meant it. I know she thinks it even now that she's run up the driveway before anyone here can yell at her, to where she left her mom's car parked on the next street. All this effort just to see me for a few minutes from the lawn.

We got you. It isn't anything I can feel.

But when I looked down into Xi's eyes, I could almost believe it. What I'm sure about is that she and Rex love me as much as I love them.

And I'm also sure, in knowing too little and loving me too much, they'll try to prove they got me. They'll want to save me, which means they'll let themselves get dragged down. They got me? No, I would get them, the way a monster gets you, like an anchor with its thick rope tied around their legs before plunging into the sea.

The plan is to live, but I can't promise that, and I can't let them go down with me. If I'm going to see the other side of this, I have to do it myself. Xi and Rex have futures, while I have a mystery.

But I've figured out at least one part of what's to come.

I won't be the key.

I tried to take control of the dreams, like lucid dreaming, but they're not mine, so I can't change them. They come from that other place. Cape Morning's Ghost Cat Island dreams up its mountain, and it sends the dreams here on the devils' backs. I can't fight a mountain's dreams, especially where the devils share one sleep, one thought, one desire.

All I have is me, in this body, and I won't give any of it to them. They can't have my name, my flesh, my me. I won't be their key.

Instead, I'm going to give them back what's theirs. Not at their place, their island, but the Ghost Cat Island in my world. Our little bit of rock isn't much, but neither am I. Maybe together, we can do something right.

~~To make me was wrong.~~
~~To remake me is wrong.~~
Too repetitious.
~~Let me live.~~ I want to live.
I cannot become what they'll make me,
Even if I'm less than I was, less than I could be.
~~This is my choice.~~ I just chose this death over another.
~~She has already taken me.~~ They have already taken me.
Getting closer.

<u>The Future, Version A</u>
I bring the devils back what I swallowed and I live

<u>The Future, Version B</u>
I bring the devils back what I swallowed and I die

Leave the dreams of that island behind and head to the beach here and now. Another dive into the dark sea, and then it's over. It's a risk, getting close to where they sleep in that other Ghost Cat Island.

But haven't I always taken risks? If I throw up the ocean heart I drank at the beach that night, it should be no harm, no foul. Like we never started this ritual, and I don't have to be a ghost, a key, or a beast. I can be a girlfriend, a student, an optimist. Even a daughter.

If nothing else, I need to do the right thing. Especially when no one else can or will.

Okay, I have it all figured out. I'll write these poems again on a new page, but they should stay in the book, too. In case I come back, or in case I don't, I might want to read them again, contrasted with each other, to see that I was wrong. One way or another.

The Future, Version A
If I can be nothing else, then I will be love.
Pure, unstoppable love.
Endless love.
To everyone I can.
To everyone who lets me.
Time is finite,
But I am an ocean of love,
And there is no emptying my affection.
Even in life, even in death.
The love is everything.
—Cabrina Aphrodite Brite

The Future, Version B
Don't call me a suicide. I want to live.
I've simply chosen one death over another
After I've been robbed of life.
—Cabrina Aphrodite Brite

[a section is missing, torn out by hand]

43. THE BROKEN

No one ever really got what they wanted. And no one should. Ivory had been kidding herself thinking this journey could end any other way when she first went looking for ghosts. Every step since she spotted Cabrina's body in the surf had led to this moment. Maybe since that April day nineteen years ago when Cabrina was born, a stranger to Ivory until now. Or maybe since Ivory moved to Cape Morning, or since she became a creature of life, or since those kids at the trick campfire taught her the cruelty behind a friendly smile.

So many possible beginnings. Only one end.

Ivory lay reclining on the stone steps of Ghost Cat Island, waiting for that finality to strike. It would come in a sound first, and then a sight. Another Cape Shadow awakening.

Thinning moonlight reached hollow fingers down her sea-green wounds, into the tide pool that first showed her the shaping power of this dreamlike place. Its toothy rocks were cracked now, much like the mountain behind her.

Much like herself. She doubled over from the steps and coughed a puddle of blood into the tide pool waters below. Hard surfaces rubbed at the back of her throat, as if growing the same greenstone that peeked through the open wounds down her body. One of them had first been carved by Viola and a scissor blade. It hadn't healed, had instead transcended ordinary flesh, and there was nothing Viola could do about it.

"Take it easy," Ivory whispered to herself.

A dull pain clenched at her middle and then branched through her bones. Were they all turning to oceanic stone? Transformation did not promise immortality, and immortality did not promise an organic nature. She might be calcifying, her body becoming a literal stone key. Because she'd dared return to Cape Shadow? Honey had refused to step through the new doorway after she'd carved it into the wall of Cabrina's house for Ivory.

Maybe Ivory should have guessed there would be a personal cost to what she'd done. Her body was a key in the sleepers' ritual, but it might be the kind to break upon use, only good for one unlocking.

Her skin prickled—there were eyes on her, watching from the cavern atop the stone steps. Even with the mountain having split open when she freed the sleepers, its hall and caverns remained, and the depths of Ghost Cat Island gaped open to its heart of sea and rock.

Ivory had visited here twice before, the second time following Honey's lead, but the first time was to chase a ghost. That ghost had not been here that night. Now things were different.

"Soon," Ivory said. "There's no rush now."

Honey had called the guest from the sky while she and Ivory were still making their way to Cabrina's house. The guest and Ivory had only briefly met with windows between them, and the morning a body washed ashore, but Ivory could make everything right. Or at least some things.

"I might've gotten carried away." Ivory reclined again over the steps. Their stone dug grooves into her back, but she scarcely felt them. Her skin sank beneath her touch, malleable like putty. "Nobody's ever made me the center of attention before, unless they wanted to hurt me. I didn't think everything through."

Deep shadows climbed the distant sea-risen monoliths off the island's shore. The moonlight was dimming by faint degrees. Cape Shadow had been stable when Ivory first dreamed of it, and the times she'd come here before, but now that the sleepers were gone, this world seemed an empty shell, fracturing around its newfound hollowness. Another victim.

"I can at least get this part right," Ivory said. "The world has always been hopelessly fucked for us, but there can be a little justice at the end. For you. For me."

A body stirred against stone at the top of the steps, between where Ivory reclined and where her special guest hid in the cavernous darkness. Groaning followed, and then coughing. The sounds of a promise coming true.

Ivory forced her aching body off the steps, turned around, and staggered toward the top. She cast eyes at the cavern only a moment, where a pale shape stared back, and then she loomed over the prone woman she'd brought here, her light hair clouding around her head.

"Viola." Ivory knelt at Viola's side and spoke in a gentle tone. "Awake at last."

Viola strained to sit up. A purpling welt spread over her temple and into her hairline. Her fingernails scratched at stone, and cloudy confusion haunted her eyes.

"No judgment here," Ivory said. "Not for sleepiness, I mean. It's hard to wake up on this side of the worlds. Sometimes it can take centuries. Eons. Now the whole place is ready to sleep. Even the moon can't keep its eye open."

She cocked her head to one side, casting a glance at the fading circle in the sky.

"I'm dead," Viola said. Her voice came creaky and monotone, as if she'd forgotten how to speak while unconscious. She looked left and right and all around, taking in the gray island, the black sea, and the bleak stars. "It's a dead place."

"You're not dead. One thing at a time." Ivory gestured to their surroundings with an open palm. "I wanted to take you somewhere empty, with no interruptions this time. And nowhere's as empty as here anymore. It's a world all about you now. You, me, and my secret guest."

Viola drew her limbs against her torso, curling up like a dying cockroach. She was paler than usual, as if Honey had let her drink bestial blood, made her part of the brood.

Ivory scooted closer, putting herself into Viola's swaying gaze. "Did you hurt Xi? I didn't want to abandon her, but I couldn't fight you then. Part of me must've trusted you not to shed another teenage girl's blood. One's an occasion, but two's a habit."

Viola kept glancing every which way. A wildness stirred in her wide eyes, gaping jaw, the tremble in her lips. One ear was bare; the other's turquoise earring glinted in the starlight. She must have lost its twin in the trip between worlds.

"You remind me of the kids from back then," Ivory said, wistful.

Viola clawed at her hair. "Never hurt anyone. Never."

Ivory leaned closer. "I didn't have a little nightmare house when I was a kid. My parents gave up loving each other, never split up, but they let me be. I could survive that benign purgatory. But school was a hell of rumors, bruises, and hate—at least until two girls tried to make nice in early junior year. Shannon and Carrie. I thought, hey, I'm sixteen, we're all growing up a little. Or maybe they understood I was just another girl like them, trying to live."

"I was friends with Delia, and Mariah, and Caitlin," Viola said, her voice frail. "I didn't, I wasn't—"

"This isn't about you, Viola." Ivory scratched at the ground. "I don't know if anyone can get it through your skull, but not everything's about you."

Viola thrashed her head from side to side, desperate to wake from an awful dream. She might have understood Cape Shadow better than she realized.

"One autumn night, those girls took me to a party by the woods," Ivory said. "Near one of their houses, to drink horse-piss beer and roast gummy marshmallows around a backyard campfire. Small gathering, a few kids from school. I figured having new friends meant I could make a few more. I never thought it was a trick campfire, trick friendship, somewhere to get me tipsy and weak. They held me down and came at me with fiery branches. *A faggot is only good for burning*, they told me. To keep everyone else warm."

Ivory leaned back and parted her knees, spreading her legs to reveal her inner thigh. She expected a grimace, any reaction, but Viola was a trembling mess. Was she even listening?

"They burned me here." Ivory traced a finger along her tattoo, hoping to guide Viola's eyes. The words *I am a creature of life* were as deep and certain as her stonelike wounds. "Hitting my thighs, same as you. But they tried to burn my cheek, too. My throat and hair. I fought loose and took off into the dark before they could hurt me again. I've done a lot of running away at night. Kept it locked inside, and even with that anger, I played nice, played pretty. Otherwise everyone would decide I was only good for burning. When the scar formed, I buried it in ink, and when high school ended, I threw my senior yearbook off a bridge to bury those monsters at sea. For a long time, I didn't remember their names."

Viola tore her gaze from the ground and looked at the starry sky.

"But then I found out about your daughter, and you," Ivory went on. "And it woke something up inside. Tonight isn't about you, but it isn't about me, either. I only bring up my past so you'll understand, back then, I never wanted to hurt anyone. And Cabrina never wanted to hurt anyone either." She inched close again, and mirth filled her voice. "But now I do. I think I've been waiting for it a long time."

A scraping footstep jerked Viola's attention from unfamiliar constellations to the cavern behind Ivory. Her lips peeled back, baring her teeth. There was something feline about her. Yes, if she deserved it, she would have made a welcome addition to Honey's nest of creatures.

"Can you see my guest?" Ivory leaned sideways, blocking Viola's view. "Don't look at her yet. Look at me."

"Stop." Viola's voice came wet and hitched. "It can stop. Anyone can stop it. Just stop."

"Anyone," Ivory said, tasting the word. She fingered at a greenstone wound between her breasts. "Do you see me as anyone? As a person? Even now?"

Viola's head rose and fell, maybe bobbing *Yes* to Ivory's questions.

"Huh." Ivory took a deep breath to digest this, and then she cast a look of feigned sympathy. "Well. I guess you should've done that for Cabrina. Maybe none of this would've happened to you."

Viola's breath quickened, and beneath it Ivory made out a racing heartbeat, the thick sweet music of surging blood. Seawater slid down her inner thigh, coating her tattoo. She was a creature of life, yes, but also wind and teeth and fury, and this moment of transcendent, ferocious beauty had been a long time coming. A joyous laugh quaked in her chest.

"Look. At me."

Ivory clenched her muscles, pressing claws up from half her fingertips. Red hair bloomed down her spine like a row of flowers on a vine, and her gums ached to grow her canines into fangs. Her limbs corded, meaning to stretch and bend in new ways. She could be a laughing beast like Honey, a monster of forgotten worlds and times.

And then she twisted and spat up another crimson glob. Her tensing body squeezed murky water from her greenstone wounds, and the scents of salt and metal mixed in the air.

She was too weak. There was a cost to this existence, and she hadn't paid it correctly. She was hungry, too.

But Viola's blood was not for Ivory. They would each have to make do until the end, as Cape Shadow darkened around them. Ivory would worry about the future later.

She turned again to Viola. "You told me real women don't threaten—we act. Is dragging you here ladylike enough for you?"

Viola reached for her hair and clawed at her head again. This was going nowhere.

"I tried to talk it out. Really tried. I wanted you to understand, but you wouldn't." Ivory bared sharp teeth. "My mistake. Like you, I wasn't being fair to Cabrina. If she couldn't make you understand across years—*years*—what hope did I have in minutes? I'm not too bright. But you are; it's kind of in your name. Maybe that's why you married your husband, just to get that name."

"Husband," Viola chirped. "Gary? Gary, there's someone in the house."

"Viola," Ivory sang. "He isn't alive anymore. Will you cry for him? You wouldn't cry for her, but maybe it's different when it's your husband. Or is it for yourself? You can't help making everything about you."

Viola's eyes were two wide saucers, her mouth a gaping pit.

"What do you think is the difference between you and her?" Ivory prodded a claw into Viola's flesh. She didn't even flinch, and Ivory gritted her teeth. "Your parts, is that it? What if I start tearing parts out of you? And after each one, you can tell me if you still feel like a woman, or a human, or even if you still feel like living. Oh, and *she* is going to watch."

Ivory leered over her shoulder, back at the cavern, and hissed into the wind.

A lighter hiss answered. Scraping footsteps shuffled from the inside of the cavern and toward its mouth, out into the starlight.

"I had no idea this fury lived inside me," Ivory said. "Honey wanted me to open a door, but you're the one who showed me what was behind it—not just the sleepers. I thought it was pain, but no. I was angry like I never knew. It was small and dark inside me before, but Honey made it big and bright. And now I get to show it. Lucky that way. Some people destroy themselves for that anger, but you showed me how to let it out. Thank God for you, Viola."

Ivory's guest approached at a glacial pace. She wasn't entirely herself right now, starving in more ways than one. They would both be healed soon.

"She needed you," Ivory said. "And she thought she'd get through to you someday, that was the last thing she meant to do, but you wouldn't listen for the thousandth time, and that was the end of her. Until she came back."

"It wasn't—I didn't—" Viola's voice gave out, but she went on mouthing silent words. Tears dotted her unblinking eyes.

"You and I met at her grave," Ivory went on. "I wanted to know what kept her ghost unsettled, and the answer was staring me in the face. You're pretty twisted, Viola. To a mother like you, a dead child is easier on a political campaign than a freak."

"Mine." Viola wrapped her arms tight around her gut. "Mine, mine."

"I know you grew her. But I want her here to see what happens to you. She'll feel better. We all will. I tried to get through to you, too, but you don't love her enough to care, even after she's died." Ivory pried herself from the stone and slid to one side, clearing the way for Viola to see. "But she can watch, and hopefully that'll be enough."

Bare feet paused a few steps behind where Ivory had blocked the way. Soil and grass stains blotted the knees of sweatpants, and a dark valley of dried blood cast a V-shaped stain down a once-gray hoodie. The hood was up, tufting out wavy locks of auburn hair around chalk-white cheeks. A shadow coated the face, as if she still hid in Ghost Cat Island's cavern, but the tip of her nose peeked into starlight, and her irises glowed golden with inborn sunshine.

There was a blankness to her gaze, an animal stare both pensive and ravenous, bound to Honey and Ivory and the sleepers' great hunger. But for all that, Viola couldn't mistake the girl standing ahead.

Her only daughter. Cabrina Brite.

44. A CREATURE OF DEATH

Ivory flinched as Viola stood on shaky legs. The cat in her wanted to chase, and she had to remind herself that Viola wasn't going anywhere, that she could take her time.

"Baby?" Viola said, disbelieving. "Is that my baby? My—mine—"

Ivory crept closer. "My lover, Honey—you two didn't consciously meet. She wasn't interested in you. But she wanted to do right by me, so she called Cabrina to follow us here."

"Can't be. It can't." Viola lost her footing as she approached Cabrina, but she kept staggering forward, one arm reaching out with tentative fingers. "Baby?"

She fell to her knees at Cabrina's feet and pawed at the bloodstained hoodie, its sleeves, the baggy sweatpants. Her fingers briefly pincered around Cabrina's left wrist, and then she crawled up Cabrina's front and dove her hands under the gray hood, into Cabrina's hair.

There was nothing in Cabrina's eyes. No hunger, but no love.

"Don't look at me that way," Viola said, drawing back her arms. "No, it can't be. You can't be."

"You'd like that, wouldn't you?" Ivory asked. "To pretend she's impossible."

Viola collapsed against Cabrina and wrapped both arms around her trunk. Cabrina's arms hung at her sides. She didn't move to touch her mother.

"It was a relief for you, when she died," Ivory went on. "The shame of having a daughter like her—like me—was over. No more worrying if she'd stain your reelection campaign. You could cauterize your kid's memory into whatever shape of scar you wanted, and then you could make that life all about you. Never thought you'd meet her again. Never thought you'd face what you'd done to her."

An earth-deep chuckle seeped from Ivory's chest. She wanted to be more solemn, but the laughter came unbidden, and why not enjoy the victorious moment? Viola must've done the same when she heard her daughter was dead. One less problem for her. No one left to argue, no one to challenge unless they shared a ballot.

Everything since Cabrina's death must have gone right as rain for Viola Brite until she lost her temper and shoved those scissors between Ivory's legs. For one moment, she must've realized the monster she was, the monster she'd always been.

And now she could find solace in knowing she was not the only monster from Cape Morning. To be relieved of solitude before death was a beautiful sentiment.

"Viola," Ivory said, calm and almost patronizing. "I'm not going to pull parts out of you. I wanted to, with my bare hands and claws. You would deserve it." She scraped two sharp points against each other to demonstrate. "But that wouldn't be fair to Cabrina, after everything you put her through."

Viola had quit moving. She clung to Cabrina, and Cabrina stood motionless, as if mother and daughter formed a statue together.

Ivory slinked close. "You kept her from medicine and friendship and love. From her own name. You tried to destroy her. For maybe a moment, when I called you *he*, you understood the tiniest scrap of how broken she felt when she lived with you. And now you're going to understand how she felt when she died. When I drown you."

Viola did not turn to Ivory. A rigidity had spread through her limbs; she wasn't even trembling. Her face had crushed against Cabrina's chest, peppering Viola's blond curls with flakes of dried blood. Was she in shock? Or was this remorse?

Ivory froze inches from Viola and Cabrina. Had she gone too far? Tearing open the worlds again, watching Cape Shadow die from within, dragging Viola here—this should be enough. Hadn't Ivory made her point? Maybe she should stop now, let this be the end of it.

Except she couldn't. It was too late for Viola to seek penance and forgiveness. A whole daughter's death too late.

"When someone burns a girl like me." Ivory glanced at Cabrina's blank expression and then turned to Viola again. "When a girl like Cabrina washes ashore. These things—no one cares. But someone like you? A town councilmember? A cop's wife? They'll care. That's my gift to you, Viola. When our dear Cape Morning forgets what they saw in the sky tonight, when they stop caring once they've buried their own dead and realize it's the rest of the world's problem, they will think of you. Who drowned you? And why? The rest of town council will be forgotten, but the questions about you will run on and on for years. Your death will haunt this town, same as your daughter. You get to be the center of attention long after you're dead."

Ivory placed her palm between Viola's shoulder blades and clenched her fingers into a fist, grasping Viola's top.

"Think of Cabrina in the water," Ivory said. "Trying to breathe. Choking on the waves. Looking to the shore and not sure if she wanted to return, because there was you, Viola. You and your empty heart were her terror." She tugged, prying Viola from Cabrina.

Viola fell against stone. She lay on her side and curled her limbs toward her body until she was a rigid comma on the ground.

Ivory unclenched her fist and circled Viola. Her wounds bled seawater, and her gut twisted to push black bile up her throat, but she forced it back down. There were more important troubles here than any ritual-borne sickness.

"Viola?" Ivory snapped. "Viola, can you hear me?" She dug a foot into Viola's middle and rolled her on her back.

Her expression had frozen into a statue. Mouth hanging open, breath whistling through her teeth. Her stilled eyes shimmered with starlight—and nothing else.

"Viola?" Ivory said again, and she gave a firmer kick. "Viola!"

No wincing at being jostled. Not even when the next kick rolled Viola close to the steps. Gravity should have tugged her nervous system into some kind of twitching reaction, but she was like a loose rock. Like someone who wasn't in there anymore.

"No, no, no." Ivory fell to her knees and began shaking Viola. "You can't do that."

She dragged one claw across Viola's arm, scratching through skin and fabric—nothing. No one home.

"You can't take this from me, understand? Not after everything." Ivory leaned over Viola's face, teeth clenched, skin beating with heat. "You have to be present! Face what you've done! Do you hear me? You can't just check out. You have to know what's happening to you—all the wrong you did to Cabrina. Now, Viola. Wake the fuck up!"

Viola remained still. Not a word. No movement but her subtle breath and the trickle of blood sliding down her arm, as if the woman who'd tormented her daughter and threatened Ivory had shattered to pieces inside.

Maybe it was the blow to the head. Or Cape Shadow's dreamy influence. Or seeing Cabrina. Maybe all of it at once—it had been too much for simple Viola Brite.

Ivory jerked back and shrieked rage at Cape Shadow's dimming sky. She then pulled her knees to her chest and folded her arms around them, ducking her head against her curled legs. Hot tears coated her cheeks, and she knew what was happening here, had to suffer with that knowledge. The universal unfairness of it. The injustice of it.

After everything Ivory had done and everything Cabrina had lived through, it wasn't right for Viola's mind to snap, for her to escape this end.

To drown her now would be to drown nothing. Not unless she woke up.

"I promised you, Cabrina," Ivory whispered. "And I'll keep that promise, really. I'll make it right."

Footsteps scraped the island's stone. Not from behind with Cabrina. Somewhere near.

What now? Ivory looked up, and her reddened eyes glared over her crossed forearms and bent knees.

Down the stony steps and along the island's lip, two figures approached beneath the fading moon and glittering stars—Xi, coated in blood, carrying a dark bundle in her arms. Rex trailed behind her, one arm hanging limp, the other tensed with a gleaming blade. He bared his teeth when he spotted Ivory. His rage pounded across Cape Shadow's impressionable atmosphere. Ivory might have worn the same look when she stood over Viola.

But Rex didn't look like he would explain his reasons or hear her out. He had no eyes for the future, only retribution for the past.

Xi neared the stone steps, where the shrinking moonlight crossed the bundle in her arms. Golden fur, a thick snout, blood-caked teeth straining to part.

Honey's head. Alive, fighting, but severed from her body by two vengeful teenagers.

Oh, these two had decided to toughen up, had they? Certainly they'd walked a tragic road to reach this point, washed in offal and death, and now they were here to spread the same.

Ivory could meet them at their worst. She made to uncurl herself and stand, but her gut's weakness had seeped into her limbs, forcing her down. If she couldn't rise, she needed to at least look like she could put up a fight.

And if she had to, she would show them a wounded animal was the most dangerous kind.

45. REVENGE

The head fussed harder as Xi reached the ascending steps. Puddles dotted the lumpy stone, and the rhythmic *slop-slop* noises of ascent seemed to rouse Honey's remains.

Or maybe Ivory's presence was enough. She loomed atop the steps on all fours, a white leopard ready to pounce. Her eyes glared dark, and her nose was scrunched in a way that might have looked cute if not for her fearsome bared teeth. Red locks draped either side of her cheeks and stiffened down her neck and spine. Claws jutted from some of her fingers.

She was different from Cabrina, and certainly nothing like Honey. If vampires turned in differing stages, Ivory's nature as the key set her apart, some mysterious incarnation between creatures, binding together their worlds of morning and shadow. What Cabrina would have become had she given in to Honey's desires, meant not for riding a fearful wind out of town with the other monsters, but for opening the way and then—what was to become of her?

Xi finished climbing the steps, where she found another figure, this one lying on the ground. Ivory hunkered over Viola Brite, a carnivore guarding her eventual kill. She looked empty, a husk of a woman.

And behind them stood Cabrina, shadowed by a cavern set in the island's mountain. She wore the same bloodstained clothing Xi had lent at that first appearance outside her window. The same empty expression haunted Cabrina's eyes as when the wind had stolen her out of Xi's arms.

Go to her, Xi thought.

But she couldn't. Her legs froze in place at the top of the steps, where Rex joined her. One beast twisted in Xi's arms, and another blocked the path to Cabrina. She looked a million miles away.

"I've been so quiet and nice for them," Ivory said, her voice forlorn.

Black mouths opened down her pale skin. Green-tinted bone peeked through each wound, where murky water dribbled out. Becoming the key looked to have consequences.

"Everything they wanted," Ivory went on. "They tell you it gets better, and you believe it, until you see the future is a cemetery ruled by people like Viola Brite. You'll see. Out there, they'll get you, and they'll gut your soul, same as they did to Cabrina. They'll hose you down like her bedroom, and drain you, and lock you up, take everything, and none of your sweet naïve ideals will save you or anyone you love. When they're cutting you, burning you, starving you, you'll know better. Before you die, you'll remember, I was right to do what I've done tonight."

Xi stood motionless. Rex was the same. The head began fussing again, but Xi buried her nails in Honey's flesh until she stilled.

Ivory lurched to one side and spewed red-black muck onto the stony ground. Her body convulsed as she wiped her mouth. The whites of her eyes had turned crimson.

Xi almost wanted to ask if Ivory was okay, but she knew the answer. The way Ivory moved, the hesitation in her voice—there was a slow wariness unlike the woman who'd answered her door this morning. Before, she had been a lioness sleeping off a meal.

Now she was a feral cat, isolated and half-starved, who'd snagged some vital organ on a barbed-wire fence. Her fear and anger only made her unpredictable.

The moon darkened a little deeper, and the stars followed. Cape Shadow would lose all its light before long.

The head wrestled in Xi's grasp. Invisible muscles kept her strong, and Xi imagined Honey bound to the great hunger, draining other vampires to feed herself. Draining Cabrina.

Maybe Ivory, too. "Yes, my love, always yours," she said, as if answering an unspoken question. Her gaze slid from Honey to Xi. "She likes you. Don't you want to help me? You hate Viola too, and I won't leave you this time, I promise. Be one of us. Help me help Cabrina give Viola the punishment she deserves."

Every word beat an exhausted drum down Xi's muscles. She was tired. More tired than she ever thought she could be. She wanted to go home, go to *bed*, dream of better vistas than Cape Shadow. To wake up with Cabrina cuddled in her arms and Rex at her back, the three of them together again. She wanted this nightmare to end.

"What are you staring for? What, you want me to feel sorry?" Ivory looked like she was going to be sick again. "Is there some point in regretting what I did? Saying sorry won't change what'll happen to the world any more than it'll help Cabrina. But I can make them wish their worst problems were a girl like Cabrina. They let her die. We all did. She deserves revenge, and I'm the one to give it." A trembling finger aimed at Viola. "She deserves it."

"Don't care about Viola," Rex muttered.

"We want Cab," Xi said. She hefted the head. "And we'll trade you. Honey for Cabrina."

"Why can't I just take the head from you?" Ivory's gaze flickered between Rex and Xi. "She's mine. My love."

"Because Cab's ours," Rex said, quieter. "Our love."

"Because you're not okay," Xi added. "Do you know what a thrall is? It's you. It's what Honey's made of you."

"I made my own choice," Ivory said.

"You don't know what you've made." Xi took a cautious step toward Viola. *The lonely tear the world down*. Those are Cab's words. Did you know that?"

"It's different now." Greenstone pulsed in Ivory's wounds like eyes full of menace. "You've never hurt anyone before tonight, have you? For all you know, you'd like the way revenge feels. Honey can help. Everything gets easier when she's on your side. Aren't the both of you angry?"

Xi held her tongue again, and Rex became a machete-wielding statue beside her. They were angry, yes, but they weren't going to give Ivory the satisfaction of seeing it. A tether seemed to run between them. Xi imagined hers and Rex's hearts beating in time as they stared down their last chance of getting Cabrina back. All of them bitten by monsters, each of them entwined in the dream of Cape Shadow. The romantic in Xi saw a beautiful death here, but the reality would be grisly and merciless.

"I'm exhausted," Ivory said. "All the time. Hopelessness is contagious, and I'd caught it. Sure, fine, the lonely tear the world down. But if I could help one of us, that'd be something." She turned to unmoving Viola. "But she had to ruin it by losing her goddamn mind. What would you two do better?"

"We made our offer," Rex said.

"We're here for Cab," Xi said. "You say you made your own choice? Then make another. If you want to sit here and nurse your grudges, do it. Build a church and pray to them."

"Got nothing to do with us." Rex aimed his machete at the severed head. "Take your fucked-up girlfriend, give us Cab, and do whatever you want in your dead little world."

Ivory reared up, muscles cording over her body. "And what the hell do you know?" Her greenish wounds widened, and Xi thought she saw the shadows of kelp and coral within. "You're just kids! The whole world's still out there waiting to gnaw on your heart. A decade from now, you'll turn out like me."

"Selfish. Narcissistic." Xi curled her upper lip. "Taking your shit out on everyone else."

"No." Ivory's claws danced at her sides, ready to slash. "No, they deserved it."

"It's nothing to do with being trans, or being alone," Xi said. "You're making everything about you."

"That's not true," Ivory said. "I understand Cabrina."

"Self-centered bitch," Rex growled.

Ivory growled back at him, all teeth and tension. Her rising body was a cobra hood, warning Xi and Rex of a deadly bite to come.

But Xi couldn't stop. "What, did you think Cabrina was like you? That you're the same?"

Ivory didn't answer. Harsh breath hissed through her clenched teeth.

"You can't see her right," Xi said. "You're too much like Viola."

"I'm not!" Ivory shouted, teeth clacking together. "She didn't give a damn about Cabrina, but I did all this for her! I'm nothing like Viola. She'd never give her heart away, but I'm going to cut it out for you. For all of us. That's why I need Cabrina here, why she can't go with you. She needs to watch her mother die."

"How can you pretend Cab's even her own anymore?" Xi snapped.

Rex made a quick step forward. "You forced her to come here."

He kept his eyes locked to Ivory, but Xi glanced at Cabrina. She hadn't moved through Ivory's bluster, a stiff white tree on this desolate island.

Ivory followed Xi's gaze and hunched her body toward Cabrina. "They don't understand. No one does, except me. I was exactly like you when I was younger, and I didn't have anyone. But things are going to be different. You can be like us." She gestured to Honey's head, grinning with her hyena teeth. "Strong like us. Sweet Honey has given me what she would've given you, but this is a shaping place. Your body is yours to change, easy as flexing a muscle. It can be better here than everything you had before."

Xi's heart thundered. She couldn't remember the last time she'd felt so angry, and she almost couldn't believe such fury was possible after tonight's terror. Ivory thinking she had a connection with Cabrina was worse than a delusion—it was insulting. Did she genuinely believe she could visit a deadnamed grave and parse through a few flowery pages and learn everything about Cabrina Brite, in and out? That diary was a fingernail to the entirety of Cabrina's life.

Xi stamped her foot. "You don't understand shit!"

Ivory's attention broke from Cabrina back to Xi and Rex. They were standing closer now, shaking together, their conjoined rage seething between them into a tangible storm cloud.

"Did you talk to her on the phone at night when she cried until she passed out?" Xi asked, every word boiling off her tongue.

"Did you know she likes seashells, and hates fishing?" Rex snapped.

"That she can't pay attention through a movie to save her life?"

"How far she can walk down the beach before she starts whining?"

"How much she loves her mother, and how much she hates her?"

Ivory glanced from one to the other. Her teeth parted like she meant to answer them, but nothing came out.

"Did you know she's full of love?" Rex asked. "Do you even know what the fuck her voice sounds like?"

Xi shook her head in disgust. "You boiled her down to one thing, like that's all she's ever been, but Cab has a whole universe inside."

Ivory stood as stiff as Cabrina. Her eyes jittered in her skull, white and gleaming wet. A crack had broken through some unseen resolve.

"You don't know what she needs." Xi's voice quieted, almost patient. "But maybe I was wrong about you. Viola wants to make the world a hard dull place. That isn't you. But you're not like Cabrina either. She wants a future. You, Ivory? You just want chaos." Her fists clenched at her sides. "You just want blood."

46. ANOTHER BITE

Ivory shrank back a step. Her jaw worked up and down, chewing the air for an answer that wouldn't come, and she stumbled again as if weathering a sudden wave.

"But I'm helping her," she tried to say, but only a meek whisper slipped out.

"We're *saving* her," Xi said, her words spitting tired and aching. "From you."

Rex was an earthquake at her side, his machete smiling in the frail light. He was ready to dive into Ivory, slash her throat, spill her intestines, one more beheaded beast under his blade.

She should rise against him. Stand tall, dare him to come for her.

Instead she faltered again, another wave of misery threatening to erode her smooth like a tidal stone, not across decades but all at once. What did she really know about Cabrina? Everything, they were the same.

Almost exactly the same.

They had to be.

Ivory grasped the sides of her head and shrank against the ground. A rhythmic tide washed up from memory, the sense of the push-and-shove that morning in the water when she saw that pale body in the surf. That was the only moment Cabrina had approached her, and it was in death. Nothing else had bound them beyond Ivory forcing it.

She had plucked up the death poem.

And she had mistaken the visitor outside Wolf's house and hers for Cabrina when it had only been—what? A dream cast by Chasm Cat, and a nothing in real life. She'd let wishful thinking sway uncertain darkness to her hope of being chosen by a dead girl as posthumous guardian. Like Ivory was special.

There was also the life poem, and she was a creature of life. Didn't that count for something?

She hadn't known that other poem until she found the diary. And she never would have found the diary if she'd ignored Xi at the door, or tossed aside the plan to steal said diary, or given herself up at Viola's house to let Xi more easily escape. No, it had been more important for Ivory to take center stage.

And she could've listened to herself when she wondered what right she had to sink into Cabrina's life.

The girl was dead. What had Ivory thought she could do? What the hell could she do now?

Footsteps clacked on stone as Xi and Rex pressed forward, their attention aiming at Cabrina. They had the right to take her in. She had genuinely visited them; Ivory and Honey had only led her out of the sky. Away from friends, away from the other beasts, needing her to spill blood here and validate Ivory's delusion of guardianship. How could Ivory justify it? Over Viola? Where was her justice?

A desire for blood remained at the root of every choice.

Ivory's thoughts tingled at a sudden scraping prick, and she tensed beneath the point of Honey's mental claw.

Ivory, no.

She waited for a command to flit through her nerves. To be commanded right now would be easiest. Honey had always made it easier. Ivory only needed to choose to submit.

Couldn't help myself, she thought. *Couldn't eat another bite.*

Her gaze fixed on Honey's remaining golden eye. "Do it," she whispered. "Help me."

Xi turned to her, face full of worry.

Honey's claw scraped again, deeper, angrier.

Ivory, wronged.

Ivory, take.

A honey-thick heat spilled down Ivory's muscles, tensing hard and squeezing seawater from the dark slitted wounds across her body. This sensation was different from Honey's command—this was righteous, an adrenaline rush. One heart pounded down her thoughts and charged fury into her chest.

It was Honey's anger at seeing Ivory's pain, at feeling it. A protective lover, pushing her paired heart to stand up for herself.

Ivory, fight.

Ivory, rage.

Ivory, kill.

Another destructive wave swept away the shattered glass of Ivory's belief. Yes, Honey was right. What did Ivory have to lose now? She'd already ravaged everything else.

"I'm nothing special," she whispered.

Now Rex paused, a couple steps from Xi. His fingers tensed around his machete, and Honey glowed with yellow-sick fire.

"I want blood," Ivory said, scratching her claws across stone. "Don't you? And don't we deserve it?"

Xi dragged her heel back, retreating to Rex's side. Was that prey-like fear in her eyes? *Prey* fear? Ivory knew that nervous expression, had felt it every day of her life since a pack of feral high-schoolers took fire to her skin. These two teenagers had underestimated Ivory. Their mistake. Her advantage.

Ivory's mouth twisted in a snarl. The last flat teeth came falling from her lips, where knifelike replacements jutted through her gums.

Her heart thundered, ready to burst. One half of every heart was a giver of blood to the rest of the body, the other half was the taker.

Honey's love thrust deeper into Ivory's thoughts, fucking the back of Ivory's mind with savage need. Each of them was a half-heart, every beast taking and taking.

Ivory was no different. It didn't matter that Xi and Rex were Cabrina's friends. They had broken a cherished illusion, and the little sliver of reality left to Ivory formed in glass-sharp teeth, stone-hard claws, and a bloodlust older than the human race.

So Rex wanted to kill somebody? Ivory's claws could do the same. They thought she wanted blood? She could let them be right. A bloodlust inside would make her the same as the sea, older than she looked, deeper too, and dangerous like no mortal could comprehend. Her claws could echo those shredding waves. She could rend and tear until Xi lost Rex, and Ivory would still be here, lapping up his blood to grow as strong as Honey.

And what of Xi then? What of her smart mouth and sharp insight? She couldn't beat Ivory by herself. She could scarcely keep hold of this severed head in her arms. In a battle of blades and claws and teeth, Xi would lose, would sink beneath the bloodthirsty waves, and before they clotted her lungs and forever painted her consciousness with abyssal nothingness, she would realize she was wrong about Ivory. About everything.

Ivory thrust across the ground and crashed into Rex, knocking him back. He swept his arm in a short arc, digging his machete against her side, but its blade sang against the sea-hardened bone inside, no better at killing her than Viola's scissor blades.

Honey's head jittered in Xi's arms, her lips peeling back in a fit of shrieking laughter.

Rex tried to slip back, but he wasn't getting away. No doubt he was the one who'd cut Honey's head off, and he dared come for Ivory too, and now he was going to pay for it with another broken arm, and then a broken face, and maybe Ivory would take enough time pulling him apart for his heart to break.

He let go of the machete and grabbed onto her hair, tugging her down with him as he fell. They rolled, her over him, him over her, the hard stone digging into their flesh.

White flashed across her vision as his head struck hers. She rolled atop him again as she tried to skitter back, and a rush of black blood surged out of her mouth and over his legs. If all she wanted was blood, why couldn't she keep hers?

"I'm sorry!" Xi shouted.

Ivory hesitated, caught between Xi, grasping Honey's head, and Rex, ready to pounce on three limbs.

Xi's eyes narrowed. "I didn't know you'd staked your soul on thinking you and she were the same."

"No!" Ivory snapped. "It was for her!" But she couldn't be certain anymore. Her world teetered on the ocean's rolling surface.

Maybe she was wrong about Cabrina, maybe they weren't the same, but these two didn't know Ivory either. She wanted more than blood. She wanted a thousand things. Loving arms, a peacefulness when she looked down at her body, to feel like someone loved her when they kept her. Not tolerated her when she was easy, not disregarded her when she wasn't, but genuinely loved her. These two might have been that love for Cabrina. Maybe the three of them once had the power to take on the world and mean it.

But they were two. Cabrina was dead, and they had come to a dead and broken place. What hope could they have now?

Why not become like the sea and crave all the blood you could drink?

"Prove it!"

Xi's cracking roar shot through Ivory's thoughts, spoiling Honey's mood and breaking her claw from the back of Ivory's mind. She stirred on the ground, disoriented—she'd been a beast for one glorious moment. Honey had pushed too far, but Ivory had begged for help. It wasn't Honey's fault that she only knew a handful of choices. Flee, hide, cut, kill, fuck, love, survive. And what did that make Ivory now?

She looked to Xi for an answer. Hers was a simple body, slowly curling into beasthood yet never reaching for it. She could be a fighter if she wanted.

But she challenged Ivory in this human form, on a battlefield that would entice her. Not the loving heart who craved blood for the wronged, not the beast who'd take any blood she could get, but appealing to the woman who'd believed she could be Cabrina's savior.

"If it's not about you, then prove it," Xi said, severe and undaunted. "Let Cab decide her future."

47. THE BRITE GIRL

Xi studied Ivory's muscles as she swiveled to look at Cabrina and then back again. The anxious tremble settled, a momentary hesitation against any coming transformation. Xi could've collapsed in relief, but she needed to stand firm, pretend she wasn't exhausted from fighting and bleeding tonight.

"You did this for Cab, right?" Xi asked. "Or were those just words?"

Ivory looked at Xi with wavering eyes, still reeling from the laughing influence of that murderous severed head. Xi knew the feeling. Hated it. That vampire influence could drown a mind in sweet enticement, but Honey must have tried a more primal ferocity on Ivory.

She didn't pounce on Xi, or Rex again. She only sat in a daze in the same way Cabrina stood nearby. Their unified craving might bind them together in stronger ways than the past. Than friendship.

Was there any coming back from this?

Xi stepped to one side and set Honey's head down on the stone. She thrashed at first, as if still caught, and then settled into place, her remaining eye glaring up at Xi.

Cabrina lingered at the cavern's edge, unmoving without the wind and sun to urge her. This empty thing seemed a Cabrina-looking mannequin, not Cabrina herself.

But then, when was the last time Cabrina had seemed like herself? When she had been stuck in her bedroom while Xi spoke to her from the lawn? That spring break night at the beach? Cabrina had been lost for weeks before she died. How could Xi expect her to now become the same girl who would struggle to write poetry at Xi's tutelage, or come up with screaming games by the seaside?

Cabrina held still, her expression eternally sedate. Bound to that cosmic hunger, tied to this shadow place, she didn't seem to have heard Xi, Ivory, anyone.

Xi gestured for Rex to step near the head, where he could guard it from Ivory, and then she approached Cabrina. She needed more than Xi's words. She needed to touch her, feel her warmth. Remember her.

A sense of animal breath resurrected down Xi's neck, where Honey's slobber had gone cold and sticky. She almost felt that monster's head smile from the ground behind her.

Both Ivory and Honey had every reason to gloat. Xi could give whatever impassioned speech she liked, but they had Cabrina by the soul.

Xi set her hands on Cabrina's shoulders. "Cab? When I thought you were a ghost, I wanted you to leave. To rest. But if there's any shot at you being part of our lives again, or having something for yourself, you should have it. You never wanted to hurt anyone, I should've remembered that. And it's not like that woman could've known. She was never your friend."

Cabrina gave a hollow stare, as if a taxidermist had plugged marbles into her eye sockets. Xi's reflection formed a dark silhouette within them. The moon and stars faded another degree.

"You're not like her," Xi said, her voice urgent. She pressed her forehead to Cabrina's, warmth against cold. "And you're not your mother. You're like me and Rex. We got each other, remember?"

Cabrina said nothing. Xi wrapped her arms around Cabrina's shoulders and held her close like it might be the last time. She couldn't let Cabrina slip into ghostly darkness like some Gothic heroine, even if Cabrina might never be herself again.

But then, if she couldn't be her old self, Xi could at least give what this new Cabrina needed.

One arm clung to Cabrina; the other slid away. Xi's right hand glistened where a shard of photo-frame glass had lacerated her palm. Honey had licked at it, but the blood was never meant for her. Cabrina was a different story.

Xi drew her hand close to her mouth and dragged her front teeth over the cut, reopening its tender flesh and drawing crimson droplets down her palm.

Rex's steps clacked behind her. "The fuck, Xi?"

"She never wanted to take this," Xi said. "But I can choose to give it."

"Don't you get what you're doing?" Rex snapped. "You'll keep turning. Won't be you anymore."

Xi tensed her arm, forcing the blood to run thicker. "I'll be me." She wasn't sure she believed herself.

Rex certainly didn't. "You'll be Xi on rabies, all high on blood. Out of your fucking mind. Worse than whatever the hell's happened to Viola. An animal. How can you come back from that? What about your mother?"

Xi glanced over her shoulder. "I need you to respect me enough for this."

Rex looked stunned. His mouth opened and shut with almost-excuses, but instead he hugged her from behind. She slid her free arm over his and hoped he could forgive the blood dripping onto his jeans.

It was the first time since before Cabrina's death that the three of them had held each other, clumsy and hurt and perfect in their own way. Some embraces shouldn't end. To let this one break apart was to accept there might never be another. There would always be a final time to put arms around a loved one, and usually there was no way to know when that final time had come. You let them go, like any other hug, and then you walked away. Maybe you hurried back for another, just to show how much you loved them, but eventually the closeness would become distance, first for a while, and then forever.

Rex at last slipped back. He stepped in front of Honey's head and aimed his machete at Ivory, daring her to interrupt.

Xi tugged her hand toward her teeth again and finished opening the wound. She then pressed her bleeding palm to Cabrina's lips.

A guttural hiss slid up Cabrina's throat, and her nostrils flared. She could taste the metal in the air, could smell it, and being inhaled by her didn't upset Xi the same way as Ivory's doorway, or Cabrina's house. This was Cabrina herself.

Even if, in some ways, she wasn't.

Soundless beyond the unsticking of her dry lips, Xi mouthed, "It's yours."

A twitch fought the corners of Cabrina's eyes the second before she sank sharp points into Xi's open palm.

Xi gritted her teeth against a pained squeal. She didn't like that Ivory and Viola were present for this intimate exchange, but it was what Cabrina needed. The blood of friends.

Another vision seeped over Xi's thoughts, clouded in mist and regret.

A dark sky hung thin with flying bodies. They swooped down on the world like vultures admiring a ripe carcass, and their cravings pulsed through Cabrina, through Xi. All Cabrina needed was to play their game. She hated how much she wanted tender flesh between her teeth. The beasts may not have taken her for their key like they tried, but they'd caught her in the end.

"It's not your fault," Xi said, wincing in pain.

The clouded vision thinned, but Cape Shadow did not return to Xi's sight. One image peeled away, and another lurked beneath—the beach, the ocean, and then Ghost Cat Island. It was at once Cape Shadow's otherworldly mountain and the pathetic scrap of rock off Cape Morning, one acting as the veil to the other's face at a funeral.

Xi watched a familiar figure shed her clothes on the dry sand, tuck two slips of pink paper beneath a tree of scarred driftwood, and then dive into the tide. One was a prayer, the other a eulogy. Cabrina meant to swim for the island.

She fought hard to break the waves. They were choppy and unpleasant, but she'd known this shore her whole life, and sometimes that couldn't save anyone from drowning, and sometimes it kept someone alive long enough to die another way.

At Ghost Cat Island, Cabrina climbed onto the rough rock. It cut at her hands and feet, but she needed to be here. She had come to give something back that she'd never meant to take.

Xi was not surprised to see Honey's golden eyes climb from the island's darkness. The monster was something she'd half-expected in the depth of thought.

This Honey couldn't leave her shadow world yet. Some smaller facet of her crawled between instances of Ghost Cat Island instead—a tawny cat with a black chasm of fur dividing her in two, crossing the veil of worlds. She met Cabrina first, pensive and sweet, and then she lured Cabrina into the breach.

The illusion seemed so obvious to Xi, but Cabrina would have had no reason to mistrust what looked like an ordinary cat. She couldn't have known that little animal was only the tip of a greater whole, the way a scrap of rock might be all a beachgoer saw of what was once a mountain.

And she followed. Slipped at least partway toward Cape Shadow, with every intent to give that devil her due.

Cabrina only learned better once she'd crossed into that dark yet starlit place. She found skin stretching, and ribs splitting apart, and a chest thumping with the catalyst for beautiful and terrible transformation, the power to reshape form and flesh. One last offer to Cabrina Brite.

And when she tried to slip back, the monster had bitten down on her and dragged her into the sea. To drown.

Xi squirmed—that moment's every sensation crowded in her head. Thrashing at the water. Biting at the monster and tasting blood, and then the sea, the endless sea. The burning in her lungs, in her sinuses, an agony she would sell her soul to end.

And then, it ended.

In that dark place, a shard of Cabrina watched her remains drift ashore. The rest came clouded with seafloor sediment and briny darkness. She had clawed up an earthen grave; she had fought from a watery grave. Nothing was true, and all things were true, and none of them could save Cabrina in the end. She was undead, and there was no changing it.

And that was her fate. Ivory, Xi—they had wondered again and again what had happened to Cabrina Brite. Now Xi knew, and it made her heart ache and scream.

She pulled her hand away, breaking from Cabrina's mouth, and the mist of vision slid away from her senses. She could hear Rex fighting not to cry, and Ivory's tense breath. A subtle whistle sang in and out through Viola's teeth, and then Honey's head boomed with ungodly laughter.

A wild shine stole over Cabrina's eyes. She leaned back a step, growling through her reddened teeth, and then pounced onto Xi, knocking her to the ground.

Xi crossed her arms in front of her, one locked over Cabrina's collarbone, the other against her throat. Cabrina's jaw snapped open and shut, lunging past forearm and wrist, craving the red nectar of life from Xi's neck. She would break through Xi's exhaustion soon, and that would be another ending between them.

Unless Xi joined her.

This morning at the beach, Rex had said that someone bitten only believed they wanted to help their undead feeder, that Xi had been caught as a vampire's thrall. But Xi could make a choice. She was bitten. What if she gave everything up and fell to these visions, this wildness?

She could lap the blood from Honey's head. Devour Viola's flesh. Become like the other vampires. Her own monster, stronger than Cabrina, maybe strong enough to save her.

There was a romance to tearing herself from one world and chasing another. Forget the future; cling to ever-present death. Xi could craft never-dreamed poetry amid the clouds and fall in love with the sky, and the coast, and with the sweeping beauty of untouchable infinity.

Cabrina's teeth spread wide. In the blackness of her throat, Xi felt the pull of the other vampires, their united thirst for blood opening a deep pit within her. They could flit across the country. Across the world, the way Cabrina used to dream.

No, Xi couldn't turn into this. A poem was not a person, and pretty immortal ideas ignored cruel realities. Whatever promises Honey had made to Cabrina and then Ivory, she hid the truth of the hungering brood, as deceitful as a war propaganda poster plastered over the blood and death and hell.

Evading one goodbye would mean bringing many more. Easy to imagine feeding from Viola when someone else had broken her. Pouncing from body to body in a ravenous tempest was another thing entirely.

To be that kind of creature, you had to end futures. End dreams.

Xi's arms crushed against her chest, losing the fight with Cabrina. Sharp teeth glistened, already tasting Xi's neck, and saliva dotted Xi's glasses. Rex was shouting from nearby, where Ivory barred his way. This struggle was between Xi and Cabrina, and they would bathe in blood together and join the beastly flock that would spread death into the west. Nothing Rex could stop.

Except Cabrina had never chosen that road, never deserved it. There had to be a detour. Xi had seen Cabrina's death—wasn't that good for anything? Didn't understanding it matter? She wanted to grab Cabrina's shoulders again, shake her, even bite her if she had to, anything to wake her out of this bloodthirsty fugue.

Bite her, Xi thought.

She ran her tongue over her teeth and lips. They tasted of salt and blood. When she sank her teeth into Honey's neck back at Cabrina's house, Honey had quit thrashing, distracted not by pain, but a sense of Xi's intrusion and influence.

Xi was on her way to turning, if Rex was right. A journey she was only starting. Monstrous Honey waited at the end, but between her and Xi, there was the cosmic hunger that had dragged Cabrina into the sky. They were all connected to it.

And influence worked both ways.

"We had your back when you'd run away from home," Xi said, letting Cabrina snap a little closer to her neck. "We're the times you'd hide in our rooms, or the times we'd head off to the beach, and maybe there would be a bunch of people or an empty shore, but it was the three of us in the middle. We're that night when you and I kissed. And we're that night you were with Rex. We're the nights we drank and talked about what happens after we die. We had you, every time."

One hand shoved under Cabrina's jaw, jamming her teeth together and baring her throat.

"We got you now."

Xi's mouth trailed down Cabrina's hair, past her jaw, nuzzling through her hoodie, where Xi clenched her teeth around the flesh of Cabrina's neck.

She didn't think about the taste. She didn't think about how she'd bitten Honey with these teeth and what it meant to pass this blood around.

Her thoughts ran toward the good times. That Frankenstein-themed Halloween. The days Rex convinced Cabrina to start eating again. Magic spells by the sea, math tests, goofy tenth-grade poetry that went stale by junior year, and the poetry from junior year that had aged poorly by senior year.

She thought of kissing Cabrina, and Cabrina's head between her legs. She thought of them coiled together. And she thought of Cabrina and Rex. Xi hadn't been there, but she had a good imagination, and she could conjure it in her head and pour adoration over them.

The intimate moments, the silly afternoons, the free times. Every adoring sight and sound, taste and scent—Xi couldn't keep hold of any single one for too long, but she could keep them cycling through her mind, down her teeth, into Cabrina, and hope like hell her friend felt every sensation.

Cabrina flinched against Xi's teeth.

Not yet, Xi thought, and she kept her mind cruising over dress shopping with Josephine. Through beach fires. Dozens of moments when Xi would warm Cabrina's icicle fingers between her thighs. It wasn't enough for Cabrina to see their bonds together. She needed to see herself the way Xi saw her. Feel herself, and remember.

A dreamer. Frustrating. Out of her mind. Beautiful. Full of love. Deep as the ocean.

Your mind, Xi thought, desperate, ferocious. And then, *You're mine. And Rex's. Not anyone's but ours. You're our love. Ours.*

Cabrina tore from Xi's teeth and fell back with a heavy gasp. She propped up on her arms, her startled eyes darting every which way. Shallow breaths rushed in and out from her lips, and the stained hoodie quivered over her rising and falling chest.

Xi caught her breath too and watched. Waited.

Cabrina noticed her watching. She stared at Xi, glanced at Rex, and then turned back to Xi. The deadness had gone out of her eyes, and now they stretched wide and wild, as if she were about to be hunted.

Xi sat up against Cabrina and pulled her close again. "Cab, it's okay."

Cabrina glanced to Rex again, and then thick tears filled her eyes. Her body went slack, and she crashed face first into Xi's chest, quaking with heavy sobs.

"Sorry," she choked out. "I'm. So sorry."

The sudden apology pricked tears in Xi's eyes. Cabrina. *Her* Cabrina. Haunted by bad dreams, wronged by her family, taken by monsters, failed by her friends, and still she thought she was to blame.

But that was part of what made her Cabrina. Overthinking yet impulsive. Brooding yet affectionate. Hopeless yet endless Cabrina.

"It's okay," Xi said again, petting Cabrina's hair while crying into it.

Another figure folded around them as Rex joined the embrace with his good arm. He was hushing Cabrina, and also kissing her temple, and also crying with Xi. Cabrina lifted her head to look at them again, her wariness fading to disbelief.

Xi told both of them that everything would be okay. She kept telling them, over and over. And after she said it enough times, she started to believe it.

48. IN THE EARTH

Rex could have held onto Xi the rest of the night. He could have soaked in Cabrina forever, with that look in her eyes that was no animal or monster, but wholly her.

But he heard Ivory's claws scraping against stone. He didn't know if she was going for the machete or for Honey's head, but he didn't trust her with either.

Lurching up from Xi and Cabrina, Rex shambled toward the head, swept his machete off the ground, and froze beside Honey's snout.

Ivory slowed two feet away. "You're taking Cabrina," she said. "Give me the head."

"You still care about this?" Rex asked, astonished. "Don't you get it? They used you."

Ivory was crying again in twin streams of darkness. "Give Honey back to me."

"Walk away," Rex said. "Leave it."

"Rex," Xi said, her voice heavy. "Let her have it."

Rex flashed her an incredulous look. A small part of him hoped to help Ivory, get her out with them, even if she didn't deserve it.

But Xi was right. Let Ivory keep her beast. So long as she didn't keep Cab.

Rex retreated one careful step at a time, circling the head, wary of Ivory trying anything. A warning cry jerked his attention to Xi, where she was rising from Cabrina, reaching out like she could catch Rex and freeze him in place.

Too late, he felt what she meant to warn him about—Honey's head, twisting in place. Her teeth spreading apart.

And then crunching down on his leg.

The pain was brief, hardly butterfly lashes as the island and sea crumbled from sight. Darkness took over like the sky had finished shutting down its lights.

There was only the eye, its iris forming a hideous golden halo. *World, fair?* it asked. *World, right? Rex doubts. Rex sees.*

This had to be Honey. Always Honey. Not enough for her to take Marla from him. She wanted his soul.

He fought to surface from the darkness, but it dragged him down like an anchor chained around his leg. Grim light outlined shadow figures, each pantomiming familiar memories—Cabrina fleeing her house and rushing toward a firelit beach. Xi and her mother, fleeing her father.

And Rex, facing down a high school full of teeth, their threat forming a carapace around his heart. There was warmth in his mothers' home. Would that warmth be waiting for him now that Marla was dead? How could he go home again knowing Joan would have to watch the sunrise without her wife? The world had ravaged that peace, and Rex might never again feel whole.

Blackness welled in Honey's baleful eye. *Wrong world*, she said. *Hate world. Take world.* Her gaze faded, and a new vision overtook Rex's sight.

The shadow puppets flitted into the sky, painting it black around countless stars. They wouldn't return to Cape Morning, but anywhere else could found their kingdom. Beneath them, an amalgamation of buildings lay piled together, shingled rooftops and convenience store windows clawing up skyscrapers and fusing into a bizarre temple with stone steps running up its every side.

The stairways converged at a plateauing peak, where Rex stood triumphant over a shattered world. He was older, hairy, and unclothed. Muscles corded beneath every inch of skin, and ripe red blood wept from his fists in crimson rivers, raining down and down upon a world he'd brought to its knees.

On the far side of the vision, Honey smirked. *Break world. Rex, king. Rex, god.*

Rex grinned against the red-black temple. How simple it would be. Much easier to destroy than to create.

Likely Ivory had come to the same desperate conclusion. Honey must've said her pain could be deflected onto the world and everyone in it. Animal-like simplicity would numb Rex to what he would do and become. The vampire brood would protect him from remorse, cushioned by their hunger and cruelty.

An unfeeling monster, crushing every life beneath him.

The shadow world snapped back to him, a place of Xi's screams, Ivory's watchful eyes, and Honey's infectious bite. Her head could hurt him, but it wasn't as strong as when it had stretched from her neck.

Rex leaned into his aching leg and slammed his free foot down, snapping Honey's jaw.

"Don't hurt her!" Ivory cried.

Rex dropped his machete and lifted Honey's head by her golden hair. Oh, she was good at temptation, had probably been seducing hearts and souls since long before empires were forged, and she had slept through their ruin. Her strength was nothing to her cleverness. The best road to immortality was bounding from life to life. Early mankind, to Cabrina, to Ivory.

But she couldn't have Rex.

He swung Honey's head back and then forward, tossing it

past the descending stone steps, toward the water. It hit the waves with a rough splash.

Ivory bounded down the steps, shrieking after the head. Her neck was thin and tempting, but to rush after her, machete in hand, was beyond Rex's limits. He watched her scramble into the tide. The water looked nearly black under the darkening sky.

Xi approached the top of the steps and paused at Rex's side. She swayed, ready to lean against him, but her gaze caught his leg. They ended up leaning against each other.

Beside them, Cabrina crouched down, her arms reaching for prone Viola. Rex had almost forgotten her. Cabrina's hand patted at her shoulders, and then she drew her mother close.

Rex stared blank-faced. "Are you fucking serious?"

They didn't have time for this. They needed to leave before Ivory returned. Before this world faded away, and them with it.

But Cabrina looked up with pleading eyes. "Rex?"

Her needfulness shot a quiver through his limbs. Best to keep his mouth shut for once. He watched Cabrina lift Viola against her chest, limbs bracing her sides, as if Cabrina were the mother and Viola were her child.

Xi then started down the stone steps, and Rex and Cabrina followed. Ivory was still splashing in and out of the darkening sea, desperate to find what was left of Honey.

She was pathetic. Had probably thought Rex and Xi meant nothing, and Cabrina wouldn't care about them anymore. They were high school, something to leave behind along with homework, bullying, all the shitty parts. Ivory had thought she'd won. Better she be left behind, one more bad memory to let disappear.

But watching her kill whatever remained of her strength, Rex understood her in ways he didn't like. Impermanence blurred her skin, her body readying to fall apart. Fading like the rest of the place under its dimming moon and stars.

Holding onto anything was better than nothing. Even if all you had was a monster.

Before you die, you'll remember, I was right to do what I've done tonight, Ivory had said, glaring defiance into Rex's soul.

The words sent a chill through him now. He could only hope she was wrong about the future.

The return journey felt too quick, as if a beast were ushering them forward. Every few steps, Rex looked back to make sure Ivory wasn't following—or worse, hunting—but the only trace of her was a cry over the waves. The farther the trio carried Viola, the less Rex paid attention to what they left behind.

Blackness had stolen over the cave where they had first emerged from Cabrina's house. The opening was small now, shrinking with the night, like a saloon door Honey had swung open that was now swinging shut. Xi slid inside first, and then Cabrina carried Viola through.

Rex lingered, wondering if every path to Cape Morning would soon close. This shadow island must've been sealed up before Honey lured Cabrina, before Ivory fell for a vampire's trick.

And maybe another few centuries would pass before anyone fell for it again.

Rex stepped through behind the others and took a moment to breathe the stuffy air of the house. His eyes then settled on the wriggling mess at the living room's center.

Honey's body. Still alive. This relentless monster, no longer able to hunt them, and yet leaving her writhing horror behind.

A second wind hit Rex's limbs. Fine, he had weathered worse tonight, and he would weather this. Honey had seduced Ivory into inviting those things into the world, maybe even to end the world— that was fine, too. But the beast wouldn't enjoy that catastrophe. Rex couldn't allow it.

"Cab," he said. "Put your—put Viola in the kitchen, out of the way, and stay put. Xi, help me find bandages?"

They found what they needed in the downstairs bathroom and tended to their wounds as best they could. After taking a moment to breathe, Rex turned to Xi again, and asked for a harder kind of help.

They found tools hanging from the garage wall beside the workbench and took them to the backyard, near the cover of trees where they wouldn't accidently unearth a septic tank or a pet cat's grave. The sky looked clear now. Most of the vampires must have finished drifting from Cape Morning, seeking hiding places for the day to come outside of Cape Shadow's reach. Doubtful that place would ever catch them again.

Rex hacked one-armed at the ground with a pickaxe. Xi took a shovel to the broken soil and dug away dirt and stones. He was injured, and she was exhausted, but she never argued with him or told him they should wait. This needed to be done, or the night wouldn't end at sunrise.

Cabrina soon joined them with another shovel. She kept silent, but she pointed and gestured, and Rex and Xi fell into a rhythm with her. Pickaxe, shovel, shovel, on and on until they had a stretch of earth dug wide and deep enough to hold a monster.

Honey's body had lost much of its strength by the time they dragged it outside. Their limbs were raw and screaming with worn-out muscle, but the trio tugged and rolled her toward the grave, and she fell inside with a dry thump.

"Hold this here," Rex said, aiming one shovel at a tree.

Xi held the shaft with both hands. Cabrina held the shovel's head against the tree trunk. Rex kicked where the wood met iron until the shovel snapped inches beneath its head. It wasn't perfect, but it would do.

He then carried the wooden shaft to the grave, hopped inside, and stabbed the pointed end into Honey's chest.

Cabrina passed down the unbroken shovel. Rex raised it over the jutting shaft with his uninjured arm as if readying a hammer to pound a nail and then tapped against the makeshift stake. Xi held it still for him. The shaft ground deeper into Honey's chest.

Rex kept pounding, a steady, firm beat against the stake. He felt it sliding through Honey's heart, past her spine, out her back, its broken end driving into the soil. He remembered his *stay here and wait for Jesus* joke he'd made to Marla a few nights ago. Couldn't find humor in it anymore. In his weariness, he started to imagine himself as Blade again, or Van Helsing, like on the beach, and then as the vampiric god from Honey's vision, but he shook every illusion away.

He had to be himself right now, and this had to be Honey. Not in a comic book or a movie, but on this night, in the earth.

This moment had to be real.

He drove the shaft down until a third of it jutted from Honey's chest and the rest pinned her to the dirt. She was too weak to thump around and dislodge the makeshift stake, let alone fight the man pinning her. All she could do was squirm as dark blood seeped into her once-golden fur.

Xi grasped Rex's uninjured arm, and Cabrina helped haul him back up to the yard. Together, by shovel, and kicked dirt, and fistfuls of soil and stone, they buried Honey wriggling in her grave. Finally, Rex gathered gravel from beneath the swing set, one fistful at a time, to coat the disturbed soil, and dragged bits of brush from the woods, laying them on top.

Xi slid to Rex's side and kissed his cheek beneath a smudge of dirt. Cabrina tucked her face against his shoulder and wrapped both arms around his middle. He thought he could stand resolute between them, but their hearts thudded together in some tryptic of strength beyond his understanding, and they all fell to their knees together in a tight cluster.

They stared at the grave as one. A tremble in Cabrina said she was waiting for something terrible to happen. Rex gripped her against him, and then he pressed into Xi too.

The earth lay still. Nothing happened, and nothing was going to happen. If Rex, Xi, and Cabrina had any say, this grave would look like an overgrown section of backyard, as if the world itself meant to hold Honey down. She was packed in tight. The soil had never known mercy, not even in whatever forgotten century first saw this monster's birth.

Rex didn't believe in souls waiting in the ground for resurrection as Marla had described it. Doubtful that Honey cared; there was a good chance she predated that religious belief and many others. He wasn't even sure a thing like her could die the same as the other vampires. No day of judgment or Christ awaited her.

Still, Rex could believe her suffering would carry on for decades and decades. It wasn't a faith he could prove kneeling in this backyard right now between his friends. No scientific evidence for it either. They had left biology behind.

But as orange tongues of light lapped the clearing sky with dawn, he could choose this vengeful belief in his heart as he and the girls laid stones over Honey's grave.

A faith that she would writhe in the earth until long after he died an old, old man.

49. A SHARD OF IVORY

Cape Shadow was a near-black world when Ivory crawled ashore. She had cried herself into a dazed state while tossing in the waves, and then at last her fingers snatched at damp hair and ragged flesh.

Honey's head. Cold and soggy, but enough to drag ashore.

Ivory, go, Honey's claw insisted. *Ivory, fast. Ivory, abandon.*

But Ivory sat at the bottom of the stone steps and cradled the head in her lap. A fetid disposition rotted its insides. One eye still blinked at her, but Honey offered no comfort or laughter now, only frantic urgency.

Ivory, leave. Ivory, NOW.

Sitting as still as stone, Ivory's thoughts turned from Honey and drifted to Cabrina. The heartbreak in her eyes had been an echo of Ivory's own. This was not a triumph for either of them. Ivory knew that much from the diary.

But a lonely life did not mean Cabrina was alone. Her past might have echoed Ivory's, but they had no twinned future. She and Ivory were strangers. Always had been. Small wonder Cabrina had joined her friends.

In the end, she had never even known Ivory's name.

"It's Ivory." Her words came in a whisper, and she couldn't tell whether her throat was weak or if the dimming of Cape Shadow had stolen her voice with the starlight. She tried again, clearer now. "It's Ivory. Cabrina, my name's Ivory! I meant to help."

No voice answered. Not even her echo.

Only Honey's claw, digging with panic into Ivory's mind. *Ivory, drop. Ivory, RUN.*

Ivory clambered onto her feet and dragged Honey's head off the ground. She wasn't going to drop anyone. Her insides had turned to aching green tar, and every uncertain step threatened to spill her and Honey into the sea, but she forced herself past the tide pool to chase the island's edge, seeking a way back to Cape Morning.

A hole opened at the foot of Ghost Cat Island's mountain, but it did not lead to flat stones or a living room with a stereo system. The way to Ivory's house had congealed into a rock wall hidden by deep shadows.

She followed the island's perimeter to where she had journeyed from Cabrina's house. Honey had opened that path more recently, and maybe it would take longer to decay as Cape Shadow lost its sense of self.

This way, too, was shut. Ivory could tell before she followed the trail of flat submerged stones leading to the small nub of rock jutting from the sea. No light there. No way back.

Honey's head weighed in Ivory's weakening arms. She had let Cabrina go for this head. And she might have made other trades without meaning to. Every choice since spotting Cabrina's body had led to this fate.

In Ivory's hasty glee to trade away parts of herself she wouldn't miss, she might also have traded away parts she would.

Cape Shadow had likewise lost a piece of itself. The sleepers had abandoned their nightmare, and now its details washed from this small world. Honey hadn't warned her about that.

But then, Honey hadn't warned her about a lot of things.

Ivory eyed the sea again. She could no longer make out the monoliths or skeletons that once climbed from the waves, let alone the bone-dotted beach from which she'd first witnessed Ghost Cat Island in its mountainous truth. No telling if that beach still existed. Cape Shadow looked to be curling in on itself, a charred lock of hair retreating from a flame.

If another way home existed, Ivory would never make the journey. She had spent herself searching for Honey's head. Now she barely had the strength to reach the mountain again.

She fell to crawling at the stone steps, three limbs propping her up, one arm cradling Honey at her underside. Failure to walk, failure to anticipate the night. To help Cabrina had been impossible after death, even when bringing a dream to the waking world. To believe otherwise was to live as one damned, and perhaps to die that way.

Honey's surviving eye shined as Ivory reached the top step, where the mountain's cavern gaped open.

"I know." Ivory buried her face against the head's damp fur.

Honey gurgled and licked her teeth. If she was fed, she might regrow herself. She could become strong again, and maybe the way between worlds was still thin enough for her claws to carve through, she and her key. Honey only wanted blood.

But so did the sea. And it was much older and stronger than Honey could ever be.

"You would've ridden one of them out of here," Ivory said, inching toward Ghost Cat Island's cavern. "Me instead of Cabrina. And then Rex or Xi instead of me."

A claw scratched at Ivory's mind. *Ivory, choose.*

"I know, it was my choice," Ivory said. "Couldn't help myself. Couldn't eat another bite. They're all excuses from beginning to end."

She dragged herself into the cavern, where the floor scraped the sea-slick stone poking from her wounds. The ocean might sharpen every part of her, given time. Through eons of undeath, she would become an island herself, with Honey in her grasp.

The claw scratched again. *Ivory—*

"Tell me, love," Ivory said. "Are you mine? Or should I have buried you at sea?"

Ivory, yes. And yes.

The head settled into the crook of Ivory's arm, the eye still glaring. This was her Honey, who sent a Chasm Cat vision pawing at Ivory's dreams, who'd given a small heart and led her to Cape Shadow. But those memories of blood couldn't wipe away the inky sky.

Shadows tossed at the shattered center of Ghost Cat Island. Its mountain lay in ruins, but the round chamber remained. Doorways once offered choices to Ivory here. What would she have found if she'd settled on the lioness path, the saber-toothed doorway, or any of the others? Maybe nothing would have changed. None of them had called out; only Honey had been desperate to end the long sleep and awaken ancient hunger.

Fallen rock now barred the doorways. The only paths from here were back the way Ivory had come, or down the gaping throat in the chamber's floor, rounded by descending stone steps.

Ivory began the downward crawl. *Make me a devil, too*, she'd said. Had she really considered what that meant?

She thought of the enormous driftwood tree where she had found Cabrina's death poem days ago. Scars marked its trunk the way greenstone wounds now gaped across Ivory's body, and she understood the dead tree's long voyage better than before. To die and then carry on was a hard existence.

Hadn't she been haunted by a night like this before? A night when she was drawn into a collective who had known each other before they knew her, acting like she could be one of them. Ones who pretended they could love her, care about her, only to instead use and hurt her for their own desires. A collective happy to discard her once they'd had their fun.

How achingly familiar.

"Looking back on it all," Ivory said, reaching halfway down the spiral steps. "I think I'm not too willful, and I'm not too smart. And I wish part of me didn't care about you anyway."

She paused to lift Honey's head and plant kisses along clenched sharp teeth. Her lips touched the ravaged eye socket, and the lid of the intact eye. The hyena-like snout. The matted hair. She did not want the end to come without Honey knowing she was cared about, even if she could not find it in herself to care in return. Love could be evil that way.

"If I'd chosen the same as Cabrina, would I be dead now?" Ivory asked. "Another ghost for Cape Morning? Was that really a choice? Is there any such thing?"

Honey closed her eye. Ribbons of flesh dangled from her head wounds. She was a broken fragment pressed to Ivory's chest. Or maybe Ivory was the broken shard.

She leaned up and kissed Honey's damp fur. "You wouldn't have loved me if I wasn't the kind to make that choice."

The throat's descent ended at the pool of Ivory's becoming. Its waters settled in Cape Shadow's dying breath, no longer an orgy of beasts and blood. Crevices opened the rock along the throat's walls, where the sleepers had once nestled together and blanketed every surface for countless years.

Ivory didn't want to think about them anymore. They certainly weren't going to think about her. The beasts already had what they wanted.

She slid into one crevice and let her body rest around Honey's head. Soft breath filled the narrow place as the last light died away. The remainder of Cape Shadow was melting into the same blackness she'd seen overtaking the moon, stars, and distant beach. A dream of nothingness encircled her and Honey, leaving only enough space for two souls to linger.

Ivory, end? The claw dug at Ivory's mind. *Ivory*—

Ivory leaned down and kissed Honey's forehead. She tasted of salt and blood—not the sugary distortion, but the real thing, the flavor no longer masked by sweet illusion. Her lips slid down Honey's brow, past her ruin of an eye. Their noses touched briefly before Ivory's breath crossed Honey's snout, and a desperate stirring worked in her jaw. The head edged closer from between Ivory's palms, and Honey licked Ivory's face, sent her tongue running hot into Ivory's mouth, her muscles, branching across her body.

Liquid warmth trickled down Ivory's throat and spread through her chest. A minor sun still burned inside Honey.

Ivory, love, she said. *Ivory, mine.*

Her eager tongue lapped at the gaping greenstone wound between Ivory's breasts. Its edges stung at the pressure and trembled at new pleasure, and a calm swept into Ivory's skin. Not a carnal thrill, but a sensual comfort that she was not alone, and she was not uncared for.

And she let Honey give that comfort. Maybe a pretend love, the only kind this monster knew, or maybe a real love simpler and more striking in its bestial nature than any in human understanding, but that would have to be enough in this dying little world. To punish was to welcome loneliness, and Ivory couldn't have that.

She loved Honey, but she loved Honey's lies even more.

Their touches soon eased into the same darkness that had taken Cape Shadow. Whatever magic remained to Honey could not revive the dream. Only rest could bring them elsewhere.

And so they rested. Ivory's limbs curled around Honey's head. This last shred of Honey nestled against her breasts. Consciousness slipped away on an ebbing tide, and Ivory hoped as she drifted off that the ocean remained here, with her and Honey, despite all sensations to the contrary.

If nothing else, she could imagine the sea while she slept.

In this sleep, Ivory dreamed she was a cat who climbed from a fissure in the small Ghost Cat Island off Cape Morning. Her fur was short and white across most of her body, with calico patches around her ears and neck.

Along one hindleg, where a tattoo on her human body once hid an age-old burn scar, a line now stretched blurry and smudged, as if it had never said anything. The words ran lost in a narrow smattering of black fur.

She was the odd cat who liked the water. In the early mornings, before the beach filled with people, she would chase the tide into the sea and pounce at tiny fish or swim in the froth.

It was a way of holding onto a memory, already sliding off her like dripping water.

But in other ways, she was purely a cat. She saw the world through a cat's eyes, and she caught a cat's prey, and she wandered from home to home with a cat's nomadic pride. She was a small thing now. A tip to her own iceberg. Vulnerable and incomplete. Always careful with her surroundings. Even more careful with her heart.

And behind that cat, in the dream, she doubted she was a creature of life anymore. Not a creature of the dead either. Something in between, then. A memory, maybe, or a haunting. One more ghost in the water.

Or the remnant of a bad dream, with only two sleepers left to dream it.

ACKNOWLEDGEMENTS

Thank you to the whole wonderful team at Titan, especially my excellent editor Daniel Carpenter, and to my stellar agent Lane Heymont. To everyone who's read this and lent their kindness toward it. To my family, and to my friends, and to my cherished Cina, Suzan, Sara, Claire, Cass. To my glorious wife, J, always. And to young Hailey. Thanks for sticking it out, little one, even when you didn't want to. I hope this book puts your demons to rest.

ABOUT THE AUTHOR

Hailey Piper is the Bram Stoker Award®-winning author of *Queen of Teeth*, *A Light Most Hateful*, *Cranberry Cove*, *No Gods for Drowning*, *Cruel Angels Past Sundown*, *Unfortunate Elements of My Anatomy*, *The Worm and His Kings* and its sequels, and other books of dark fiction. She is an active member of the Horror Writers Association, with over 100 short stories appearing in *Weird Tales*, *Pseudopod*, *Cosmic Horror Monthly*, and other publications. Her non-fiction appears in *Writer's Digest*, *Library Journal*, *CrimeReads*, and elsewhere. A former New York resident, she now lives with her wife in Maryland, where they keep the supernatural a secret.

Find Hailey at haileypiper.com.

COUP DE GRÂCE
Sofia Ajram

"Alienating, exquisite, and disturbing; a poem in blood and concrete." **Gretchen Felker-Martin, author of *Manhunt* and *Cuckoo***

Vicken has a plan: throw himself into the Saint Lawrence River in Montreal and end it all for good, believing it to be the only way out for him after a lifetime of depression and pain. But, stepping off the subway, he finds himself in an endless, looping station.

Determined to find a way out again, he starts to explore the rooms and corridors ahead of him. But no matter how many claustrophobic hallways or vast cathedral-esque rooms he passes through, the exit is nowhere in sight.

The more he explores his strange new prison, the more he becomes convinced that he hasn't been trapped there accidentally, and amongst the shadows and concrete, he comes to realise that he almost certainly is not alone.

A terrifying psychological nightmare from a powerful new voice in horror.

A BOTANICAL DAUGHTER
Noah Medlock

It is an unusual thing, to live in a botanical garden. But Simon and Gregor are an unusual pair of gentlemen. Hidden away in their glass sanctuary from the disapproving tattle of Victorian London, they are free to follow their own interests without interference. For Simon, this means long hours in the dark basement workshop, working his taxidermical art. Gregor's business is exotic plants – lucrative, but harmless enough. Until his latest acquisition, a strange fungus which shows signs of intellect beyond any plant he's seen, inspires him to attempt a masterwork: true intelligent life from plant matter.

Driven by the glory he'll earn from the Royal Horticultural Society for such an achievement, Gregor ignores the flaws in his plan: that intelligence cannot be controlled; that plants cannot be reasoned with; and that the only way his plant-beast will flourish is if he uses a recently deceased corpse for the substrate.

The experiment – or Chloe, as she is named – outstrips even Gregor's expectations, entangling their strange household. But as Gregor's experiment flourishes, he wilts under the cost of keeping it hidden from jealous eyes. The mycelium grows apace in this sultry greenhouse. But who is cultivating whom?

Told with wit and warmth, this is an extraordinary tale of family, fungus and more than a dash of bloody revenge from an exciting new voice in queer horror.

MYRRH
Polly Hall

"For every woman with a goblin inside her. This dark, lonely, yearning, twisty book is not for the faint of heart, and boy did I love it." **CJ Leede, author of *Maeve Fly***

Myrrh has a goblin inside her, a voice in her head that tells her all the things she's done wrong, that berates her and drags her down. Desperately searching for her birth-parents across dilapidated seaside towns in the South coast of England, she finds herself silenced and cut off at every step.

Cayenne is trapped in a loveless marriage, the distance between her and her husband growing further and further each day. Longing for a child, she has visions promising her a baby.

As Myrrh's frustrations grow, the goblin in her grows louder and louder, threatening to tear apart the few relationships she holds dear and destroy everything around her. When Cayenne finds her husband growing closer to his daughter – Cayenne's stepdaughter – and pushing her further out of his life, she makes a decision that sends her into a terrible spiral.

The stories of these women will unlock a past filled with dark secrets and strange connections, all leading to an unforgettable, horrific climax.

THIS SKIN WAS ONCE MINE AND OTHER DISTURBANCES
Eric LaRocca

THIS SKIN WAS ONCE MINE

When her father dies under mysterious circumstances, Jillian Finch finds herself grieving the man she idolized while struggling to feel comfortable in the childhood home she was sent away from nearly twenty years ago. Then Jillian discovers a dark secret that will threaten to undo everything she has ever known about her father.

SEEDLING

A young man's father calls him early in the morning to say that his mother has passed away. He arrives home to find his mother's body still in the house. Struggling to process what has happened he notices a small black wound appear on his wrist. Then he discovers his father is cursed with the same affliction.

ALL THE PARTS OF YOU THAT WON'T EASILY BURN

Enoch Leadbetter goes to buy a knife for his husband to use at a forthcoming dinner party. He encounters a strange shopkeeper who draws him into an intoxicating new obsession and sets him on a path towards mutilation and destruction...

PRICKLE

Two old men revive a cruel game with devastating consequences...

ALSO BY HAILEY PIPER AND
AVAILABLE FROM TITAN BOOKS

A LIGHT MOST HATEFUL
Hailey Piper

"A juicy horror tale you'll want to sink your teeth into, before
it sinks its teeth into you." **Rachel Harrison**

Three years after running away from home, Olivia is stuck with
a dead-end job in nowhere town Chapel Hill, Pennsylvania.
At least she has her best friend, Sunflower.

Olivia figures she'll die in Chapel Hill, if not from boredom,
then the summer night storm which crashes into town with
a mind-bending monster in tow.

If Olivia's going to escape Chapel Hill and someday reconcile
with her parents, she'll need to dodge residents enslaved by the
storm's otherworldly powers and find Sunflower.

But as the night strains friendships and reality itself,
Olivia suspects the storm, and its monster, may have its
eyes on Sunflower and everything she loves.

Including Olivia.

TITANBOOKS.COM

For more fantastic fiction, author events,
exclusive excerpts, competitions, limited editions and more

VISIT OUR WEBSITE
titanbooks.com

LIKE US ON FACEBOOK
facebook.com/titanbooks

FOLLOW US ON TWITTER AND INSTAGRAM
@TitanBooks

EMAIL US
readerfeedback@titanemail.com